This Champagne Mojito is the
Last Thing I Own

This Champagne Mojito is the Last Thing I Own

ROSS O'CARROLL-KELLY
(AS TOLD TO PAUL HOWARD)

Illustrated by Alan Clarke

PENGUIN
IRELAND

PENGUIN IRELAND

Published by the Penguin Group
Penguin Ireland, 25 St Stephen's Green, Dublin 2, Ireland (a division of Penguin Books Ltd)
Penguin Books Ltd, 80 Strand, London WC2R ORL, England
Penguin Group (USA) Inc., 375 Hudson Street, New York, New York 10014, USA
Penguin Group (Canada), 90 Eglinton Avenue East, Suite 700, Toronto, Ontario, Canada M4P 2Y3
(a division of Pearson Penguin Canada Inc.)
Penguin Group (Australia), 250 Camberwell Road, Camberwell, Victoria 3124, Australia
(a division of Pearson Australia Group Pty Ltd)
Penguin Books India Pvt Ltd, 11 Community Centre, Panchsheel Park, New Delhi – 110 017, India
Penguin Group (NZ), 67 Apollo Drive, Rosedale, North Shore 0632, New Zealand
(a division of Pearson New Zealand Ltd)
Penguin Books (South Africa) (Pty) Ltd, 24 Sturdee Avenue, Rosebank, Johannesburg 2196, South Africa

Penguin Books Ltd, Registered Offices: 80 Strand, London WC2R ORL, England

www.penguin.com

First published 2007
1

Copyright © Paul Howard, 2007
Illustration copyright © Alan Clarke, 2007

The moral right of the author has been asserted

Set in 12.5/14.75pt Monotype Garamond
Typeset by Palimpsest Book Production Limited, Grangemouth, Stirlingshire
Printed in England by Clays Ltd, St Ives plc

A CIP catalogue record for this book is available from the British Library

ISBN: 978-1-844-88124-6

Contents

Prologue

Who the fock is Edna O'Brien?

I've never heard of her. That's if it even is a her. Oh, it must *actually* be, roysh, because it says,

> *'As a writer, Fionnuala O'Carroll-Kelly has challenged our sexual mores like no Irish woman since Edna O'Brien. And it turns out that the forty-five-year-old South Dublin housewife …'*

Forty-five! Are you yanking my focking chain? The woman's got facial warts that are forty-five. I'm never buying the *Times* again. That's it – game over.

> *'. . . is a huge fan of the author, whose* Country Girls *trilogy caused outrage in the less permissive Ireland of the early 1960s with its graphic sex scenes, even prompting book-burnings in churchyards the length and breadth of the country. Fionnuala admits she feared similar public conflagrations of her work in the car park of Avoca Handweavers, the popular shop and café whose clientele she has captured so magnificently in her sexual-political thriller,* Criminal Assets. *The response to her book, though, has been overwhelmingly positive, according to the stunningly attractive grandmother …'*

Stunningly attractive! What the fock are these people looking at? She's uglier than a kitten in a blender.

> *'. . . who admits that the book's heroine, the sexually insatiable Valerie Amburn-James, is largely a self-portrait. "I can't believe how many people*

have come up to me after reading the book and told me they identify with her. I could literally be anywhere – the Westbury, Pia Bang, the Laura Mercier counter in BTs – and someone I've never met before will approach me and tell me they really love VAJ. Men especially seem to enjoy VAJ, and obviously women are partial to a bit of VAJ themselves."'

This shit is beyond funny.

'While there have been no public burnings of her searingly honest portrayal of Foxrock's own Desperate Housewives, she has set the literary world ablaze, so much so that advance orders of the sequel, Legal Affairs, *have sent it rocketing to the top of Amazon's bestseller list – and Fionnuala admits she hasn't even finished the first chapter yet. She's understandably reluctant to give away the plot, but she does say that Valerie's post-menopausal sexual reawakening continues with a vengeance . . .'*

Oh, fock!

'Wherever the ride takes us, it's unlikely to be dull – much like Fionnuala's own life, which is beginning to resemble the old cliché about life imitating art. Her husband, the controversial county councillor Charles O'Carroll-Kelly, is awaiting trial on 143 charges, including corruption and tax evasion. He is currently on remand after it was discovered that he was planning to flee the country . . .'

Of course, at this stage I'm thinking, and when is she going to mention her son, who captained Castlerock College to the Leinster Schools Senior Cup in 1999?

'Fionnuala dead-bats questions about her husband, whose contro-versial campaign to stop the link-up of the city's two Luas lines coined the slogan, Different Nations, Different Stations. *Her*

literary agent, Lance Rogan, interrupted to say the interview would be terminated if she was asked any more questions about her marriage.'

Er, *hello*? Any mention of me?

'She will, however, answer questions about her famous style. When we met, she was wearing a stunning black cashmere twinset by Hermès, black trousers by Alessandro Dell'Acqua and a magnificent pair of leopard-print Salvatore Ferragamo shoes. So where does her wonderful fashion sense come from?

"I hate this the-new-Jackie-Onassis tag that the press have labelled me with," she says, demurely. "I think what I wear is quite ordinary. It's very expensive, but ordinary at the same time. I suppose, there's a group of us really – yummy-mummies, you might call us – Mary Kennedy, Liz O'Donnell, Sheana Keane, myself and, you know, I'd look at what they wear and they'd look at what I wear and I suppose we influence each other quite a bit."

It also helps that her daughter-in-law is Sorcha Lalor, owner and manager of Sorcha's Fashions in Dublin's Powerscourt Townhouse Centre, one of the hottest boutiques in the city right now, with its exclusive Chloé and LoveKylie ranges.'

And then I see it, roysh, way down at the bottom of the piece. The last paragraph, in fact. Five measly focking words.

'She also has a son.'

1. On Us Thy Rich Children

He looks like shit, it has to be said. Wouldn't say the food in here is hectic, but all the same, it looks like he's lost a stone, even two, in the – what? – six weeks he's been here.

'Any word from Michael Cheika yet?' he goes, straight away trying to strike up the old pals act.

I don't say anything, roysh, just give him the hord stare and eventually he goes, 'He'll see the light. I don't think Leinster are sufficiently well-off for players that they can afford to ignore the claims of – in this humble observer's view – the finest out-half this country has produced since Campbell, quote-unquote . . .'

The focker's chicken oriental. It's like he's totally oblivious to where he is and shit? It's probably, like, a defence mechanism. Wouldn't envy him the next few years in here. I'm looking around the visiting room and I've never seen so much CHV in one place. It's like the Ilac Centre, but with focking bors on the windows. We're talking Adidas everything and Lizzy Duke bling and it hums of, I don't know, defeat – defeat and desperation and Lynx.

There's some random skobe at the next table and his eyes are all over my Henri Lloyd. Probably has a buyer lined up for it already – not that he can do shit about it in here, but I suppose old habits die hord.

It's weird seeing the old man in his own clobber. I thought these places would give you, I don't know, a suit with arrows on it or something.

I whip the little box out of my Davy Crockett and push it across the table to him. Then I go, 'Here, I brought you something,' and somehow – don't ask me how – I manage to keep a straight face. He looks at the box, then at me and his face lights up like a focking slot-machine.

'Kicker's brought me a present,' he goes, turning around, looking for someone to tell. No one's interested.

I can't believe some focker hasn't stuck a knife in him yet.

'Open it,' I go, which he does. He whips off the lid, pushes aside the tissue paper and pulls it out.

It's a harmonica.

He studies my boat, trying to work out if it's, like, a genuine gift or if I'm just, like, ripping the piss.

I'm there, 'An innocent man facing a ten-stretch? You've got to have a focking harmonica, don't you? It's like in the movies.'

He looks down, all sad. Then he goes, 'Oh, I'm not innocent, Ross. Not by a long chalk. No, no, no. This time they've got what are popularly known as "the goods" on me, I'm afraid. Full stop, new par. Two-and-a-half million salted away in a bank account in Jersey, soliciting bribes from two property developers, paying bribes to two council officials . . .

'Hennessy reckons two to five years,' he goes, giving me the big cow eyes, feeling all sorry for himself. 'I do appreciate your efforts to cheer me up, though. Look, the boy's brought me a harmonica,' he goes, turning to the pair at the next table, who are in the middle of a serious borney. Then at the top of his voice, he's like, 'Oh, that's something you're all going to have to get used to in here over the next few years, I'm afraid, the constant, inverted commas, *joshing* between Ross and myself. Oh, we're famous for it. Like

6

Jury's cabaret. Although I'm a Berkeley Court man myself, and you'll get no apology from me on that score . . .'

The pair beside us are staring at him with their mouths open, like he's a personal injuries compensation cheque.

He's going, 'Be warned – earplugs are advisable when we get going. One will say one thing and the other will say something back and on and on it goes, with a heavy emphasis on hilarity . . .'

The two of them are still just staring. Then, without saying anything, they go back to whatever they were arguing about. I'd imagine she's been boning some other Ken Acker while he's been inside, probably his best mate or his brother, knowing these kinds of people, which I'm happy to say I don't.

I look at the old man and I go, 'Are you not . . . *scared* in here?' and he's there, 'Scared? What's there to be scared about?' and I suppose if he doesn't know, there's no point me telling him. He goes, 'Scared? No. Sad? Yes. Sad that I'm going to miss the first few years of my beautiful grand-daughter's life. How *is* lovely little Honor?' and I just go, 'She's fine,' and he nods, as if he's trying to, like, process this information.

He's there, 'I meant to warn you, Ross, not to bring her in here,' and I'm like, 'I had no focking intention of it,' and he's going, 'It's no place for a baby. A photograph of her would be nice, though,' and I just shrug, roysh, as if to say, I'll see what I can do.

Suddenly, roysh, he looks over both shoulders, then he goes, 'Of course, you know the *real* reason I'm in here today, don't you?'

I'm like, 'Er, because you're a focking crook?' and he's there, 'Well, yes, obviously. But why did they decide to step up their investigations? Think about it . . .'

7

See, I actually don't *give* a fock?

I go, 'Presumably because the old dear wrote a supposed book about some sexless trout whose husband was on the take. Wouldn't take Columbo to work out that she was writing about her own miserable focking life . . .'

The old man's just, like, shaking his head, with his eyes closed. 'Must I remind you,' he goes, 'of the whispers in the wind *vis-à-vis* rugby football at Croke Park?'

I'm there, 'Yeah? And?'

He's like, '*And* they want me out of the way, of course. Stands to reason, does it not? What, the *chairperson* of Keep It South Side? *At large* at this pivotal moment in Mr Bertie Ahern's big plan to bring rugby to the northside of the city? No, no, no, no, no. Couldn't happen, see. The enemy had to be neutralized – with a capital N, if necessary. Oh, Hennessy and I were planning all sorts – protest golf outings and so forth. Our friend didn't want that . . .'

Actually, this is storting to seriously bore me. I wonder would it be rude just to fock off now.

He goes, 'Now I can see the light going out in your eyes, Kicker. You're thinking, but who will lead us now? Well, fret not. Answer – *I* will. Because I'm not giving up. Oh, no. Sure, you can cage me. That's easy. But your chap Ahern will find out, as Ceaușescu did, as F. W. de Klerk did, to say nothing of Papa Doc Duvalier, that you can't cage a feeling. You can't lock up popular sentiment.'

Out of the blue then, he suddenly goes, 'So, how's your mother, Ross? She bearing up okay?' and – genuinely, roysh – I'm like, 'What are you focking banging on about?'

He goes, 'Well, just that. Give her my love, will you? Tell her I'm sorry about . . . all this . . .'

I don't know why I *give* a fock, but I end up going, 'Are

you *actually* telling me she hasn't been to see you yet?' and suddenly he's back on the defensive, going, 'She's busy, I understand that. She's doing the publicity work for that book of hers. It's flying off the shelves, apparently. Wonderful article about her in the paper. They're calling her the new Edna O'Brien.'

I've never seen him look so sad. He goes, 'Then she has her charity work. When I read about that earthquake in Pakistan, I thought, oh, there'll be a roulade sale in a certain house on Brighton Road before the week's out. And don't forget her campaigns. Nobody said political marriages were a bed of roses . . .'

I'm just, like, staring at him, hating him for talking like this, hating him for being so focking weak.

'And I expect she's still doing that Yogalates programme with the girls. That's three mornings a week, Ross, it's a big commitment.'

And that's when I end up totally losing it with him.

I'm like, 'She's a focking hound. *She's* the reason you're in here and now she's just, like, leaving you to rot? When are you going to, like, cop onto yourself and shit?'

I know I'm going to have to watch this, roysh, but for probably the first time in my life I find myself actually feeling sorry for him.

The dickhead.

Her ears are so tiny, her nose, her little hands. She's so peaceful when she sleeps.

I'm kneeling down, roysh, looking into her crib, watching her little chest fill up and then empty, watching her breathe in and out, in and out, in and out . . .

It's, like, totally mesmerizing. I suppose you could say I'm having one of my famous intellectual moments, thinking basically that life is such an amazing thing when you, like, think about it and shit?

It has to be said, she's an actual ringer for me, though you do have to be careful who you say that to, especially around here.

When she was born, Sorcha's old pair – who hate my guts – were like, 'Oh Sorcha, she's the image of *you*,' like it was a major relief all round, roysh, and of course I was there thinking, er, I'm not exactly Martin Johnson, in case you haven't noticed, though I didn't need to say it because deep down, I know – and they know – that it wasn't true, roysh, because deep down, I know – and they know – that Honor looks like me.

Says in one of Sorcha's magazines – might have been *Mother & Baby* – that in the first six months of their lives babies usually resemble their dads and this is, like, nature's way of persuading the father – in other words, the bread-winner – not to abandon his, like, offspring.

Not that there's any danger of that happening in this case. I'm looking at her, roysh, and I'm thinking, I would actually do anything for you – we're talking clean toilets, we're talking stack shelves in Lidl . . . We're obviously not talking literally, but you get my point.

And God help the boys when they stort calling to this door for her.

It's just, like, the most amazing feeling in the world to have this little, I don't know, bundle of life basically, that is, like, totally dependent on you and you can't fock up anymore because there's, like, no excuses, it's too important.

But the next thing . . .

She's suddenly awake and she's staring at me, roysh, and

as usual this look of, like, total panic crosses her face. I'm there going, 'Ssshhh! Ssshhh! It's okay – it's me. You *know* me . . .' but her face just, like, creases up and then the crying storts.

I pick her out of the crib and I'm going, 'Please don't cry, baby. Come on, you *know* who I am. *Ssshhh! Ssshhh! . . .*' but that's when the howling storts, and suddenly I hear the sound of Sorcha pounding up the stairs, followed by her old pair and her focking granny, which is a bit OTT, you'd have to say.

Sorcha's there, 'I thought you said you were going to the toilet?' and I'm like, 'I was . . . I . . . just decided to look in on her,' and she's like, 'Oh my *God*, Ross, it took me *ages* to put her down,' and she pretty much tears her out of my orms, and I notice I'm getting major filthies from everyone in the room.

Her old man's there, 'Your dinner's going cold,' basically telling me to get out of here.

Sorcha's sort of, like, gently bouncing her up and down in her orms, trying to calm her, but Honor keeps turning her head in my direction and just, like, screaming her lungs out.

'She doesn't like him,' the granny goes and they all look at her, roysh, as if to go, that's the thing we all think but we're not allowed to say. Then she says it again. She's like, 'I'm telling you – that baby does *not* like him,' and I try to laugh it off by going, 'Well, she would be the first member of the female population to feel that way . . .'

Sorcha's old dear goes, 'Don't be silly, Mum. They just haven't bonded yet. Fathers and daughters – it's more common than you think,' and I have to get the fock out of there, roysh, because I don't want to give that family the pleasure of seeing me upset.

*

It's focking weird, Fionn being back at Castlerock, although he's not repeating – he's actually gone back as a teacher, we're talking English and History. Seems happy enough, though. He's sitting there – get this – preparing a class, in the middle of focking Lillie's.

At one point he catches me staring at him and holds up his book – *Modern Irish History* or some shit – and goes, 'Brings back memories, doesn't it?' and I swear to God, roysh, I have never seen the book before in my life.

Of course, then he remembers who he's talking to and he goes, 'Well, for *some* of us . . .' and I'm like, 'Yeah, the focking nerds among us. I didn't own a single book in school – and look at me now. It's a Friday afternoon and here I am, kicking back, enjoying a pint of Ken in a club I own – sorry, *portly* own – while watching a bunch of immigrants do the focking work . . .'

Fionn storts giving it, 'I suppose it's true that the simpler you are, the less you want from life . . .' and I'm just like, 'Do you want to end up having to go back to SpecSavers?'

'Ah, get a focking room, you two,' One F goes. He walks in wearing his Cher *Heart of Stone* Tour 1990 T-shirt and I'm thinking, it won't be long before we're celebrating its twenty-first. 'Listening to you two bitching – it's like being back in Cam Ranh Bay,' which goes totally over our heads, even Fionn's.

'Well said, One F,' Oisinn goes. 'Hey, did you bring a paper?' and One F throws him a copy of *The Stor*, or whatever factory-canteen gazette he's working for these days. Then he disappears behind the bor and storts fixing his Tony Blair in the mirror.

Christian's on the Wolfe to Lauren. What the fock do those two find to talk about? I mean, they've just spent the morning together, roysh, then he comes in here and spends, like, twenty minutes on the phone to her.

I suppose it's like, whatever you're into – even if it does make him a focking sap.

When he hangs up, I go, 'Hey, any word from your mystery woman?'

He suddenly gets all fidgety. See, the rest of the goys aren't supposed to know.

'Christian's been getting these calls,' I go. 'Hang-ups, basically. They've been going on for, like, months. Some bird. She never says anything – oh, except his name – and aport from that all he can hear is, like, crying. Have you any idea who it is yet?'

Christian goes, 'Er, no,' like he's actually embarrassed by it. I wouldn't be. Then again, I've burned a lot of girls in my time. I'm, like, no stranger to their middle-of-the-night agonies.

I'm there, 'I bet it's that Susan Sandys – *was* headgirl in Loreto Foxrock. She always had the big-time hots for you. Or who was that bird from Muckross, asked you to her debs? Oisinn, you remember, she used to turn up in Herbert Pork every Sunday afternoon to watch us throw the ball about, used to hang around with Pagan Hicklin . . .'

Fionn sticks his oar in then. He looks up from his book and goes, 'Ross, I don't think Christian is comfortable talking about this,' and I swear to God, roysh, I'm about to go, oh and you know my best friend better than I do, do you? But I don't, roysh, instead I go, 'God knows what those kids are going to turn out like having *you* for a focking teacher.'

I end up nearly spitting Heineken all over the gaff when he turns around and goes, 'Well, you'll get to see for yourself, because I'm teaching Ronan.'

When I've finished coughing and spluttering, I'm there,

'Ro? You're *actually* teaching Ro?' and he's like, 'Yeah, History,' and I'm there, 'Don't you go filling his head with facts and figures. Not everyone wants to turn out like you. And I swear to God, if his rugby suffers . . .'

'What's the story with JP?' One F goes suddenly. I turn around and he's still fixing his hair. The funny thing is, roysh, it looks exactly the same as it did when he storted – in other words, big.

We're all like, 'JP?' and he goes, 'Yeah, have you not noticed that he's been acting weird?' One F thinks he fought in Vietnam – if *he* reckons you're weird, you must be in serious focking trouble.

'He does seem a bit preoccupied,' Fionn goes. Him and his big words and stupid focking glasses. 'I rang him last night. Look, he's probably just thinking about Monday . . .'

Monday is the day they're bringing Fehily back from France. The Feds have decided not to chorge him with war crimes after all. Whatever shit he was up to in Paris all those years ago, he's going to get away with, roysh, because he's too old and too sick to stand trial. So sick, roysh, that Fionn and JP are going to have to go over and bring him back. They're saying he's only got weeks left.

All of a sudden, roysh, Oisinn goes, 'Hey, Ross, look at this,' and he holds up the paper, roysh, and there's, like, a double-page spread and I have to strain my eyes to read the headline. All the goys crack their holes laughing. It's like, 'CO'CK OF FOCKROCK FACES TOUGH TIME IN THE DOCK' and then underneath it's like, 'Controversial Councillor Looking At Lengthy Jail Term,' and I'm just there, 'I don't care what they write – I hate the stupid tool as much as anyone. More, actually,' but Oisinn goes, 'No, listen to this. They've done a panel. *The Wisdom Of Charles O'Carroll-Kelly – Quote Unquote.*'

Then he storts reading. It's like, 'On teenage mothers – they should be forcibly sterilized to ensure they don't produce any further burdens on the State,' and of course that gets a big laugh, even from me, because we all remember him saying that.

Then it's like, 'On the National Lottery – an ingenious way of giving poor people dole money and then taking it back from them again. On heroin – God's way of culling the package-holiday classes . . .

'On the hospital crisis – if these so-called patients can afford cigarettes, scratch-cards and Sky Television, they can afford private health insurance. What's wrong with sleeping on a hospital trolley anyway? Think of it as a bed with wheels . . .'

I swear to God, roysh, we're all cracking our holes laughing now. I'd forgotten what a funny focker he can be sometimes.

'On Travellers – I don't know why they call them Travellers. The ones on the Sandyford Road have been there for fourteen years. They never travel anywhere. On the Hill of Tara – why is something worth keeping just because it's old? If I'd adopted the same attitude to my Lexus GS 430, well, then I would never have driven the Lexus IS 300. And you can quote me on that . . .'

We're laughing so much, we're all going to need oxygen in a minute.

Oisinn goes, 'Oh, I love this one. On Funderland – what are the Gardaí doing about it? Surely, there must be bench warrants out on most of the people who go there. On Christmas clubs – they encourage criminality by putting temptation in the way of the poorer classes . . .'

One F finishes doing whatever he was doing to his hair and storts reading over Oisinn's shoulder.

Oisinn's there, 'On Grafton Street – it's time to put a checkpoint at either end of the street. These mini-supermarkets and mobile phone shops are drawing – and let's not mince our words here – *peasants* to what was once Europe's most fashionably upmarket shopping street. On Ringsend – one of the benefits of global warming and the melting of the polar icecap is that this aberration, this awful experiment in environmental engineering, will soon be reclaimed by the sea, forgotten by the rest of Dublin 4 as some God-awful, working-class Atlantis . . .'

I swear to God, roysh, I'm pretty much on the floor, I'm laughing that much. I'm wondering do they get *The Stor* in the Joy. What am I saying – of course they focking do!

'I don't believe it,' One F goes. 'They didn't even give me a byline.'

And we all crack up laughing again.

I'm gagging for my bit. I haven't actually had it since about eight months before Honor was born.

Well, not with Sorcha anyway.

The thing is, roysh, she's looking pretty incredible at the moment and she must have noticed that I'm on for it because I made her, like, two cups of tea this afternoon and then tonight, after she put Honor down, I suggested we watch *You've Got Mail* on DVD.

So when it's over, roysh, we go up to bed and – without painting you a picture – I stort throwing the lips on her and all of a sudden she goes, 'Wait, I've got to put something on,' and she disappears into the *en suite* and I'm thinking, bit of lingerie action, happy days.

I grab two or three candles out of her drawer, because I know she likes that. I light them and then I hop into the sack.

I'm focking horder than honours physics here.

And I wait. And wait. And wait.

Twenty minutes later she comes out, with her face covered in Sudacream. Of course, she cops my reaction straight away. 'Sorry, Ross, my skin is in ribbons,' she goes. 'It's like, *oh* my God . . .'

The thing is, roysh, she's never had a Randolph Scott as long as I've known her.

I'm like, 'I thought we were gonna, you know . . .'

And she goes, 'I'm not in the mood anyway.'

What do people actually mean when they say they slept like a baby? Do they mean they woke up every hour, on the hour, screaming for focking food?

I'm just wondering because that's how mine sleeps.

All focking night she had me up, screaming her little hort out, which probably explains why I'm unusually cranky today. I had to keep hopping up out of the scratcher and grabbing the shit Sorcha had left for her in the fridge – formula, it's called – and of course by the time I got back upstairs with it she was out of the game again, spitting zeds.

And if it wasn't Honor keeping me awake, then it was Sorcha, who's in Wicklow with her old dear, enjoying another of their pampering weekends. She was the one who thought it'd be a good idea leaving me and Honor alone for the weekend. 'Might help you bond,' she goes.

No exaggeration, roysh, she must have rung, like, eight times during the night, bawling her eyes out, telling me how unnatural it is for a child to be separated from her mother so early and, well, she might have said the words *oh my God* once or twice as well.

She was like, 'I can't believe you actually let me go away and leave her,' like it's my focking fault.

She was also the one who decided not to breastfeed, *supposedly* because Honor has infant eczema and needs a prebiotic supplement in her milk, but *really*, I suspect, because Chloe told her that it would make her Walter Mitties sag and her chest would end up looking like – and I quote – two rocks in a hammock. As if Chloe can afford to talk! She's still wearing a training bra. But what the whole bottle-feeding thing means is that *I'm* having to work my orse off, roysh, especially since Honor is still going totally ballistic at the very sight of me. And we are talking *totally* here.

So with all that going down, you can only imagine how cream-crackered I am today and I don't think anyone would call me a bad father for putting Honor down a little bit earlier than usual in the afternoon, whipping the batteries out of the baby monitor and crashing out on the sofa in front of *Ricki Lake*, *Meg & Mog* and *SpongeBob SquarePants*.

I totally conk out, of course, and eventually, roysh, when I open my eyes I notice two things at the same time, the first being that *Hollyoaks* is just finishing, which means it's, like, half six in the evening, the second being that the door-bell is ringing, as in somebody has their finger pressed on it, we're talking constantly?

I'm thinking, fock, it's probably that painter Sorcha asked to do the nursery. He said he'd call around to check out the room, see how many tins he's going to need.

So I get my shit together and go out to answer the door, roysh, but I can see through the glass that it's not him at all, it's Christian and Lauren – and at least one of them isn't a happy bunny to see me.

'Can you not focking hear that?' Lauren goes – there's no, Hi, Ross, how are you? Are the rumours true that you might be going back playing rugby? – she just, like, pushes past me and disappears up the stairs and it's only then that I notice that Honor's awake again and screaming the basic house down.

Christian gives me a look that says, you're in serious shit, Dude. I go, 'I ended up sleeping through *Hollyoaks* – you didn't hear who the father of Dawn's baby is, did you?' but before he gets a chance to say anything Lauren's shouting down the stairs, 'She's soaking wet, Ross! Have you changed her at all in the last twenty-four hours?' and I hear her stomping around upstairs, looking for nappies.

I don't like the mince pies Christian's giving me either. I look at him and go, 'The short answer to that question is no. You've no idea, Christian. I mean, you change her and literally an hour later, she's pissed herself again. I mean, you could end up changing her, like, six or seven times a day. No point, in other words. I'd prefer to do just one big serious change a day.'

Christian just, like, stares me down and goes, 'Ross, whatever you do, do *not* repeat that within earshot of Lauren,' and what can I do, roysh, except nod, I suppose you'd have to say sympathetically, as in, she must be, like, menstrually disturbed at the moment.

He's there, 'I'd probably keep your questions about *Hollyoaks* to yourself as well, just until she calms down,' and I offer him the high-five, just to say, it's good to see you, Dude, and we go into the kitchen and I stick on the kettle.

I'm there, 'So how many weeks is it now?' and as he sits

down at the island, he goes, 'Four,' and I'm like, 'Four weeks to live,' and then I laugh and I go, 'I'm only yanking your chain, of course. No, marriage has actually surprised me, as in, like, a good way? Aport from the first few months obviously, when Sorcha was trying to get an annulment.'

So we sit there, shooting the shit, me talking mostly about Leinster and how it's a huge test for Dorce against Glasgow this weekend, Christian talking mostly about how climate change on the planet Hoth has decimated the Tauntaun population and how Wampas are adapting to the new environment by becoming scavengers, as opposed to pred-ators, which they've been for, like, millions of years – the usual shit really.

Lauren arrives back downstairs just as I'm pouring the coffee. She doesn't look at me, which means she's not a happy camper, and I'm thinking, I might actually open the Fox's Golden Crunch Creams, get back in her good books.

I turn to Christian and I go, 'Hey, I'm sorry I brought up that shit yesterday, about the crank calls?' and I can tell from both their reactions that I'm on thin ice here.

The thing is, roysh, I have the answer to the problem. 'Hey, I've got something for you,' I go, and I open, like, the third drawer down, under the hob, and whip out this little box.

I'm like, 'This is turning out to be a week for presents,' and I hand it across the island to Christian and, looking at Lauren, nervously it has to be said, he goes, 'This is very Luke and Obi Wan in the hovel on Tatooine, isn't it?' and he takes off the lid, looks inside and goes, 'What is it, Ross?'

Lauren has a look in and she goes, 'It's . . . a whistle.'

I'm there, 'Correction – it's a *pest* whistle,' and Lauren, who in fairness has never had any time for my shit, goes, 'Ross, are you actually suggesting that Christian deafens this poor girl?'

I'm like, 'Absolutely – blow her focking eardrums out,' and she just looks at me in, like, total disgust.

I go, 'I don't understand how you're being so cool about it. This bird is trying to basically muscle in on your patch,' and I turn to Christian and I go, 'I bought it off the internet. It's banned in, like, America, Europe and loads of other countries. Whatever, I don't know, frequency it is, the person on the other end of the phone will end up with basically a perforated eardrum,' and I turn back to Lauren and go, 'But the *good* news is that the eardrum eventually repairs itself.'

'This girl needs sympathy,' she goes. 'Not . . . *this*,' and then, roysh, out of the blue Christian goes, 'Lauren thinks she knows who it is,' and of course my jaw just drops.

I'm like, 'Is she from, like, Cabinteely?' thinking, Christian used to score a bird from there who's a bit Baghdad.

'She won't tell me,' he goes and Lauren's like, 'Well, it would be unfair if I was wrong . . .'

I'm definitely not getting out the good biscuits without a focking name.

I'm like, 'Did she sing "Time of Your Life" by Green Day at the Rathdown graduation a few years ago?' and of course Lauren flips. She's like, 'Ross, this isn't a game. This girl is in love with Christian. She can't help that. She doesn't deserve to be . . . *maimed*. And I'm certainly not going to give her name to you to spread all over town.'

The girl can read me like a book. I was actually just thinking who I'd text first with it.

I'm like, 'Okay, just tell me did she ever play hockey for Three Rock?' but she just gives me a look that means I should shut the fock up, as in now.

I pour us each another coffee and Lauren's eyes suddenly fix on the big pile of Laura Ashley shit for the nursery that Sorcha has piled up by the back door. That gets the first smile of the day out of her.

She's going, 'Aw, this stuff is so cute,' sorting through the bedding sets, dust ruffles, diaper stacker, window valance, musical mobile, lamp base, mirrors, wallpaper borders and other shit that cost me the guts of a grand. She's going, 'She went for the Hello Kitty Princess range in the end? I knew she had her heart set on that beautiful blue whale crib set, but I suppose it has to be pink for a girl.'

Suddenly, I hear a cor pulling up outside. I look out the window. It's the painter. He turns out to be working class, but then I suppose they all are, aren't they?

I let him in and follow him up the stairs – mostly to make sure he doesn't focking half-inch anything. Seven and a half litres should do the job, he reckons, and then he asks – he *actually* has the cheek to ask – for a cup of coffee because it smells so good and, fair enough, roysh, it *is* the Gloria Jeans southern pecan, but you're supposed to wait until you're focking offered.

We go down to the kitchen and I pour him one anyway – nice to be nice – while Lauren's going, 'Oh, these little pink picture frames are SO gorgeous. Sorcha has SUCH good taste,' and I automatically go, 'Exactly, that's how she ended up with me,' and I've got a big, stupid grin on my face, but nobody acknowledges the line. After downing his coffee in two mouthfuls, the painter goy goes, 'Right, I better make tracks. So it's seven and a half litres of the Raspberry Crush . . .' and I don't know why, roysh – well, I do, it's me playing Jack the Lad as usual – I go, 'Actually, no. Change of plan . . .'

He's there, 'But your missus said——' and I'm like, 'Doesn't

matter what *she* said. I make decisions in this house, too. I'm thinking, how about Leinster Blue?' and that's got Christian and Lauren's attention.

The painter's like, 'What's Leinster blue?' and I grab a handful of my shirt and go, 'You're telling me you've never heard of the Leinster Lions?' and he scratches his head and goes, 'That looks like maybe a Windsor or a Peacock Blue. Be very dark for that room now, especially with only the one window.'

And of course Johnny Big Potatoes here has to go, 'Sorry, who the fock are you – Laurence Llewelyn-Bowen all of a sudden?'

He's just there, 'Okay, okay, you're the boss. Peacock Blue it is. I'll see you in the morning,' and as he's making his exit, roysh, Lauren says that they'd better make tracks, too, and as they're heading out the door, I turn to Christian, grab another handful of shirt and go, 'If it's good enough for Drico, huh?'

'Do you know the difference between a hamburger and a blowjob?'

I doubt if JP's old man will ever change. The bird he's shouting at – she's actually a ringer for Adele Silva – is standing behind a table with a poster behind her that says, 'Turkey – A Land Of New Horizons,' and she's doing her best to ignore him, roysh, but he's not going to let it go and, well, he's drawing a bit of an audience, so when he turns around for, like, the third time and goes, 'Do you know the difference between a hamburger and a blowjob?' she looks at him all flustered and goes, 'No. No, I don't,' and of course he gives her the punchline then.

'Good – do you want to have lunch?'

It gets a few laughs, roysh, but most people walk away muttering words like 'obscene' and 'disgusting' under their breaths, but he's as oblivious to it as ever. At no one in particular, he shouts, 'I never wanted to play doctors and nurses when I was a kid – I wanted to play gynaecologists.'

The Conrad is focking rammers for a Saturday afternoon. They're hosting one of those, like, foreign property exhibitions and there must be, like, a thousand people milling about the place, talking investment funds, spa resorts and, I don't know, advantageous offers.

I've got Honor with me – she's out for the count for once – so I wouldn't mind splitting pretty soon.

I go, 'So what's the Jack, Mr Conroy. What did you want to talk to me about?' and he looks at me like it's the most ridiculous question in the world. He sort of, like, sweeps his orm around the room and goes, 'You're saying *this* hasn't got your haemoglobin pumping?'

I'm like, 'Well . . . no, actually,' and he shakes his head, roysh, like he's disappointed and shit? He goes, 'Look around you, Ross. Doesn't it make you proud? Not content with having the fastest-growing economy in the world, the Irish are buying up Europe. We're colonizing this continent on a scale not done since . . . well, Hitler.'

I'm there, 'And this affects me *how* exactly?' and he's like, 'Mark my words, Ross, it'll affect you when you wake up in a couple of years' time and realize that you're the only one of your friends without, shall we say, a place in the sun.' He flicks his thumb at Honor and goes, 'And how's this little princess going to feel, the only girl in Mount Anville without a place on the Black Sea to go to for an Easter study break? There's no telling how that might scar a girl.'

I suppose he has a point.

I go, 'Where are we talking exactly?' and with his two hands he sort of, like, traces the outline of a woman's body and goes, 'Bulgaria.'

I'm there, 'Bulgaria? You're saying that's an actual place? You haven't just made that up?' and he goes, 'No, I haven't. Believe me, it's there, where it's always been, in the south-east corner of Europe – as sure I'll be in Joy's at three o'clock tomorrow morning, wrapping myself around a €70 bottle of sauvignon blanc and a fifty-year-old divorcée. It borders Macedonia, Serbia and Montenegro, Romania, Greece and Turkey. Stinking hot, but the Rila, Pirin and Stara Planina are snow-capped all year round. Surf in the morning and ski in the afternoon . . .'

He puts a brochure down on the table in front of me and goes, 'Talking of skiing, look at the tits on that! Does she sleep on her back or what?' There's a cracking-looking bird on the cover alright, we're talking Naomi Watts except, like, hotter?

He goes, 'The Black Sea coast is made up mostly of long, white sandy beaches and the water is even warmer than the Med. Inland, you've got quiet, rural scenery, spectacular mountain ranges . . .' and I cut him off halfway through his spiel and remind him that I was an estate agent once, too.

All I want to know is how much a gaff over there will set me back and how I could, like, make a few shekels from it.

He goes, 'Well, for the pure investor, I have quite a number of prestige apartments in established complexes in Pleven, Varna and Burgas.'

I'm like, 'They sound like sexually transmitted diseases.'

He's there, 'That's funny, I always think gonorrhoea, chancroid and trichomoniasis sound like Balkan holiday resorts.

Anyway, for a two-bedroom apartment, it could cost you as little as fifty Ks.'

He lets it hang in the air, then he goes, 'Out of your league?' and I'm there, 'No way,' suddenly sounding more John B. than I actually am.

He goes, 'You're a smart guy, Ross. That's why I wanted you in on the ground floor of this idea. For fifty Ks, remember, you're getting a prime property in an area with a six- to seven-month rental season, giving you a guaranteed annual yield from your investment, as well as an asset that might even quadruple in value when Bulgaria joins the European Union.'

I have to say, roysh, my head is focking spinning at this stage. I've been out of the game too long.

I go, 'I probably should, er, think about it,' and he's there, 'Of course. It's a big step. You want to kick its tyres, see how they stand up. Take the brochure away. Actually, I'll give you another. The cover of that one's a bit, eh, sticky. Bit of a spillage. We're all adults here.'

I'm there, 'Yeah, cool. I'll, er, take these home and give you a bell in maybe a couple of weeks . . .' and he goes, 'Yeah, have a talk with your wife and let me know what she decides.'

I'd forgotten how good he is – the focker knows exactly what buttons to press.

I'm there, 'My wife? As in Sorcha?' and he goes, 'Yeah, *she's* a smart girl – a businesswoman. It's understandable that you'd want *her* to make the final decision,' and of course he knows he has me by the knackers now.

I end up going, 'Hey, *I* wear the trousers in my gaff,' and he nods, like he doesn't believe me.

I'm there, 'Sorry, how much did you say these aportments cost?' and he goes, 'Well, I've got two beautiful prime properties in the exciting city of Sofia,' and straight away I'm like, 'Okay, I'll take them . . .'

He goes, 'Er, great. Now, the mortgage . . .'

'Mortgage?' I go, sort of, like, snorting at him at the same time. 'I'm not one of your mortgage-paying classes. I'll pay cash . . .'

We have exactly €127,660 in our current account.

He's there, 'Cash?' totally thrown by it. He's never had a client like me before. 'Excellent.'

I'm there, 'I've actually been with a *bird* called Sofia,' and he puts his orm around me and leads me over to a table with a laptop on it, to do the paperwork.

'I bet you have,' he goes. 'I bet you have.'

Fionn rings from, like, Paris. He's there, 'Hey, Ross, how are you?' and I'm like, 'Ah, Sorcha's focked off down to BrookLodge again for the weekend, leaving me with a baby who hates my guts. Don't ask basically. How's Fehily? Have you picked him up yet?'

'He's in good spirits,' he goes, 'considering. He looks like shit, but he knows what's happening to him. You know – he knows he's coming home to die . . .'

The way he says it leaves me cold.

Then he goes, 'But it's not Fehily I'm worried about . . .' and straight away I'm like, 'You're talking about JP, I presume?'

He's there, 'Ross, he hasn't said a word to me since we left Ireland. I wondered was it just grief, but it seems somehow more than that. I'm sensing, I don't know, a deeper distress in him. Once or twice I've looked at him and I'm sure he's been crying . . . I think he's having some kind of crisis of faith.'

27

I ask Fionn when they're, like, coming back and he says they're about to leave for Charles de Gaulle. He goes, 'We're going to take Fehily to the nursing home next to the school. Give him a day or two to get settled in before you come and see him, yeah?'

She bursts through the front door, as in literally, as in nearly takes the thing off its focking hinges. It's like watching those Septic soldiers on *Sky News* searching a house in, like, Iran or Iraq or wherever it is they've bombed the shit out of.

She sticks her head around the kitchen door and it's like . . . CLEAR!

Sitting room . . . CLEAR!

Study . . . CLEAR!

We're actually out in the conservatory. I'm holding Honor, who, after crying for seven hours non-stop, has slipped into what I presume is a coma due to sheer exhaustion. I'm reading *The Hungry Caterpillar*, which is the only book I've ever actually finished, aport from Drico's, of course.

Sorcha comes in and I'm there, 'Hey, Babes, did you have a good time in—' and before I've even finished the sentence, roysh, she's whipped her out of my hands, like I've just tried to, I don't know, abduct her or something, and then she bursts into tears and goes, 'I'm so sorry, my baby. Mummy will never go away again. Promise. I'll *never* leave you on your own again.'

She's, like, hugging her really tight and Honor wakes up and suddenly storts getting really, like, distressed, obviously picking up that her mother's upset, but I keep the old Von Trapp shut.

'Now, you picked her up whenever she cried,' she goes,

'and comforted her, like we agreed?' and I'm there, 'Of course.'

She goes, 'And you changed her nappy whenever it was dirty?' and I'm like, 'Hey, what do you take me for, Sorcha?' and she's there, 'I'm sorry, I'm just feeling SO guilty for leaving her. I shouldn't take it out on you.'

Then, all of a sudden, she remembers something. 'The nursery?' she goes. 'Oh my God, is it done?' and I'm there, 'Er, yeah. One or two changes of plan, though. That Raspberry Crush, they don't do it anymore, so obviously I had to go for the nearest thing to it. Now, it looks unusual, but it actually grows on you,' but she's not listening, roysh, she's taking the stairs like I'd take the Seoige sisters – in other words, two at a time – and when I hear nothing for, like, thirty seconds, I make the mistake of thinking she loves it.

Like a fool, I'm shouting up the stairs, 'You heard they beat Glasgow, I presume. You'd want to see D'Arcy's try. It'll be a focking disgrace if me and him never get to play on the same team together . . .'

And that's when Sorcha appears at the top of the stairs, looking like she wants to tear my focking head off.

It's probably not the time to tell her we're also the proud owners of two prestige investment properties in the exciting town of Sofia. I decide to go out for a coffee, give her time to cool off, otherwise it's another night in the spare room.

I hate putting her in there, but when she's in this kind of form, what can I do?

I'm sitting in the window of Café Java in Blackrock, knocking back a couple of espresso mollotinas and reading Gerry Thornley's view of the weekend's events. He thinks that a lot of the questions regarding the hardiness, or lack thereof, of Leinster's pack were put to bed once and for all, blahdy blahdy blah, which is pretty much what I think as well.

Suddenly, roysh, out of the blue, my phone rings and I look at the caller ID and it's Jilly focking Cooper herself, not a care in the world on her, playing it cool as a fish's fart.

She's like, 'Ross, I'm in Thomas's. Just getting some goose fat and some stem-ginger cookies. Ask Sorcha does she want me to pick up some of that muesli she likes – the one with the figs,' and for some reason, I end up totally losing it – and we're *talking* totally here. I just flip out.

I'm there, 'Your husband's in the slammer and all you can think about is feeding your focking face?' and in the background I can hear her going, 'Yes, I'll take the muesli as well. And three or four slices of prosciutto there . . .'

When she's finally finished I turn around and go, 'Why haven't you been to see him yet?' and she's there, 'Ross, your father understands, I'm a very busy woman. I have *two* fundraisers coming up. Angela's pulled out of Meringues for Meningitis brackets Bacterial. I'm having to organize *that* now, on top of Panna Cotta for Pakistan . . .' and all of a sudden, roysh, I realize she's hung up on me, she's *actually* hung up on me.

If there's one thing I hate, roysh, it's rudeness, especially from a focking wagon like that, so after paying for my coffee – and, it has to be said, flirting my orse off with the bird behind the counter, who's SO like Faye Tozer they could be, like, cousins – I end up jumping into the old BMW Z4 and pointing the beast in the direction of Foxrock.

My first stop is the gaff, but she's not home yet, and then I remember it's Tuesday morning, roysh, which is when she meets her mates in The Gables. So I hit the village and pork the cor Storskey and Hutch-style on the kerb outside.

As soon as I open the door, roysh, the hum of *Chanel No. 5* hits me like the heat from an oven. I hear the stupid bitch before I see her. She's going, 'Bacterial meningitis is all I have time for, Susan. If Delma wants to do something for viral, she can organize it herself,' and this waitress – think Kayleigh Pearson – comes at me with a menu, going, 'Table for one, is it?' and I'm like, 'Don't worry, I'm not staying,' and I head straight for the table where the focking noise is coming from.

The old dear is in, like, total shock when she sees me, but I don't let her get a word in edgeways. I just go, 'Look at you – stuffing carrot cake into your fat focking face while your husband wastes away in prison,' and I swear to God, roysh, the whole place just goes silent.

Some jazz track that was playing in the background suddenly stops and so has every conversation in the place.

The stupid bitch storts looking around her – her head spinning three-hundred-and-however-many degrees – to see who's watching and, of course, the answer is everyone.

But she doesn't open her mouth, roysh, just sits there staring at me. One of her mates – I'm pretty sure it's Delma – goes, 'Ross, this isn't the time . . .' and I just give her a two-finger salute and carry on staring the old dear down.

In the background someone goes, 'I'll call the Gords.'

I'm there, 'I can't believe you've turned your back on him, leaving it to focking muggins here to visit the sad prick. Who paid for your focking gym membership?'

I look up, and through the window I can see her new Hyundai Santa Fe 4x4 outside. I'm there, 'Who paid for your new cor?' but still she doesn't answer me, roysh, and it's then that I realize that for some reason she doesn't want to open her Von Trapp.

I'm there, 'What's the focking Jack with your gob?' but there's no response.

I'm there, 'Open your mouth!' but she just, like, shakes her head. I go, 'OPEN YOUR FOCKING MOUTH, YOU WAGON!' and all of a sudden, roysh, she flips.

She goes, 'I AM *NOT* GOING TO THAT WRETCHED PRISON,' and suddenly, roysh, this flash of light blinds me and I stagger backwards into the table behind me, knocking over two cappuccinos and a vanilla latte and sending foam everywhere.

I'm literally lying on the deck. I manage to struggle up onto my elbows and I go, 'You've . . . you've had your focking Taylor Keith done . . .'

She goes, 'I have a publicity tour to do, Ross,' as if *that's* any kind of answer, and she picks up her fork and goes back to her carrot cake and that's the signal for normality to return. The waitress goes, 'Okay, free refills for everyone,' and suddenly the music comes back on.

I climb to my feet, picking bits of scone out of my Tony Blair. I'm not letting this go, though.

I'm like, 'The old man's looking at a ten-stretch while you're getting your Da Vinci Verneers done,' and she sort of, like, studies me – coldly, you'd have to say – while she finishes what she has in her mouth.

Then she goes, 'I *had* to, Ross. God knows what we're going to be left with by the time the Criminal Assets Bureau are through with us.'

Chloe goes, '*Oh* my God, that goy is, like, SO checking me out,' which he actually isn't, roysh, certainly no more than anyone else in here because that's what the Ice Bor is like – everyone just automatically checking each other out. You walk through the door and you can feel twenty pairs of eyes looking at you, from your face to your crotch and back again.

But Chloe's going, 'Oh my *God*, this is, like, SO embarrassing? I'm tempted to go over there and tell him that I actually have a boyfriend,' and I realize that this is just Chloe's way of reminding everyone in the group that she's actually going out with somebody.

Of course, Sorcha takes the bait.

She's like, 'Oh my God, how *is* Shawn? I saw you in Bleu the other day. I was going to call in, but I had the stroller. Oh my God, you looked SO cute together. It was, like, *awww*!' and Sophie and Emer and Claire from Bray all go, '*Awww*,' and Chloe cracks on to be embarrassed when she goes, 'I know. We are, like, SO happy together. He is SUCH a nice goy.'

Shawn turns out to be Shawn Hotten, as in Hottie, who I know pretty well – and I don't think even his old pair would say he was a nice goy. He was on the Ireland schools team with me in sixth year. Went to Belvo. I mean, he was sound *and* a wanker, if that makes any sense.

I remember a couple of years ago, roysh, he was going out with Becky Scarne – as in second-year Event Management in DBS – and he ended up boning some bird from Liverpool he met in Club M one night. Anyway, roysh, he didn't bag it up before they did the deed and he ends up getting gonorrhoea. Of course, not only does he tell Becky that he has it, roysh, he manages to persuade her that *she* gave it to him. He told her that birds can be carriers without actually suffering the symptoms, and it had probably been dormant in her for years, which Becky totally bought. So she ends up on a course of Ceftriaxone that she doesn't actually need, while Hottie – total legend that he is – can't resist telling pretty much everyone in Annabel's the story. Naturally it got back to Becky, who flipped.

So that's Shawn Hotten. I'm tempted to say something – it's actually unfair on *him*, all these birds thinking he's something he's not – but I keep the old beak closed.

'Oh my God,' Sophie suddenly goes, 'has anyone heard about this new carrot-fume diet? It's, like, a bowl of carrot soup for breakfast, one for lunch and one for dinner. But you don't drink it – you just, like, breathe in the fumes from it. It's supposed to, like, *totally* suppress your appetite?'

Oisinn calls Sophie, Chloe and Emer 'the ladies who *don't* lunch'.

Erika eventually arrives. It's typical of her to tell us to be here for nine, then to make her entrance an hour late. She looks incredible. She always does.

We're all sitting there on tenterhooks, wondering what this news of hers is, when she eventually goes, 'Clifford and I have set a date for the engagement party. It's on the twelfth of October – two weeks' time,' and I go, 'Whoa! So you're still marrying that goy who's minted then – Lord whatever-he's-called,' and she looks at me, roysh, the way she has always looked at me, like she's totally and utterly bored by my presence.

She goes, 'It's at Hathbury House, in Cambridgeshire. It has eighty-seven bedrooms, so we should be able to put up all of you.'

Sorcha turns to me and under her breath she goes, 'I can't actually believe we got my mum to babysit for *this*,' but she still says the *oh-my-Gods* in all the right places when Erika goes, 'It's not going to be so much a dinner as a banquet. I've decided on oyster cream soup, followed by a quail and *foie gras* terrine that Clifford usually has imported from France, then roast loin of venison with cracked black pepper and juniper, followed by bread pudding, which, as you know, in normal circumstances I would dismiss as being totally WC, except this one is made with blueberry whiskey sabayon . . .'

Erika storts dishing out the invites. She gives me an extra one. She's like, 'This one's for Ronan. He *can* come, can he?' and I'm there wondering does she know what she's doing, letting that one-man crimewave loose in a stately home.

Totally out of the blue, roysh, Chloe goes, 'Are Charles and Camilla going to be there?' and every mouth around the table just drops, roysh, because she's basically being a bitch here and no one – and I mean *no one* – ever does that to Erika. Chloe goes, 'It's just that this goy is – what? – ninety-eighth in line to the throne. You said yourself that they might be there,' and I'm rubbing my hands, roysh, expecting fireworks here.

But there's none. Erika just, like, stares her out of it, then goes, 'They might. Obviously they have a lot of engagements,' and Chloe goes, 'I bet they have. And it's not as if you're marrying Prince William. Or any member of the royal family who actually matters . . .'

And Erika says nothing, as in she *actually* lets it go – obviously not on her game tonight.

I stand up, roysh, and Sophie goes, 'Are you going to the bor, Ross?' and I'm like, 'Yeah, I'm getting a pint in,' and she goes, 'Oh my God, I would *love* a Champagne Mojito?' and I'm thinking, at nineteen euro a pop, I wouldn't focking blame you.

Chloe goes, 'I'll have one as well, Ross,' and Sorcha goes, 'Get a round of them, Ross. One, two, three, four, five, six, seven, eight, nine . . .' and I go, 'Why don't I just get one in and you can all breathe in the fumes?' which – in the absence of anything from Erika's mouth – is the best line of the night.

It's fair to say, roysh, that none of us was ready to see him looking like that, even though we all knew he had the old Kerry Dancer.

See, Fehily was always a bit on the, I don't know, portly side, if that's the word. Now, his cheekbones look like they're going to burst out of his face and his skin isn't red any more but a sort of, like, yellowy-grey colour.

Me and the goys – we're talking Christian, Oisinn, Fionn and JP – sit there making awkward conversation, afraid to look at him for more than a few seconds, ashamed I suppose. Of what? That's the question. Of being alive.

And the only one of us acting in any way natural is an eight-year-old boy, who talks to Fehily in the same way that he's always talked to him.

'What's the story, Fadder? I hear you refused chemo . . .'

Fehily smiles. You can tell it takes a lot of effort. 'I'm eighty-nine years old,' he goes. 'Dying is something I'm going to have to get around to eventually, don't you think?'

Ronan just shrugs his shoulders.

'I'll put it to you another way,' Fehily goes. 'Brother Ignatius, he spent thirty years of his life in the Congo, and they have a saying there that he likes to use – a dead fish won't swim, no matter how hard you throw it into the water. Do you know what that means?'

Ronan looks at us, then at Fehily. 'Haven't a fooken clue, Fadder,' and what does Fehily do but smile and go, 'You know, I've just realized, neither have I . . .'

Ronan pulls up a chair and the rest of us just sit there,

roysh, listening to the two of them just, like, vibing off each other, like they always do.

'Are you in pain?' Ronan goes. 'If the drugs aren't doing anything for you, I can get you something. I'm not without contacts. A shut mouth catches no flies . . .'

'No,' Fehily goes, basically chuckling to himself, 'the morphine's good,' and Ronan goes, 'So I believe, Fadder. So I believe.'

I look at Fionn and I roll my eyes. Fionn smiles.

'Tell me everything,' Fehily goes. 'How's the rugby going?'

Ronan's captain of the Castlerock Junior School team this year. Like father, like son.

He's there, 'One or two not pulling their weight. I'm not naming names – it's not my style – but I'm going to have to start cracking skulls . . .'

Fionn catches my eye and nods towards the door. He wants a word in private. We go outside and he goes, 'I found Vianne.'

Vianne was the love of Fehily's life, before God obviously. They were shacked up together in Paris during the War. Her old man was a Nazi collaborator basically. That's how Fehily ended up in shit. It was also the reason he left France in a hurry all those years ago.

I'm like, 'Vianne? She's not brown bread then?' and he goes, 'No, she's alive. Wasn't that difficult to find her either. Fehily said she was from Clermont-Ferrand. There were only four Heisserers listed in the phone directory in that area. The first one I phoned turned out to be a cousin, who said she was living in Bordeaux. Turns out she married a Swiss guy – Hans-Pieter – and they ran a vineyard together. He died about twenty years ago. They had three sons . . .'

I'm there, 'So, like, where is this all going?' and he goes,

39

'I'm going to write her a letter. It's been sixty years, Ross. Can you imagine being separated from someone you love for that length of time? There's so much between them that was never resolved. But there's still time for them to say goodbye . . .'

I give Fionn a hord time and everything, but he's actually got a hort of gold.

We go back into the ward. JP's got tears streaming down his face. I'm about to ask him if he's okay, but then I notice, roysh, that Christian and Oisinn are crying as well. Fehily's telling Ronan that his favourite film is *I Never Sang For My Father*, that he likes the bit where Gene Hackman says, 'Death ends a life, but it doesn't end a relationship . . .'

2. A New Queen B.

There's no doubt she's a natural with kids. Well, with Ronan, anyway.

He's going, 'Gimme the glasses again, Erika,' and without losing her patience she goes, 'Sherry glass . . . red wine glass . . . white wine glass . . . water goblet,' and he's just like, 'Sherry, red, white, water – game-ball.'

Erika's been teaching etiquette to the transition-year birds in Mount Anville two days a week, roysh, and I thought it'd be a good idea if she gave Ronan a pretty much crash course in table manners before this porty of hers. Imagine the shame of it if he storted eating with his focking hands in front of that whole horsey set.

So she's, like, laid the table in the dining room for him, and me and Sorcha are in the kitchen, listening in. Well, I am. Sorcha's got her nose in one of her child-rearing books and she's telling me that, in their first few weeks of life, baby girls smile nearly twice as often as baby boys and it's important that we encourage Honor to laugh, roysh, because laughter stimulates the immune system and triggers the release of endorphins, which are our body's natural pain-killer.

I go, 'If it's a laugh she wants, I'll show her my credit cord statement – she can see how much all that Laura Ashley shit set me back,' and as soon as I've said it, I realize that the nursery is still a sore point with her. She gives me a look and I go, 'Well, how much it set my old man back . . .'

In the next room I can hear Erika going, 'Dining is an

art, Ronan. And laying a table is like putting paint on a canvas. You don't just trowel it on, like little Claire does her make-up . . .'

Ronan laughs. I think he's in love with this girl as much as I am.

She goes, 'The distance between places at the table should be about two feet from plate centre to plate centre. Cutlery is placed in order of its use, with the pieces to be used first placed farthest from the plate. Remember, you work inwards. Now, *this* . . . is a salad fork. You'll always find it to the outermost left of the plate, with the dinner fork inside it. *This* is a soup spoon. It goes to the outermost right of the plate, outside the salad knife – which is here – and the dinner knife, which looks like *this*. The cutting edge of the knives always faces towards the plate. The dessert spoon and the fork will either be directly above your plate or brought out when the dessert is being served . . .'

I turn to Sorcha and I'm like, 'Is it my imagination or is that girl, like, mellowing?'

She doesn't answer me.

'Now, there are two ways to use a knife and fork – Continental Style and American Style. I like to call them right and wrong, respectively. These people we're dining with are *not* Americans, Ronan. The fork should remain in your left hand at all times, with the tines facing down, and the knife in your right hand.'

She goes, 'Now, any questions?'

Ronan's like, 'Why wasn't I born twenty years ago?' and she just gives him this sort of, like, flirty laugh, then goes, 'You're so sweet. Concentrate, now. Your father's worried you might embarrass him, though it'll more likely be the other way round,' which is bang out of order.

'Your bread roll goes on your butter plate, which you'll

find here, above the forks, to the left of the place setting. Your butter knife will be laid, slightly diagonally, across it, from upper left to lower right, with the sharp edge of the blade facing towards the edge of the table.'

She goes, 'What do you know about napkins?' and Ronan's there, 'Just that we have them at Christmas. And you stick them in the front of your jumper,' and Erika's there, 'I *do* hope you're joking, Ronan. You place your napkin on your lap: if it's a small luncheon napkin, completely unfolded; if it's a large dinner napkin, in half, lengthways. The exception is if the napkin has already been placed in a glass, which means a servant or wait-person will place it in your lap for you.

'Your napkin is for use in gently blotting your mouth. Use it sparingly, although always use it to dab your mouth before you take a drink, in order to avoid leaving marks on the glass. Don't use it to wipe your nose, face or forehead. Never spit food into it. If you must remove food from your mouth for whatever reason, you must do so with the implement with which you put it in, placing it on the edge of the plate. The only circumstance in which you may remove something from your mouth using your fingers is if the offending item is either a fish bone or a seed.'

Sorcha looks up from her book and goes, 'Ross, did you pick up that Bosieboo TummyTub?'

Haven't a Betty Blue what she's talking about, although the name rings a bell. Best to bluff. 'Er, sometimes,' I go.

She sees straight through it.

She's like, 'Ross, I *asked* you to go to Mothercare when you were in town this morning. You know how much Honor hates her regular bath.'

I tell her I'll pick one up tomorrow and she tells me that I'm useless, that I am SO useless, it's like, *Oh* my God!

43

Erika's going, 'The napkin sets the parameters of the meal. When the host unfolds his or her napkin, you should take it as a signal to do the same. If for any reason you must leave the table during the meal, place your napkin on your chair as a sign to the serving staff that you intend to return. The host will signal the end of the meal by placing his or her napkin on the table. You should do likewise, placing the napkin to the right of your dinner plate, being careful not to refold it or to wad it up.'

Ronan goes, 'Here, any birds up in that Mount Anville interested in becoming a gangster's moll, is there?' and Erika cracks up laughing again, then goes, 'Now, when you've finished with a course, never push your plate away. Leave it where it is in the place setting, laying your fork and knife diagonally across the plate as if pointing to the numbers ten and four on a clock face, with the sharp side of the knife facing inwards and the fork to the left of the knife with the tines down. Any unused silverware should be simply left on the table.

'Now, conversation. Remember, Darling, you're going to be dining with the bourgeois. They *always* begin the dinner-table conversation with a discussion about the weather, because it's an inclusive topic that it's virtually impossible not to have an opinion on.'

She's there, 'So, let's recap then, shall we. You begin eating . . .'

Ronan's like, 'Only after everyone has been served.'

'Bread rolls . . .'

'Should be broken – never sliced – into small pieces and buttered only one or two bits at a time. Butter should be taken from the butter-dish and placed on the bread plate, not directly on the bread.'

'Soup should be drunk . . .'

'Quietly. And don't blow on it to make it cooler. Simply engage in conversation, about, for instance, the weather, taking occasional sips, until it has reached a bearable temperature. And when you're finished, you don't put yisser spoons in the bowl. Put them down on the flat plate on which the soup bowl was presented to you.'

She claps her hands together in excitement and goes, 'You are my *best ever* student, do you know that? Now, I want to talk to you about cheese . . .'

It's some stack of breeze-blocks, I'll say that. The girl has fallen on her Deep Heat in a major way. I know she said it was big, but I didn't expect it to be Buckingham focking Palace. The entrance hall itself has got, like, paintings and statues and fountains everywhere and it's so focking huge, roysh, that we're all just standing there with our mouths open.

I turn around to JP and, out of the corner of my mouth, I go, 'A celebrated fifteenth-century Jacobean-style house set on two thousand acres of lavish parkland in the Cambridgeshire countryside,' trying to get us buzzing off each other, like we used to when we worked for his old man. I'm like, 'The hall, with its wonderfully extravagant oak carvings, features a unique set of tapestries featuring characters from popular mythology . . .'

But it's no good, roysh, he just sort of, like, smiles weakly at me, then carries on staring into space.

Erika goes, 'I'll show you to your rooms. Don't worry about your bags, the servants will bring them,' and she leads us up this huge, sweeping staircase, roysh, and one by one shows me, Sorcha, Ronan, Christian, Lauren, Fionn, JP, Oisinn and the girls where we're all sleeping.

Our so-called room is actually a suite with, like, two bedrooms, we're talking one for me and Sorcha with a big four-poster bed in it, the other for Ronan, roysh, not to mention our own private kitchen and living room and a crib for Honor. Erika says she'll leave us to get settled and see us for drinks in the King James Drawing Room, wherever the fock that is. All I know is it could take us a week to find it in this place.

So the servants – *actual* servants – drop our bags up to us and there we are, roysh, as in me and Sorcha, unpacking them, when all of a sudden out of the corner of my eye I notice Ronan, chilling out on this chaise longue in the corner, wearing what I suppose would have to be described as a quilted dressing-gown.

I go, 'Why don't you take it easy there, Ro. You'll give yourself a hort attack,' and he laughs and goes, 'What do you think of me smoking jacket?'

I'm there, 'Where did *you* get a smoking jacket?' and he goes, 'Nudger and Gull gev it to me. They did that last raid on Russborough House,' and I swear to God, roysh, my hort does a focking somersault.

'Ah, I'm only pulling your wire, Rosser,' he goes. 'They bought it offa the internet for me. Said all the big knobs in England is wearing them. Jaysus, look! There's a cigarette-holder in the pocket,' and suddenly, roysh, he's lit up one of his rollies, as he calls them, and he's, like, smoking it through this long piece of plastic.

I go, 'Hey, Ro, maybe you shouldn't be, like, smoking around the baby and shit,' and Sorcha goes, 'Oh my God, Ross, would you stop being SUCH a stick in the mud!' and she tells Ronan not to listen to me and she tells him he looks very bourgeois, which seems to be a good thing.

The next thing, roysh, there's a knock on the door and

who is it only Erika and she's going, 'Hello?' in this, like, posh English voice. 'I wanted you to meet Clifford,' and this goy walks into the room behind her and I swear to God, roysh, my jaw hits the focking floor. The goy must be, like, sixty if he's a day, we're talking, like, old and grey here? He actually looks a little bit like Donald Sutherland.

He goes, 'So *you're* the famous Sorcha,' and he takes her hand, roysh, and kisses it.

It's like something out of a focking movie.

He goes, 'My gosh, you *are* beautiful,' and it's pretty clear the goy could give me a good run for my money in the old chorm stakes.

'And look at this beautiful baby,' he goes, leaning over the crib. 'Obviously inherited her mother's good looks,' and I'm there thinking, HELLO? I wasn't exactly beaten with the ugly stick myself.

He shakes my hand, a good firm one, and he goes, 'Ah! Ross O'Carroll-Kelly. I've heard great stories of your exploits on the rugby field. I played myself, you know. Second row. For Oxford.'

Oxford? Didn't even know they were a team. He mustn't have been much good, though I don't pull him up on it. You don't want to rub the dude's nose in it.

He goes, 'I loved it, of course. Played with some crashingly great blokes. Nothing in your class, obviously,' and I'm like, 'Well, I don't want to come across as big-headed or anything, but I was actually good. I was going to be the next Brian O'Driscoll even before there *was* a Brian O'Driscoll.'

He's like, 'How wonderful!'

Then he looks over my shoulder and goes, 'And you must be . . . Ronan,' and Ro hops up off the chaise longue and goes, 'Howiya. What do I call you – Me Lord?' and the goy goes, 'Oh good God, no. It's Clifford. Always has been, always will be. I adore your smoking jacket by the way. I've got one just like it. What say I put it on later and we puff our way through a box of ten-year-old Ecuadorian Sun-Growns?' and I'm looking around me, roysh, wondering am I the only one in the room who thinks it's basically wrong for an eight-year-old kid to be smoking?

Ronan's like, 'Now you're talkin', Clifford,' and then he goes, 'Some gaff this, but,' and he's sort of, like, nodding at the ceiling. Clifford goes, 'Come, I'll give you the grand tour,' and I look at Erika, roysh, and she looks as happy as I've ever seen her.

He's leading us down this corridor and he's going, 'The house has been in our family only two hundred years. It's changed hands quite a bit down through the centuries, which accounts for the foreign embellishments to the original Jacobean structure . . .

'For instance, the main staircase is classic Italian Renaissance. Much of the interior decoration is French style. But its history of changed ownership has left it rich in paintings, furnishings and fine tapestries from different countries and different eras, not to mention the finest collection of suits of armour in all of England . . .'

He leads us down the staircase, through the entrance hall and down another hallway and, while he's doing this, he's going, 'The ceilings and walls here were painted by Giulio Taldini. Now I'm going to show you the Long Gallery . . .' and he opens the door into this room that must be the length of, like, two rugby pitches, roysh, and it's got, like, oak-panelled walls and oak floors and these humungous paintings of men, a fair few of them wearing tights I might add, and maybe twenty or thirty chandeliers hanging from the ceiling and, like, six or seven fireplaces on either side and antique tables and chairs everywhere.

I'm looking at Erika walking ahead of us and I'm thinking, she has struck focking gold here. By the looks of him, it won't be too long before Clifford drops off the perch. Then all this'll end up being hers.

'The Long Gallery was created some time in the early seventeenth century by knocking down several interior walls,' the goy is going. 'It runs the entire length of the south front of the house. The ceiling, as you can see, was covered by gold leaf shortly afterwards, at the instigation of Lady Dowager Gwenyvere Reddyhough . . .' and I catch Ronan's eye and I go, 'Don't you focking tell Nudger and Gull about this place,' and he cracks up laughing.

I notice that he's carrying Honor and that she's awake and that she's, like, gurgling away happily in his orms.

Clifford goes, 'Now, this room here is the King James Drawing Room . . .' and it's more of the same, roysh, probably five times the size of our entire gaff at home and stuffed to the focking gills with paintings and chandeliers and furniture, none of which I would say came from Habitat.

He goes, 'James the first spent a lot of time here and this was rumoured to be his favourite room . . .'

Erika goes, 'Why don't we have a drink?' and Clifford's there, 'A splendid idea,' and he looks at me and Ronan and goes, 'Chaps, what'll you have?'

I'm there, 'Pint of Ken – that's if you've got it,' and I see him and the servant exchange what I think is called a quizzical look. I'm there, 'As in Heineken?' and Clifford goes, 'Oh, good heavens, yes. It's one of these *laggers*. Dutch, if I'm not mistaken. Some of the chaps used to drink it at Oxford. We'll see what we can rustle up. And you, Ronan?' and Ronan goes, 'Brandy for me please, Clifford,' helping himself to a chair.

I'm about to say something, roysh, but Sorcha gives me

this filthy, telling me basically to keep the old Von Trapp shut.

Clifford goes, 'What about a nice '58 Armagnac?' and Ronan's there, 'See, now you're speakin' my language.'

Clifford's like, 'I'll get it. It's in my study,' and Erika goes, 'And I'll go and round up the rest of the chaps,' which is a word I've never actually heard her use before.

When she's gone, I turn around to Sorcha and Ronan and say that I've never seen her so happy.

'I take it you're joking?' Sorcha goes and I'm like, 'Er, no?' She's there, 'She's miserable, Ross. Oh my God, can't you see it?' and Ronan's like, 'Sorcha's right, Rosser. That girl is not happy.'

I'm looking up at the ceiling in, like, total awe. I'm there, 'You've got to be kidding me. Who wouldn't be happy in this gaff?'

Ronan suddenly whips out his phone and dials a number.

I'm there, 'Who are you ringing?' and he goes, 'The Met Office.'

I probably should ask, but I decide it's best not to even go there.

We're sitting around in the armoury, having a few looseners before we get ready for dinner, when all of a sudden Christian turns around and goes, 'Our room has a Rubens – an *actual* Rubens. Lauren knows her art and she says it's an original. And a Hobbema,' and I'm thinking, what's the focking Jack with *them* getting the best room in the gaff?

Chloe says she's just finished reading my old dear's book and it's, like, big laughs all round. 'Who would have thought she had that stuff in her head?' she goes, with a big shit-eating grin. And then she's like, 'I saw her coming out of The Unicorn last week with her new boyfriend. Oh my God, a ponytail – it's like, okaaay. . . innnnteresting . . .' and I'm there, 'He's *not* her boyfriend. He's her focking agent. He's actually supposed to be the best in the business,' and she does that thing that birds do when they set out to piss you off and then get the reaction from you that they were looking for all along. She goes, 'Oh my God, why are you being so defensive?'

So I end up going, 'How's, em . . .' and I nod towards her you-know-what and go, '. . . Shawn?' and that wipes the focking smile off her face. The word is he dropped her like a hot snot, ended up scoring Aisha Robb in Dakota two Saturdays ago, pretty much in front of her.

And Aisha Robb of all people. She's had more bones in her than Deansgrange cemetery.

Sophie comes chorging to the rescue, of course. '*Oh* my God,' she goes. 'He turned out to be a TOTAL wanker,' and I'm like, 'What do you mean, *turned out to be*? In fairness to the dude, he's never claimed to be anything else,' and I turn around and Oisinn and Fionn are both nodding their heads. I'm there, 'In fact, I'd say that's why you were into him in the first place.'

Emer mentions then that she, oh my God, SO loves Chloe's pumps and Chloe stops giving me filthies and mentions that they were €380 and Emer asks her if they're, like, Eileen Shields and Chloe says they are and Emer says she saw them herself in Horvey Nichs and was going to get them, but didn't in the end, roysh, and while Chloe stares at her trying to work out whether that was a bitchy comment or not, Claire from Brayruit says she got an, *oh my God*, amazing pair of, like, Allura sparkle ones in, like, Nine West and also a pair of Yaney black patent ones that she got in, like, House of Fraser, which are cool because she can wear them to work *or* on a night out.

JP used to have a word for birds when they talked like this – shoecotic.

The next thing, roysh, the door opens and in he walks – JP himself – and it's weird, roysh, because I was just about to ask the goys if anyone had, like, seen him and shit. There's something different about him – something different about his boat race – and I'm staring at him for ages trying to work out what it is, and then it hits me. He's shaved off his focking eyebrows. I turn around to Fionn and he's noticed as well. He just gives me a little shake of his head.

No one says a word to him. He just sits down in the rocker next to me, in front of the fire.

Emer asks Oisinn if it's true that he scored Melinda Clarke – as in, like, *the* Melinda Clarke, from *The OC*? – and Oisinn tells her that she shouldn't believe everything she reads in the papers, which is what he said to me when I asked him as well. There *was* a picture of them together, but I don't know if that means anything.

'Speaking of weight,' Chloe goes, which no one actually was at the time, 'has anyone seen Aoife since she got out of hospital?'

Sophie's like, '*I know*!' and Chloe goes, '*Oh* my God, SUCH a porker. I thought the girl was supposed to be, like, anorexic?' and I'm about to say something, roysh – because I know if Sorcha wasn't up in our room feeding Honor, *she* definitely would – but, as it turns out, Fionn gets in there before me.

He goes, 'I don't focking believe you,' and he's obviously pissed off, roysh, because Fionn never swears. He's there, 'Aoife's sick. She's been sick for as long as we've known her . . .'

Chloe goes, 'I'm just saying, how has she gone from being such a skinny bitch to being . . .' and she puffs out her cheeks and puts her hands out in front of her, like she's holding a big Ned Kelly.

I forgot that Fionn has history there. I actually think he's still in love with Aoife. Fair focks to him for standing up for her, though, because he just goes, 'Chloe, it doesn't matter what you weigh – you'll always be shallow and point-less,' and he gets up and walks out.

Chloe goes, 'Oh my God, why is everyone being SO defensive today?'

I've a pain in my Jacksons listening to her. I stand up and follow Fionn out of the room, and then Christian and Oisinn follow us out too.

'Sit fully erect in your chair . . . keeping your feet squarely and firmly on the floor . . .'

Ronan's having a great old chat with himself.

'Chest approximately eight inches from the table . . .'

It has to be said, roysh, he looks the part in that tux that Erika bought him and his little step haircut Brylcreemed over to one side.

It's the longest table I've ever seen in my life. You could sail the focking Pacific on the thing. There's, like, thirty-six of us sitting at it – all of our crew obviously, as well as Clifford and shitloads of his relatives and friends, roysh, who are basically like him, all very *la de da* but unbelievably sound.

Looking at the birds in their ball gowns and all the goys in their tuxes, it actually feels like the debs all over again, though I doubt if we'll be focking food around the place at any stage of the evening.

I kid you not, there is a string quartet playing focking Pachelbel and, I don't know, Vivaldi in the corner of the room.

Clifford takes off his napkin, unfolds it and lays it across his lap and just happens to mention that the weather's been pretty mild for October, at which point Ronan – totally out of the blue – goes, 'Today was mild, windy, but mostly dry, with light rain over the western part of the UK. Tomorrow will be less mild, with a belt of rain edging its way across from Ireland during the night, with the rain heaviest in the south-west, particularly along the coast,' and there's, like, total silence for about twenty seconds and then Clifford's brother – don't remember the dude's name – at the top of his voice goes, 'I say, what an *extraordinary* child!' and suddenly everyone around the table's, like, looking at each other, nodding and going, 'Extraordinary, yes . . .'

Erika had her dress made by David Sassoon. Eighty focking Ks it's supposed to have cost her – and that's, like, sterling – but the dude used to make dresses for Princess Diana, so it's not like picking one off the focking rack in Oasis. He obviously knows what he's doing as well, this goy, because every time Erika moves, I'm getting a focking helicopter view of her top tens.

I go, 'Your dress is amazing, Erika,' and I can feel Sorcha staring at me, giving me big-time filthies on a major scale.

The oyster cream soup arrives. I go to pick up my spoon and, beside me, Ronan goes, 'Wrong one, Rosser,' and I grab the other one and hold it up and Ronan gives me a little nod.

The goy opposite me – I'm pretty sure he was introduced to me as Clifford's best man – says something to me, roysh, which is so posh that it just comes out as, like, noise and I end up having to ask him to repeat himself seven times before I cop that he's asking me if I like cricket. He doesn't really talk in, like, full sentences, this dude. It's just, like, a rumbling noise and then a couple of, I suppose, key words popping their heads up here and there. It's like, '*Rrrrrrrrrrrr* . . . Australia . . . *Rrrrrrrrr* . . . Ashes . . .*'

I don't want to go all philosophical on you, but I suppose when you're that loaded, you've always got someone there to do shit for you. I mean, if I had that kind of wonga, I probably wouldn't bother my orse talking in full sentences either.

I go, 'Cricket's not my game. Fionn's your man there,' and Fionn goes, 'Yeah, I enjoy it. Played quite a bit when I was in Trinity last year. I'm thinking of joining Pembroke next summer,' and I kind of snigger, roysh, but no one else does and suddenly everyone's banging on about LBWs and googlies and all sorts of shit that you don't have in rugby.

It's actually a relief when Erika storts telling us about the plans for the wedding. They're basically going to have it in a marquee in the winter garden, roysh, the day before Christmas Eve.

Just to make conversation, I end up going, 'So, have you been married before, Clifford?' and I get a seriously hord kick on the shin for my troubles, presumably from Sorcha. I doubt if it was the brother, what with him being in a wheelchair and everything.

Clifford goes, 'I have actually. Four times, I'm afraid, but all for love, I'm rather happier to report,' and I'm looking at Sorcha as if to say, see, no big deal.

I don't think I've ever met a sounder goy.

Somewhere towards the middle of the table I hear some old bird, the sister of one of Clifford's mates, go, 'Scented holy water? What a *wonderful* idea!' Oisinn's working his magic, the focking chormer.

'I'm actually experimenting with chilled yuzu and pomegranate at the moment,' he goes. 'Sorry, I couldn't help but notice that you're wearing *Versace Bright Crystal* . . .'

She puts her hand up to her mouth and she goes, 'He's right! He's absolutely right!' and then she gives him this real, like, flirty laugh and goes, 'Oh my, you *are* extraordinary. No, really. You fascinate me . . .'

Oisinn would actually give me a run for my money when he's on form, which he certainly is tonight.

'Sorry I'm late, everyone.'

We all look up. It's Chloe. I didn't even notice she wasn't here. She missed the soup. I'm trying to think up a really funny gag to whisper to Fionn when . . .

Jesus Christ!

I think those two words actually come out of my mouth. I'm not the only one either.

Where the *fock* did she get those? Every focker knows that Chloe's flatter than a carpenter's dream – or rather *was*. I've never seen a rack like it. We're talking focking huge. They're so big they should have traffic cones and a focking guardrail around them.

'What's everyone staring at?' she goes, cracking on she doesn't know.

Well, now we know where she disappeared to last week. And why she's been wearing her Abercrombie hoody ever since we got here – obviously wanted to unveil them at the dinner and totally steal Erika's thunder.

'*Ross!*' Sorcha goes. I'm sorry, I just can't stop staring, but then, neither can anyone else. Even Clifford's mince pies keep getting drawn to them.

Chloe sits down. 'So, Lauren,' she goes, as casual as you like, 'how are the plans for your wedding coming along?' and of course, with the way she's been acting lately, we're all immediately wondering, what's her focking angle here? Then I'm thinking, hang on, has she got anything to do with those crank calls? Maybe it's her.

The venison is unbelievable.

Some solicitor friend of Clifford's, who obviously knows his shit, storts telling me and the goys that we really should stort thinking about getting a foreign property portfolio together. 'It's the only fail-safe investment option,' he goes, which is music to *my* ears and probably Oisinn's as well. He's bought up half of Poland and I know that Fionn has two aportments, one in Turkey and one in, like, Spain, both of which he's rented out.

I'm wondering is this the time to tell Sorcha about the two aportments I bought with our money, because the goy seems to be saying we can't lose. In the end, though, I lose my bottle. Don't know what it is. Just lately, I can't do anything right in her eyes.

The cheese arrives. I didn't realize there were so many kinds. There must be, like, twenty on each platter and there's, like, fruit and crackers with it as well. I grab a lump of the one nearest to me, roysh, and a couple of Digestives and Ronan just, like, shakes his head at me.

I'm there, 'What?'

He's like, 'That's camembert, Rosser. Goes with the water biscuits there. You need something a bit stronger for Digestives, like the cheddar,' and of course everyone's getting great amusement out of this. It's like watching a monkey smoking.

Clifford's like, 'Quite right, Ronan. Quite right. And that there's Unpasteurized Montgomery. The King of Cheddars. They make it in Somerset. I see *you've* gone for the maconnais,' and Ronan goes, 'Indeed an' I have. Here, you wouldn't have any *charcoal* crackers, would you, Clifford?'

I'm thinking, he must be the first cheese snob ever to come out of Pram Springs. Still, it's good news that him and Clifford have hit it off. I can see us spending a lot of holiday time over here. Servants looking after our every whim.

Clifford goes, 'Yes, I rather suspect there's some in the pantry. Millers Damsel, unless I'm very much mistaken,' and he calls over a servant and tells him to fetch them, which I have to say is seriously impressive.

So anyway, roysh, again, just trying to make conversation, I go, 'So . . . *four* ex-wives, Clifford? Have to admit, I've left a fair bit of emotional wreckage on the road myself,' and I lift up my glass and go, 'Here's to love, though,' and that's when Clifford – totally out of the blue – turns around and goes, 'Love? I don't know about that, Ross . . .'

Everyone – and I mean *everyone* – stops talking.

He's there, 'Well . . . you know . . . I'm a bit too wise in the ways of the world to believe that a beautiful young girl like Erika could fall in love with an old fart like me, let alone find me physically attractive,' and I crack up laughing, roysh, mainly because he did first.

He goes, 'But, well, I do know she *likes* me very, very much indeed. And I like her. And, well, I'm sixty-three now – no children – and I should think it's bally well time I sired a son and heir.'

And I'm looking at Erika, roysh, and she looks pretty embarrassed. Actually, worse, she looks like she's about to cry.

'The stock on these things is quite similar to the stock on the Security S-5 blaster – although I seriously doubt whether this has a liquid cable shooter.' They're the first words out of Christian's mouth when Clifford puts the double-barrelled shotgun in his hands.

The birds are all up in the gaff, looking at Erika's plans for the wedding. I swear to God, roysh, there's focking maps and everything.

Clifford gives me my gun and I have to say, roysh, it's a major buzz having it in my hands. Oisinn turns around to me and goes, 'Sorcha has no problem with you doing this, then?' and I'm like, 'Why would she have a problem?' and Fionn goes, 'Well, clay pigeons – everyone knows how she feels about animals!' and I laugh and high-five him, roysh, and then about five minutes later I manage to get the joke.

McGahy, our old prick of a geography teacher, used to say that my brain was slower than my digestive system.

Clifford goes to give JP a gun and Oisinn steps in front of him and goes, 'Er, not a good idea. You might want to sit this one out, eh, JP?' and JP just nods, roysh, and it's like he's five years old and it just, like, breaks my hort to see him like that.

I wondered should I ring his old man, to let him know that me and the goys are worried about him, but Oisinn reminded me that he went into a similar, like, trance the time in Israel when he found God and that he'd eventually snap out of it, like he did then.

Clifford's going around, roysh, making sure everyone has, like, ear muffs and goggles.

Then he goes, 'First of all, for those of you who have never shot trap before, a few rules. Treat every gun as if it is loaded, which is to say with the utmost respect at all times. *Never* point or fire your gun at anything other than a clay. When carrying the gun, it should be broken – like this – with the chambers empty at all times. And always check that your barrels are clear after any gun malfunction . . .'

He puts us standing in a line, with me next to Fionn. And I think to myself, I should really say something to him about that scene with Chloe yesterday and I end up going, 'I just wanted to say, what Chloe said, you know, she was, like, bang out of order and it took a lot of balls for you to say what you did . . .'

He goes, 'Thanks, Ross,' and I'm like, 'I mean, what the fock is that girl's problem. She's turned out to be a bigger bitch than Erika,' and then – *Oh, fock!* – I remember that Clifford is standing only a few feet away. He didn't hear me, though. He's too busy giving us our instructions – dos and don'ts basically.

'Have you ever heard of supersedure?' Fionn goes.

How do I answer that? Of course I focking haven't. I don't say that, though. I pull the same face I used to at school when I was cracking on that the answer was on the tip of my tongue. Of course, he knows me too well.

'Supersedure,' he goes, 'is the process by which an old queen bee is replaced by a new queen. You see, bees communicate by way of pheromones. In every hive you've got a queen, who, by emitting various chemical scents, tells the entire fifty-thousand-strong population when to work, sleep, eat, shit.

'When a queen gets old, her egg-laying ability diminishes and at the same time so does her pheromone output. When the other bees sense this, they create a new queen, killing the old one.'

I should maybe listen to Fionn a bit more – he's actually a pretty interesting goy when you, like, concentrate on what he's saying and shit.

'So basically Chloe reckons Erika's there for the taking?' I go. 'And she wants to be the queen bee . . .'

He shrugs his shoulders and goes, 'What else are we, Ross,

but animals? We spend so much time examining our higher motives while all the time ignoring our fundamental animalistic ones . . .'

I'm definitely going to stort reading. I might even buy a focking book in Heathrow on the way home.

Clifford's still banging on.

He's going, 'Trap-shooting involves, quite simply, shooting at small, saucer-shaped discs that are fired into the air at various angles of elevation by this machine here.'

I'm a bit John B. to get on with it, to be honest. I don't think I'm the only one either.

'Now, your guns – which you should all have broken at this time – take two cartridges, which means you have two shots at each clay, or bird, whatever you want to call them. Now, has anyone here ever shot a gun before?'

And it's at that exact point, roysh, that we hear this little voice going, '*Pull!*' and there's, like, two *massive* explosions, and I am NOT exaggerating when I say we all immediately hit the focking deck.

There's smoke everywhere. My first thought is, JP's got his hands on a gun and gone postal, but when it finally clears, roysh, there's Ronan standing there with his gun in his hands – this'd be his own one now, as in the sawn-off? – and he's blowing into the barrels and sort of, like, staring into the distance at the little bits of clay still falling to the ground.

Clifford gets up off the ground and goes, 'By jove, Ronan, you're a natural,' and Ronan sort of, like, shrugs modestly and goes, 'I'm shooting guns me whole life, so I am,' and Clifford reacts like that's the most natural thing in the world.

He goes, 'Excellent! I see your gun is missing its barrels. We had a robbery here at the house once. Awfully exciting.

The chap had a gun just like that. Supposed to give a bigger kick, is that so?'

Ronan's there, 'You'd certainly feel it in your shoulder, alreet,' and as he's saying this he's breaking the gun, putting two more cartridges into it and snapping it shut again.

Of course, I'm straight over to him.

I pull him to one side and I go, 'Where the *fock* did you get that gun?' and of course, the way everyone's looking at me all of a sudden, you'd swear *I* was the focking villain here.

'No names, no pack drill,' Ronan goes.

Then he thinks better of it and goes, 'Winker gev it to me. I was saying there was probably going to be clay-pigeon shooting. It was a present.'

I'm there, 'Whoa, Horsey, who the fock is Winker?' and he goes, 'He's Nudger's brother,' as if that's supposed to mean something to me. 'Mention that name to Plod, by the way, and it might be the last conversation you ever have. *Capisce?*'

I'm like, 'Don't *capisce* me. I'm taking that gun off you,' but before I can prise it from his hands, he goes, 'What if I told you this piece may or may not have been used in a recent robbery on a post office in Dunboyne?'

Of course, I just freeze.

He gives me a wink, turns on his heel, then goes, 'PULL!' and there's two more blasts. The clay, or the bird, or whatever the fock you want to call it doesn't stand a chance.

Clifford looks at me and goes, 'It's like he was born to it,' and I'm just there thinking, never was a truer word spoken.

'*Oh* my God, she's SO good,' Sorcha's going. 'She sleeps right through. I put her down in the evening and I *actually* have to wake her myself in the morning,' and I don't know whose baby she's talking about, roysh, but it couldn't be ours.

I pick her little Eeyore up off the floor where she threw it and I bring it over to where she's lying on the bed and hold it in front of her, roysh, and do one of those funny voices that babies usually focking love. But Honor looks not at Eeyore but at me, with what would have to be described as fear in her eyes. She's terrified of me.

She scrunches up her face, roysh, like she's about to scream the house down. Of course, Sorcha would go ballistic, so I move away, roysh, and the second I do – the *very* second – she relaxes again.

I go into the *en suite*, roysh, because for a moment I actually think I'm going to cry. In the end I don't, but I sit there on the bowl for twenty minutes, wondering what the fock is wrong with me? What's there for a baby to hate about me?

When I come out, Sorcha's going, 'It won't be long now, Lauren. I presume everything's arranged,' and Lauren laughs and goes, 'Yeah, you know me – military precision . . .'

Sorcha goes, 'Weren't you going to get married in Lahinch? What happened there?' and Lauren sort of, like, throws her eyes up to heaven and goes, 'Well, you remember I told you I had all those wonderful childhood memories of holidays down there? Well, when I phoned the hotel to book the reception, they remembered the name Coghlan-O'Hara. I mean, you would, wouldn't you?

'It seems the last time we were there, we left with certain bills unpaid. I wondered why we came in through the revolving doors at the front and left by the kitchen and an emergency exit . . .'

The two of them crack up laughing.

'Which was alarmed, by the way . . .'

I don't know whether I, like, misgauge the mood of the conversation, but I thought it would have been perfectly acceptable to go, 'Good old Hennessy – he never changes, does he?' But when I do, Sorcha suddenly gets all, like, serious with me and goes, 'People in glass houses? *Hello?*' which is a reference to my old man and totally bang out of order.

Lauren goes, 'So it's Foxrock Church and then the Four Seasons,' and Sorcha says the Four Seasons is SUCH an amazing hotel and Lauren says *oh my God* it is and then, after a couple of gags about Chloe's new top tens, Lauren heads off.

And not before time either. I actually really like Lauren – even though she's not exactly my number-one fan – but I'm actually gagging for my bit here, which I always am when I'm feeling a bit down.

And Sorcha is looking incredible, it has to be said. She's shed a fair bit of the cargo she piled on when she was up the Ballyjames and I'm thinking I'm going to have another crack at the title this afternoon.

So you can imagine that it's, like, music to my ears, roysh, when she turns around to me, the second Lauren's gone, and goes, 'Ross, I think it's time we got things back to normal on the homefront, if you know what I mean . . .'

I actually go, 'Live the focking dream!' and stort unbuttoning my chinos.

But then she's suddenly like, 'Er, what are you doing?'

I'm there, 'Well, I wouldn't mind getting straight into it actually. I was hoping we could put off that whole foreplay thing until we, I don't know, find our feet again . . .'

So there I am, roysh, standing there with my kacks around my ankles, trying to get my Dubes off without undoing the laces, and I realize that Sorcha's giving me serious filthies.

She goes, 'When I said *back to normal*, Ross, I meant I was thinking of going back to work. Aoife can't manage the shop on her own, Ross. She has problems enough managing herself . . .'

It's actually *his* voice I hear first. He's going, 'He *is* a lovely bloke. That's why it's only fair to tell him,' and I'm thinking, who the fock is Ronan dishing out advice to now?

I'm standing outside this sort of, like, drawing room, listening at the half-opened door and I'm actually finding this hord to believe, roysh, but it turns out to be, like, Erika pouring her hort out to him.

She's going, 'I just don't want to hurt him . . .'

I haven't heard her sound this upset since she found out that Mount Anville storted out life in Glasnevin.

Ronan's there, 'You've got to think about yourself. Here, give that nose a good blow,' which she does, because I can hear it.

Then she goes, 'I can't believe I'm unloading on you. You're – what? – eight years old?' and he's there, 'I've been around the track a time or two meself. I know what it's like to have your heart kicked round in the dirt.'

You have to give it to him, he's a focking comedian, this kid.

'Looks fairly simple from where I'm sitting,' he goes then. 'The houses, the money, the fancy paintings, they don't matter a damn,' and I'm thinking, what the fock is he saying? I'm actually tempted to burst in there to tell him to stop talking out of his orse.

He's going, 'Clifford's a great bloke. Not a bad bone in his body . . .'

Erika's there, 'But what if I can't have the person I *really*

67

love?' and it's, like, HOLY FOCK! Suddenly, all I can hear is my own breathing.

Ronan goes, 'You're in love with someone else?'

'It's not an issue,' she goes. 'He's taken. The die is cast . . .'

I have to say, roysh, I honestly had no idea she felt this way about me.

'I've been in love with him since I was fifteen.'

'Jaysus,' Ronan goes.

I've got my ear roysh up against the door for this bit.

She goes, 'I'm too much of a hard bitch, though. Well, that's what I send out. My signals, they frighten boys away – the nice ones, anyway . . .'

There's, like, a lull in the conversation. I wonder should I make my entrance now.

'My parents split up when I was thirteen,' she goes.

I'm thinking, I actually remember that.

'My dad, he was such a focking pillar of the community. Minister for the Eucharist. *Huh!* He was a focking fraud. He cheated on my mum. He cheated on her all their married life, but it took her years to get the goods on him. When she did, she took him to the cleaners. I get my hard streak from her, see. Always look after number one. That's how I end up in places like . . . like *this* . . .'

There's, like, silence again. And then before I know what I'm doing, I've, like, borged through the door and gone, 'It's too late for regrets, Erika,' and they both spin around in, like, total shock to find me standing there.

'I'm actually *with* someone now?' I go. 'And in case you haven't noticed, she's *supposed* to be your best friend?'

Erika's just staring at me, roysh, lost for words.

I'm there, 'You've missed the boat, Babes. You had your chance. Loads of focking chances. How many times did I make a move on you over the years and you burned me? You nearly broke my fingers at Louise Prunty's twenty first, in case you've forgotten. And all because you thought you could do SO much better . . .'

Erika's like, 'Ross . . .' and I'm going, 'Save it. Hord and all as it is, Erika, you're just going to have to try and get over me.'

It's at that point, roysh, that she storts totally losing it. At the top of her voice, roysh, she goes, 'I'm not talking about *you*, you focking idiot!'

Of course, that stops me dead in my tracks. If it's not me . . .

And then it suddenly hits me, like I've just jumped into an ice bath after a really hord training session – obviously in which I've played really, really well.

I'm like, 'Christian! It was *you* . . .'

She's there, 'How long were you standing outside?' and I go, '*That's* why you gave him the room with the Rubens,' and she doesn't answer, roysh, just looks away.

I go, 'Oh my God, this is, like, too weird. The godmother and godfather of my daughter. That's, like . . . incest,' and Ronan's giving me daggers, roysh, as if to say, go easy, Rosser.

I'm there, 'Those phone calls . . . they were, like, wrecking the dude's head,' but again she doesn't answer and I end up going, '*Christian!* I mean, Christian? He's my best friend and everything, but, well, it's a strange one, I'll give you that. I mean, you could have anyone you wanted.'

She just, like, spins around, roysh, suddenly looking more like the old Erika, and goes, 'Like *you*, for instance?' and I'm like, 'Well, in a word, pretty much, yeah. Before I got married obviously.'

She looks at me like she's just wiped me off the sole of

her best Manolos. 'How could you think I'd be interested in you?' she goes.

I'm thinking, I don't have to stand here selling myself to anyone.

I'm there, 'Well, it can't have escaped your attention that I wasn't exactly at the back of the queue when God was handing out looks. I mean, *Christian* . . . the dude's on another focking planet,' and I actually feel bad for, like, dissing my best friend here, but the whole thing is just, like, weirding me out?

Erika stands up.

I'm like, 'Where are you going?' and she goes, 'It's about time I told him the truth,' and I go, 'HELLO? He's marrying Lauren. Okay, she might not be in your league looks-wise, but he loves the girl . . .'

She goes, 'I'm not going to tell *Christian*! I'm going to tell Clifford.'

I turn around to Ronan and give him one of my disappointed looks. Then I go, 'That's *you*, that is. Filling her head with all that focking happy-ever-after bullshit. You've a lot to learn, kid. I was looking forward to holidays over here – drinking and shooting, servants looking after my every whim. That's pretty much gone out the window now.'

Erika sits down again and goes, 'Ross, will you shut up!' and all of a sudden, roysh, she looks up in surprise and I'm suddenly aware of another presence in the room. I spin around, expecting to see Clifford standing there, except it's not, roysh.

It's Lauren.

Erika puts her head in her hands, roysh, and bursts into tears. I turn around to Lauren and I go, 'Is that who you suspected it was all along?' and she gives me this look, roysh, which basically says, get the fock out of here now.

She just sits down next to Erika on the old chaise and, instead of scratching her eyes out, which she has every right to do, she puts her orms around her and pulls her close to her and suddenly Erika's sobbing away on her chest and Lauren's stroking her hair, telling her everything's going to be okay.

Erika keeps apologizing to her, roysh, presumably for the phone calls, then she goes, 'Lauren, please don't tell Christian. I know it's a lot to ask but . . .'

Lauren goes, 'Erika, I—' and then she looks up, over my shoulder, and I whip around and who's standing there, roysh, only the man himself.

It's like an episode of focking *Hollyoaks*, this.

I turn around to him and I go, 'You're a focking dark horse, aren't you?' but he walks straight past me, roysh, over to where Erika and Lauren are sitting.

'Christian,' she goes, 'I'm so sorry. The way I felt . . . the way I feel . . . I was desperate . . .' and she's so upset, she can hordly string the words together.

I'm expecting him to come back with something from focking *Star Wars* – this happened to Han and Leia on the planet whatever-the-fock — but he doesn't, roysh, he just goes, 'I had no idea, Erika . . .'

She goes, 'I didn't tell you. And now I've caused all this. What are people going to say?'

Christian takes hold of her hand. It's pretty focking emotional stuff, it has to be said.

'There's no real harm done,' Lauren goes. 'There's no need for anyone to know about this – anyone outside this room . . .' and for some reason, roysh, she shoots me a look.

Erika goes, 'It's too late. Chloe knows. Stupid – I told her about it when we were fifteen. When she heard about the phone calls, she worked it out . . .'

All fits into place now. Explains why Erika's been letting that wagon away with murder. I mean, in a fair fight she'd, like, break in two.

One thing's for sure, though – there's not going to be any wedding now. I turn around to Ronan and I'm there, 'Come on, you. I suppose we'd better stort packing.'

I'm standing at the carousel, waiting for our bags.

'Erika in love with Christian,' I go. 'Who would have believed it?'

Sorcha's there, '*I* knew.'

I'm like, 'You?'

She goes, 'She's my best friend, Ross. Do you think there's anything about that girl that I don't know?'

I'm there, 'I suppose. So where's she gone then?'

'America,' she goes. 'Just for a few weeks. Get her head straight.'

She has a sister in New York who works for Goldman Sachs. Earns a focking fortune apparently.

I spot Ronan's case. It's got, like, a sticker on it that says, 'Property of Prisoner #30725'. I lift it off the conveyor belt.

I hear Chloe telling Sophie that we won't be seeing Erika again. She goes, 'How could she even, like, show her face?'

3. Fever

'For God's sake,' Sorcha's old man goes and he stops cutting his steak, grabs the napkin up off his lap and focks it down on the table. 'How much more of *this* do we have to listen to?'

I was actually halfway through telling a story about the time we played Clongowes and I sold Gordon D'Arcy an unbelievable dummy and the goy ended up doing his actual hernia.

'Why does the conversation always have to revolve around *you*?' he goes.

I have to say, roysh, I didn't realize he was such a big Dorce fan. Sorcha's old man went to Mary's. But then, I suppose it might have something to do with the fact that he hates my *actual* guts?

Sorcha's old dear turns around and goes, 'Edmund! Don't spoil the day – this is *supposed* to be a celebration,' and the goy just gives me a filthy, then takes his napkin up again and goes back to his steak.

We're having Sunday lunch in LePanto, roysh, in the Radisson in Booterstown, and what we're celebrating is the fact that, from tomorrow, Sorcha's shop is going to be the first in Ireland to sell Rock & Republic jeans, which is like, big swinging mickey.

Portly to piss off her old man, and portly to show that I am actually a nice goy, I turn around to her and go, 'Tell us a bit more about these jeans, Babes,' and without looking up, roysh, I can tell that her old man is staring at me like he wants to rip my orms out of my focking sockets.

Sorcha looks up from her chicken liver terrine with balsamic reduction – which she's having as, like, a main course – and goes, 'They cost four hundred and fifty euro a pair and I cannot believe the demand for them already. We've got, like, twenty pairs of VB Rocks arriving in tomorrow and orders for, like, forty-five. It's like, *oh my God!*' and I'm there, 'I'd imagine it is – they're the ones that that focking Posh Spice wears, aren't they?' laying it on with a focking trowel now.

She nods and I raise my glass and propose a toast to my wonderful wife and her great business brain, roysh, and her prick of an old man has no choice but to join in.

'Speaking of which,' Sorcha goes, and then she pauses, like she's got some big focking announcement to make. I can't think what it could be. 'Ross and I have been talking and we've decided that I should go back to work.'

Her old pair immediately look at me and I'm tempted to go, whoa, that's *not* how it focking happened.

'Don't blame Ross,' Sorcha goes. 'This was a decision we arrived at together. It's like, oh my God, I don't want to lose my PBI . . .'

Sorcha's old dear gets there before me. 'What's a PBI?'

'My Pre-Baby Identity,' Sorcha goes. 'You have to make time and energy for the things that you used to do. Oh my God, I'm thinking of taking up reiki again. Or even Indian head massage . . .'

Her old man is not a happy bunny.

'I thought you *wanted* to be a full-time mum,' he goes. 'You said it yourself, stay-at-home mums form a bond with their children that working mums don't. Your words, Princess . . .'

Sorcha goes, 'But that was before I was talking to Sophie's

mum – she's, like, a midwife? – and she says that new mums have to be careful that their lives don't become entirely defined by nappy changes and feeding times. Oh my God, I don't want to end up, like, *resenting* Honor . . .'

'And *you're* happy with this?' the old man goes, turning to me. 'Seven o'clock every morning, your daughter plonked in the hands of some . . . crèche worker?' and before I can think of an answer, roysh, Sorcha's gone, 'Dad, we're going to hire a nanny,' which again is news to me. 'And I actually don't want to discuss it any more . . .'

Sorcha's sister – Oonagh, or Asia, or whatever-the-fock she's called – takes that as an opportunity to turn around and go, 'Sorcha, did I tell you I got that basque in the end?'

Sorcha, who's still in a bit of a snot, goes, 'The *Agent Provocateur* one?' and the sister nods her head and she's like, 'Yeah – in baby pink, though.'

While this conversation is taking place, I should add that the sister has, like, kicked off one of her Dubes and stuck her foot in my crotch and is doing her usual trick of trying to bring me off under the table.

She's going, 'It's really soft. I'll have to show it to you,' and she looks at me when she says it and I swear to God, roysh, I've got a baton on me that could put manners on a Reclaim the Streets rally.

I take a drink of water and try to think about some of the birds Oisinn has been with over the years, to try to, like, bring down the swelling, but it's no good.

She's there, 'I bought a balcony bra as well. It's amazing. It sort of, like, pushes everything up,' and she actually grabs her top tens and storts, like, massaging them.

And of course nobody says a focking Charlie Bird to her.

At the same time she's sort of, like, flicking me with her big toe, roysh, and I try to pull my chair back a bit, but she's got a pair of legs on her like Shane Horgan.

There's no getting away from her. She's going, 'When I put it on, my breasts are up *here*. And they feel SO firm.'

I swear to God, roysh, I'm going to blow my muck roysh here at this focking table.

Suddenly, roysh, just in the nick of time, the old Wolfe Tone rings – the *Hawaii Five-O* theme tune, which no one in LePanto seems to love, it has to be said – and, without thinking, I jump to my feet.

'I have to take this,' I go. 'It could be Michael Cheika.'

And of course, in these beige chinos, it's pretty obvious to everyone around the table that I'm horder than Phil Mitchell.

'Oh, for heaven's sakes,' Sorcha's old man goes, putting his hand up to his eyes and making a big focking drama out of it. Sorcha goes, '*Oh my God!*' eight times and I'm actually tempted – while we're on the subject – to point out that this is the most sexual experience I've had involving *any* member of her family since the day she found out she was up the Damien with Honor.

But I don't, roysh, because it's nice to be nice – *and* because I've got a call to take.

It's Oisinn.

Actually, I meant to send him a text earlier. Heard he's been Moby since we got back from England.

I'm like, 'Dude, how the fock are you? I met that Clara Balfe – used to be deputy headgirl in Loreto on the Green, *was* Malahide Festival Queen two years running – coming out of Blue Eriu. What the fock is mono?'

'Mononucleosis,' he goes. 'It's American for glandular fever.'

76

I'm like, 'She said you'd lost, like, two stone,' and as I'm saying this, roysh, I'm deciding to hit the Orangerie for a cheeky JD. I deserve it after an hour with that family.

'It's not quite two stone, but it's in that ballpark,' he goes.

I'm there, 'You must be focking miserable,' and he's like, 'Er, not exactly. Ross, you've got to get out here . . .' and I'm like, 'Why?' and he's there, 'You've got to see it for yourself,' and I'm like, 'Bit difficult at the mo – having Sunday lunch with the Lalors.'

'Focking mare,' he goes.

I'm like, 'Tell me about it. Look, I'll swing out tonight,' and he goes, 'Later, Dude.'

I hit Oisinn's new gaff on Shrewsbury Road, roysh, with a DVD of Ireland's 2004 Triple Crown win and twelve cans of Ken, only to discover that the dude's got company. Bad focking company.

It's, like, Chloe who answers the door – Chloe, of all people – and she goes, 'Oh my God, Ross, *hi*!' and she air-kisses, then hugs me, like she hasn't seen me in two years. I saw her in focking Superquinn yesterday and she pretty much blanked me.

I'm looking at her, roysh, thinking, what's *her* focking game? Is Oisinn throwing her a bone now?

That's when I smell Dettol.

'Come in,' she goes, like I *need* an actual invitation to walk into one of my best friend's gaffs.

I head straight for the kitchen, where the hum is coming from, and there, roysh, is Emer . . . scrubbing the focking floor.

It wouldn't be the first time I've seen Emer down on her

hands and knees, but it *is* the first time I've seen her with a focking J Cloth in her hand.

This totally weird feeling comes over me.

I'm there, 'Okay, what the *fock* have you done to my friend?' presuming – naturally enough – that the only reason Chloe and Emer would be in here, wearing rubber gloves, is that they've killed Oisinn and now they're, like, cleaning up the crime scene.

'Oisinn's *upstairs*, Ross,' Chloe goes. '*Oh* my God – *what* is your problem?'

Yeah, I'm actually going to have to *stop* watching *CSI* before I go to bed.

Suddenly, roysh, Amie with an ie arrives into the kitchen with an iron in her hand. She's like, 'Okay, that's all three bags finished. I am, like, SO tired . . .' but she says it, roysh, like it's a good thing?

Then she cops me standing there and goes, 'Oh, hi, Ross. Oh my God, so Erika was in love with Christian. That's like, HELLO?'

'Sad, sad, sad,' Chloe goes and Emer's there, 'I heard she had a *total* meltdown,' and she says it with a big focking smile on her face. 'She thought she was all that. About time she was taken down a peg or two. What's Sorcha saying about it?'

I'm like, 'Why don't you ask her yourself?'

'Hey,' she goes, 'will I tell him about Aoife?' and Chloe and Amie with an ie both laugh, which she takes as a yes.

'I'm not being a bitch or anything,' she goes, 'but I saw her in, like, Café Java . . . *stuffing* her face with carrot cake. *And* she had an espresso mallowchino . . .'

'Well,' Chloe goes, 'she's certainly fighting the good fight against anorexia,' and the three of them crack their holes laughing.

I don't know why I'm still standing here.

Emer goes, 'That girl *never* had any willpower.'

'Pathetic,' Amie with an ie goes.

Chloe looks at me and she's like, 'Your wife's two best friends are . . . *losers*,' and she makes an L shape with her finger and thumb.

I hate myself for not being able to think of a decent comeback. Instead, I head upstairs to Oisinn's room. He's watching the news, of all things. Have to say, though, there *is* something about that Anne Cassin.

'Hey, Ross, what's the Jack?' he goes and I'm like, 'I might ask you the same thing. What are *they* doing here?'

He mutes the old Liza and goes, 'You probably wouldn't believe me, even if it was in my nature to tell tales . . .'

I'm just, like, staring at him.

'No focking way,' I go. 'All three . . .'

He just smiles.

I'm like, 'At the same time?'

He shakes his head.

'One after the other?' I go. 'Oisinn, I need to know – *what the fock?*'

'It's glandular fever,' he goes. 'You might say it's *in* this year. I mean, I've lost over a stone and a half in a week. Every bird wants to catch it. And it's spread by kissing . . .'

'Three birds in one day!' I go. 'Who do you think you are – me?'

He's like, 'You don't know the half of it. I actually started to feel a bit Moby the night we got back from England. Went to the doctor the next day and he says I've got glandular fever. Tells me to go home to bed. Now, I told one person – Barbara Bannon – because she texted me and I just happened to mention it to her . . .'

I'm there, 'Is this Barbara Bannon who looks like Simon Cowell?' and he goes, 'Yeah.'

He's in love with her.

'Anyway,' he goes, 'within an hour the news that I'm glandular is all over town. Two hours later – I shit you not – I'm lying here in the scratcher, watching *Family Affairs*, when all of a sudden the doorbell rings . . .'

'*No* focking way . . .'

'I shit you not. It's Maolisa.'

I'm there, 'Violin Maolisa?'

He's like, 'Flugelhorn.'

I'm there, 'I don't know her,' and he goes, 'I don't either. I mean, I've been with her five or six times, but I don't actually know her, as in *know* know. So she says she heard I was sick and – get this, Ross – she made me some chicken soup, her mum's secret recipe, blahdy blahdy blah. We're standing in the hall downstairs and she looks at me and goes, *oh my God*, you *have* lost weight, and before I can say anything she's storted sucking the lips off me. Focking soup everywhere . . .'

I'm like, 'No way!'

He's like, '*Way!* Anyway, I don't need to paint you a picture. An hour later, she's getting dressed . . .'

'And she turns around to me and she asks me what I think of Anna Finnegan, as in her best friend . . .'

I'm like, 'I know her. Fock, she looks like Samia Ghadie.'

Oisinn goes, 'Well, I nearly fell out of the bed when she asked me if I was interested in being with her. She must have seen the look of shock on my face because she said, "Hey, you have glandular fever, that makes you SO hot at the moment." The next morning, Anna calls around . . .'

'Holy shit.'

'That night, Sara Crook *and* Maria Munn. Then, about eleven o'clock, some bird who I swear to God I've never clapped eyes on in my life – said we met at some twenty-first or other in Sandycove Tennis Club. Anyway, she seemed pretty concerned about me, so I let her in.

'By Thursday night the living room down there was like a focking doctor's waiting room. I actually threw a few *OK*s and a couple of *Woman's Way*s in there – one or two *Newsweek*s as well – just to help them all pass the time.'

He's a funny focker, it has to be said.

So anyway, roysh, I stick the DVD in and sit on the end of the bed and we crack open a couple of cans and watch Gordon D'Arcy rip the total piss out of the Welsh midfield.

Oisinn goes, 'And just to think, that goy there envies *you*,' which he didn't have to say, roysh, but it's nice to hear all the same – and it *is* actually true. I've lost count of the number of times I've wiped that goy's eye on the scenario-front over the years.

Oisinn's suddenly there, 'How's your old man, by the way?' and straight away I'm like, 'Couldn't give a fock. If they give him twenty years, it'd be no skin off my nose.'

He's like, 'You've been to see him, though?' and I'm there, 'Just the once. More out of guilt than anything . . .'

Whoa! Big Mal's just creamed Mork Regan – how did that goy ever walk again?

Oisinn goes, 'Bit horsh, Ross. I mean, you're all he's got. You and your old dear,' and I consider telling him about that focking wagon, but then I don't bother. It'd only bring us both down.

Go on, Strings, you little focker!

'By the way,' he goes, deciding it's wise to change the subject, 'you know JP's back talking again?'

'As in properly back talking? Are you serious?'

'Can't shut him up,' he goes, 'and I don't mean in a good way. He rang here the other night, storted ranting and raving, throwing Matthew, Mark, Luke and John at me. I told him I preferred the silence. I mean, the goy should be *in* somewhere, Ross . . .'

I think we've all come to that conclusion.

When it's over, I decide to hit the road. I leave the rest of the cans with him.

I don't know why, but I stick my head around the kitchen door to say goodbye. Emer is checking Chloe's glands. She's going, '*Oh* my God! They're *actually* swollen.'

Two hundred squids for electricity. A grand for my mobile bill. Three and a half Ks for my cor insurance. Plus there's four Ks on my credit cord that Visa seem anxious about getting cleared.

He answers on the third ring.

I'm like, 'Hennessy, how the fock are you?' and he storts telling me that his back's a bit sore but that he's really looking forward to Lauren and Christian's wedding. I go, 'Hey, Dude, it's a figure of speech, I don't actually give a shit how you are,' and then I'm like, 'I've a few Jack and Jills here that need paying. I presume you'll be doing that for me while focking Shawshank's away?'

He goes, 'Yes, your father transferred some money into an account to look after your bills,' and I'm there, 'There better be a lot of it. I'm not scrimping and saving for the next twenty years just because that focker's a crook.'

'I need to talk to you about that,' he goes.

It's a pretty crap reception, it has to be said. He's breaking up left, roysh and centre.

'I'm in the humidor,' he goes. 'Probably going to lose you altogether in a minute,' and of course I'm thinking, what the fock is a humidor?

He's like, 'I'm in that little cigar shop at the top of Grafton Street. Up the stairs,' and as it happens, roysh, I'm in the club, so I go, 'Stay there. I'll be up to you in five minutes.'

A humidor turns out to be an airtight room they use to keep the tobacco moist. I find Hennessy in there, sniffing a focking Cohiba the size of Paul O'Connell's orm.

'Pure quality,' he goes to me. 'Must have been *some* harvest,' and I end up just, like, shrugging my shoulders, as if to say, er, this affects me *how*?

He puts the cigar back and he goes, 'I want you to brace yourself, Ross. I've got some good news . . . but also some bad news.'

I sit down in the big leather ormchair in the corner and go, 'Shoot.'

He's there, 'You're not going to see your father again for a very long time,' and I'm just, like, staring into the distance, nodding. Then I go, 'Sorry, can I just check with you – is that the good news or the bad news?'

Of course he looks at me like I'm chicken oriental. 'That's the *bad* news,' he goes. 'Heavens above!'

I suppose it all depends on your POV.

He picks a cigar out of an open box and waves it at me. 'You know what this is?' and I don't answer. 'It's a 1983 Cuban Davidoff, manufactured before old Zino fell out with Castro and shifted his entire operation to the Dominican Republic. Publicly burned a hundred thousand of his Cuban stock before he left Havana. Very rare. A hundred and fifty euros each . . .'

I go, 'You said there was *good* news as well?' and he stops and stares at me and goes, 'Good news? Did I?' and then he shakes his head. 'No, Ross, there's no good news, I'm afraid. Probably just offered you that as a palliative – help you swallow the bad news . . .'

The manager sticks his head around the door and asks if I'd like a cup of Cuban coffee. I could get used to this place.

Hennessy goes, 'What year was young Christian born?' and I'm there, 'What year? It was 1982 – same as me,' and when the goy arrives in with my coffee, Hennessy goes to him, 'I'm going to take twenty Davidoffs from Eighty-Two,' and then he turns to me and he's like, 'I'm meeting him during the week for a little, er, chat. Want to make sure he looks after my little girl.'

When the goy hands him the box, he taps the top of it and goes, 'He can smoke one of these every year on his birthday.'

I take a sip of my coffee.

For some reason, I go, 'What kind of stretch is the old man looking at?' and Hennessy sort of, like, blows hord through his lips. 'It's not looking good, Ross,' he goes. 'As his solicitor, obviously my advice would be to cut a deal. Name names. The problem is, Charles O'Carroll-Kelly is a name. And with the blasted meter running so high on all these tribunals, the public wants to see *someone* go to jail. Unfortunately, it's going to be poor old Charles.'

He hands the goy his credit cord.

I go, 'Well, he can focking rot in there for all I care. Don't forget to give me a bell if he dies. Let me know what's coming to me.'

He's like, 'You mean you're not going to visit him?'

I'm there, 'Already did. Once was enough. That focking mutt he's married to can look after him.'

He sits down in the other ormchair, serious all of a sudden. 'You know,' he goes, 'I'll never for the life of me understand why he allowed your mother to write that book. She put everything down. All his questionable business details. In black and white. I've known your mother almost as long as I've known Charles, so it's hard for me to say this, but, well, it's almost like she wanted him to go to jail . . .'

I'm there, 'She hasn't even been to focking see him, as in not even once.'

He goes, 'It sounds very much to me, Ross, like your mother's got herself a solicitor.'

I'm just, like, staring into space, roysh, trying to take all this shit in. He goes, 'Honestly? If I was representing her, with the Criminal Assets people sniffing around the family accounts, I'd advise her to put as much distance between herself and Charles as she possibly could.'

He stands up, takes the bills out of my hand and, without looking at them, folds them in three and slips them into the inside pocket of his Cole Haan sheepskin coat.

'Look, this is going to get a lot uglier,' he goes, 'especially with the Criminal Assets Bureau involved. You're going to have to get used to the idea that there might be some changes in your life, Ross.'

He taps the top of the box again and goes, '*A woman is only a woman – but a good cigar is a smoke*. Rudyard Kipling said that.'

I'm like, 'Yeah? I can't wait for your father-of-the-bride speech.'

Has to be said, Fionn's in his focking element teaching.

He's going, 'It's unbelievably rewarding, especially when

you find a group who are really interested. Like my sixth-year English class. I've even been teaching them a few rudiments of philosophy . . .'

I'm looking around. Everyone – Sorcha, Aoife, Lauren, Christian – they're all hanging on his every word.

'Like the other day, I put that classic Heraclitus question to them: can you step into the same river twice, or does the constant flow of water mean that it's a different river the second time around? And this kid – he's a great student – he says, well, if that's the case, is it possible to step into the same river once?'

We all crack our holes laughing. I'll Google that later, find out what the fock is funny about it.

They've all turned out for Oisinn in fairness. I'm looking around me and I can't believe who's here – we're talking Andrea Roche, we're talking Caroline Morahan, we're talking Rosanna Davison.

In fact, the Merrion Hotel is, like, wall-to-wall scenario. There's these huge purple silk ribbons everywhere, with Holy$_2$O written on them, and there's, like, five or six Barbie dolls handing out free sample bottles of Oisinn's new holy water.

You've got to say fair focks to the goy.

Whoa – there's Glenda. I think I'm actually in love with that girl. I'm about to go over and use one or two of my lines on her, roysh, when all of a sudden focking JP sidles up to me and the first words he's spoken to me in probably a month are, '*I am He who lives, and was dead, and behold, I am alive forevermore. Amen. And I have the keys of Hades and of Death . . .*'

I'm like, 'Well, that's all good news,' basically humouring the mad focker.

I notice his eyebrows still haven't grown back.

'How's your father?' he goes then, out of the blue.

'Don't know,' I go. 'Only been to see him the once.'

He's there, 'And did you have some words of comfort for him? From Psalms, perhaps? Or Proverbs? *He who walks with integrity walks securely,*' and I'm there, 'Er, no. I called him a stupid penis a couple of times, though . . .'

I try to change the subject. I'm like, 'Some focking turnout for Oisinn, isn't it? All the papers and everything are here. I'm telling you, he's going to be focking coining it in . . .'

JP doesn't bat an eyelid, just goes, 'Our generation, we're so obsessed with money, we've lost sight of what's important. We need to refix our focus and trust that God will provide for us. *Your heavenly Father already knows all you need and he will give you all you need from day to day if you live for him and make the Kingdom of God your primary concern.* That's Matthew 6:32.'

And this from the man who used to drive around Tallaght with Oisinn, shouting 'Poverty!' and 'Eat your young!' through the sunroof of his old man's Beamer.

I can't listen to any more of his shit. Fionn's right. He needs help, but we can't, like, *force* him to get it?

I give Laura Woods a wink.

The next thing, roysh, Oisinn's at the mic, thanking us for coming and cracking a gag about how when he was at Castlerock, the teachers were constantly telling him that what he wrote didn't make sense – and now, by some weird twist of fate, he makes 'scents' for a living.

That gets a humungous cheer. He could have any bird in this room he wants and wait'll you see, roysh, he'll go home tonight with something that looks like a bucket of burnt Lego.

That's Oisinn.

He goes, 'Consider, if you will, the centrality of holy water in our everyday lives. Like most of you, I'm sure, I keep a font in my hallway . . .'

I actually laugh out loud at that. The goy's got balls like focking Space Hoppers.

'. . . and whenever I dip my fingers in there on my way out the door, I'm reminded of baptism, my initiation into the wonderful Christian faith. Another rite that many of us perform before we leave the house is a social one – the spraying on of perfume or aftershave. And the two are linked. After all, did not John the Baptist tell, I don't know, Moses at the Wedding Feast of Cana that cleanliness is next to Godliness?

'And so I got to thinking, why not combine the two rituals? We all lead busy lives. The Celtic Tiger, blah blah blah. One splash instead of two before going out the door would surely leave us all with a lot more time for sporting and leisure activities.'

Everyone claps.

'Most of you will have got your little aspersoriums of *Love One Another As I Have Loved Yuzu*, which is the first in the Holy$_2$O range. It's a scent for men and women, and one I'm particularly proud of . . .'

He finishes with, 'May God bless you – and keep you fragrant.'

Incredible. No other word for it. I'm there lapping the focker up, roysh, when all of a sudden I hear all these, like, cameras clicking away behind me. I spin around, roysh, and who's walked in, stealing Oisinn's big moment? My old dear.

She's tarted up like a skobe's chariot, of course. Must be four or five grand's worth of designer clobber hanging off her mangy body, and whatever perfume she's wearing smells like Toilet Duck and roadkill. Big focking pouty lips on her, probably the result of collagen implants.

The photographers are all over her, roysh, and she's loving it, sucking in her cheeks and giving them that faraway stare, so caught up in herself that she doesn't even hear me when I shout over to her, 'What the fock are you doing here, you miserable mangebag?' although that agent of hers definitely hears me and tries to stare me out of it.

'He's so handsome, isn't he?' I hear Glenda go and I turn around to her and I'm like, 'What are you looking at? He's got grey hair in a ponytail, for fock's sake,' but she says she thinks it makes him look distinguished. Then she goes, '*You'll* be happy if you have a body like that at his age.'

If I have, I certainly won't be wearing tight-fitting white T-shirts.

Two or three reporters stort firing questions at her. It's like, how's the new book coming along? How's her husband? What designer is she wearing?

All she says is, 'Alexander McQueen,' and then, 'Another time – this isn't *my* day,' and I'm about to shout, why the fock did you gatecrash it then, when my eyes are suddenly drawn to Lance's hand, on the small of her back, guiding her through the crowd.

And that hand, I can't take my eyes off it.

'So,' I go, 'two weeks to go. Any nerves?'

Christian sort of, like, pulls a face and goes, 'Not nerves as such. But, well, there's a couple of things on my mind,' and he thinks for a couple of seconds, roysh, then picks this big whack of A4 paper off the stool beside him and slams it down on the bor.

I'm there, 'What the fock is that?'

There must be, like, five hundred pages there.

He goes, 'It's my prenuptial agreement,' and of course he must cop the look of shock on my face because he goes, 'I'm as serious as an Imperial Star Destroyer,' which means very.

He goes, 'Lauren's old man took me out to Portmarnock the other night for the big fatherly chat. Nice meal. Gave me some cigars. Then he produced this. Said he'd no intention of giving his daughter away unless it was signed.'

Hennessy's some focking operator. I go, 'What's in it?' and Christian storts flicking through the pages, picking out lines at random.

He goes, '*In the event of the first party* – that's Lauren, by the way – *wishing to bear a child, I, the undersigned, pledge that conception – that is, fertilization of the female egg – will take place within six months of the assertion of such a desire and that failure to honour this commitment will result in any marital agreement being declared null and void.*'

I'm there, 'That's focking outrageous. I can't believe Lauren's pulling this shit on you this close to the wedding?'

'Lauren knows nothing about it,' he goes. '*Knew* nothing about it. Hennessy didn't want her to. Said it was to protect her.'

I go, 'But you told her?' and he nods. He's like, 'She wasn't happy either. She's gone to see him tonight . . .'

'Well, I presume you get to keep the cigars,' I go, 'whether you sign it or not?' but he just, like, shrugs his shoulders. It's obviously not that important to him.

I order two more pints. We're tanning them tonight, it has to be said.

I go, 'You said there were a *couple* of things on your mind?' and suddenly he's all, I don't know, awkward with me.

He's there, 'Yeah, look, Ross, obviously my old pair are going to be at the wedding. And, well, obviously it's going to be difficult for everyone, but I've spoken to them both and, well, you know they're making a go of things and . . . well . . . it's far from perfect, but I'd really appreciate it if . . .'

I do not believe this. He's asking me not to bang his old dear. Not to bang his old dear *again*.

I'm like, 'Dude, you don't have to say it. That shit's way in the past – and we're *talking* way. I'm just happy that our friendship survived it, gay as that sounds. And I wouldn't do anything to, like, jeopardize it again.'

He seems happy enough with that.

He focks off then for a hit and miss, roysh, and when he's gone, I'm thinking that, as his best man, I should probably offer him a few words of advice about the whole marriage thing, benefit of my experience, blahdy blahdy blah.

That's when my phone rings. I check the screen and it's, like, Bianca, as in Bianca Luykx. She's supposed to be editing that focking *VIP* now. Of course I give her the big flirty, 'Hey, B, how the hell are you?' but she goes, 'Quit the shit, Ross. The word is you're a father again,' and that totally wrongfoots me.

I'm there, 'Er . . . yeah. A little girl. Honor,' and she laughs, roysh, obviously thinking I'm ripping the piss.

Of course, then she realizes I'm not.

She goes, 'I was wondering would you and Sorcha be interested in doing a photo feature for the magazine,' and I'm sort of, like humming and hawing, roysh, going, 'Well, I'm actually up to my towns at the moment. Spending a lot of time in the gym. I'm not sure if you heard, but I might be going back playing rugby again,' laying it on seriously thick with her.

She goes – and this is out of order, roysh – she goes, 'Well, it's more Sorcha we're interested in. Everyone's talking about her shop. She's doing Rock & Republic now . . .' and I'm thinking, she can actually fock off after that.

I'm there, 'To be honest, Babes, I've no interest in prostituting my wife and daughter just to sell a few copies of your—'

She goes, 'We'll pay you fifty thousand euros.'

I'm like, 'I'll see you the day after tomorrow.'

I hang up and punch the air. Christian sees me on his way back from the TK Maxx.

'Good news, young Skywalker?' he goes.

I'm there, 'Could even be *great* news. I've just got to think of a way of getting Sorcha to pose for a glossy magazine shoot without her knowing it.'

Then I tell him that the secret of a happy marriage is to tell the wife only what she needs to know. And admit nothing, until denying it storts to embarrass you.

There's one thing I'm never going to get used to and that's the hum of this place. Smells of piss basically, which is why I'm wondering what the goy's got to be so cheery about. It's like, does he even know where he is and shit?

'Hasn't escaped my attention, Kicker, that the squad for the autumn internationals is being announced this afternoon,' he goes, before he's even sat down at the table. 'Come on, don't keep me in suspense – have you had a call?'

I go, 'Cop the fock on, will you?' and he's there, 'It's just our friend from Youghal is talking about new faces and I figured . . . well, I'm sure I'll find out in time. Excuse me if I'm sounding a bit chipper today, by the way.'

I'm like, 'Don't tell me – you've storted digging a focking tunnel, have you?' and he laughs as he pulls out his chair and docks his orse opposite me. I go, 'Trust me, there isn't a reason in the world for you to feel chipper in this shithole. I don't even know what I'm doing here. Take my word for it, though. I won't be coming back.'

I look around me. The visiting room's full of scaldy faces, skinny bodies and chunky gold everywhere. It's like Hill 16 on heroin. Except you can never leave.

'Oh, don't believe anything you read in the papers about this place,' he goes. 'It's a cracking little prison, Ross, full of tremendous characters. You see that chap over there?'

I'm like, 'I don't think you should be *actually* pointing in here?' and I look around and the goy he's talking about is a wiry little focker with greased-down hair and a Dublin football jersey.

'He's called Git,' the old man goes. 'First or last name, I'm not sure. I mean, I can ask him later if it's important to you – pop around to his cell and so forth. But he's a fascinating character, Ross – smuggles all sorts of contraband into the prison, see . . .'

I'm looking over both shoulders, going, 'Not that I care one way or the other whether you get a kicking in here, but you should probably keep your voice down?'

He's not listening, though.

He's going, 'Puts it up his, er, you-know-what . . . The Keester Bunny, they call him. I wanted to have a word with him, see could he get me *The Irish Times* in. I mean, the *Indo* would probably be easier, given that you can get it in tabloid now, but I'm desperate to know how a certain G. Thornley Esquire thinks we'll acquit ourselves against New Zealand and Australia, fullstop, new par.'

I'm there, 'How the fock are you still alive?'

Suddenly, his head goes up and he's obviously spotted someone he knows.

'Lex!' he storts shouting. 'Lex!'

Then he stands up and it's like, 'Lex! Lex, old chap!'

Then he goes, 'Oh, he hasn't heard me,' all disappointed. And he sits down again and goes, 'Lex is my new cellie, Ross. Hard as old boots. Armed robbery. Malicious wounding. Whatever you're having yourself. They've just shanghaied the chap up from Cork. He must have been inside a long time – would you believe, he'd never heard of Peter Stringer?'

I'm there, 'Sorry, did I just *actually* hear you use prison slang?' and he goes, 'What, Shanghai? Oh, yes, you pick it up. Don't worry, though, I'm not about to get *strung out on gear*, quote-unquote. Ross, I haven't told you the reason yet for my jollity and mirth. I'm expecting a visitor . . .'

I'm like, 'At last. You probably won't recognize her. She's been botoxed that much, her eyebrows have slipped down the back of her neck . . .'

He goes, 'Er, no, not your mother, Ross. I'm talking about that little chap of yours, young Ronan.'

I'm like, '*Ronan?*' as in the child whose existence this focker denied for years. I'm like, 'Why would Ronan want to visit you?'

'He's been here twice already,' he goes. 'Brought me pictures of Honor and everything.'

'Ronan? He's been here *twice?*'

He's like, 'Yes! Very concerned about his granddad, he was. He knew I was a drive-up, you see. That's prison-speak for a new inmate. I think he was afraid they were going to walk the dogs on me. Seems he's not without friends on the, inverted commas, inside. He put the word about – lay off Charles O'Carroll-Kelly, Independent, Foxrock.'

I'm there, 'Yeah, whatever. What's the Jack with the old dear? You know Hennessy thinks this was her plan all along?'

'Oh, Hennessy and his conspiracy theories,' he goes. 'If your mother doesn't want to see me, Ross, I can't force her. Look, I could be facing a dime here. That's a long time to wait for someone. Your mother's still an attractive woman,' and I'm there, 'No, she's not. She's a focking hound. I've actually seen better-looking things on the end of a fishing line.'

He goes, 'Ross, I'm not cappin' your mother. Yes, I could sit around in my Peter all night, bitchin' up. But what would be the point? Your mother's in a different space right now and I am, too. Being in here has opened my eyes, Ross . . .'

All of a sudden his face lights up. 'Here he comes.'

'Alreet, Grandda,' I hear.

Ronan in the house.

'Story? Alreet, Rosser?'

I'm like, 'Hey, Ro, how the hell are you?' and he turns to the old man and goes, 'See? Didn't I tell you he'd be back?'

'You did that,' he goes. 'You most certainly did.'

Ronan leans in close to him and goes, 'Here, what's the SP? I hear someone bugged out this morning – Baldy Bracken . . .'

'Your information's correct,' the old man goes. 'Seems young Cozzy doowopped the food line and Baldy came at him with a shank. Bladed him up in a big-time way.'

'Baldy's in serious shit, I hear.'

The old man nods. 'Took him straight to bing. Look like he gonna do Buck Rogers time.'

I'm just like, 'Whoa, whoa, whoa – I didn't understand a single focking word of that.'

'Oh, sorry, Ross,' the old man goes. 'It means our friend is looking at an EPRD – that's an Earliest Possible Release Date, to you and I and the chaps from Portmarnock – some time in the twenty-fifth century.'

The next thing, roysh, Ronan goes, 'LOB – bird on the line,' and I look up just as a screw walks past our table.

When he's gone, the old man goes, 'I was telling Ronan the last day – wasn't I, Ronan? – being in here, it's really opened my eyes. Did you know there are people in the world who've never tasted Osso Bucco? Who've never golfed, Ross? Who don't own shares? A whole hidden Ireland I never knew existed. See this chap here?' he goes and he points at this, like, really emaciated-looking goy three or four tables down. 'He got a Jones . . .'

Ronan goes, 'A drug problem, Rosser.'

'That's right. Now it's nigh on impossible to get a new syringe – or, quote-unquote, works – in here. So this chap, he fashions them himself, using the tube of a simple, common-or-garden biro. Well, you know how much I admire ingenuity. Imagine what this chap could do on the outside . . .'

Presumably he's *in here* for what he did on the outside.

I'm there, 'Dad' – and I must be worried about him, roysh, because I never call him that – I go, 'just be careful, will you?' but he doesn't acknowledge it.

Ronan – the voice of experience – goes, 'Doing time is a case of mind over matter. You have to understand that they don't mind and you don't matter.'

The old man goes, 'That's right. Baldy himself gave me two pieces of advice when I arrived here – drink plenty of water and walk slowly.'

I'm there, 'Walk slowly?'

He goes, 'Yes. Because none of us is going anywhere.'

I'm there, 'Just be careful,' as I get up to go. 'You could get hurt in here.'

He looks as happy as I've ever seen him. So does Ronan. How focked up is that?

'Me? Hurt?' he goes. 'I don't think so, Ross. Then who would talk to the Governor about getting us some extra TV time for the forthcoming internationals?'

'Who's this *friend* of yours anyway?' Sorcha goes to me as she's slipping Honor into the JLO Baby three-piece eyelet sundress set that Aoife bought. She goes, 'I don't remember you ever being friends with a photographer,' and I nearly kack it, roysh, thinking she's obviously seen through my – I have to say – pretty clever cover story.

I'm there, 'He's, er, more of a friend of a friend really. He knows Kenny, who used to be on the S with me?' and she just stares at me, roysh, putting pressure on me to, like, add a couple more lines to the story, which I'm already losing track of.

I go, 'He set up his own studio. Doing mostly, like, family portraits and shit? He's won, like, awards,' which is all total horseshit, of course.

But she won't let it go. Your typical Mountie, see – focking dogged.

She goes, 'Awards?' and I'm there, 'Yeah, em, just last week actually . . . he won the Cutest Baby Picture in the Basic World Award. The second time he's won it, according to Kenny. Might actually have been the third. I mean, I can check if you like . . .' and I go to leave the room, roysh, just to get away from the looks she's giving me. It's like she can see straight through me.

She can, of course.

'Because this awful thought struck me,' she goes, 'that maybe you'd gone behind my back and invited, say, *VIP* magazine to come to the house and take pictures of our daughter? For money . . .'

Of course I freeze. I can't even turn around and look at her.

She goes, 'I mean, you were the captain of the Senior Cup team in Castlerock. I run a successful fashion boutique in the Powerscourt Townhouse Centre. That makes us, I suppose, a celebrity couple. I'm sure *VIP* would pay in the region of, I don't know, fifty thousand for a spread with us? If we were interested in prostituting ourselves, that is . . .'

I spin around, roysh, and crack on to be all, like, wounded and shit?

I'm going, 'You think I'd be . . . *capable* of actually doing something like that?' and I sort of, like, turn away from her again, roysh, but out of the corner of my eye I can see that she's not buying it.

I make my voice go all wobbly, cracking on that I'm upset. I'm like, 'I just thought it would be nice to get a family portrait done – as in professionally – of the three of us together. Me being thoughtful for once.'

The next thing, roysh, the doorbell rings. I peg it to the front door and it's Patrick, roysh, as in the photographer, who I've never met before in my life.

It's, like, first things first. I'm there, 'Have you got the shekels?' and he goes, 'Shekels? Well, no. What, you think the magazine would give me fifty thousand euro to drive around with in the boot of my car?'

I'm there, 'Keep your focking voice down, will you?' stepping out onto the doorstep and, like, pulling the door shut behind me.

I'm there, 'Listen, there's one or two things I need to put

you wide on. Sorcha, as in my – I suppose – wife, she's been a bit, I don't know, funny since the baby was born.'

'As in, funny peculiar?' he goes and I'm there, 'Prrr-etty much. Keeps forgetting things. I mean, I mentioned this photo shoot to her a few minutes ago and she couldn't even remember agreeing to it . . .'

I laugh – nervously, you could say.

He takes a step backwards and he goes, 'But she *did* agree to it, didn't she? I mean, I saw her signature on the consent form,' and of course I can't look the dude straight in the face. I'm like, 'She agreed to it alroysh. It's just that, well, like I said, she forgets things . . .'

So suddenly he's nodding all sympathetically and going, 'That might be a touch of post-natal depression. My wife had it after *our* first – mood swings, exhaustion, depression, lack of concentration . . .'

And I just, like, throw my eyes up to heaven and go, 'They're a focking nightmare, women, aren't they? Anyway, it's best just to humour mine. If she storts, like, babbling, as in not making any sense, just nod your head at her,' and he says okay and then heads back out to the cor to fetch his cameras and his lights and his various other bits of shit.

I give him the guided tour of downstairs, roysh, and he decides the sunroom at the back of the gaff is the best place for the shoot.

So Sorcha comes in and introduces herself and, of course, Honor to him as he's setting up the lights. She's still big-time Scooby Dubious, though, because she goes, 'Hey, congrats, by the way,' and Patrick looks at her, roysh, like he hasn't a focking bog what she's banging on about, which of course he hasn't.

Sorcha goes, 'I mean, we are, like, SO honoured that you

could fit us into your busy schedule of awards ceremonies and whatever else,' and I'm standing directly behind her, roysh, and I'm, like, making that twirling motion at the side of my forehead, as if to go, I told you – Baghdad.

So anyway, roysh, he tells us just to relax and be ourselves, and he ends up taking a shitload of snaps of the three of us, then a load of just Sorcha and the baby. Then he says, 'What about a picture of the doting dad in his Castlerock colours?'

Of course, I'm up them focking stairs like I've just found out Nell McAndrew's in the bed waiting for me. I'm out of my light blue Ralph and straight into my old red-and-black rugby shirt.

I have to move fast, of course, because who knows what's being said downstairs. I stick the collar up and then I'm back down, to discover that Patrick has decided to shoot a few in the gorden.

He's setting up the tripod and Sorcha's still in the poor goy's ear. She's going, 'So, how's Kenny?' and of course Patrick doesn't know anyone called Kenny.

'Er, fine,' he goes, basically humouring her.

Sorcha's there, 'His brother was supposed to do the music at our wedding, except the reception didn't last that long. You probably heard, did you?'

I go, 'Sorcha, the goy's trying to actually work,' but she totally ignores me.

She's like, 'Do you *see* much of Karl? Is he still going out with Kate, as in used to be headgirl in Rathdown but left halfway through sixth year to go to the Institute?'

Patrick's so lost, he doesn't even know it's a focking question. He just, like, nods his head like Sorcha's said something really deep and meaningful and then, roysh, when he's showing me the exact pose he wants from me, he whispers in my ear, 'It's definitely post-natal.'

I go, 'I know, mad as a box of frogs. Hey, do you want a get a couple of me with my shirt off?'

Fair play to the dude, roysh, he hangs around for two hours, taking photographs of us from every possible angle, and Honor, roysh, she didn't cry once. Obviously loves having her photo taken – like her old man.

But as Patrick's packing up his shit, Sorcha tells him she is SO going to have to visit his studio, see some of these awards of his for herself, and I manage to prise him away from her and get him out the front door.

I close it behind him and turn around to find Sorcha standing roysh behind me in what has to be said is a threatening way, like Kathy Bates in *Misery*, giving me without doubt the worst filthy in the history of filthies.

She holds up an envelope and goes, 'Did I mention that this came for you this morning? It's a cheque, Ross. For fifty thousand euros. Any idea who it's from?'

I go, 'It's a, er, signing-on fee. Munster are trying to tempt me to play for them. It'll never happen, though. Actually, give it to me there and I'll tell Declan Kidney what he can do with it.'

I make a move to grab the chicken's neck off her, but she's too quick for me. She whips it away and goes, 'I *know* who it's from, Ross. I got maximum points in my Leaving Cert., you got minimum. Has something happened in the meantime to persuade you that you're smorter than me?'

I don't answer.

She goes, 'Have you forgotten that Bianca comes into the shop at least once a week?'

Oh, *fock!*

She's there, 'I'm going to put this money in a savings account. It'll help put Honor through Mount Anville. I want her to have the education I had, so that she can see through men like you as well.'

I just stand there with my stupid focking mouth open and Sorcha going, '*Oh* my God, Ross, you should *see* your face. I wish I had a camera.'

4. Alright to Be Sad

'How are you, my child?'

It's unbelievable. Fehily's at death's door and he wants to know how *I* am. I'm there, 'I'd be more concerned with how *you* are,' and he laughs, roysh, he laughs so hord that it turns into a cough and I end up having to get the nurse for him.

Nuala is a focking miracle-worker, having single-handedly cured me of a lifelong fetish for women in uniform. She has a face that would make the Luas cut through a field.

She sits him up in the bed, roysh, while he coughs up a load of guck and spits it into a little plastic bucket she puts in front of him. Then she plumps up his pillows and he lies back down again.

'Thank you,' he goes and she smiles at him – not pretty – and then focks off to, I don't know, buy men's shoes or whatever birds like that do when they finish work.

'The boy,' Fehily goes. 'Look after the boy.'

I'm there, 'Ronan?'

He's like, 'He'll be better than Gibson. Ah, I wish I could be there to see it . . .'

I'm there, 'Don't talk rubbish. There's, like, years left in you,' but I know it's not true and I can't even make myself sound like I believe it.

Fehily goes, 'Well, there's not many live to the age I am . . . except in the Old Testament,' and he sort of, like, chuckles, I suppose you'd have to call it.

After a while, he goes, 'She's coming, you know.'

I look at him blankly.

He goes, 'Vianne. She's coming here. Fionn wrote her a letter.'

It's hord to tell whether he's happy or sad about this. Maybe he doesn't know what to feel.

He's there, 'The most beautiful woman I've ever set eyes on. She was like Constance Bennett.'

I've heard all this before, but it's almost nice to listen to it again.

'She worked in the box office of a little theatre in Vienna,' he goes, 'where I had an audition. I had big dreams, you see. I wanted to be a tenor. I did César Franck's 'Panis Angelicus' – the one that John McCormack did in the Park in 1932. I had quite a high opinion of myself in those days . . .'

He laughs and I laugh with him.

'They hated me,' he goes. 'I thought I did quite well, but I was the only one. I saw Vianne on the way out. A split second and that was me – smitten, as we used to say. I asked if I could take her for coffee. She looked at me like I was quite mad. Turned out she was from France. She was like me, travelling Europe, looking for, I don't know . . . something to move her.

'We went to a little coffee house on Gumpendorfer Strasse. She had a sad face, but when she smiled . . . Oh, how I worked for those smiles.

'It was the twenty-eighth of February 1938. Two weeks before the Anschluss. Vienna was abuzz because we knew it was coming. Everyone was tired of listening to Schuschnigg – they wanted Hitler. I saw grown men weep tears of happiness the day he drove into the city . . .

'Vianne took me to Paris after France fell. Her father was high up in the Vichy government. Knew Philippe Pétain.

Well, you know the rest . . . I got a job with the Milice française, typing up statements from members of the Resistance who'd been tortured, some of Vianne's father's closest friends. I tried to blank that side of it out until . . . Well, it gets to the point where you can't bear to look at yourself long enough to shave your face in the morning. So one day I told Vianne I had to go. She said she understood. Never saw or heard from her again.'

'How do you feel about seeing her now?' I go.

He's like, 'Embarrassed,' and he laughs. 'I mean, look at me. Wait till you see her, Ross. She's like a film star . . .'

It's amazing, roysh, because he seems to think he's the only one who's gotten old.

He thinks of something then and storts feeling around the top of his locker. 'Look what Ronan brought,' he goes.

I go over to the locker and find it for him. It's a videotape. It's a tape of the 1999 schools cup final. I'm a bit taken aback, roysh, because I gave that to Ro over a year ago and he told me he accidentally recorded *The Sopranos* over it.

'We sat here, watched it together,' he goes. Then he shakes his head. 'You boys, you brought me such happiness. Highs I never thought I'd know again. By the age of twenty-five, I'd done it all. I sang with José Luccioni. Shook Georges Carpentier's hand. I'd met kings and queens. I'd fallen in love. Lived through a war. Saw the world. And it burnt me out. What was there left to impress me after that?'

This is heavy shit.

'And though it's been my pleasure to serve the Lord,' he goes, 'it's a terribly lonely feeling to be twenty-five and to know you've already lived your life. But then, you boys came along . . .

'All those battles . . . Belvedere. Mary's. Newbridge. I knew what it was to be Rommel. Von Leeb . . .'

He's there, 'Watching you in action was like watching a great orchestra play . . .' and that makes me sad, roysh, because I know it's always been a bit of a disappointment to him that I never got an IRFU contract.

I don't know what to say next.

I'm thinking of mentioning the All Blacks giving us the focking hammering of a lifetime last weekend and how the Irish players are going to have to learn to be a bit more composed with the ball in hand, but in the end I don't.

'I was von Leeb,' he goes and he looks me hard in the eye. It's a look full of meaning and what it means is, goodbye. Because somehow we both know that this is the last conversation we're ever going to have.

Honor is screaming the house down again and I'm basically at my wits' end.

I've tried everything. I've turned up the Liza. Tried listening to my iPod at full blast. I've even thought about trying to soundproof the nursery, but it would have taken, like, two or three hundred egg boxes and *Ross Kemp On Gangs* has already storted on Sky Two.

In the end I decide to bring her downstairs, roysh, and it's then I notice that the pen is Padraig and her nappy needs changing. I probably should add at this point that for the past two days she's had Chris Rea's Welsh cousin around – in other words, Dia – and I realize I'm going to have to do a pretty quick emergency nappy change here, because I've a Chinese ordered and I am SO not going to be able to eat it with that smell in the room.

Sorcha is out, by the way, looking after her PBI, which

means a sunbed session in Blockbuster Video and then a couple of glasses of wine with Aoife, over which she plans to break the news that she's coming back to the shop earlier than planned, as in the first week in January.

I put a towel down on the good Italian leather sofa and I get the nappy off and it has to be said, roysh, it's not a pretty sight. I'll spare you the details, but basically we've all been there ourselves. Shitting Baileys.

I go into the kitchen and grab a packet of baby wipes. Then I've got to go back because what I actually picked up were Domestos Wipes and I'm sure there *is* an actual difference.

So there I am, roysh, cleaning up and I'm thinking, some focking Friday night this is. I should be in Lillie's, filling birds' heads with shit, breaking horts left, roysh and centre.

Instead I'm listening to, *Wwwaaahhh!*

I try to put the clean nappy on her, unsuccessfully it has to be said, because Sorcha's decided we're not using disposables and even if Honor was lying still for me – which she certainly isn't – I'm all fingers and thumbs anyway.

Wwwaaahhh!

It's *actually* wrecking my head? In the end, I give up and leave the nappy off her.

Now, Christian, roysh, he bought her this, like, Tigger baby bouncer, which you sort of, like, hang out of the frame of the door, then sit a baby in it and let her basically bounce up and down.

It's supposed to be, like, soothing and shit, but it's never been taken out of the box, roysh, because Sorcha reckons Honor's still too young for it. But ten o'clock on a Friday night, with a sweet-and-sour pork and special fried rice going cold on the table, I'm prepared to try anything.

So I whip the thing out of the box, roysh, and set it up.

It's actually pretty cool. It makes this, like, *boing-boing* sound effect as it goes up and down and, despite her kicking, screaming and fighting me all the way, I manage to get Honor into the little horness and I stort bouncing her up and down in it and – it's a focking miracle, roysh – she actually stops crying.

It's at that exact moment, roysh, that One F rings me and goes, 'Ross, stick on RTÉ. Your old dear's on the *Late Late*,' and of course I hit the channel straight away and up comes her stupid focking face – ugly as a shot dog.

'Now, you're the first of the new wave of women's fiction writers,' Pat's going, 'to grasp the . . . *sexual* nettle and write, well, steamy love scenes. That must have taken a lot of courage . . .'

Courage! I'll have words with that focker next time I see him in The Queens.

The old dear goes, 'I think I'm a very . . . *sensuous* woman,' which is her new catchphrase, and suddenly there's all this, like, whooping and hollering from the audience.

'I know it's easy to look at me and think of me as some kind of sex goddess,' she goes, 'but I don't think any one of us is ever finished exploring his or her sexuality. And I wrote *Criminal Assets* really as part of my own continuing efforts to understand the roots of desire and arousal . . .'

I can't believe I'm focking hearing this.

'Now, you're not only an international best-selling author,' Pat goes, 'you're also something of a fashion icon. You're the new face of Crème de la Mér. *And* you're going to be modelling some of Paul Costello's new designs at London Fashion Week. Has success changed you in any way?'

Yes, Pat, she's become an even bigger focking weapon.

'If it has, I would say only for the better,' she goes, sitting there like focking Cruella de Ville. 'All this success, the things you mentioned there, have come as a result of hard work. I think I've always been very driven . . .'

'You trained as a florist?'

'That's right,' she goes. 'I don't come from a wealthy background. We were just an ordinary upper middle-class family really. My father was just a bank manager. I think he would have liked me to follow him into the branch, but I wanted to plough my own furrow. So, like you said, I got into the flower business. A florist's not far from here, in Stillorgan. And, well, I suppose I started at the bottom. And it was hard work. I'm not going to try to make it sound glamorous. You're talking long days – 9.30 start every morning and most days I was still there at 4.30 in the afternoon, and that's with only an hour for lunch . . .'

'But the hard work paid off,' Pat goes, 'because within a year, you *owned* the business?'

She's there, 'Yes, I suppose I always had a vision of how I could grow the business, but of course it wasn't mine at the time. So I served my time, saved up some money, and then one day when the owner announced that she wanted to sell, I put in a bid and, well, Pat, I was flabbergasted when it was accepted. There I was, owner of my own florist shop at nineteen . . .'

A round of applause from the audience.

That's the biggest pile of shit I've ever heard. She focking conned that Mrs Goad out of her business, her and her old man. The poor woman was, like, sixty – hadn't a focking Betty Boo what was going on. Piece of piss for a shark like my old dear. The old man told me the Jackanory the day they had that sale in Terroirs and him and Hennessy ended up getting mullered in the study.

Basically, what happened was, she storted creaming money off the top. It wasn't simple thievery, though – no, that'd be working class. Half of everything that went through the till she was siphoning off into a separate bank account. So, of course, within a year this once highly successful florist's shop, despite being busier than ever, was suddenly showing a loss. Mrs Goad missed a couple of mortgage repayments and the banks storted coming down heavy on her. Well, *one* bank. Do I need to tell you who the manager was?

Poor cow. It happened so fast, she barely knew it happened at all. She died about two years later, a broken woman. Meanwhile, that focking trout there did what she said she would – grew the business – and sold it for a couple of million the year we moved to Foxrock.

'Looking back,' she goes, 'it was character-building. It helped define the person I became, the woman I am today. One afternoon in particular. I was sweeping the floor, of all things, and I remember thinking, right, Fionnuala, this is the lowest you're ever going to get. Remember this moment. And it's what spurred me on. It's where I get my drive, my independence.'

Pat goes, 'Now, you're married to Charles O'Carroll-Kelly, the, er, *controversial* businessman and independent councillor, who has been charged with various offences. Now, I understand the matter is sub judice . . .' and then, roysh, totally out of the blue, the old dear goes, 'My marriage is over . . .'

There's, like, total silence from the audience.

Then she goes, 'Charles and I had long ceased to be intimate . . .'

I whip out the old moby. I've got RTÉ on speed-dial from ringing Ryle. Some bird answers and I go, 'I want to be put through to the *Late Late Show*,' and she goes, 'Is it a question or a comment you have?'

I'm like, 'A question. I just wanted to ask her, er, who her major influences are, as a writer,' and she goes, 'And your name is . . .' and I'm there, 'Ross.'

And it's amazing, roysh, because I end up getting put through and the next thing Pat Kenny's going, 'Okay, we have a caller with a question. Ross, is it?' and I can actually see the old dear's face drop.

She's thinking, *uh oh!*

I go, 'Yeah, my question is this. Why don't you deal with your sexual frustrations like other women – get yourself something battery-operated, sort yourself out and stop bothering the rest of us with your sick shit, you pug-faced, back-stabbing, mange-ridden weapon of mass destruction.'

Then I hang up.

The only thing is, roysh, I hadn't realized that I was taking my anger and frustration out on the baby bouncer and Honor's spent the last ten minutes bungee-jumping up and down at, like, ninety miles an hour. I mean, she seems happy enough, but something tells me, roysh, that with her stomach in the shape it's in, it can't be a good thing for her.

I think it'd be wise to get another nappy on her, fast, so I whip her out of the little horness, but it's too late. I hear this, like, gurgling sound and then she just, like, explodes, sending a spray of you-know-what – shit, basically – everywhere, pebble-dashing the toasted almond, matt-finished walls.

My phone beeps. It's a text from Sorcha. Fock. Her and Aoife have obviously been watching the show.

It's like, 'OMG, that was SO not a cool thing to do, Ross,' and I'm looking at the living-room walls – it's like some kind of dirty protest – and I'm thinking, you don't *actually* know the half of it.

*

I give Christian a sideways look and I go, 'You okay?' and I expect him to say that he now knows how Han felt when, I don't know, the Millennium Falcon was caught in the Death Stor tractor beam, but he doesn't, roysh, he just sort of, like, swallows hord and nods his head.

I go, 'Dude, you have to relax. You are actually *allowed* to enjoy the day, remember?'

I have a quick George Hook over my shoulder. It's great to see everyone here. Oisinn, who's back on his feet again, is doing groomsman with JP, One F and Fionn, who gives me a little thumbs-up, as if to say, basically, good luck, which is nice, given our whole history.

And speaking of history . . .

I cop a sly look at Christian's old pair. *She's* looking seriously hot, it has to be said, even though I've promised to be on my best behaviour. I actually don't know what the Jack is there. They're back under the same roof, but the word is they're, like, living pretty much separate lives, although there's a big show of unity today, of course, hand-holding, the lot.

She has her hair cut short and it makes her look, like, I don't know, thirty-five maybe, and she's wearing this black silk dress that really shows off her top tens and actually her legs are . . .

Fock! Christian's old man catches me scoping her, so suddenly it's like, eyes front!

But then I feel a hand on my shoulder, and a voice – his voice – in my ear going, 'Your duties as best man do not include checking out the groom's mother,' and then he turns to Christian, who hasn't heard it, shakes his hand and wishes him luck.

So I'm there kacking it, roysh, wondering did Sorcha notice as well.

There's going to be fock-all else to look at today, it has to be said. I met the bridesmaids earlier and they're a focking disgrace. What was Lauren thinking? Abby – as in her best friend – has a face like a burst couch, and believe it or not she's actually the best of the four. It's a focking shambles.

'Lauren has a surprise for me,' Christian goes. I'm there, 'A surprise? As in?' and he's like, 'Well, I don't know. It's a surprise. But she said she wants her entrance to be something I'll remember for the rest of my life,' and I'm there thinking, I bet her dress is going to be, like, red-and-black stripes – as in the Castlerock colours? – and then I'm thinking what a serious turn-on that would actually be.

The next thing, roysh, this hush sweeps through the church – as in Foxrock Church – and the doors swing open and then, roysh, the music storts up and it's not 'Here Comes the Bride', roysh, it's the focking Dorth Vader morching tune.

I turn to Christian and he's already got, like, tears streaming down his face.

I have a quick look over my left shoulder and first it's the bridesmaids – I swear to God, they'd scare a pack of wild dogs out of a focking butcher's shop – and then behind them I see Hennessy and he's linking Lauren and she looks un-focking-believable, not that it'd be hord among that lot.

All you can hear, aport from the organist banging out Christian's favourite tune of all time, is birds going, '*Oh my God, oh my God, oh my God*,' and without looking around, Christian goes to me, 'Well?' and I go, 'She looks incredible. Dude, you are the luckiest goy in the world.'

So then it's, like, ladies and gentlemen, we are gathered here today, blahdy blahdy blah – the whole Mass bit of the ceremony.

And it all runs pretty smoothly – boring, but smoothly – except for this bit in the middle, when the priest calls JP up to do the first reading.

Christian had asked him to do it, like, ages ago, as in before he went chicken oriental, and I suppose, as Christian's best man, I probably should have sacked him and asked somebody else.

So JP stands up there and he's like, 'A reading from the Book of Corinthians,' but then he suddenly looks up and he goes, 'This isn't my own personal choice. I'd have probably picked something from Leviticus. The sacrament of marriage has become a mockery in Ireland in recent years . . .' and we're all thinking, *Oh, fock!*

The priest, roysh, he actually stands up and goes, 'Would you mind just reading the text, please?' which is, like, a serious slap in the face – the equivalent of being red-corded by a bird, for those of us who *are* still into them.

So what happens then? Nothing. For the next thirty seconds, roysh, JP just stands there, staring into the congregation. It's like he's stuck. Suspended, if that's the actual word. Until Fionn goes up to the basically pulpit, puts his orm around him and helps him off the altar and in the end, roysh, the priest has to do the reading himself.

Someone must have phoned JP's old man, roysh, because he came and collected him. By the time we were all outside in the cor pork, he was gone and I suppose we all knew that it'd be a while before any of us would see him again.

There's nothing any of us can say, roysh, except, poor goy. First Erika, now JP . . . Who's next?

I'm there, 'Have you lot seen the focking bridesmaids? One of them has a beard,' and that actually lightens the mood a bit.

'Oh, I've seen them, alright,' Oisinn goes. 'Ugly beyond reproach,' and he sort of, like, rubs his hands together, and of course, to him, that's an actual good thing.

Oisinn focks off to try to chat up the ugliest of the four, leaving me with Fionn.

'Can we bum a lift to the hotel off you goys?' he goes – it's in, like, the Four Seasons – and I'm like, 'Yeah, cool,' and then I'm thinking, who's *we*?

The next thing, roysh, Sorcha and Aoife are walking across the cor pork towards us and Aoife's going, 'Have you told him?' and Fionn's giving it, 'No, I was just about to,' and then he turns to me and he goes, 'Aoife and I are, em . . . we're together. We're a couple – again.'

For some reason, I'm suddenly grinning like a monkey shitting a wheelbrace.

It's weird, roysh, but I can't explain how happy this makes me feel. I mean, I wouldn't exactly be Fionn's number one fan, even though he *is* one of my best friends. But still, I've always thought that him and Aoife were made for each other, even though it's, like, five years or whatever since they last went out.

I give Aoife a hug and tell her she looks amazing, which is actually true. I always thought Aoife was a ringer for Katie Holmes and she actually looks even better with a bit of weight on. She squeezes my hand and goes, 'Thanks, Ross. I'm going to *stay* well this time.'

Then I shake Fionn's hand and I go, 'I'm really happy for you, Dude, even if you are a steamer and you're living a lie,' and Fionn laughs and points out that everyone else is gone and we're the last ones to leave the cor pork and, as best man, I'm probably supposed to be with the happy couple for the photographs.

I ask Sorcha if she wants me to take the carrycot for her

and she hands it to me and goes, 'But don't let Honor see your face – you know it scares her.'

Apparently, over dinner, all the talk was about Erika.

I say apparently because obviously I was at the top table, roysh, but Sorcha filled me in on everything, including the stand-up row she had with Chloe, who storted the whole thing by talking about this new diet she's on – you eat and drink nothing for four days and then, just before you slip into a coma, you lick a sprout – and how the weight is falling off her, and all this within earshot of Aoife. She was doing it just to be a bitch, of course.

So Sorcha pulled her up on it, roysh, and Chloe went, 'Look, I'm sure it's all in a good cause, but I refuse to tiptoe around you just because you've chosen to be friends with the psychiatrically ill.'

'Meaning?' Sorcha went and Chloe was like, 'Well, Erika, for one – *Oh* my God, a *total* basket-case. It's like, *Hell-o!* I don't think anyone's going to make any great claims for Aoife's sanity. And I see you've got Ross in on the act now as well – *what* was that with JP?'

Sorcha apparently went, 'You know what, Chloe? Steve knew what he was doing getting rid of you,' which in normal circumstances would be way horsh, roysh, because they were living together and were actually engaged when Steve gave her the Spanish archer. Had to sell their gaff in Greystones and everything.

Of course, then Sorcha storts to feel guilty about having said it. I tell her to forget about it.

We're all sitting around watching Christian and Lauren do the whole first dance thing – 'You're Beautiful' by James Blunt – and having a few scoops.

Aoife tells Sorcha that 'You're Beautiful' is probably her favourite song of all time, apart from   maybe – 'The Scientist' by Coldplay, or 'Dancing In The Moonlight' by Top Loader.

My speech went down pretty well, it has to be said. Everyone sat listening to the stories with their, like, mouths open, especially the one about the time me, Christian and Oisinn broke into Blackrock College and made shit of the sixth-year common room.

I end up getting very, very drunk. And it's probably *because* I'm mullered, roysh, but at some point in the evening I stort bad-mouthing my old dear, saying what a tit she made of herself on the telly the other night, and Sorcha, seeing how upset I am, puts her hand on top of my hand and goes, 'Lots of marriages break up, Ross.'

I pull my hand away and tell her I'm going to hit the bor.

I ask the borman for a pint of Ken and a sambuca and I immediately throw the sambuca into me, and that's when I notice Christian's old dear, standing at the bor, just a few feet away.

I look over both shoulders. Make sure the coast's clear. Christian's old man is over in the far corner, boring the ear off one of Hennessy's brothers about, I don't know, protected consensus bonds or whatever the fock he's into these days.

So I sidle up to her and go, 'Hey,' playing it too cool for school, because I'm not trying to get in there, remember. If anything I'm just trying to prove that I could if I actually wanted to.

She's there, 'Hi,' making it pretty clear that I'm going to have to work hord for anything I get here tonight.

I'm like, 'Still drinking wine, huh?' which is a subtle

reminder that that's exactly what she was drinking the night I threw her a length. She's there, 'Yes, Ross. Still drinking wine,' and I sort of, like, raise one eyebrow, James Bond-style.

I have this unbelievable urge to kiss the point where her neck and shoulder meet.

I go, 'We shouldn't be ashamed about the way we feel,' and she suddenly gives me this, like, hord stare. She's like, 'What are you talking about?' and I'm there, 'Wounded innocence. Cute. Look, I'm not saying anything's going to happen between us tonight, but there *is* an actual attraction and I know it's, like, mutual. We should both at least admit it's there. Makes it easier to control if we acknowledge it.'

She looks away.

Her left hand is on the bor. She's not wearing her sporkler, which, to me, is proof that the whole making-a-go-of-it thing is a total sham. I stroke her long, slender orm with the back of my hand and she doesn't pull away, roysh, just takes a deep breath. Then she goes, 'I admit it. I haven't stopped thinking about seeing you here today. Dreading it, but at the same time excited by it . . .'

I give her a big understanding nod – a trick I've learned with birds – then I go, 'Look, I know I said a second ago that nothing was going to happen between us, but I think there should also be an element of, like, go with the flow here?'

I feel shit for doing this to Christian, but I am seriously gagging for my bit.

'I saw you looking at me in the church,' she goes.

We're standing side by side, barely looking at each other, trying to *not* make it obvious?

I'm there, 'I have to tell you, the thoughts going through my brain weren't exactly pure.'

'Oh?' she goes, then takes a sip of her wine, then with her finger she dabs away the little red Ronnie it leaves on her upper lip.

I go, 'I was actually thinking about undressing you. Caressing your body . . .'

'Keep your voice down, Ross,' she goes.

I'm there, 'Then doing you, in just that hat you had on in the church. I'm presuming it was a Philip Treacy?'

'Yes, it was,' she goes, her voice all trembly. She wants me bad. There's no doubt that this is going to happen.

I have another quick George over the shoulder. Christian and Lauren are still on the dancefloor, lost in each other's eyes.

Actually, there is one thing I need to square away first . . .

'Look, I'm sorry about the last time,' I go. 'You know, about . . . like, I usually last way longer than that. But I suppose it was because I was so turned on by you.'

That old lie.

I'm there, 'You should take it as a compliment.'

'All this talk, Ross,' she goes, looking around her, 'it's making me want you even more.'

She turns and she faces me for the first time.

She goes, 'I'm in room 207. Follow me up,' and before I have a chance to say anything she goes, 'Don't worry. Christian's father and I have separate rooms. Follow me up. No one will miss us for an hour.'

An hour? She's focking pushing it there, but I don't say anything.

I'm like, 'I'll go and get a pack of Johnny B. Goodes,' and then I'm there, 'Although . . .' and I nearly end up saying that I probably won't need them, what with her being the wrong side of the menopause, blahdy blahdy blah, but I stop myself, which is probably a sign that I'm finally growing up.

She knocks back the rest of her wine and I stare at her orse as she leaves and her unbelievable legs, which in a few minutes from now are going to be wrapped around me.

I wait ten minutes, though it's probably actually two, then I slip out of the function room, head for the lift and hit the button for the second floor. I get out and practically run the short distance to 207 and knock on the door.

I hear Christian's old dear go, 'Just a minute, Ross,' and I'm standing there, roysh – as happy as Lucy Kennedy's cor seat – when all of a sudden the door opens, roysh, and this fist comes flying through the gap and knocks me flat on my orse.

When I look up, she's standing over me. 'I wanted to do that downstairs,' she goes, 'but I didn't want to spoil Christian and Lauren's day.'

I'm cut under the left eye. I remember now, she actually wears her diamond on her right hand.

Fock!

She's there, 'Best man? You disgust me!'

I get to my feet and put my hand to my cheek. There's a fair bit of blood. I'm like, 'Hey, you can't afford to be so high and mighty. You'd no problem being with me the last time.'

'*Being* with you?' she goes. 'Oh, please! I've had hiccups that lasted longer than you. And were more enjoyable . . .'

Buying the pack of twelve instead of six seems insanely optimistic at this point in time.

'When are you going to grow up?' she goes. 'You have a *wife* downstairs! *And* a baby!'

I'm there, 'So?'

She's like, '*So?* Have you any idea of the pain that comes

with a marital break-up? The depression, the guilt, the sense of failure? The loneliness? Would you like to have to go through that? Sit down at a table and divide your possessions, your friends, your family photographs. Is that what you want? To have your daughter call another man Daddy? To have another man give her birthdays and Christmases and holidays, while you're just a man she vaguely knows who takes her out on a Sunday afternoon?'

'All I want with you is an hour,' I go. 'Not even an hour – what am I saying? All that other stuff's not going to happen.'

She's there, 'Oh, it is, Ross. That's as sure as I'm standing here. Because you can't help yourself. You're going to end up sad and on your own.'

I'm like, 'With this face? Somehow I *don't* think so.'

'You make me sick to my stomach,' she goes, and then she walks out of the room, past me and back downstairs.

I sit on the sofa opposite the lift and, I suppose, contemplate my life for a few minutes. Then I go back down to the reception, hitting the jacks on the way to clean up the old Ricky Gervais.

It's a pretty nasty cut.

When she sees me, Sorcha goes, 'Oh my God, Ross, what happened?'

I'm there, 'Er, I had a bit of a disagreement with a couple of Clongowes heads. They said I was a has-been in terms of rugby. Ended up having to deck both of them.'

Old. That's my first impression of Vianne. And we're not talking old in a Dame Judi Dench sort of way, where you don't care what age she is, you still would, if only for your country.

No, she's nothing at all like I expected. Forget Constance whatever-she's-called – this bird must have had *some* focking personality for Fehily to have gone there.

We end up having to take the lift because she can't, like, get up stairs and shit? She links Oisinn with one orm and Fionn with the other and the goys walk her down the corridor, until Fionn goes, '*Il est dans cette chambre, Vianne,*' and we stop outside Fehily's door.

Fionn knocks and they all go in, roysh, and all I can hear from outside is her going, 'Denis! Denis!' except, the way she says it, it sounds like '*Denise! Denise!*'

Then I hear Oisinn go, '*Vianne, nous attendrons en dehors de la porte,*' and I'm thinking, how did those two fockers win Senior Cup medals *and* end up being good at French?

Fionn gives me this little half-smile, then goes over to the seating area and docks his orse. I'm like, 'Well? Don't keep me in suspense,' and he looks around him, roysh, like he hasn't a focking clue what I'm talking about.

I'm there, 'Was he disappointed?'

Fionn goes, 'Disappointed? What do you mean?' and I'm like, 'Well, let's be honest, she's not exactly Eva Mendes, is she? I'm wondering is that how he remembered her?' and he looks across at Oisinn as if to say, is this goy for real?

He's like, 'The woman's in her *eighties*, Ross. We're not trying to get them back together. They have things they want to say to each other, things they've been holding onto for over sixty years. Do you not get that?'

I go, 'Hey, take a chill pill, will you?' because they're trying to make me feel like a total wanker for bringing it up.

I take a walk past the door and look in through the window. Vianne's sitting on the side of the bed, roysh, and the two of them are just, like, holding hands, not even talking.

I go back and sit down.

I'm like, 'So, what's her story again? Owns her own vine-yard. Married some Swiss dude . . .'

Fionn goes, 'Three sons. That was one of them, Didier, who you met at the hotel this morning.'

Yeah, they're staying in the Merrion. I wouldn't say they're short of a few shekels.

We can suddenly hear laughter coming from the room, from her *and* Fehily, which can only be a good thing.

An hour passes. Then another. I take another subtle look in through the window and they're, like, gabbing away.

I can't believe I'm sitting in a focking nursing home with Ireland just about to kick off against Australia. I ended up giving my tickets to Ronan, as did my old man, who pointed out that there's been a member of the O'Carroll-Kelly family at every home Ireland rugby international going back to 1963. So Ro's flying the flag for us today, and he's brought Nudger, Gull and Buckets of Blood along for the ride. I just hope they don't disgrace us by acting like soccer fans and, I don't know, shitting in gardens on the way to the ground.

I get a text. It's actually from Ronan. Bollocks. It's 3-3 and Rog is having a focking mare. My mind is suddenly racing with the possibilities. I have to get to a Liza Minnelli.

I turn around to the goys and I go, 'Em, should we go in there and rescue the goy?' and Fionn and Oisinn are just, like, shaking their heads in, I suppose, disbelief.

Fionn goes, 'Are you that focking insensitive, Ross? Can you even begin to imagine what's going on in there? And does it not gladden every fibre of your being? Years and years of longing finally coming to an end. Now, they can finally reach an accommodation with themselves over what happened . . .'

Of course, Oisinn backs him up. He's like, 'Shit the bed,

they have to squeeze an entire lifetime of conversations into one afternoon. If we end up having to bunk down here for the night, so be it,' and I'm thinking, yeah, roysh, you're on your own there.

Another text. Ireland are 6-3 up at half-time, but they're playing kack.

The next thing, roysh, Didier arrives in. It's, like, *bonjours* all round at the beginning, roysh, but then all of a sudden it's, like, really awkward and shit? There's just, like, total silence, which really wrecks my head.

I'm trying to think what this must be like for him. The dude's probably in his fifties himself. His old man's brown bread, what, thirty years? And then his old dear drags him halfway across the world to Ireland to meet some goy she was shacked up with in her twenties. That shit's focked-up in anyone's language.

As much to break the tension as anything else, I go, '*Voulez-vous coffee?*' because I happen to know there's a machine down the corridor that dispenses shitty water that smells vaguely of coffee.

Fionn and Oisinn look at me, obviously surprised that I know a bit of French.

Didier, though, hasn't a focking bog what I'm talking about. I suppose there's different, like, dialects, depending on where you live and shit?

Fionn goes, '*Est-ce que vous aimez une tasse de café?*' and Didier goes, 'Oh, I see. No. No, thank you very much.'

Silence again.

Another text. Ireland are 25-9 down. What? Two tries for Drew Mitchell and a cracker by Chris Latham. Rog's been taken off and Humphreys is on. I mention it, but no one seems to actually *give* a shit?

Didier suddenly goes, 'All my life, my mother tells me

about *Denise*. What a wonderful man. Her special friend. The first man she loves, yes?'

He walks over to the door and, like, peers in the window. Then he turns around and goes, 'They are asking me to go in,' and we all just nod and in he goes.

Then another hour passes. Maybe two. I've lost all track of time. Finally, the door opens and suddenly Didier appears with Vianne, who's obviously been crying quite a bit. She turns to Fionn and she keeps going, '*Merci. Merci beaucoup*,' and Fionn's giving it, '*Vous êtes bienvenu*,' whatever that means, and then we all say our goodbyes.

We go into Fehily. At first I think he's asleep, but then I realize he's just, like, staring into space. He's been crying as well, but there's a little smile on his lips. And we leave without saying anything to him because it's obvious he just wants to be left there with his thoughts.

So the next thing, roysh, me, Fionn and Oisinn are walking down the corridor and I'm going, 'Eddie O'Sullivan's going to have some focking job rebuilding that team's confidence for the Six Nations,' and – this is really weird, roysh – Fionn stops walking and he sort of, like, pins my orms to my sides and he goes, 'Ross, it's alright to be sad,' and the next thing, roysh, for no reason at all, I just feel my eyes storting to fill up.

'Feel it, Ross,' he goes. 'This is real. This is happening,' and I end up just, like, bursting into tears, there in the middle of the corridor in front of everyone.

Oisinn says we should find somewhere to sit down and we do. And I end up just, like, blubbing like a focking bird for maybe an hour, roysh, and Fionn's got his orm around my shoulder going, 'It's okay, big man. It's okay.'

*

We're in the scratcher, roysh – as in me and Sorcha – and we're watching, like, *X Factor*. When the ads come on, I move over beside her, kiss her on the side of the face and stort getting busy with my hands, my usual manoeuvre, tried and trusted.

'Ross,' she goes, 'I'm not interested.'

I roll away from her. I'm like, 'Not interested tonight, or not interested in general?'

She doesn't answer me.

Look at the two of them – thick as thieves.

'Howiya, Rosser,' one shouts. 'You fooken benny.'

'Here he comes,' the other goes. 'It's taken the greatest outhalf this country has ever produced to keep this chap out of the Ireland team. Not my words – the words of no less a judge than Tom McGurk, who came to see me yesterday.'

Of course, every head in the place shoots up, but it's weird, roysh, because the atmos is different today – as in lighter, if that makes any sense? I'm sure I even hear one or two people go, 'Howiya, Ross,' on the walk to the table.

'Looks like this fella can't stay away,' Ronan goes.

The old man's like, 'Yes, I wasn't expecting to see you again so soon,' and I'm there, 'Yeah, big focking deal. Don't keep banging on about it . . .'

'Sorry, Ross,' he goes. 'Me just bumping me gums here. Hey, look what young Ronan bought me.'

He holds up a brand new Mont Blanc, so focking hot I'd say you'd need asbestos gloves just to write your name with it.

'Yeah, for his birthday,' Ronan goes to me.

I didn't know the old man had a birthday in November. Didn't know he had a birthday at all actually.

'What's that, Charlie?' this voice behind me goes. I look around and it's Lex, the old man's cellmate, an absolute focking gorilla, who I've noticed has this habit of, like, checking out your two shoulders when he meets you. Apparently his porty piece is tearing off people's orms.

'It's a Mont Blanc,' the old man goes. 'Young Ronan's brought it in for me,' and Lex looks at Ro and goes, 'Good man. You look after your grandda, you hear me?' and then he turns around to, I presume, his wife, and I hear him go, 'That's him – that's Charlie,' in sort of, like, awe, if that's the actual word?

And as I'm sitting there in the visiting room, watching various Ken Ackers come and go, saying hello – well, it's more, 'Howiya, Charlie' – I'm thinking about something One F said to me recently. I was telling him the old man was shouting his Von Trapp off in here, acting like he was in the members' bor in Portmornock and was going to end up getting himself killed. One F shook his head and went, 'See, the thing you don't realize about your old man is that people actually like him. He topped the poll in Dún Laoghaire in the local elections. They'll love him in there, Ross. He's a leader, see.'

All of a sudden, roysh, Lex's bird is standing over our table – she could go on a focking double-date with Janis Battersby, this one, and still not be the looker – and she goes, 'Charlie, I just wanted to say thank you,' and the old man's there going, 'Oh, stop that. Anyone would have done the same,' and she's like, 'No, he'd be dead today if it wasn't for you.'

When she's focked off, roysh, me and Ronan are suddenly both looking at him for an explanation.

'It was the strangest thing,' he goes. 'As you know, Lex has something of a past, quote-unquote. Armed robbery, aggravated assault and what-not. See, I'm one of the lucky ones – I'm here for coffee and a day. Lex will be in his fifties by the time he's bag and baggage. A stretch like that . . . well, poor Lex has his days. I usually try to keep his spirits up, telling him about some of the great rugby matches I've seen over the years and the great players – yourself included, Ross.

'Then sometimes we play a round of virtual golf – just us and our imaginations. *Oops, I've skewed my tee shot off the notoriously tricky third, Lex. It's going to take some shot to get me out of that rough* . . . One day we'll play the K Club. The next it'll be Elm Park . . .'

I'm there, 'So, where is all this actually going?'

He's like, 'Well, I wasn't the only one to notice he'd been down in the dumps the last couple of days. One or two of the, inverted commas, screws asked me to keep an eye on him. "Come on, old chap," I said to him a few nights ago, "let's play Milltown," but he didn't want to know, Ross – and that's his favourite. "Morning, Minister," he likes to say as we're walking the fairways. "Morning, Chief Justice."

'So the following morning, seven o'clock, I try to wake him, but I can't. The screws hear my screams coming from the Peter and they naturally assume the chap has flipped out and bladed me up. One of them has a look through the bean chute – of course, they don't know what they're going to find – and I tell them, "It's Lex – he's unconscious."

'So in they come – medics and so forth – and they're asking me, "What did he take? What did he take?" and I'm saying, "I didn't see the chap take a thing," and they're slapping his face and talking to him and trying to bring him around and then it suddenly hits me. He has diabetes.'

Ronan goes, 'How did you know, Grandda?'

He's suddenly turned into the kid off the fockling Werther's Original ad.

'I didn't know,' he goes. 'But my brother, Alisdair, who'd be your grand-uncle, he went into a diabetic coma one night, when we were boys, you see. Went the same white colour as Lex. So I'm sitting on my bed, listening to the medics – they're saying, rapid heartbeat, breathing normal, severe perspiration – and suddenly it's all coming back to me.

'"It's hypoglycaemia," I said. They all looked at me. "Are you sure?" one of them said. "Positive," I said. "Trust me." So they took him off to the hospital, gave him a hit of Glucagon and twenty-four hours later, well, he's birdying the horrible seventh in Elm Park . . .'

A screw touches me and Ronan on the shoulder and tells us visiting time's over.

As we're walking away, he goes, 'Thanks for the pen, Ronan,' and then, 'I might write one of my world-famous letters to *The Irish Times* tonight. I wonder what Madam will think when she sees the headed notepaper from this place, eh, Ross?'

Father Fehily used to tell this joke. There's a priest sitting on the platform of a train station. We'll call it Dalkey, for the sake of argument. All of a sudden this drunk comes along and sits beside him. The goy is totally horrendufied and he reeks of, like, whiskey and cheap perfume. He has a newspaper with him, which he opens and storts reading.

Eventually, roysh, he turns to the priest and he goes, 'Father, what causes arthritis?' and the priest pretty much flips. He's like, 'It's caused by loose living, by drinking that filthy rotgut and spending time with women of no moral virtue. *That's* what causes it,' and the goy goes, 'Fair enough, Father,' and he goes back to reading his paper.

So a few minutes later, roysh, the priest is feeling bad for losing the rag with the goy and he apologizes. 'It was very wrong of me to be so judgemental. Tell me, how long have you had arthritis?' and the drunk goes, 'I don't have it, Father. I was just reading here that the Pope does.'

I'm actually discovering that I've got a bit of a talent for this public-speaking. The whole church cracks up laughing, then bursts into a round of applause. I have notes, which I scribbled down last night, but I don't even look at them – it's like the momentum of the occasion takes over and the words just come.

I go, 'I guess the moral of the story is that you never can tell with people. Father Fehily loved people. He never believed that the world was a bad place. "No," he used to say in that big, booming voice of his, "it's a wonderful world – full of kindness and hope and love and charity."

'When we were in transition year, we sold Christmas trees for St Vincent de Paul, so that families in places like Neilstown, Cabra and Bray might eat. I suppose we've all seen the images on television. We raised a hundred and ten Ks and I remember Father Fehily saying to me, "You see, Ross. People – they'll confound your worst expectations."'

I look down at the goys and they're all, like, nodding back at me.

I go, 'When it comes to, like, belief in God, I wouldn't exactly be top of the chorts. And if it's big words you want to hear, then Fionn should be up here, not me. But on behalf of the past pupils of Castlerock College, I've been asked to say a few words about this man we were all so lucky to know.

'The first time I ever met him was my first day in the

school. I was kacking it, it has to be said. The strange faces. The big echoey corridors full of photographs of all the famous people who went there. Rugby players. Politicians. Businessmen. And then Father Fehily's big voice at our first assembly. He asked me my name and then he asked if I was Charles O'Carroll-Kelly's son. I said yes and he said, "How terribly unfortunate,"' and that gets a good laugh, roysh, because pretty much everyone knows my old man and what he's like.

I go, 'The night before the Schools Cup final, Father Fehily came to see me because he knew I was nervous, even though it was only, like, Newbridge we were playing and they were a boggers and a joke and basically a disgrace to the competition. "The only instruction I'm going to give you," he said, "is when you walk out on that pitch tomorrow, do it with your back straight and your chin up high. And, whatever happens over the course of the next two hours, I want you to walk off the same way."'

I look down at Ronan. He's sat in between Sorcha and Aoife, crying his little hort out. He's really going to miss him.

I go, 'I think we'd all agree that the world is a poorer place without him today,' and then I go and sit down.

On the way back to my seat, all the goys stand up. Oisinn and Christian, who's just got back from his honeymoon, are going, 'Well done, Ross,' and Fionn, who I've had my differences with, just goes, 'Thanks,' which is unbelievable to hear and then Ronan leans across Sorcha, taps me on the knee and goes, 'Good man, Rosser.'

When it's all over, we follow the coffin outside and we all stand around talking about old times, like the day we all bunked off school early and went to Greystones to see the Ireland team train. On the way home, roysh, on the Dort, we wouldn't let anyone into our carriage. We had, like, Oisinn on one door and JP on the other, and any time anyone tried to get in, they were like, 'Sorry, this is a Rock carriage.'

Of course, someone complained to the driver, roysh, and he tried to get in, but we actually held the doors shut and he ended up calling the Feds, who were waiting for us at, like, Booterstown. It was Fehily who persuaded them not to press chorges.

So we're standing there, roysh, and this goy all of a sudden comes over to us — this really old dude — and tells me he really enjoyed my oration.

I'm there, 'It was more a speech than anything. Were you, like, related to Fehily?' and he goes, 'No, I was not. In fact, I had not seen him for many years,' and he has this, like, weird accent, roysh, that I can't quite place. Might be French.

To cut a long story short, he says his name is Daniel. Daniel Shum, I think. And he knew Fehily during the War. Turns out his father ran, like, a patisserie in Paris, in a place called St Paul. Then one day he was taken away on a train, never to be seen again.

He goes, 'Denis — your Father Fehily — he drank coffee in our father's shop, perhaps every day. We knew he was Vichy. It didn't matter. He was a nice man. He liked to sing, like my father. For hours they would talk about the great tenors. He knew my father was a member of the Resistance. So one day, he comes to see my father with the news that they are coming for him. The Milice. He said to go, far away from Paris. But my father was proud — to be a Jew and to be a member of the Resistance. He say *non*. He would not run. He stayed.'

He goes, 'We never saw him again. Denis came to the shop that night and collected us — my brother and I. He arranged for us to come here, to Ireland. He had friends. They looked after us.'

Fionn goes, 'Wait a minute, are you saying that Father Fehily was a kind of Oscar Schindler?' and the goy storts laughing and goes, 'He didn't have Schindler's numbers, no? Two people – not enough for a movie, I think,' and he sort of, like, chuckles to himself.

Then he turns around to me and goes, 'He was a very special man and your speech did him justice.'

The coffin is loaded into the cor as the school choir forms a gord of honour, singing *Be Not Afraid*, which was the goy's favourite hymn.

> *If you pass through raging waters,*
> *In the sea you shall not drown.*
> *If you walk amid the burning flames,*
> *You shall not be harmed.*
> *If you stand before the power of Hell,*
> *And death is at your side,*
> *Know that I am with you through it all…*

And we all stare into the distance, roysh, knowing that a little bit of all of us is being taken away in that wooden box.

5. Counting Cranes

'Will I read her a story, will I?' Ronan goes.

He's holding Honor and there's not a peep out of her.

I'm like, 'You can read her a story, but not from one of your Chopper books,' and he laughs, roysh, then he goes, 'Not from one of me Chopper books – I like that, Rosser,' and he not-very-subtly sticks the book he had in his hand up his hoody.

It's Christmas Eve and he thinks we're bringing him to Dundrum Town Centre to choose his present, but that was, like, a ruse to get him here? Sorcha's at the window, watching. I hear a cor pull up outside and she goes, 'It's him.'

'Who?' Ronan goes. 'Who are you looking out for, Sorcha?'

I'm there, 'Ro, we have a little surprise for you. We didn't know what to get you for Christmas. You *have* a replica pistol. You *have* what I thought until recently was a replica sawn-off shotgun. You *have* those Ronnie Kray half-glasses I bought you for your birthday . . .'

His face is all lit up.

Sorcha takes the baby out of his orms, then goes back to the window. She's like, 'He's coming up the path, Ross. Oh my God, he's, like, SO much taller than I expected.'

The doorbell rings and I stand behind the door and open it, leaving Ronan staring into the eyes of . . . The Monk.

I watch his jaw drop until his mouth is just like a big O and the goy, in fairness to him, goes, 'Howiya, Ronan. You comin' for a spin?' and Ronan looks over the Monk's shoulder at the big stretch Hummer, which is blocking an entire lane of traffic on Newtownpork Avenue.

'Merry Christmas,' Sorcha goes and I honestly have never seen the kid more happy.

The Monk shakes my hand, then Sorcha's and goes, 'It's lovely to meet you,' and it's true what they say, roysh, he is a total focking gentleman.

He goes, 'Come on so, let's hit the road,' and I tell Sorcha I'll see her in the afternoon, roysh, and The Monk's already halfway up the path, with Ronan running alongside him, trying to match the length of his stride.

'Do you want to sit up front with me or in the back?' The Monk goes. 'There's a telly in there, drinks cabinet . . .' and Ronan's rubbing his hands together, going, 'If it's all the same with you, I think I'll sit up front,' and he climbs in, then turns around to me and goes, 'Get in here, Rosser, there's three seats,' which there is.

The Monk asks where we want to go first and without even, like, thinking about it, Ronan goes, 'Wanderers Rugby Club — it's on Ailesbury Road,' and I have to say, roysh, I haven't a bog why he wants to go there.

It's only when we're pulling into the cor pork that I remember that Shane Danaher, the Wanderers prop, has a saucepan, I think called Ollie, who's Ronan's main rival for the outhalf position on the Castlerock College under-eleven team. A little prick, by all accounts.

In the distance, on the main pitch, I can just about make out Shane, spotting balls for Ollie to put between the posts from different angles. It's Christmas Eve, for fock's sake. It's, like, give the kid a day off.

Ronan goes, 'I want to have a quick word in this fella's shell-like,' and The Monk obviously cops what's going on, roysh, because he goes, 'Let's get a bit closer, then,' and he drives up onto the grass and across the pitch to the twenty-two-metre line, where little Ollie is posing over the ball, thinking he's Rog himself.

Of course, him and his old man stop dead in their tracks when they see the limo. Ronan hits the button and the electric window rolls down.

Shane looks in and gives me a nod. He'd obviously have a lot of respect for me as a player. Ronan goes, 'Story, Ollie?' and Ollie's like, 'Oh, er, hi, Ronan,' obviously, like, stuck for words.

'I just wanted to say I hope you enjoy yisser Christmas,' Ronan goes, 'and to say that whoever gets the number-ten shirt, well, there's no hard feelings on my part,' and Ollie's just, like, nodding and looking at his old man, as if to say, what's the Jack here?

'I want you to meet a friend of mine,' he goes and he points at The Monk, who gives them a little wave and wishes them a Merry Christmas.

'By the way,' Ronan goes, 'you're leaning back too far when you address the ball. Just a word from the wise.'

And when we drive away, roysh, I take a look in the rear-view and Shane and his kid are just, like, rooted to the spot, watching the cor disappear.

We get back on the road and we end up having this amazing conversation about which of Tony Soprano's *capos* we like the best. Me and Ro are both huge Paulie fans, but The Monk likes Silvio, roysh, because he's loyal, keeps his trap shut and never rats anyone out.

'Same as me grandda,' Ronan goes. 'He's in the Joy, so he is. They've told him – name names and you'll do your porridge on his pillow. But he won't. He's not a tout.'

I'm thinking, how does he know all that shit?

The next stop is Ro's estate. I always think 'estate' a

hilarious name for that council-built shantytown he grew up in.

It's amazing, roysh, but everyone seems to recognize the cor. Malnourished men in hoodies, fat birds in leggings, fifteen-year-old girls pushing prams – they all stop and stare, roysh, in respectful silence, like you would if a funeral car passed by.

So Ronan has the window down again and he's borking out various instructions to people, going, 'Oi, leave that alone,' at these two older kids who are siphoning petrol out of a Suburu Signet, presumably to sniff. Two other kids go by on a horse – it's like *Into The* focking *West* around here – and he goes, 'That animal looks tired, give him a break,' and in the rearview I watch them climb down off the horse's back, roysh, and stare at us with their mouths open, like a couple of focking cod, as we disappear around the corner, and I can only imagine what this is doing for Ronan's street-cred.

'Would you mind popping into me Ma to say hello?' and The Monk goes, 'No problem,' because, like I said, roysh, he's actually a really nice goy.

Of course, when she meets him, Tina turns into Mrs focking Doyle. It's like, *Tea? Sandwiches?* I've never got a welcome like that.

The focking dirt of the place, though. It's the kind of gaff where you wipe your feet on the way *out*.

The morning ends with the four of us – we're talking me, Ro, The Monk and Tina – sitting around the table, eating sandwiches of tomorrow's turkey, drinking tea and just, like, shooting the breeze.

I mention the names of the ten or fifteen people I met on a holiday to Playa del Ingles who claimed to be friends – no, *personiddle* friends – of his, but surprise, surprise The Monk had never focking heard of any of them.

Then Ronan asks him does he know The Terminator, a local hood who Ronan, I suppose you'd have to say, looks up to in a big way. It's amazing. The Monk just stops chewing, roysh, puts his sandwich down and goes, 'Why do you idolize people like that?' and Ronan's like, 'Ah, I've heard the rumours meself. He touted on someone when he was sixteen. But they're apposed to have grilled him like a salmon steak. We're all hard men until they stick a hundred watts in yisser face.'

'I don't mean that,' The Monk goes. 'Ronan, what do you want to do when you leave school?'

'Honestly?' Ronan goes. He looks at me, then at Tina. 'The Bank of Ireland, College Green. That's the dream, but.'

The Monk nods his head, really slowly, like he's about to say something pretty serious. 'You know there's cleverer ways – legit ways – of making a fortune without sticking a gun in some poor teller's face,' he goes. 'The people who hold up banks are the ones who aren't clever enough to know that.'

I look at Ronan as if to say, that's exactly what I've been telling you.

Ronan goes, 'But I'm underworruld – throo and throo.'

The Monk can't help but laugh at that. The kid's a focking comedian.

'Your da here tells me that you're the smartest kid in your class,' The Monk goes, because I did, roysh, when I rang him to make the booking. 'In every subject. Maths, English, History . . . so you don't need to go waving guns around, kid. Why would you want to be the next Jesse James when you can be the next Sean Dunne?'

It's unbelievable, roysh, I wouldn't have thought the goy was so deep. Ronan's just, like, staring at him, nodding.

Fair focks to him, The Monk drops me all the way back into town. I pay the dude and tell him how much I enjoyed the morning.

'Me too,' he goes. 'That's a great kid you have there,' and ten minutes later, roysh, I'm standing on the Stephen's Green rank, thinking, yeah, he *is* actually a great kid, when my phone suddenly beeps and it's a text from Tina, telling me that Ronan's in his room, reading – of all things – his school books.

She seems to think this is a bad thing.

I'm in a Jo, heading home, dreading Christmas dinner tomorrow in the Lalors', when all of a sudden I get another text from, like, Jonny Cassidy, who was on the Ireland under-nineteen team with me – he's, like, Clongowes, but he's still sound – and he's working in Maxwell Motors these days.

Anyway, roysh, his text is just like, 'Ross im in work get ur orse out here now.'

Now as it happens, roysh, we've actually just passed the Frascati Centre and I tell the driver to drop me at the next lights.

I'm not *actually* ready for the scene that greets me when I walk into the showroom. My old dear and some other old biddy have been having a scrap in the middle of the floor. I know this because they both have a grip on each other's hair and five or six members of staff are still trying to prise the two of them aport, roysh, and with no success.

I just wade in there, of course, grab the old dear's two little fingers and bend them right back until I hear them crack and she suddenly lets go, howling with the focking pain.

Then the staff drag them a safe distance from each other.

I look at them both. I have to say, roysh, I barely recognize my own mother, the stupid bitch. She's been focking botoxed that much her tears are coming out of her eyes sideways.

The other old dear has scratchmorks on her face. I actually recognize her. Turns out her son, Barry, was on the same Clongowes team as Jonny. Her husband's, like, a consultant in, I don't know, Blackrock Clinic or one of those.

'So, is anyone going to tell me what the *fock* this is about?' I go.

When neither of them answers, Jonny, who has a good hold of my old dear, goes, 'They were fighting. Over who's going to get the first o6 D BMW X5 with sat nav,' and I swear to God, roysh, I'm pretty much speechless.

At the mention of satellite navigation, the old dear wants to go at it again, roysh, and she storts screaming and kicking, sending one of her Salvatore Ferragamos flying across the showroom, nearly taking the focking eye out of the poor goy who has Barry's old dear in a headlock.

'You're a focking disgrace,' I turn around and go to the old dear. 'You've lost all focking respect for yourself,' and she's absolutely focking bulling, roysh.

She goes, 'What do you care?' She absolutely spits it at me. She's there, 'You've never had any respect for me anyway,' and, quick as a flash, I go, 'That's because you're a focking trout,' and the next thing, roysh, this voice behind me goes, 'Don't speak to your mother like that.'

I spin around and who is it only that agent of hers.

'What's it to you?' I go.

He doesn't answer, roysh, but then he doesn't need to. I look at the old dear and I just shake my head.

Jonny goes, 'Look, it's Christmas. If everyone leaves now, I won't call the Gords.'

I just, like, stare Lance out of it, then I sort of, like, flick my thumb in the old dear's direction and I go, 'If you can't control your dog, at least put a focking muzzle on it,' and I give him a good, hord shoulder on my way out the door.

Christmas is barely over and Sorcha's already got the ad in the paper. The Rock & Republic shit is flying out the door and it's like she's going to die if she doesn't get back to the shop. So we end up spending the week after Christmas interviewing nannies, roysh, most of them immigrants it has to be said. Or what is it Sorcha calls them? Non-nationals.

Anyway, roysh, after much careful consideration, we've whittled the candidates down to two – Anka and Eskaterina.

You would presume, of course, that, being Dutch, Anka would be the nicer of the two, but I have to say, roysh, I've never been so disappointed in my life as I was to see her. She's actually uglier than Parnell Street. A real focking mess.

Eskaterina, on the other hand, is from a place called Belarus, which sounded like a bit of a makey-up place to me, like something from the 'Lord of the Rings', but Sorcha *had* heard of it and she did honours geography – and she got an A in it, as she did in pretty much honours everything.

She's a serious honey, this Eskaterina – a ringer for Liv Tyler – and I'm just, like, staring at her, thinking, I should have bought two aportments in *your* town, wherever that is.

She focking aces the interview from my point of view.

'Well, it's no contest, really,' I go to Sorcha after I've followed Eskaterina's orse down the garden and halfway up Newtownpork Avenue.

'I agree,' she goes. 'Have you seen Anka's references? The last little girl she nannied for was a member of the Dutch royal family,' and I make a face as if to say, and your point is?

She's there, 'I don't believe it – you're thinking about Eskaterina, aren't you?'

She knows me only too well.

'She just seemed cool,' I go. 'And Anka, well, she's not exactly easy on the eye, is she? Not that looks are that important. But we don't want Honor waking up screaming with nightmares . . .'

Sorcha knows I have a point, but at the same time, roysh, she knows that bringing Eskaterina into the house is putting temptation in my way. Like I said, she knows me too well.

'Look,' I end up going, 'why don't we call them back for second interviews,' thinking, at least I'll get another look at Eskaterina, even if we end up hiring the other wreck.

'Second interviews? Ross, it's a nanny's job – not head of research at GlaxoSmithKlein.'

But eventually, roysh, she agrees and she phones the two of them up and asks them to come back out to the gaff tomorrow afternoon.

Anka mustn't be a happy camper because I hear Sorcha go, 'Yes, I *have* read your references, but we still have one or two questions,' and when she hangs up I go, 'Sounds like she has a problem with authority,' really sowing the doubts in her head.

Of course, there's no way that focking whelk is looking after a kid of mine. I wouldn't even be a hundred per cent sure she's a woman.

So the following morning I get up early – we're talking ten o'clock – and I point the old love-machine in the direction of Shankill – focking *Skankill* – where Anka lives in an aportment. I press the intercom button, but she doesn't buzz me in, roysh, she says she'll come down to the front door.

Probably can't trust herself not to try to be with me. But when she arrives down, roysh, she's straight on the attack.

She's like, 'What is this *second* interview? So I am good enough for the cousin of Princess Maxima, but not good enough for you, yes?' and I stort nodding, roysh, sort of, like, sympathizing with her? I notice she wears those big focking Nana Mouskouri glasses, something she failed to mention at her first interview.

I go, 'Look, my wife's a pretty tough cookie. I'm only here because I want *you* to get the job.'

She's there, 'This is something that surprises me. You did not look at me even one time during the interview,' and I actually laugh out loud at that. I'm terrible around birds I've no interest in.

She's like, 'In my interview, you were – how do you say? – throwing your eyes up to the sky.'

Yeah, I can actually believe that.

But of course, Slick Mick here ends up going, 'That's because I thought interviewing you was a waste of time. If it was left to me, I'd have given you the job on the strength of your references. I mean, what was it the cousin of that princess called you? Punctual?'

She goes, 'Yes, and resourceful,' and I'm there,

'Resourceful, yeah. And I looked all those up and they're all good shit, which is why I'm offering you a word of advice. The area you're falling down on, believe it or not, is hobbies.'

'Hobbies?' she goes, looking seriously Scooby Dubious. 'Hobbies. *Pah!* I write down badminton, reading . . .' and I go, '*Everyone* puts badminton and reading – it's one of those lies you put on your CV when you realize you actually *do* fock-all, except work and drink . . .'

'So,' she goes, 'what, you think I should make something up?' and I'm like, 'Exactly. You wouldn't believe how seriously Sorcha takes this hobbies shit. It's important for her to feel she has a connection to whoever's minding her baby, if that makes any sense to you.'

I let that sink in. Then I go, 'Sorcha really enjoys hunting.'

She looks surprised.

I'm there, 'Yeah, five or six times a year, we're out there in, I don't know, Wicklow or somewhere like that, riding around on horses, looking for foxes to kill.'

She goes, 'In Holland, many of the royal family like this. I go maybe one or two times . . .'

I'm thinking, yeah, with a set of teeth like that, I'd say you led the focking pack.

I don't say that, though. What I say is, 'Well, why not mention that – that's *if* hobbies come up this afternoon? Give yourself the best chance,' and she thanks me, roysh, she actually focking thanks me.

So three o'clock rolls around and we're all back in the living room, Anka sitting in the ormchair, me and Sorcha asking the questions from the sofa like Mark Cagney and Sinead what's-her-face.

We pussyfoot around for a few minutes, until I decide

this bird's face is too focking offensive for me to look at it for a minute longer.

I give her a little wink, roysh, then I go, 'Let's talk about your hobbies. What actually are they, aport from badminton and reading, which sound pretty interesting by themselves?'

I can feel Sorcha looking at me.

'Em, I like to hunt the animals,' Anka goes and suddenly Sorcha's looking at *her*.

Sorcha's there, 'Sorry, can you *actually* repeat that?' and Anka looks at me, then back at Sorcha, and goes, 'The royal family, they like to hunt. Many times I go with them. I like it, too. The dogs, they like to run after the fox especially. When they catch the fox, it make me so happy . . .'

'No offence,' Sorcha goes, 'but I don't think you're a suitable person to look after my daughter,' and she stands up, roysh, and opens the living-room door, doesn't offer to shake her hand or anything.

Of course, Anka doesn't move. She sits there, roysh, with her mouth open, looking at me for back-up, but I'm just, like, blanking her, all of a sudden taking a huge interest in the palm of my hand.

'I'd like you to leave,' Sorcha goes and Anka gets up slowly, probably dizzy at how quickly that just happened, and she heads for the door.

When she's gone, I turn around to Sorcha and I'm like, 'You'd think she'd have a bit more sympathy for animals – looking like that.'

Claire, as in Claire from, like, Bray of all placcs, turns up in Lillie's on New Year's Eve wearing a flat cap, having apparently seen Keira Knightley wearing one in *Heat* magazine.

'Wow!' Chloe's supposed to have gone. 'Where are the auditions for *Oliver Twist* going on?'

Oisinn rings me up and asks me if I fancy going for a shave, as in a proper shave, like we used to in the old days, on the morning of a big game.

So we end up hitting Knight's in Stephen's Green, roysh, and it's just like old times, except, of course, I end up having this attack of paranoia walking through the door of the place, remembering how the papers stitched up the Dricster the last time he got his Tony Blair cut.

Four focking hours *is* a long time, in fairness.

Oisinn's already lathered up when I arrive – and I don't mean that in a gay way. 'Hey, happy new year, Dude. I'm just looking out for the paparazzi,' I go. 'I thought I saw one back there, outside Argos,' and of course the focker has to go, 'Ross, you won a Schools Cup medal in 1999. I think the tabloids have bigger fish to fry,' meaning *him*, of course.

There was a picture yesterday of him with Donatella Versace, coming out of RPG's.

I'm not usually a last-word freak, but I end up going, 'Well, they're bound to have gotten wind of the fact that I'm thinking of going back playing rugby,' and Oisinn sort of, like, snorts at me and tells me to sit down, which I do, then one of the birds storts rubbing eucalyptus into my Ricky Gervais.

Even under all that foam, you can tell that Oisinn's looking well. That's what being loaded does for you.

That scented holy water of his is walking off the shelves. Next month he's launching two more, I suppose, varieties, we're talking *An Eye For An Iris*, and then another which has, like, bamboo in it, called *The Mark of Cane*. And if yesterday's paper is to be believed, Versace are paying him an advance of, like, two million sheets for his next fragrance, which he gets in his Davy Crockett before he even turns on a bunsen burner.

I'm not going to give him the pleasure of asking him about it. Instead I ask him about JP, roysh, has he heard any word?

'Met his old dear in Donnybrook Fare,' he goes. 'She said he's coming around. I said we wouldn't mind seeing him, but she didn't think it was a good idea.'

I'm there, 'Yeah, I phoned the gaff a couple of times over Chrimbo. His old man said pretty much the same to me. He was like, not at the moment. So what's the Jackanory? Did she say what happened?'

He shrugs his shoulders. 'Just a nervous breakdown,' he goes. 'No big mystery.'

Then, totally out the blue, Oisinn goes, 'Ross, I want to sell the club.'

I grab the bird's hand, just as she's about to go at me with the open razor, and I'm like, 'Say that again,' and suddenly, from under a pile of hot towels, he's going, 'I'm serious. Lillie's — I want out,' and I'm so in shock, roysh, I can't think of a single thing to say.

He goes, 'I'm focked, Ross. Totally creamed. That's how I ended up with glandular fever. The last couple of years have been . . . well, there was *Eau d'Affluence*, now the holy water and I've, er, one or two other things in the pipeline . . .'

Yeah, one or two million.

The bird takes the towels off his face. He's there, 'Look, I'm spending a lot more time away, now. Shit the bed, Dude, I just don't need the stress of owning a nightclub any more . . .'

I go, 'Why don't you just sell your stake? There's one or two of the Ireland players might be interested. Shaggy, for one . . .'

That's when Oisinn goes, 'Have you spoken to the goys?' and I'm like, 'Are you saying you've all decided this behind my back and shit?'

He's there, 'Look, Fionn's teaching fulltime now – he doesn't have time to run a club. JP's old man would think it's a good idea to sell. Christian's a family man now – of course he wants out . . .'

'That'd be more Lauren than him,' I go. 'I'd have focking words with that girl if I wasn't so scared of her. What about One F?'

He laughs and he goes, 'Derek's got this theory that the bubble's about to burst. Wants to put his money into ketchup.'

I'm like, 'Ketchup? Explain that to me.'

He goes, 'Well, believe it or not, it *is* the biggest growth industry in times of recession. When people are poorer, they eat more junk, more frozen food.'

I'm there, 'He actually believes that shit?'

He's like, 'Well, as he says himself, do you think Tony O'Reilly ever wears the same pair of kacks twice?'

It's out of order.

Correction – it's bang out of order.

I can't get Christian on the Wolfe. Fionn, either. Then I remember, roysh, that Fionn'll be back at work today, so I end up pointing the old BMW Z4 in the direction of Castlerock with the intention of, like, confronting the four-eyed focker, we're talking face to face.

Have to say, roysh, it's always a huge thrill going back to

the old school, but it feels, like, weird with Fehily not being around. I keep expecting to hear that voice of his come booming down the corridor.

McGahy is the new man, the first lay principal in the history of the school and he hates my actual guts. He used to teach me geography. Or try. I used to give him, like, dog's abuse and there was fock-all he could do to me, roysh, what with me being on the S and shit.

I notice that his poxy little Nissan Sunny isn't outside, so I lash my cor into his porking space, roysh, just for the buzz, just for old times' sake.

I wander down to the secretary's office, as in Ms Butler. She's always had a thing for me, if I'm being honest.

I'm just like, 'Hey! I'd say you never thought you'd clock this ugly mug around here again,' and when she doesn't answer, roysh, I go, 'I'm actually looking for Fionn . . .'

She's like, 'Fionn? Oh, you mean Mr de Barra?' and I'm there, 'Er, no? I mean Fionn,' and she goes, 'Oh, he's, em, in A34. Fifth-year History,' and I'm like, 'Kool *and* the Gang.'

He's not a happy bunny when he sees me walk through the door. I could hear him from outside, banging on, giving it, 'The provisional Government were becoming more and more impatient with the failure of Seán Mac Eoin's command to quieten disturbances in the north-west, in particular Mayo and Sligo . . .' and when I burst in, roysh, I wasn't expecting to find anyone still awake.

But they were and one of them went, 'Oh my God, there's Ross O'Carroll-Kelly,' and of course, within five seconds the whole room is going, 'Leg-end! Leg-end! Leg-end!'

I'm like, ah stop goys, but at the same time, roysh, it is nice that people remember.

Fionn's fit to be tied, of course. He sort of, like, ushers

me out the door, then goes, 'How dare you barge into my classroom like that!'

I'm just like, 'Hey, you're not talking to some spotty little transition-year kid now. How about I break every pane of glass in your face?'

He's there, 'Ross, I'm at work. I don't barge in on you when you're . . . doing whatever it is *you* do all day.'

Barge is a real teacher's word.

I'm there, 'That's what I actually want to talk to you about. What do you mean deciding to sell the club behind my back?'

He shrugs. 'I just want out,' he goes. 'Look, Ross, it was fun for a couple of years. But I've got a career now. Aoife and I want to spend Friday and Saturday nights together. We've a lot of catching up to do . . .'

I have to say, roysh, I'm pretty crushed.

I'm there, 'It's just that everyone seems to be, I don't know, moving on.'

'And what's wrong with that?' he goes. 'Aoife and I, we want to get married, buy a house — you can't begrudge us that,' and he's actually roysh. I can't. Certainly not Aoife. And not Fionn either.

'Look at all *you've* got,' he goes.

He means Sorcha, Honor, blahdy blahdy blah.

But I just don't know what I'm going to do with my days now.

I decide to let him go back into class. 'Hey,' I go, 'I bet those kids have never chanted that to you,' and he laughs, in fairness to him, and he says he'll see me around.

I head outside, roysh, and I see something that I have to say immediately cheers me up. McGahy's walking around my cor, looking at it like he's just found a pube in his egg sandwich.

I saunter on over there, giving it loads, it's got to be said

'Is this *your* car?' he goes and I'm like, 'Oh, you mean the BMW Z4 convertible?' really rubbing his nose in it. Bear in mind, roysh, that he's still driving the same focking bucket of rust he was six or seven years ago.

He's actually bulling, roysh, we're talking red in the face. It's not my fault he's a schoolteacher. He's just another well-meaning fool who chose to take a vow of poverty. No point taking it out on me.

'It's in *my* parking space,' he goes. 'Move it!'

And what do I say, roysh, as, like, a comeback? Nothing. I just slip my hand into the inside pocket of my Henri Lloyd, whip out my platinum cord and for, like, ten seconds, I just hold it right in front of the focker's face.

Eskaterina's telling me a bit about her country — as in, like, Belarus? — and if the truth be told, it's a bit focking boring, roysh, but I suppose a major port of conversation is actually listening to what the other person's saying.

So, like, one third of the country is made up of forest apparently and their equivalent of the euro is the rouble.

I'm there, 'Is it anywhere near Bulgaria?' and she's like, 'No, is between Poland and Russia, yes?' Which of course means little or nothing to me.

She's like, 'The town zat I come from is called Brest,' and of course when she says that I'm trying not to smile, but I'm failing miserably. Eventually, I just crack up laughing in her face.

'What is it?' she goes. 'What is funny?' and I go, 'Just the name of your town. Brest. I mean, in our country that means basically tit,' and she laughs and goes, 'You are very funny man,' and I'm thinking, yeah, I suppose my sense of humour *is* one of the things I really love about myself.

She goes, 'So, how voz your day today?' and I'm like, 'Pretty crap actually. Ah, the rest of the goys want to sell the club, as in Lillie's, the nightclub we own?'

She mutes *Extreme Makeover* and she looks at me sort of, like, sympathetically. She goes, 'And zis makes you sad, yes?' and I'm like, 'Yeah, pretty much. Aport from anything else it's, like, my base of operations. Lillie's to me is like the Bada Bing is to Tony Soprano . . .'

She's nodding like she understands.

I'm there, 'When it's sold, I'll have no reason to get up in the afternoons. And on top of that, it just feels like everyone's, I don't know, drifting away in different directions.'

So out of the blue, roysh, she goes, '*Zer are no conditions of life to which man cannot get accustomed, especially if he sees them accepted by everyone around him.* Zat is Tolstoy, Russ. From *Anna Karenina.*'

I suppose it's another way of saying, basically, build a bridge and get over it.

I'm like, 'One of the, I suppose, downsides of being a really good-looking goy is that people think life is easy for you. And that's not me trying to sound big-headed,' and she goes, 'Yes, everyone, no matter who, have problems . . .'

I'm suddenly like, 'And here's me banging on about mine. What about you? What kind of a day did you have?' and she goes, 'Good. Honor, she sleep for four hours in ze afternoon, letting me catch up on ze college work . . .'

She's studying Russian literature. Waste of focking time, obviously, but this Tolstoy must be one of that crew.

'Zen, in ze afternoon,' she goes, 'I have a phone call from Yevgeni.'

Yevgeni is, like, her ex. I get the impression she only came to Ireland to, like, get away from him.

'Zis phone call, it make me very sad. He say he want me to go back to Belarus, to lif wiz him in Minsk – he is lecturer in university, yes? – and for to marry and make baby wiz . . .'

I'm like, 'Whoa, heavy shit.'

She goes, 'Yes, heavy sheet, like you say it.'

She seems really sad, but this is good, roysh, because we're really, like, bonding.

'Pardon me for saying it,' I go, 'but you actually look like Liv Tyler. Take my advice. You're young, free and single – you just got to mingle. That's Kool and the Gang said that, I think,' and that puts the smile back on her boat race.

The next thing, roysh, there's a key in the door and we both automatically jump up from the sofa, even though there's, like, nothing going on here. Eskaterina storts checking on Honor, who's in, like, her carrycot on the floor, roysh, and I crack on that I'm looking through my DVDs.

Sorcha opens the door of the living room and I look around and go, 'Hey, Babes, how was your sunbed?' but she doesn't answer, roysh, she just, like, glowers at me, which means she's pissed off with me – and the worst thing is, roysh, she doesn't even know why yet.

I'm having one last mooch around the Library and it has to be said it's pretty hord-going. It's, like, everywhere I look there's a memory. Lying across the grand piano while Rosanna Davison played 'The Lady in Red' and Amanda Brunker fed me chocolate-covered strawberries. Then me and the Irv pretty much coming to blows over Lady Isabella

Hervey, then getting it on with Atomic Kitten in the pool room.

Never did get those stains out of the table.

The fake tan, I mean.

The Irv's.

Happy days. Yeah, we're leaving some amount of ghosts behind.

Suddenly, roysh, I hear shooting – as in actual focking machine guns – coming from the penthouse upstairs and I automatically go, 'Is Oisinn trying to get McWilliams to settle his tab?' but there's actually no one around to hear what I have to admit is a cracking one-liner.

Anyway, I take the stairs the same way I took the Kittens – quickly – and, up in the penthouse, who do I find but One F, the focking Ketchup King, stretched out in the giant jacuzzi, knocking back a bottle of JD by the neck and watching what turns out to be *Platoon* on the giant plasma screen.

Without looking at me, he goes, 'The Hueys are here, are they?'

I really like One F, roysh, but I've only understood about five per cent of the things he's ever said to me.

'Hueys!' he goes, looking at me in, like, total disgust. 'I'm talking helicopters. It's what the Septics used to call the UH-1s. Are you telling me you've never seen footage of the evacuation of Saigon?'

I just go, 'Er, we're all downstairs, Dude, clearing out our desks, having a few scoops . . .'

Lillie's sold unbelievably quickly, as in two days after we put it on the morket. It works out at, like, three-quarters of a million each, which is, like, two hundred and fifty thousand sheets more than we each paid for our stake, but it's still sad to be leaving – and in a major way.

One F goes, 'They want to plant the Revolutionary Forces flag on the roof tonight, do they?' and of course there's no answer to that except, 'Yeah, whatever.'

I go back downstairs to the main bor.

Fionn goes, 'Where's Duong Van Minh?' and before I get a chance to answer, One F walks through the door behind me with only a towel around his waist, still necking the JD from the bottle. He doesn't say anything, roysh, just gets to work, first taking his picture of Cher down off the wall, then packing the rest of his possessions – mostly hair products – into what his readers would probably refer to as 'a holdall'.

'Whose is this?' Christian goes, holding up what looks like a BlackBerry.

Oisinn goes, 'It's Drico's. It was found on the floor of the Library a couple of months ago. I just never got around to giving it back to him,' and I go, 'Don't! Not until I grab a few numbers off it,' and suddenly I'm going through his phonebook, thinking, I can't fucking *believe* the birds this goy knows. If the IRFU had given me a contract, my life could have been SO different. But of course, I was too busy loving it, loving it, loving it, loving it like that.

Oisinn goes, 'Look at this,' and we all look up and he's, like, holding up an empty pint glass. He's there, 'Lucy Kennedy drank out of this,' and he sniffs it and he's like, 'You can actually still smell the Bulmers off it.'

Then Fionn produces the spread that *VIP* did on us when we bought the place. 'The Darling Buds of Lillie's.' And I get a bit of a slagging over my, 'I'm too cool for school – and I'm hung like a mule,' line, which earned me a slap across the old Brendan Grace from Sorcha and six nights of the silent treatment.

I always was a slave to the one-liner.

Pretty soon we're all up on the roof, drinking cocktails and watching the sun go down on our last day as the owners of Lillie's Bordello.

'It was fun,' Fionn goes and for once in my life I have to agree with him.

I'm there, 'The best time of my life – aport from winning the S obviously.'

'This can't be how it ends,' One F suddenly goes. 'Sipping cocktails like a bunch of bitches. This is the dissolution of a wonderful partnership, guys – we need to mark this moment, remember it for ever.'

I'm there, 'How?' and he's like, 'By breaking the law, of course.'

Oisinn – who's fairly hammered at this stage – stands up and goes, 'Let's break into Croke Pork and play rugby on their so-called sacred field,' and it's one of those moments, roysh, when we all look at each other and go, Oh my God, that is focking *genius*. Because it's pretty humiliating, you'd have to agree, that we're pretty much down on our knees, begging the bogball crowd to let us use their stadium – which is in focking Comanche land, let us not forget – and they're going, Oooh begorrah, we don't know if we can let ye, because rugby's a fodden game, be-to-hokey, and playing it is a mortal sin so 'tis, oooh I love a big bowl of turnips, so I do.

So we're all like, let's end the debate once and for all.

It's nine o'clock and we all pile into a Jo. We swing by Oisinn's gaff to pick up a ball, then we head for focking Crock Pork. And let me just say, roysh, driving from Shrewsbury Road to Clonliffe Road is probably the biggest culture shock any of us will ever have.

Even though I took Sorcha to the Point Depot once to

see Il Divo, I wouldn't exactly make a habit of hanging out on the northside. We've all seen the horrific images on television, though, and I have to say, roysh, it's actually a lot worse in real life. We're talking burnt-out cors, boarded-up shops, children on the street eating bread and jam.

We finally arrive at the ground and it's in, like, total dorkness, which should make getting in a piece of piss, but it turns out that it's not CCTV cameras we have to worry about – these people are muckers, remember, they're only on the electricity two years – it's the focking razor wire.

We're all standing there thinking, how are we going to get over that – especially me with my new black Hugo Boss shirt.

Of course, One F isn't fazed at all. He just goes, 'Brings me back to Hiep Hoa . . .' and then, almost in one, like, fluid movement, he whips off his leather jacket, throws it on top of the wall, managing to cover a section of spikes five feet wide, takes a run up and sort of, like, jumps and then pulls himself up onto the wall, climbs over the coat and then jumps down on the other side.

There's, like, silence from him for about thirty seconds. Christian goes, 'One F – can you hear us?' and he's like, 'Loud and clear, guys.'

I'm there, 'What's it like? Is it true it's, like, horder to breathe?' and he goes, 'No, it's just like Lansdowne Road, guys – except shit, obviously. Come on, climb over,' which we do, roysh, one by one, following the same route that One F took, the mad focker.

It actually turns out to be a pretty normal stadium. One or two of us were expecting to see, I don't know, a couple of hundred heads of cabbage growing along the sidelines and maybe a couple of rows of *shpuds*, but there's actually, like, none of that? In fact, you could basically be on the southside – if it wasn't for the constant sound of alorms and police sirens, which seems to be the focking soundtrack to life on this side of the world.

'Okay,' Oisinn goes, 'who's first?'

We're all standing on the sideline, roysh, staring out into the blackness. It's actually a little bit eerie, if that's even a word.

'What do you mean, who's first?' I go.

He's like, 'Well, one of us is going to be the *first* to take a rugby ball onto that pitch. I'm just saying, I don't mind if it's someone else . . .'

Christian goes, 'I have a baaad feeling about this.'

I'm like, 'What the fock do you think's going to happen – you're going to, like, burst into flames or something?'

I look at the goys, one by one. They're actually shitting it. I turn around to Oisinn and I go, 'Give me the ball,' and I grab it, roysh, and run onto the pitch and do a few drills.

'What's it like?' Christian shouts over to me. 'I mean, do you feel any different?'

I'm like, 'Goys, I'm telling you, it's Kool and the Gang,' but it's only after I kick a couple of really tasty penalties that they decide it's safe and they all pile onto the pitch.

So we're, like, throwing the ball around, roysh, still hammered of course, but really enjoying ourselves, when all of a sudden we hear this voice – and it's definitely a bogger – go, 'Leds, what are ye doing, begorrah?'

I look up and I end up nearly kacking myself. It's the Feds. There's, like, four Gords walking across the pitch towards us.

Oisinn goes, 'I think we need to peg it,' but I'm like, 'No

way. Goys, one of us here has the chance to score the first ever try on this focking ground. How about we see can the Castlerock backline still work that old magic?'

Fionn just smiles at me. It's one of those moments, as in, fock the consequences.

We spread out in a line and then we attack them with the ball. The first Gord is actually pretty quick on his feet for a big goy. He hits Oisinn like a focking train but, before he hits the deck, Oisinn manages to offload to Christian, who skips around the second and third Gords, like he used to back in the day, then throws an unbelievable loop pass to One F.

He quickly offloads the ball, roysh, to Fionn, who plays the most unbelievable little grubber kick forward for me. I mean, the ball stops, like, five metres short of the line, roysh, and I'm focking pegging it now.

I'm across the halfway line and I'm like Denis focking Hickie here, breaking sprint records left, right and centre. But so is the Gord who took out Oisinn. I can hear him behind me, roysh, his George Webbs going *thrump, thrump, thrump*, like a focking horse's hooves.

All I've got to do, roysh, is scoop it up and dive over the line. Doesn't even have to be under the posts, roysh, because something tells me I'm not going to be let take the conversion.

I cross the twenty-two. It's me and him now.

I can hear the goys going, 'Go on, Ross! It's your ball!' and the other Gords are like, 'Ketch him, Ned! Dawnt leshim do ish!'

I'm five yords from the ball. I'm already crouching down to scoop it up. It's like everything is happening in slow motion. I reach down. I put my palm on it. I wrap my fingers around it. I pick it up. And then . . .

BANG!

The next thing I remember, roysh, is giving my details to the desk sergeant in Store Street Gorda Station and asking him had my jaw come loose on one side. Ned, the Gord who creamed me – and who, it turns out, carried me, unconscious, over his shoulder back to the van – goes, 'Did you hear what dee were doing in dare, Peadar?'

Peadar looks up from his little focking ledger and Ned goes, 'Dee were playing rugby, bejaysus?'

'Is it havin' me on, you are?' Peadar goes. 'Rugby? On de sacred turf?'

Ned's like, 'On de sacred turf . . .'

Peadar looks me up and down and he's like, 'Ye durthy bastards, ye,' and it's like we've just been caught, I don't know, setting fire to an old-age pensioner.

I turn around to Ned and I'm like, 'That was a high focking tackle, by the way. That would actually have been a penalty try.'

He's there, 'We play by diffordent rules, begorrah.'

We're put into separate cells, like focking criminals – I hear One F screaming, 'Don't put me in a Tiger Cage!' – and we end up being kept there until seven o'clock in the morning, when Christian finally gets his father-of-law out of Joys to bail us out.

It's, like, eight o'clock when I get home, absolutely hanging, with my jaw feeling like I could snap it off without too much effort. Sorcha's on the way out of the gaff as I'm on the way in. We actually meet on the doorstep.

I'm there, 'Hey, Babes, I, er, ended up crashing at the club last night. Turned into a bit of a session. How was your night?'

'Oh, nothing too eventful,' she goes. 'Aoife called around – we're thinking of doing that wine-tasting course in the

French Paradox. Mum rang to tell me she found that article about having your baby nutrigenetically tested. Oh, and then the Gardaí in Store Street rang, just to verify that Ross O'Carroll-Kelly lived at this address . . .'

I'm like, 'Babes, I'm really sorry if they, like, woke you and shit?'

'Leave me alone,' she goes. 'Just leave me alone.'

'What are you watching?' I go and I plonk my orse down on the sofa beside her. It's *Judge Judy*. Ah, that takes me back.

She goes, 'You see zis man here?' and I'm there, 'The black one?' although I didn't mean it in a racist way. She's like, 'Yes, ze black one, he is married to zis lady here, but zen he sleeps wiz her seester,' and she shakes her head and looks at me for a reaction. I suppose, given my history, I'd be a focking hypocrite if I said anything.

'What a dirtbag,' I go and Eskaterina's like, 'Yes. A deertbag,' and then she turns back to the screen and she's there, 'Now, zey are in court fighting to see who can keep zis sheety little car. One day, zey love each other and the next day zey do all of zis, argue on television for meelions and meelions of people to watch. Americans, zey are crazy,' and I go, 'You're not wrong there,' and I end up telling her three or four of my J1 stories, and of course she totally laps them up.

'How's *she* been?' I go eventually, nodding at Honor, who's been curled up in Eskaterina's orms the whole time, not a peep out of her, happy as Larry, and we're talking Larry Flint.

She's there, 'She is such a heppy leetle girl,' and then she goes, 'You vont to go to your deddy?' and of course I'm there going, 'Er, *not* a good idea, Eskaterina. She'll only stort crying,' and Eskaterina's like, 'Plees, call me Katya. And no, she von't cry.'

I'm there, 'No, seriously, she hates my *actual* guts?' but she doesn't listen, roysh. She lifts her and puts her into my orms and I swear to God, roysh, it's amazing because she doesn't cry at all. She actually smiles at me for the first time since, I'm pretty sure, the day she was born.

Eskaterina – sorry, Katya – goes, 'You vont somesing to eat?' and I'm there, 'No, I'm cool, Sorcha will be home pretty soon,' and Katya's like, 'No, she ring to say zat she is vurking late in ze shop – till eight, yes? – zen she is having ze sunbed,' and I'm thinking, *another* sunbed? Nice of her to focking tell *me*.

'So I cook, yes?' Katya goes and I'm there, 'I don't want to put you to any, like, trouble and shit?' and she goes, 'Is no trouble and sheet. I cook traditional East Europe deener for you,' and she seems happy to do it, roysh, so I let her.

So for the next half-an-hour, roysh, I'm the happiest I've ever been, probably since the day Reggie Corrigan and Shane Byrne came up to me in Lillie's and said they couldn't believe I hadn't been called up to the Leinster team, given my natural talent, faith in my own ability, blahdy blahdy blah.

I have Honor lying, like, lengthways on my lap and I'm tickling her little belly and she's laughing, roysh – as in really, really laughing – and then suddenly we're looking into each other's eyes and I actually can't explain to you the feeling that passes between us at that moment, unless you have a daughter of your own.

Then Katya arrives back in the living room, with this amazing smell wafting in with her.

'Who is keeping ze car?' she goes. 'Ze black man or ze black woman?' and it's then I realize that I was so caught up in the moment that I actually had no interest in how the case turned out.

'The woman,' I go, because I imagine it's what she'd want to hear.

She's like, 'Gude. Now, zis is *machanka*,' she goes, putting the plate down on the coffee table in front of me. 'Is pork stew wiz – how to say – sour cream?' and I'm there, 'Cool.'

It might *look* like it came out of the orse of a shivering chihuahua, roysh, but it's actually incredible, like something you'd get in, like, a restaurant.

Katya goes, 'I'll put Honor down for ze night, zen bring for you a beer.'

He asks me to meet him in Shanahan's, of all places, and he's already there when I arrive, wrapping himself around a steak the size of Limerick. With slightly less blood obviously.

'You wanted to see me?' I go and he's like, 'Yes, sit down there, Ross,' which I do, then I grab a menu off the next table and stort studying it.

I'm like, 'I'm pretty peckish, it has to be said,' and I'm thinking, yeah, it's not often you get to stiff Hennessy for anything.

I ask the waitress – fock, she has a face like a dropped pie – to bring me the dearest steak in the house, with all the trimmings, we're talking chips, we're talking onion rings, we're talking the whole shebang.

'And to drink?' she goes and I just, like, flick to the wine list at the back, run my finger down the price column and ask for the most expensive bottle on the list, which could be paint stripper for all I know, but it's five hundred bills a bottle.

Hennessy doesn't bat an eyelid, just goes, 'Ross, I need you to talk to your father,' really, like, serious all of a sudden. 'He's talking about pleading guilty.'

I end up just giving him a shrug and I'm there, 'Er, he *is* focking guilty?'

He's like, 'You know that and I know that, but I think I could get him acquitted on most of these charges, certainly the one involving bribing county councillors. It'll be impossible to link those contributions to favours, and the DPP knows it. We can say they were campaign contributions.'

I go, 'Sorry, Hennessy, all this affects me *how* exactly?'

'It affects you in a very serious way,' he goes. 'He pleads guilty to these charges and the Criminal Assets crowd won't need to make a case against him. It'll be done for them. By my calculations, about seventy per cent of your father's assets can be linked to criminal activity . . .'

My steak arrives.

I go, 'Not being, I don't know, callous here, if that's the word, but I've got three quarters of a million coming to me. Why would I give an actual fock?'

'Which brings me on to my next point,' he goes. 'You *don't*. I mean, you don't have three quarters of a million anything coming to you . . .'

What the fock is he talking about?

'Your share of the club was in your father's name. That's how you wanted it, remember?'

I'm like, 'HELLO? Only for, like, tax reasons? I was the *actual* owner,' and he goes, 'Can you prove that? I mean, Charles gave you the money for your stake and, well, there's no evidence that you paid him a single cent back. It was in *his* name . . .'

I don't focking believe this. And then I remember something else. 'Hey, what about my bills – who's going to pay them? And my—'

'Your two thousand euros a week allowance?' he goes. 'Why don't you ask your mother – she's independently wealthy these days . . .'

I'm there, 'That trout? I wouldn't give her the pleasure . . .'

'Ross,' he goes, 'you have got to talk your father out of this madness.'

'Pleading guilty? Are you off your focking cake?'

He doesn't answer, roysh, he just stares over my shoulder, into the distance. 'You know what I miss most about the outside – maybe the only thing I miss?' he goes.

I don't even bother answering him.

He's there, 'Hennessy and I, we had this guilty little pleasure that we'd indulge in on occasional Sunday afternoons . . .'

I'm not sure if I actually want to hear this.

'We'd pick up a bottle of XO, a couple of Cohibas, sometimes even a picnic from Cavistons – well, everyone knows how much Hennessy loves their Roquefort – and we'd take the boat out, just outside Dún Laoghaire harbour, and we'd sit on deck and count the cranes on the skyline . . .'

I'm like, 'Cranes? If you'd told me you'd a couple of hookers onboard, I'd have had more respect for you. What the fock are you counting cranes for?'

He laughs. Then he goes, 'Construction is the true measure of a country's well-being, Ross. Counting cranes is like taking an economy's pulse . . .'

I'm like, 'Well, whatever pumps your nads, I suppose.'

The old man goes, 'You're too young to remember the last recession, Ross. Thank heavens for that, I used to say to your mother. Ireland was a wretched place. None of your . . . Starbucks and your . . . Tommy Hillseeker in those days, thank you very much indeed. The seventies and eighties, we were the Albania of western Europe.'

I'm like, 'Shit, in other words?'

'Oh, the word doesn't even come close to covering it. We were Third World in every way. Not just poverty but poverty of thought, poverty of imagination. Everything was shut on a Sunday. The banks closed at three o'clock. If you wanted a phoneline put in, it took four, five months. You know, I think it even got darker earlier.'

I'm like, 'And no Storbucks?'

'Why would they come here, Ross?' he goes. 'Nobody had any money. Our, inverted commas, political leaders – the same crowd who've turned their backs on me and my kind today – they couldn't have led a one-man race. They took us into an economic war with our most impor- tant trading partner – they hated Britain more than they hated being poor. You know all that, of course, from your history . . .'

What does he think I was actually doing at school?

'Ireland was run by these Ebenezer types,' he goes. 'Thin, grey men with pinched faces, writing in ledgers with quill pens. If you wanted to do anything, they'd give you a hundred reasons why you couldn't. And then, along came Ireland's first go-getter generation. Most of them – the ones with sense, you might say – got out. They emigrated. Built thriving business empires abroad.'

Lex arrives in. He has a visit. He gives us a wave from across the room and the old man waves back.

Then he's like, 'Some of us – bloody sentimentalists like Hennessy and I – well, we believed in this country enough to stay, try to make something of it.'

He laughs to himself. 'You won't remember this, Ross, but when you were a little boy I used to take you to – well, I suppose there's no harm in you knowing now, the cash-and-carry, of all places. I'd have you in my arms, like this, and we'd stand there for hours, watching, listening . . .'

I'm there, 'In the cash-and-carry? What were we focking listening to?'

'Commerce,' he goes.

I just shake my head. 'Jesus, it's a wonder I wasn't taken into focking care . . .'

'In the seventies and eighties,' he goes, 'you wouldn't believe how expensive it was just to give somebody a job in this country. We were paying crippling rates of PRSI, on top of crippling rates of taxation. Then there were unions shouting the odds, *wanting* things. You couldn't have made a success of business without keeping a few secrets from our friends – the Taxecutioners, as Hennessy and I used to call them.

'In the early nineties, when the economy was at its lowest ebb, I employed 2,478 people. I should be in the Seanad today, on the board of half-a-dozen semi-states – not in jail. Eight, maybe ten thousand people in this city had food on their table every day because of me, because I broke rules, cut corners.

'That crowd who are in power now. They knew how it worked. Ireland, remember – *independent* Ireland – was only sixty, seventy years old. Well, you name me a country that wasn't built on – as these people call it – corruption . . .'

I only know about five countries, fullstop.

'As for the, inverted commas, planning scandals, that's a

laugh. Capital L. Do you think there'd be a Celtic Tiger today without all those material contraventions of the County Development Plan? Do you think the economic turnaround would have happened had it been left to architects and town-planners to plot the future for us? There was no money in green fields, Ross. So we paid councillors – bribes, if that's what you want to call them – to turn those fields into shopping centres, factories, private housing estates . . .'

I go, 'The papers are saying you could even get ten years. You're just going to, like, accept that?'

'See, the media don't *get* it, Ross. They never did. All those little Woodwards and Bernsteins, chasing paper around and being outraged about things that happened before many of them were even born. Charlie Haughey *got* it. Fianna Fáil and Fine Gael *get* it, but of course they can't just come out and say, "Look, this is how economic booms happen. Now enjoy your lobster bisque and stop worrying your little heads about it."'

I go, 'You don't have to actually plead guilty to stand up and say all that shit in court.'

He's there, 'But I *am* guilty, according to the standards by which I'm being judged,' and I'm like, 'But you're going to lose *everything*,' and of course what I mean is, *I'm* going to lose everything.

'Not everything,' he goes. 'Just the things that don't really matter.'

I'm like, 'Oh, like that old hag you were married to?' which is a low blow, I know.

He doesn't look sad and he doesn't look happy.

'Me got the grapes on your mother,' he goes. 'Me hear she got herself a Sancho . . .'

I'm like, 'Will you stop focking talking like that. If you mean she's getting poked by someone who isn't you, you'd be right,' but there's, like, no reaction from him. He doesn't seem to actually *give* a *fock*.

The next thing, roysh, this tall, really, like, starving-looking goy on the far side of the room, shouts, 'Charlie – 28, 15, 26,' which I recognize straight away as one of Castlerock's famous lineout calls, and all of a sudden, roysh, the old man throws an imaginary rugby ball across, which this goy jumps, like, four feet in the air to catch.

The entire visiting room bursts into a cheer and then, like, a round of applause.

When the noise dies down, the old man goes, 'I've started a rugby team,' and I end up laughing in his actual face. He's there, 'I'm serious, Ross. You see that chap two tables up?'

I look, and there's what can only be described as a focking monster sitting there. The old man turns to him and goes, 'Bunter, how many cops did it take to drive you down?' and the goy goes, 'Eight,' and the old man turns back to me and goes, 'Eight, Ross. *With* truncheons. Let's not have any false modesty, thank you very much indeed. Oh, can you imagine a front row of our friend here, Lex and A.N. Other?'

He has a point actually.

He goes, 'And the competition for backs is intense – and you can drop whatever it is you're doing and cap up the I for me. All these chaps on drugs – there's not a pick on them. And boy can they move. A good grounding in shop-lifting, you see. Slippery little fellows. Oh, the people in here, Ross, they're wonderful.'

I go, 'You weren't saying that a year ago. You said that drug addiction was part of natural selection. Heroin was nature's way of culling the weak, according to you.'

He's there, 'I regret all those things I said.'

I stand up and I'm like, 'I don't know what the fock's

behind it, but I have to say, I don't like this new you. Do whatever the fock you want, but I swear to God, roysh, the Criminal Assets touch my three-quarters of a mill and it's goodnight, Vienna. You can focking rot in here for all I care.'

6. This Is the End

You'd have to get up pretty early in the morning to put one over on me. Actually, that's not strictly true, especially since I'm hordly ever out of the scratcher before *Home and Away* storts. Anytime before midday would probably do you. My point is that it's pretty much impossible to get anything past me. Lauren is away at the moment, roysh, at some training course in the UK. I know that for a fact. So when I overhear Christian on the phone, arranging to meet someone for dinner in Peploe's, I'm straightaway thinking, he's a focking dork horse. I mean, the goy's only been married a few weeks. Which means, of course, that he hasn't yet mastered the art of cheating on his wife.

Okay, brass-tacks time. You don't bring whoever you're knocking off to a good restaurant. Your bit on the side is your bit on the side, to be used, abused and eventually discorded like a focking jizz rag. Taking her to a place like Peploe's is like giving caviar to Blanchardstown – expensive, unnecessary and possibly even dangerous.

I'm tempted to point all of this out to Christian, except he's, like, playing his cords seriously close to his chest, as in he won't even tell me who he's meeting.

So my plan is, roysh, to show up at the restaurant, accidentally-on-purpose, just as they're getting their storters, to show Christian that he's got to be more careful about this kind of shit.

So half-eight, roysh, I pork the cor – as in my BMW Z4 – on Stephen's Green, mosey over to the restaurant and tip down the steps. The *maître d'* dude asks if I have a reservation and I tell him I'm looking for someone and I step past him and stort having a mooch around the place.

Imagine my shock, roysh, when I cop Christian sitting at a table in the corner with, not another bird, but with George Lucas, as in George *focking* Lucas. How the fock has this happened without his best friend even knowing about it?

I play it cool as a fish's fart, though. I go over to them. I know I shouldn't, but I do. I suppose deep down I know what's actually happening here and I want to fock it up for the goy.

'Ross?' Christian goes when he sees me. He does *not* sound a happy bunny. At the top of my voice, I'm there, 'What a focking coincidence. I just popped in for a bit of nosebag.'

Christian introduces us, roysh, and when he describes me as his friend I have to add the word 'best' to it. Then I sit down and go, 'You don't mind if I join you, do you? I see you've had the French onion soup, George. Focking great, isn't it?' and I end up asking the waiter for the same, followed by the grilled lobster with garlic butter, a bowl of *frites*, which is, like, French for chips, and some green beans with garlic and bacon, and I'm thinking, this isn't bad, two free dinners in a week.

I know I'm being a pain in the orse, roysh, but I can't help myself. It's like I'm on a mission.

I go, 'I love your movies, by the way – not as much as this focking lunatic, obviously. But I've seen them all. Can't remember much of the last one, though. I was gee-eyed. Remember that night, Christian? I got us focked out of the cinema in Dún Laoghaire.'

Christian ignores me and goes, 'George, what were you

saying earlier about the Sith?' and it's, like, okay, pretend I'm not here, then.

So George Lucas goes, 'You're not going to hear anything, I'm sure, that you don't already know. But I have a question to ask you and I'm going to come at it in a very roundabout way. As you know, the Sith are an ancient order whose history can be traced back to the time when the Jedi were the law-enforcement arm of the Old Republic. And as you also know, a dissident, who was known as the Dark Jedi, believed they couldn't fulfil their role if they remained pacifists. They would have to embrace the Dark Side – and the anger, fear and aggression that are functions of it . . .'

I'm pulling faces at Christian, to try to make him laugh. The main courses arrive. They're both having the traditional fish pie topped with mashed potato and parmesan.

George Lucas keeps going. He's like, 'The Jedi Council, not surprisingly, expelled him because of his views. Some Jedi went with him and they called themselves the Sith. But their lack of discipline led to an internecine power struggle that all but wiped them out. The only survivor was . . .'

'Darth Bane,' Christian goes.

'Absolutely. And as you know, Christian, it was Bane who decided that the Sith could only survive and perpetuate itself by limiting its numbers to two – a master and an apprentice . . .'

I yawn loudly. They both ignore me.

'When the master passed on, the apprentice would take over his role and he would himself take on an apprentice. I suppose what I'm asking you, Christian, in a very long-winded way . . .' and he laughs and goes, '. . . will you come to California to work at Lucasfilm?'

I knew it. I *focking* knew it.

Christian goes, 'What? Wow, em, I thought you weren't making any more *Star Wars* movies,' and George Lucas is like, 'Well, I've never said never. But I *have* made six and, as you know, those six have spawned an entire industry. We employ thousands of people, Christian, working on the various spin-offs – cartoons, DVDs, merchandising, conventions. What we need most is people with knowledge . . .'

He reaches under the table, where he has a bag, and he pulls out a file, roysh, thick as a DBS first-year repeat.

He goes, 'You've sent me a lot of letters over the years.'

Christian goes, 'Whoa – you kept them all?' and he's like, 'Sure. We keep all correspondence. When you sent me your draft script for a possible *Star Wars VII*, I have to tell you, it got me thinking, maybe I *do* want to do three more. I hadn't felt that way before . . . So, I had someone pull your file. Reading these, I was reminded of me as a young man. I need people like you around me, Christian.'

'It'll cost you,' I hear myself go. 'A million a year.'

George Lucas just shrugs. 'Sure.'

'Okay,' I go. 'Two million.'

He turns to Christian. 'Money is not going to be an issue,' he goes. 'I can assure you of that.'

Christian nods. He's there, 'I, er, don't know what to say. It's like a dream come true. Obviously, I have to talk it over with . . .'

I'm like, 'His friends. The people who've stuck by him through thick and thin . . .' and Christian looks at me and goes, 'I was actually going to say my wife, Ross.'

I go, 'Can I remind you, Christian, that your life is actually here. It's about time you grew up. California? You're being focking ridiculous – both of you.'

My soup arrives, but I don't even touch it because suddenly, roysh, I have to get out of here. I throw my napkin down on the table and I stand up to go.

'May the Force be with you,' they both go.

They're focking made for each other, those two. I seem to be dishing out ultimatums, if that's the word, to everyone this week.

I'm there, 'Christian, if you fock off and leave me, that's it. So bear that in mind before you make your decision.'

'Why are you wearing a man's watch?'

I think it's a reasonable enough question — I could just as easily have gone, why are you wearing sunglasses indoors in the middle of February? — but, of course, Chloe looks at me like I've just keyed her focking Mini Cooper.

'HELLO?' she goes, so loudly that pretty much everyone in the champagne bor in Ron Black's hears her. 'Do you actually *know* anything about fashion, Ross?'

I'm like, 'So when did it become fashionable to wear your old man's Cartier?' and Chloe looks at Sophie, as if to say, you answer him because it's, like, SO beneath me.

Sophie goes, 'They make your orms look thinner, Ross. It's the new thing. As in Lindsay Lohan? As in Nicole Richie? As in, like, Mischa Barton? It's, like, big sunglasses, big bags — this one's, like, Balenciaga Lariat — headscorves because they, like, keep your hair off your neck, show off your clav-icles . . . Oh and vintage dresses . . .'

Sophie's had a shitload of work done on her boat race — botox definitely. And I've heard of people getting moles removed, roysh, but she's had one put on, an actual cosmetic birthmork, in the same place as, like, Cindy Crawford's?

She turns around to Chloe goes, 'Oh my God, did you hear that Talitha — as in, Talitha Tierney who went to Alex, got maximum points in the Leaving – she got a Pucci kaftan and it was like, oh my God, *seven* grand?'

Chloe doesn't respond, roysh, just stares at her and eventually goes, 'I actually met her mum and dad coming out of Cavistons on Christmas Eve. They went home and told Talitha they were really worried about me. They thought I had anorexia,' and Sophie's there, 'Oh my God, that is SO cool,' and Chloe's like, 'I know.'

I head back over to Fionn and Oisinn and I go, 'What the fock are *they* doing here anyway? I thought we all hated them now,' and Oisinn's there, 'It's Ellie's birthday, Ross, she can invite who she likes.'

Ellie is actually Ellie Banaher. Looks like Tea Leoni. I've had my sweaty way with her twice.

Christian comes over and he storts giving it, 'Hey, goys,' but I just blank him, roysh, worse, I actually turn my back on him and walk away.

Then I wander around, looking for Sorcha. I pass Lauren. Hailey Swanton, who was on the Irish debating team with Sorcha, is telling her that she should change her name to L'Wren when she goes to the States and as I walk by, roysh, I get the evil eye from her, as in Lauren.

I notice Aoife.

I'm like, 'Hey.'

She's like, 'Hey.'

I'm there, 'How's the form?' and she goes, 'Great. Did Fionn tell you we've storted looking at houses?' and I'm like, 'No, cool though,' and she goes, 'We actually saw a really nice one in Blackrock yesterday, not far from yours,' and I'm like, 'That'll be great, pretty much neighbours,' and then I tell her how good it is to see her, you know, basically healthy again and with all her shit together.

The next thing, roysh, Chloe and Sophie arrive over and

180

Chloe goes, 'Wow, Aoife! I *love* your dress,' and Aoife doesn't answer, roysh, because she knows Chloe's being a focking wagon and she's not going to get, like, suckered in. Chloe goes, 'It's SO frustrating, though, isn't it? You buy a dress two sizes too small for you and you tell yourself, I am SO going to fit into that by the night of the porty. Doesn't always work out, huh?'

I'm about to say something really horsh, roysh, but in the end I don't have to, because from the back of the room comes this voice and it goes, '*Oh* my God, Chloe – what the *fock* are you wearing?' and I'm thinking, I'd know that voice anywhere.

It's Erika.

Every single conversation in the room stops. She looks focking unbelievable, even by her standards.

She walks straight up to Chloe – no, she focking glides up to her – and she stands, like, two inches away from her and goes, 'Well? What are you wearing?' and all Chloe can do is go, 'It's a vintage dress. It's *actually* Yves St Laurent,' and Erika looks down her nose at Chloe's scrawny little body, then up at the Jackie O shades perched on top of her head and goes, 'You look like a fly. I don't know whether to slap you with my hand or a rolled-up newspaper.'

Everyone in the place just cracks up laughing. I pull up a stool. This is going to be a good show.

Chloe goes, 'You have *such* a nerve showing your face around here. I mean, Christian – *puh-lease!*'

Erika ignores her. 'What inspired this *image*?' she just goes, looking her up and down. 'You look like something off a Trocaire box.'

Chloe's like, '*Hello?* I'm not the one who totally flipped the lid.'

Erika's there, 'You know what would be good with that look? An IV drip . . .'

I don't give a fock, she's getting a round of applause for that.

'What are you even doing here?' Chloe goes. 'I thought you'd be at a nursing home, looking for a new man . . .'

Erika's just there, 'Where did *they* come from?' and everyone cheers, roysh, because *they* obviously refers to Chloe's big silicon valleys.

Chloe's like, 'What, these? They're called breasts – haven't you heard of them?'

Erika goes, 'Chloe, there's enough rubber in your chest to tyre a fleet of off-roaders.'

'*Oh* my God! *Hello?*' Chloe goes. 'These are *actually* real?'

Erika gives her this, like, patronizing smile and goes, 'Mother nature doesn't do acorn clavicles and watermelon tits on the same body, Dear.'

We all crack our holes laughing again. That is some high-performance unpleasantness. We're talking zero to bitch in, like, two point five seconds.

Chloe's comeback is pretty lame, it has to be said. She's like, 'I'm not the one who made a total fool of myself at the engagement porty,' but Erika's just there, 'Six months ago you had bigger tits on your back than you did on your front. You could iron your shirts without taking them off. What did they do, hoover all the fat out of your orse and put it on your chest?'

Sophie's just about to say something, roysh, but Erika cuts her off by going, 'And where did that barnacle come from?'

My palms are actually sore from clapping.

Erika's there, 'Look at the two of you – you look like two

eight-year-olds dressing up in mummy's clothes. When was the last time either of you ate? Can we get a doctor in here?'

Chloe storts, like, touching her collarbone, which actually looks like it's about to burst through her skin, and she goes, 'You're just jealous. I'm *actually* a zero.'

'Yes, you are,' Erika goes, with an evil smile on her face.

Then she's like, 'You know who I met in New York? You remember Steve, the guy you were engaged to? The guy who dumped your sorry little ass – before you had it lipo-suctioned off, of course.'

Chloe's face just drops.

'I spent a very enjoyable evening in the Waldorf Astoria with him and his new girlfriend – Talitha Tierney.'

Talitha? *Whoa!*

Sophie speaks for us all when she goes, 'Oh *my* God!'

Erika's like, 'Oh, they looked so cute together. Didn't she use to be a friend of yours, Chloe?'

Chloe's just standing there with her mouth open, roysh, like a focking goldfish. She actually looks like she's about to cry.

'Well,' Erika goes, with pure focking badness on her face, 'Steve and Talitha both had a bit too much to drink that night, started telling stories out of school.'

Chloe's like, 'Stories? As in?' obviously thinking she's bluffing.

Erika gives it to her with both barrels.

'Well, it seems Steve finished it with you because you're . . . frigid.'

Whoa. There's this, like, huge intake of breath from, like, everyone in the room. I hear Oisinn telling Fionn that he heard that before, that the goys in Clongowes used to call her Godot, because you could literally wait for days and she'd never come.

Erika goes, 'What is it he calls you? Frigimortis!'

I swear to God, roysh, the whole place just, like, erupts into laughter and it must be true, roysh, because Chloe just bursts into tears in front of everyone.

Of course, Erika ends up getting a standing ovation.

Frigimortis. That's actually a cracker.

'It's great to see you back to your old self,' I go to her.

'Get a life, Ross,' she goes, 'you total loser.'

Like I said, great to have her back.

'It's like pork crackling.'

'Which one? The Vincent Girardin?'

'Yeah.'

'Oh, no, I liked it. I thought it was like, *Oh* my God!'

'I did too. When I said pork crackling, I meant it in a good way. I was talking about the nose. It's like sitting in a lemon grove eating actual pork crackling.'

'Oh, yeah – it's like, *Oh my God.*'

This is the shit I'm having to listen to in the cor – and that's after sitting outside the French Paradox for half-an-hour, roysh, waiting for them to come out.

Two Tuesday nights and the three of them think they're experts, though I'm keeping my thoughts to myself, roysh, because I get the impression that Lauren's still not a happy bunny with me.

'Oh my God,' Sorcha's going, 'do you know which one I loved? The Domaine de la Condemine Mâcon-Péronne le Clou '99,' and Aoife's giving it, 'I know. It's made from, like, super-ripe grapes,' and Sorcha turns around in the front passenger seat and goes, 'The flavours are, like, honey-streaked, but they're knotted together SO subtly,' which is all just total bullshit, of course.

Sorcha says, *oh my God*, she hadn't realized in this day and age how important it was to know something about wine and then she asks me, roysh, would I mind dropping Lauren home and, seeing as Lansdowne Square is only five minutes away, it's like, ain't no thing but a chicken wing.

She's pretty quiet in the back, it has to be said.

Out of the blue, Sorcha goes, 'Oh my God, did you hear who Erika's seeing?' and Aoife goes, 'I know. Patrick Laffin. He is actually SO hot. He used to be in the Ireland rugby squad.'

'*Development* squad,' I go.

Patrick Laffin. I ran rings around that focker when we were at school. He was more into focking cricket. Actually, I've got a video on my phone of him in Lillie's a couple of months ago, being focked out by the bouncers and you can see this, like, humungous piss-stain on the crotch of his chinos. It's a well known fact that Michael's boys can't hold their beer. I must put it on YouTube, see how focking *hot* he is then.

I pull in, roysh, opposite the Mount Herbert and the first thing Lauren says to me all night is, 'No, go into the square, Ross. Christian wants to talk to you about something. It's very important,' and I'm thinking, that's weird, because he usually has his scriptwriting class on, like, Tuesday nights.

'Is he in?' I go and she's like, 'Yeah,' and of course my instant reaction is, why didn't *he* pick Lauren up – it's only around the focking corner for him.

As I'm getting out of the cor, roysh, Aoife's telling Sorcha that she SO loves the spicy fruit and meaty tannins in the Albert I Noya Lignum '99 and Sorcha's telling Aoife that no, the wine she's *actually* thinking of is the Palacio de la Viga Tempranillo Reserva Navarra '96.

Lauren puts the key in the door and I can already see, roysh, that the gaff is in total dorkness. I go into the hall and she closes the door behind me.

I'm there, 'What's going on? Where's Christian?' and she's like, 'He's at his scriptwriting class tonight. I needed to talk to you on your own,' and of course I'm thinking, what the fock's going on here? Is she about to tell me that she has feelings for me, other than actual disgust?

It turns out it's not that at all.

She goes, 'You know about this offer that Christian's got from Lucasfilm?' and I'm like, 'Er, yeah, I did hear something about it alright,' playing it majorly cool, it has to be said. I don't know what she knows.

She's there, 'Christian's still in two minds about it. He's just torn – he's not sleeping or anything. I'd really be interested in hearing what you think?'

'Honestly?' I go. Then I lean up against the wall and sort of, like, blow my cheeks out. I'm like, 'I think he'd be crazy to take it, if you want my opinion. I mean, Lucasfilm – who knows if they'll even be around this time next year. And the States? It's, like, so far away, isn't it? I think you goys would be better off staying here – the economy, Celtic Tiger, blah blah blah . . .'

She nods, roysh, like she's taking it all in and then – so fast that I don't even see it – she grabs me by the town halls and goes, 'Listen to me, you little shithead. This is something Christian has dreamed about his entire life. There is *nothing* in the world he's better qualified to do. And the only thing stopping him saying yes to that offer is *you* . . .'

Her face is so close to mine I can smell the brie and

charcuterie off her breath. She tightens her grip and my entire body is, like, paralysed.

She's clearly learned a thing or two from her old man.

'I love Christian,' she goes. 'I love him more than anything in the world. And I won't stand by while a little focking tidemark like you tries to deny him happiness. So I'll tell you what you're going to do . . .'

Anything – just let go of my Jackson Pollocks.

'Christian will be home in an hour. You're going to call him and you're going to tell him you were wrong and you're sorry. And you're going to tell him to take the job – okay?'

I sort of, like, nod.

'*Okay?*' she goes, twisting my focking knackers and sending this, like, spasm of pain up my spine. I'm thinking, if this focks up my chances of a late call-up for the Six Nations . . .

'Okay! Okay!' I go.

She lets go.

I walk back to the cor like a man who's just shat his kacks. Sorcha and Aoife are cracking their holes laughing.

Sorcha – my *so-called* wife – goes, 'It serves you right, Ross. I heard what you said to Christian. That was, like, SO out of order.'

Aoife says she found the peach, apricot and honey flavours in the Gruner Veltliner Smaragd Freie Weingartner Wachau '98 a bit on the unctuous side.

'So she grabs me like *this*.'

Katya's face is in total shock as I make, like, an upsidedown claw with my hand. She's like, '*No!*' holding her hand up to her mouth, and I'm going, 'Actually, *yes* – by the focking knackers. And then she twists them . . .'

She's shaking her head, going, 'Zat is not right,' and I'm thinking, that's actually more support than I got from my wife.

And she makes a better fry-up, in fairness to her. She actually walks down to Superquinn every morning for these sausages.

The thing that suits me most about unemployment, I would have to say, is the hours. In fact, it's killing time that's actually the biggest problem, as pretty much the entire population of Bray will tell you. But I find that if I break the day down into, like, parcels of time, it passes basically quicker.

So I get up at, like, one o'clock in the afternoon, roysh, and Katya fixes me a humungous fry, we're talking two fried eggs, we're talking black *and* white pudding, we're talking the lot. I wolf it back while reading One F in *The Stor* or the old Thornster, who's, like, a God to me and not just because he thinks I'm one of the biggest rugby talents never to have made it.

At two o'clock, on the button, Sorcha rings to be hostile to me and make sure I'm not exceeding my happiness quota for the day. Then I do, like, half-an-hour of weights, concentrating mostly on my upper body, while Katya gets me my lunch.

Then the two of us settle down in front of the old Liza for the afternoon to watch *Murder She Wrote*, *Boston Legal* and *Hollyoaks*. We put Honor down for the night at about half-six and Sorcha gets home at, like, seven bells, which is when Katya goes home, leaving me and my wife alone to ignore each other for the evening.

The only real conversation I get these days is *from* Katya, who I can talk to about literally anything – my best friend focking off to the States, my old dear being a total hound, why I don't believe Felipe Contepomi is the answer to Leinster's problems at number ten.

It's not all one-way traffic either – sometimes she offloads on me, too. Like this afternoon, when we were watching *Tyra* – 'Girlfriend, you gone from fat . . . to phat' – she turns around to me out of the actual blue and goes, 'Yevgeni calls me today.'

'Oh, what did he want?' I go, obviously trying not to sound too Roy, and Katya sort of, like, massages her temples with the tips of her fingers and it takes her ages to answer.

Then she's like, 'He say he luff me,' and I sort of, like, nod really slowly, like the man of the world who's heard it all before.

'Love's a big word,' I go, 'even though it's only got four, maybe five letters in it . . .'

'Is a big vurd, but is easy to say,' Katya goes. 'Is too much easy to say. Oh, I luff you. Oh, I luff you. Oh, I luff you. We all say it, all ze time. But wiz Yevgeni, I never feel like he mean it. He only interested in Yevgeni. "Oh, I am beeg lecturer in Minsk – what are you?" He never listen to me like . . . you do.'

I think about mentioning the fact that I'm taken, but I don't.

'I don't know what to do,' she goes.

I'm there, 'Take my advice, Babes, drop him like Honours Irish.'

She's like, 'Is not so easy. He say he come to Island to bring me home,' and suddenly she has my attention again. I can actually feel my hands tighten into fists.

She goes, 'He say he come to Island. He haf my address in Dooblin. He say he bring me home.'

I'm just like, 'I'm *not* going to let that happen. He can take that as, like, a threat or a promise, but the basic truth is he's not going to get near you . . .'

Shit, I nearly called her Sorcha there.

She goes, 'Sank you, Russ,' breathing a sigh of, like, relief, and I go, 'Hey, it's all port of the service,' and I'm hoping that it didn't sound too cheesy.

But it obviously didn't, roysh, because we end up sitting there, just staring into each other's eyes and it's weird, roysh, because for once in my life I feel no urge to bail in. Obviously, I can't speak for Katya, but for me it's enough to just sit there, smiling at each other.

So the next thing, roysh, Honor storts bawling her eyes out. 'I sink somevun's neppy needs to change,' she goes and she jumps up off the sofa, roysh, but then suddenly stops. 'Unless you vont to change . . .' she goes.

I'm like, 'There's an awful lot of things I'm actually really, really good at, but changing nappies is SO not one of them?' but she grabs my hand and goes, 'Is easy. Come, I show. I show you how to do properly . . .'

She lays a changing mat down on the cold, wooden floor and already I'm noticing differences between the way she does it and the way I do it. She lays Honor down on the mat and it's incredible, roysh, because she stops crying immediately. A *changing* mat – I'll definitely remember that.

I undo the nappy, roysh, and I can't even begin to tell you what it smells like, and Katya tells me to use the clean side to clean off the bits of you-know-what – shit, basically – that are clinging to her.

'Take thees,' she goes, handing me a baby wipe, roysh, which I use to clean up, while Katya offers me little bits of, like, advice and encouragement.

She goes, 'Now, hold her ankles togezzer like zees, leeft her legs in ze air like zees and . . . slide ze clean neppy undernees her boom, yes?'

Of course, I'm grandstanding now. I'm there, 'I actually

wouldn't have believed it was this easy. And I can't believe she's stopped crying. She usually hates me.'

Katya looks at me, roysh, suddenly all serious. She goes, 'Honor does not hate you, Russ. It is not in a bebby to hate. But bebbies is very clever, see? Zey – how to say – *sense* when somesing is wrong between ze muzzer and ze fazzer. I sorry, I no like to make judgement, but you and Sureeka, all ze time you fight . . .'

I'm there, '*Tell* me about it. I mean, I can only put it down to post-natal depression for so long. But if she doesn't get her shit together soon, she's going to be . . . offski.'

She's like, 'A bebby which sense zees hosteelity between ze parents will take ze side of ze parent she is ze most familiar weeth. Zat is Sureeka, yes?'

I'm there, 'Well, I've been pretty busy, it has to be said, with offloading the club and then with me *possibly* going back playing rugby. I've been doing a fair bit in the gym, you've probably noticed . . .'

She goes, 'When you fight, Onair sees you as ze enemy. In Moonich, where I work one time, bebbies is swaddled in fazzer's shirt when zey is born. Zen zey are handed to ze muzzer. Hef chance to bond wiz bose parents in foorst moments, yes?'

Then she goes, 'Here,' and she hands me a tub of cream, which I apply to, let's say, the affected area, before doing up the clean nappy and getting a round of applause and a peck on the cheek from Katya, who I can't help but notice is wearing *Happy* by Clinique.

Neither of us hears the front door open, but suddenly Sorcha is standing at the door, roysh, weighing up the scene.

I go, 'Hey, Babes, I changed her nappy without her crying once,' but she just, like, glares at me and then glares at Katya, like she thinks something was going on.

I go, 'You're home early,' which I suppose isn't going to make her any less suspicious and Sorcha's there, 'Aoife said she'd look after the shop. I was missing my daughter,' except the way she says it, roysh, it comes out as *my* daughter and she gives Katya a look, then bends down and picks Honor up off the floor.

Of course, it's then that I cop what's going on here. It's the old green-eyed monster. So I try to change the subject, roysh, to try and, like, win her around?

I'm there, 'Did forty minutes of weights today, Babes. I'd tell you how many incline presses and pec dec flies I did, but you wouldn't actually believe me.'

But she doesn't answer, roysh, just gives me a look, then disappears upstairs with Honor. Katya looks at me and goes, 'Perhaps, Russ, you should poot a shirt on.'

I suppose it's, like, seeing the place so empty that gets me.

The sofa where I slept so many nights after Sorcha focked me out – there's an empty space where it used to be. The table on which I boned the two O'Prey twins on consecutive nights when Lauren was away on one of her ugly mates' hen nights – gone. Even the full-size Dorth Vader I bought for him as a wedding present has been shipped, along with everything else.

I suppose he's not going to change his mind at this late stage.

'Time's your flight?' I go.

He's like, 'Seven in the morning. Lauren's old man's coming for us at four.'

I just sort of, like, nod. Too soon. It's all too soon.

'I remember the first day I ever met you,' he goes and

I'm just there hoping that this doesn't get too gay. There's always a danger of that with Christian.

He hands me a beer. I lean against the wall and drink it from the can.

'It was our first day in Castlerock,' he goes. 'We were, what, twelve? We were in the tuck-shop queue. You wanted four packets of Meanies and a can of Coke, and you tried to pay by cheque . . .'

I laugh at that. That's actually true.

I'm there, 'The old dear had no cash that morning – the stupid focking wench,' and Christian just shakes his head. 'It was seriously impressive,' he goes.

I thought he was going to mention the time I was getting the shit kicked out of me by those three sixth years, who storted basically bullying me, if you can believe that, when the word got around that I used to live in Sallynoggin, even though it was *actually* Glenageary.

Anyway, roysh, they had me in one of the science labs and they were basically knocking seven shades out of me when all of a sudden the door opens and it's, like, Christian, who I'd never even had a conversation with at this point.

Conor Carlin, who was the biggest prick out of the three of them, goes, 'Fock off, you little squirt. Police business,' but Christian turns around, locks the door, throws his jacket – as in his good Henri Lloyd – on the ground, puts his fists up like a focking boxer and goes, 'Okay, let's go.'

I was thinking, who *is* this focking lunatic? But we fought them anyway – the two of us. They squashed us into the focking ground, roysh, but Carlin walked away with a split lip and a headache for the afternoon and it was the last time they ever laid a finger on me.

'A cheque,' I go and shake my head. 'What *was* I thinking?'

I look around the kitchen. They're actually nice gaffs these. I still think they should rent it out, roysh, but Lauren wants to sell. A clean break, she says. They've left it in JP's old man's hands.

'What about that time we played Michael's?' he goes. 'You remember Gerry Thornley said that all Castlerock had going for them was their pack? You must have ran, like, seventy yords for that try. Then you stood in front of the press box, pulled up your shirt and showed them all your abs. The crowd went ballistic.'

I nod my head and go, 'I was doing a serious amount of work in the gym that year.'

When he mentioned the Michael's match, I thought he was actually talking about my second try, roysh, when he had the ball and he waited and waited and waited, before playing me in, even though it meant him taking the most unbelievable hit I've ever seen a player take. The dude had to be, like, stretchered off.

I'm like, 'My pecs were pretty focking impressive as well that year, if I remember right,' and he agrees with me.

I'm like, 'So, uh, where's Lauren?' and he goes, 'Oh, she's just saying goodbye to a few friends.'

The cast of the focking *Rocky Horror Picture Show*, I'd say.

I'm there, 'I suppose I, uh, better hit the road before she gets back,' and he's like, 'Why? She'd want to say goodbye to you,' and I'm there, 'Look, I'd love to, but, hey, I know how she feels. About me and shit?'

He just shakes his head and goes, 'Lauren doesn't hold grudges.'

She doesn't hold grudges. Just like this man. You know it's, I don't know how many years since me and his old dear, well, I don't need to say it – basically, got it on – and he's never held it against me.

He forgot about it.

I wish I could say the same, roysh, but, I'm ashamed to say I was actually happy with the way it enhanced my street-cred. When goys I'd never met before came up to me in the battle-cruiser and went, 'Hey, are you the goy who . . .' I never told them to fock off. I just gave them a little knowing smile.

It's always been a mystery what Christian ever saw in me.

But every goy in the world knows what I know only too well at this moment, standing in the hall, saying goodbye – that you're no one without a good wingman.

Christian was my fast-gun, always watching the door for me.

And now my biggest problem is that I don't know how this scene ends. A handshake? A hug? A high-five?

None of them seems enough.

So I end up going, 'You got your reward and you're just leaving then?' and I watch his little face light up.

'That's right,' he goes. 'I got some old debts I've got to pay off with this stuff. Even if I didn't, you don't think I'd be fool enough to stick around here, do you? Why don't you come with us? You're pretty good in a fight. I could use you.'

I'm like, 'Come on! Why don't you take a look around you? You know what's about to happen, what they're up against. They could use a good pilot like you. You're turning your back on them.'

He's there, 'What good's a reward if you're not around to use it? Besides, attacking that battle station's not my idea of courage. It's more like . . . suicide.'

I step outside. It's storting to piss.

'Alright,' I go. 'Well, take care of yourself, Han. I guess

that's what you're best at, isn't it?' and I turn around, roysh, and walk sadly across Lansdowne Square and out onto Herbert Road.

Katya taps on my door at, like, half-eleven in the day.

She's like, 'Russ, can I come een?' and of course I'm there, 'Hang on a sec – I'm not decent,' and then I flex my pecs and my biceps and go, 'Okay, come in . . .'

She's looking well today, it has to be said.

'I am surry to vake you so early . . .'

I'm there, 'Hey, it's cool. What's the jack?'

'I just vont to check on you,' she goes. 'I know you are sed because your friend go avay.'

Fock, Christian's gone to the States – hordly justifies putting me on suicide watch. Anyway, if I was actually going to off myself, it'd be over the Criminal Assets crowd trying to take *my* actual money.

I'm like, 'Christian isn't the real reason I can't sleep, if you must know . . .'

'Vot is on your mind?' she goes and she sits on the side of the bed. 'Zare is somesing.'

I'm there, 'To be honest, it's the old man. It's weird, roysh, but I was actually storting to like him, if that makes any sense? Now he's talking about admitting everything – settling with the Criminal Assets Bureau. I still don't think he'll do it, but if he does – *fock!* – I could end up losing a lot of money, we're talking seven hundred and fifty Ks. And yet there's a port of me – we're talking deep, deep, deep down – that actually admires him for, like, just thinking about it. Even though he's a dickhead obviously.'

'You are gude man,' she goes.

I'm there, 'Thanks, Katya, that's really, like, decent of you and shit?'

Then I'm like, 'Where's Honor?' and I don't know why I asked that question. I must have known something was going to go down here, roysh, because all I really wanted to know was that she was out of, like, earshot?

'She is sleeping,' she goes and I'm like, 'Cool.'

She gives me a really nice smile then and she goes, 'You are ferry, ferry gude friend,' and — I am *not* yanking your cord here — she touches the top of my orm, roysh, and gives my actual bicep a squeeze.

So suddenly we're, like, staring into each other's eyes, roysh, and all I can smell is that Clinique, which, as you know, I'm a sucker for, and I can tell from her mince pies that she's already doing in her mind what we're about to do for real.

The next thing I know, roysh, I've whipped back the sheets and we're suddenly at it, in other words making bacon.

The sex is un-focking-believable, roysh — Katya has more than a few tricks in her grab-bag — and, though I don't want to sound like I'm writing my own reviews here, I think it's safe to say that she got as much out of it as I did.

Afterwards, roysh, we both drift off and I eventually wake up feeling a bit of tightness in my supraspinatus muscle and I'm just hoping that it's not going to rule me out for the knockout stages of the Heineken Cup, when I eventually get the call.

It's funny, roysh, because at that moment in time, I thought that was my biggest worry in the world.

'What time is it?' Katya goes and I have to say, roysh, my hort skips a beat when I check my phone and it's, like, four o'clock in the afternoon. We must have been out for, like, hours. But that's not the worst of it. There's, like, someone moving around downstairs. I end up nearly kacking myself.

It's Sorcha.

I throw back the covers, roysh, hop out of the bed and lash on my chinos and my blue-and-white Abercrombie T-shirt. I fix my hair, whip open the bedroom door and listen from the top of the stairs. I can hear Honor crying and Sorcha trying to, like, comfort her.

I go back into the bedroom. 'It's like, do you think she knows?' I go and Katya's like, 'I don't know. Russ, thees is ferry bed,' and I'm there, 'No, I don't think she's actually copped it – she'd have pulled both my focking testicles off by now, believe me . . .'

She looks away, roysh, lost in thought for a minute. Then she goes, 'I can go to ze spur room. I shall say I am seek. I hef to go to ze bed. You can say you were – how to say – checking on me, yes?'

She's good, this bird.

I'm there, 'Yeah, I'm actually going to play this one as I see it,' and then I go, 'That's what Fehily used to tell us before the big games – just play it as you see it,' and she nods, like someone who understands rugby, and then I tip downstairs, roysh, only remembering to button up my fly when I'm in the hall.

'Hey, Babes,' I go and I'm playing it easy like a Sunday morning.

She doesn't acknowledge me, roysh, except by going, 'Oh my God, I think she's *actually* teething already . . .'

She doesn't know. There's no way she knows.

I'm like, 'Teething? Fock – that's all we need.'

Then I go, 'I'm going to put on a pot of coffee, if you fancy some.'

She doesn't say anything, just storts making baby-talk to Honor. It's like, 'Who's the big girl? Who's the big girl? Who's getting the big teeth? Yes – you are. Yes – you . . .'

'Still no word from Michael Cheika,' I go. 'I swear to God, roysh, if Gordon D'Arcy was just ripping the piss out of me in Kiely's the other night . . .'

I tip three spoonfuls of French vanilla supreme into the pot, and then a fourth, just for the heck of it.

'In our bed, Ross?' I suddenly hear Sorcha go. 'In *our* bed?'

I spin around and she's suddenly standing right behind me. She's not crying, roysh, but I can tell from her eyes that she, like, has been?

'Sorcha,' I go, just basically stalling, trying to think of something to say, but for probably the first time in my life, there's no lie I can tell to get me out of this.

Neither of us says anything for, like, five, maybe ten minutes. Then Sorcha goes, 'I took the suitcases out of the eaves. We'll go down to Superquinn in a minute and get you some boxes.'

She's playing this one tough.

I'm like, 'Boxes?'

She's there, 'I'm going to mum and dad's for the weekend. Two days should be enough for you to get your stuff together?' and I'm like, 'Are things *that* bad?'

She doesn't give me a straight answer. She just goes, 'You know, I blame myself in a lot of ways.'

I'm thinking, whoa, there could be an out for me in this. I'm there, 'Go on – continue . . .'

She puts Honor back in her carrycot. As she does, she's going, 'I should have seen it coming – you and her. You know, I used to come home from work some days and look at the two of you and think, oh my God, *they're* like the husband and wife. Not me and Ross. It was like, *Oh! My God!*'

It's weird, roysh, because she doesn't seem angry – just, I don't know, sad.

She's there, 'You read about this stuff all the time in *Heat*. New mums who think they'll never get back to work. They hand their babies – oh my God, their homes – over to a nanny and suddenly they're not the woman of their own house anymore. I don't blame you for being confused. For the last few weeks, even I haven't known my own role, my own function here . . .'

I go, 'This *can't* be the end . . .' but she gives me this smile, roysh, a sad smile, as if to say, basically, it is.

The front door slams.

She must cop my boat race because she goes, 'Katya . . .' and I'm like, 'Too scared to face the music – typical,' trying to take some of the heat off myself.

Sorcha walks over to the sink and storts making the coffee herself. Obviously I'm in too much shock. Sorcha pours the water into the pot.

Then she goes, 'Did you check out Katya's references like I asked you?' and I'm there, 'Do you already know the answer to that question? I mean, is there any actual point in me lying here?'

She slowly plunges the coffee. While she's doing it, she goes, 'When I came home and saw the two of you in bed, I came downstairs here and pulled out her CV. I took it into the study, started phoning around some of her previous employers . . .'

I'm like, 'But they were in, like, Spain and England and shit . . .'

She goes, '*And* France. The numbers were easy to get. She gave us the names. It's just, like, 11860.'

Then she's there, 'There were a lot of others she didn't put on the list. Ross, would you believe me if I told you that this girl has left a trail of broken homes right the way across Europe?'

I swear to God, roysh, my entire body just goes cold.

She goes, 'It seems Katya has a lot of what they call issues.'

No focking way.

She pours my coffee and puts milk and two sugars in it, just the way I like it. Then she goes, 'I'm going to put Honor in the car,' as in the Peugeot 306 2.0 convertible her old pair bought her to celebrate Honor's arrival. And then she does the weirdest thing, roysh. My hand is, like, resting on the table top and she rubs it, roysh, like a mother would to her child.

She goes, 'Finish your coffee. Then we'll go and get you those boxes.'

It's, like, half-six in the evening when I walk through the front door. I drop my bags in the hall and from the old man's study, the sound of her typing stops suddenly and I hear her go, 'Oh, hello, Dorling! You wouldn't believe how much I've been looking forward to seeing you.'

Now, naturally enough, roysh, my first instinct is to tell her to quit her focking babbling and ask what's for dinner, because I'm Hank focking Morvin at this stage. That's when, totally out of the blue, she turns around and goes, 'Get *in* here, Big Boy,' and I suppose that's when I should have copped there was something NQR about the whole scene.

I push open the door of the study. She's got, like, her back to me and she goes, 'I've been a baaad girl today – come in here, you brute, and punish me,' and she suddenly spins around in the old man's swivel chair and there I am, left standing, staring, at my old dear in the total raw – and we're talking *total* raw, with no clothes on, unless of course you count her gold Marc Cain incised pattern scorf as clothes. Which I don't.

She actually focking screams – *she* screams – and I've got my hands over my eyes, going, 'Cover it up – it's focking revolting,' meaning her body.

She's going, 'I thought you were Lance! I thought you were Lance!' and I'm like, 'Just put some focking clothes on, you disgusting old hag,' which she thankfully does. She sort of, like, backs out of the room, covering her – fock, I can't even say the word – her various bits and pieces with the scorf, then I hear her tramping up the stairs, like the wagon that she is.

I feel, I don't know, violated, like I need a focking shower or something.

I look at the computer. She's still writing that focking follow-up to that piece of shit she put out last year. *Legal Affairs*, my focking Swiss.

I go to close the file on the screen and it's like, do you want to save the changes you made to this document? I hit don't save, then I click on the little spotlight thing in the top roysh-hand corner and I type the words 'legal affairs' and up comes all the focking chapters she's finished.

One by one, I delete them, roysh, then I go to the little trash basket in the bottom right-hand corner of the screen and I empty that as well.

It's like, how do you like *them* transparent, dangling carrots?

The next thing, roysh, she's back in the room, *with* clothes on this time.

I go, 'You're a focking disgrace, you know that? You've a

body like a focking walrus and you're not even embarrassed about it?'

Get this, roysh. She goes, 'Why are you even *here*, Ross?' like I'm not entitled to just walk into my own home.

I'm there, 'Sorcha's focked me out,' and she goes, 'Why?' and I'm like, 'Are you telling me that birds actually *need* a reason to do the things they do?' and she has no answer to that.

The next thing, roysh, I hear the front door slam and a voice in the hall go, 'Where are you, you bad, bad girl? Daddy's going to punish you?' and I just give her a filthy.

She quickly goes, 'Lance, Ross is here!' at the top of her voice and when he appears at the door of the study – I don't focking believe this – he's buckling his belt again.

He looks at me and he's like, 'Oh, hello,' and I'm there, 'Eat shit,' which he ignores, roysh, turns around to the old dear and goes, 'How's it coming along, Sweetheart?'

Sweetheart? I have this focking urge to cut off that ponytail and thrash him to a bloody pulp with it.

The old dear pulls a face. 'Slowly,' she goes. 'I'm writing this scene where . . . okay, Valerie's in Fallon & Byrne – enjoying a Gruyère and sundried tomato tartlet and perhaps a glass of Château Jolys Jurançon Sec – when she spots a man she recognizes as a senior officer in the Criminal Assets Bureau. He's eating alone. I don't know *what* he's eating yet – the chowder in there is wonderful – but he's had a long day and he wants a moment to himself before he goes home to his wife and children in, say, Ranelagh . . .'

Lance is going, 'This is good,' like *he'd* focking know. It's actually shit.

She's there, 'Valerie sees her chance. She undoes the top button on her blouse, takes out her make-up mirror and checks her teeth for poppy seeds, then frumps up her breasts . . .'

Out of the corner of my eye, I catch Lance licking his lips. He's actually getting his jollies listening to this.

She goes, '. . . and struts on over there. So Valerie seduces him – she *always* gets what she wants, remember – and they take photographs of each other, in various positions and stages of their fevered love-making . . .'

I'm there, 'I can't listen to any more of this shit. My marriage is over, just in case you actually *give* a shit,' and I go out into the hall, roysh, and grab my bags, while she's still going, 'Of course, Valerie's going to use the photographs to bribe him . . .' and that prick is there, 'To get back all the assets that were seized. Fionnuala, that's genius . . .'

I drag my bags up the stairs and head for my old room. There's something, I don't know, reassuringly familiar about it, if that doesn't sound too wanky – my Kylie calendar, my poster of Drico . . . I don't know what I was expecting, maybe the old dear to have turned it into a focking S&M parlour, but, no, it's still the same . . .

I throw myself down on the bed, roysh, and I just lie there, staring at the ceiling, wondering should I ring Sorcha or not. I get her number up on my phone, roysh, and I'm about to hit dial, but I wuss out.

I do the same thing, like, six or seven times in the next fifteen or twenty minutes.

Then I decide to ring Katya, port of me thinking, I need to find out if that shit Sorcha said was true, roysh, and another port of me thinking, tonight – of all nights – I need female company. Her mobile rings maybe ten or fifteen times, roysh, and just as I think it's about to go to message-minder, she answers.

She's like, 'Hello?' and I'm there, 'That did *not* go down

well, it'd be fair to say,' trying to make light of the whole thing, I'm there, 'What are you up to?'

She's like, 'Russ, I so sawry. I make things bed for you and for Sureeka. So tomorrow, I go beck to Belarus,' and I'm there, 'What? Are you yanking my actual chain?' and she goes, 'I hef to go, Russ. I make so much unhappiness. Yevgeni – he luff me, even if he know I am, how to say, crezy woman . . .'

I'm there, 'I could call up to your gaff. We could talk . . .' and she goes, 'Russ, is not good idea. I am sawry for break your merridge. I ferry sed for you and for Sureeka. She is nice girl. I not know what heppen in my head sometimes . . .' and with that, roysh, she just hangs up.

I'm about to ring her back when I hear this, like, high-pitched scream coming from the study downstairs and then all this, I suppose you'd have to say, sobbing. I walk out onto the landing, roysh, and all I can hear is the old dear, going, 'I can't understand it   where could it have *gone?*' and of course I'm thinking, this is going to big-time cheer me up.

I tip down the stairs and go into the study, where the old dear's sitting staring at the screen, sobbing like the sad sack of shit she is, mascara all over her focking Ricky Gervais.

I'm just like, 'What are you blubbering about?' and she's there, 'It's gone – weeks of work. It must be a virus . . .'

I just laugh in her face.

Speaking of viruses, Lance is rubbing her back, going, 'Macs don't really get them, Sweetheart. There must be an explanation . . .'

She loses it then, which makes me laugh even horder.

She's like, 'Well, maybe *you'll* tell that to my publisher. They want this book in two weeks' time,' and then she thinks better of it and goes, 'I'm so sorry, Darling – taking it out on you. If only I'd listened when you told me to back-up my files. But no, I was too busy baking tiramisu veloces for the Carrickmines Croquet and Lawn Tennis Club's Hurricane Katrina relief cake sale . . .'

I'm nearly on the floor laughing at this stage. They both ignore me. Lance storts massaging her shoulders, going, 'Your mind's been all over the place recently – books, publicity, your charity work. I know you're keen on getting the ladies' captaincy this year as well. Which is why . . .'

He reaches into the pocket of his Hugo Boss blazer, which he's, like, way too old to be wearing, and whips out what turns out to be one of those, like, USB memory-stick things.

'. . . I backed up your files for you,' he goes.

'Bollocks,' I go.

The old dear turns around to him and she's like, 'You . . . you didn't? Lance!'

She's a focking hound, roysh, but she looks worse – if that's even possible – when she smiles. He's nodding, going, 'You won't have lost much. I did the last back-up just after one o'clock today, when I was home for lunch.'

Home? Since when was this *his* focking home?

She puts her hands up to her face and goes, 'Oh, I was in The Gables. I'm so sorry, Lance. I never would have believed that this captaincy business would have involved having lunch with so many awful women . . .'

Then she sort of, like, smiles at him again, cocks her head and goes, 'You've saved the day, Darling,' and I look at the two of them and I'm just like, 'Pardon me, I'm just going to go and puke my focking ring up.'

7. The Worst Job in the World

'Hi, Ross.'

Fock, I didn't expect *him* to be here.

I'm like, 'Hey, Fionn,' and there's this, like, nervous silence for a few seconds before Aoife goes, 'Er, she's not *actually* working today, Ross?' and I'm like, 'I knew that. I just wanted to . . .' and then I change my mind and go, 'How's that Rock & Republic shit going, still shifting well?'

Fionn goes, 'Are you okay, Ross? I mean, how are you coping?'

Coping! Like he actually *gives* two focks?

Aoife goes, 'You just wanted to *what*, Ross? Why are you here if you know Sorcha's not *in* the shop today?'

We're talking major hostility. I suppose she *is* her friend.

I shrug my shoulders, then go, 'If you must know, I was going to ask you if you'd put a word in for me. She's not answering my calls,' and Aoife's like, 'Put a *word* in for you?' sounding, I don't know, exasperated, if that's the actual phrase.

Then she takes a deep breath, roysh, like she's stopping herself from saying more.

'It's not really anyone else's business to get involved,' Fionn goes – the voice of reason, with his stupid glasses. 'What goes on in your marriage is between you and Sorcha.'

'But I love her,' I go, hating myself for sounding so focking gay. 'And I've had to move back into the old pair's gaff, which is a focking mare . . .'

A bird walks into the shop behind me. Lia something or

other. I recognize her from Lillie's. Wouldn't mind tipping my concrete in there actually.

'I'm sorry,' Aoife goes, 'I *cannot* listen to this,' and she's holding up her hand, roysh, and jerking her neck, like one of those big black birds you see in the audience on, like, *Ricki Lake*, and that's not being racist.

Fionn goes, 'Aoife, don't,' but she's not going to be stopped.

'I'm sorry,' she goes, 'but your daughter's nanny? Your daughter's *focking* nanny? What were you thinking?' and I automatically go, 'Hey, why don't you keep your focking opinions to yourself?' and Fionn goes, 'Don't speak to Aoife like that,' fixing me with this, like, firm look, roysh, to let me know he means it.

I know I'm out of order here, so I'm just there, 'Sorry.'

'Sorry,' the bird in the shop goes, holding up a pair of House of Deréon skinny jeans, 'do you have these with a twenty-six-inch waist?'

Aoife goes, 'Um, is there a pair out there?' which is, like, one of those stupid questions that shop assistants always ask. She's a big future in this line of work.

'Er, no,' the bird goes and Aoife's like, 'We only have what's out there,' and the bird sort of, like, looks her up and down and then sort of, like, tuts to herself and when she's left the shop, Aoife goes, 'Twenty-six? Huh. That's Rachel Skarke's little sister. She has a *serious* attitude problem.'

Fionn just nods. Why isn't he at focking school today anyway?

'Why aren't you at school?' I go and he's like, 'Service day,' and I turn around to Aoife and go, 'Focking money for jam, isn't it, his job?' but she doesn't answer, roysh, because she's obviously in a snot with me and I suppose you can't blame her.

I'm like, 'Look, Aoife, I'm, er, sorry for saying that. It's just, well, I'm actually losing it here. I'm going off my rocker without her. Without them. *Them* meaning Sorcha *and* Honor . . .'

'As opposed to Sorcha and the girl you were having sex with in her bed?' which is horsh, roysh, and – I'm actually ashamed to say this – I just break down there on the spot and stort blubbing.

I'm going, 'I just focking hate myself,' and the amazing thing is, roysh, at that moment in time, I actually mean it. I really do. I hate myself. And Fionn and Aoife – in fairness to them – are trying to, like, calm me down, even comfort me.

Fionn's there, 'That doesn't sound at all like the Ross O'Carroll-Kelly that I know and love – that the rugby public knows and loves,' and it's actually nice to hear that.

Aoife looks at me sadly and goes, 'Ross, don't spend the rest of your life beating yourself up over this,' and I look at her, roysh, and her words hit me, like Paul O' focking Connell.

I'm like, '*The rest of my life?* Are you saying there's no way back?' and she storts looking around her, roysh, like she's trying to make up her mind whether she should say whatever the fock it is she knows.

Eventually, she goes, 'Look, Ross, you know this already – it wasn't just what happened with the nanny. From what I hear, it was over anyway, a long time ago . . .'

I'm looking at the table in the kitchen in, like, total disbelief. I'm like, 'What the fock is all this shit?' and he turns around and goes, 'This, may frond, is called a holthy brackfest.'

I can't believe I didn't notice it before. He's from Northern Ireland – a focking foreigner.

I give him a look, roysh, and I go, 'Let's get one thing straight, you ponytailed prick – I'm not your *frond* . . .'

He just, like, point-blank ignores me and goes, 'Pure bron,' pointing into the first bowl and then, 'That one thor is samphire, a rare seaweed rock plont – very ruch in iron. That's malt in thot thor jor. And see these wee seeds – pumpkin, sunfloor, sesamay, poppay and lonseeds. Tray some – have you shitting solid, so they will . . .'

I can't believe he actually said that. I'm like, 'Would you mind – I'm about to eat? As in, a fry-up? Speaking of which, where is that scabrous old crone?'

'She's in bod,' he goes, 'opening her mail. And I would *prefor* if you didn't speak abite her like thot.'

I can't believe the town halls on this goy.

I'm like, 'Oh, would you? I've always spoken about her in that way – and I always will. Get used to it or get the fock out.'

He goes, 'Oh, *touché*,' which is obviously French for something, a language I hordly speak a word of, so the joke is *actually* on him.

He looks over his shoulder, obviously checking that the old dear isn't behind him, then goes, 'Con't you see, she doesn't want you here? You're spoiling her hoppiness,' and I'm like, 'I'm spoiling *your* happiness more like. I'm more entitled to be here than you – it's *my* focking home.'

He goes, 'There's so many good things happening for your maw at the moment. There's even talk of *Rochard and Judy*. She doesn't need you casting your clide of unplosantness over her lafe . . .'

I go, 'Eat your birdseed, dickhead.'

He gets down off his stool, roysh, and looks at me like

he's about to throw a dig. So I just, like, flex the abs and the biceps, which I have to say look amazing in my Leinster training top, and I'm like, 'Go on then, fitness freak – your best shot,' and he thinks better of it and gets back on his stool again.

He goes, 'See you, I'll get you ite of this hice. You think thot, if it came to it, your maw would choose you over me?'

I'm like, 'Are you telling me you actually want to mix it with the Rossmeister General? You want to take me on?' and he laughs in my face, roysh, but it's a nervous laugh.

'Consider yourself totalled,' I go. 'Totally focking totalled.'

'Maybe you'd like some bubbles with that orange juice?'

I turn around. It's the old dear. She's like, 'Because I'm sure there's a bottle of Moët in the fridge.'

No, Hi, Ross, how did you sleep? or anything. Doesn't seem to give a fock that my marriage is over, let alone hers.

I'm not playing her stupid focking game, roysh, but of course *he* is.

He's like, 'Moët? What's the occasion?' and she just, like, holds up an envelope, roysh, as if that's supposed to make us any the wiser.

'*This* came from Columbia Pictures,' she goes, then pauses for, like, dramatic effect, the stupid focking hog. 'Lance, they've *doubled* Paramount's offer,' and all of a sudden, roysh, the two of them are, like, dancing around the kitchen together.

I don't even give them the pleasure of commenting.

'As your e-gent,' he goes, 'I have to recommend, of course, that you teek it,' and, if I had anything in the old Malcolm O'Kelly, I'd probably spew it all over the kitchen floor.

The old dear goes, 'My book – being made into a movie. I just can't believe it . . .'

'Who's playing you?' I go, quick as a flash. 'That pig from *Babe* must be old enough now.'

She goes, 'They're actually thinking in terms of Kim Cattrall for me – or rather Valerie,' and I just laugh out loud and go, 'In your focking dreams.'

Lance pops the cork and pours three glasses and I take mine, roysh, and tip it straight into the sink, right in front of his eyes.

The old dear tries to change the subject by going, 'Lance, how are you feeling?' and he goes, 'Went abite an oar ago, Sweethort. It was like shitting bollets, so it was. It was that wee alfalfa leaf that dod it – relaxes the moscles in the intestine, you see. And, of course, that fennel really cleared the gos ite of me . . .'

Then, all of a sudden – get this, roysh – the old dear goes, 'Oh, that's *so* good,' and, like, throws the lips on him, there in front of me. They stort kissing like a couple of focking thirteen-year-olds in Irish college.

I feel like focking a bucket of water over them.

'Hey, Kim Cattrall,' I go, and she suddenly pulls away from him, even though *he's* still got his orms around her waist. 'I'm hungry – fix me a fry,' and she looks at me, roysh, and she's about to focking do it as well, until she looks at your man and he gives her this, I suppose, sharp little shake of the head.

'No,' the old dear goes, obviously having grown a spine since she opened that letter from Hollywood. Then she's there, 'Ross, what time are you going out today?' and I'm like, 'I wasn't aware that I was,' and I look at him and then I look at her and I don't even want to think about why they suddenly want the gaff to themselves.

I just shake my head and go, 'It's like dialling a 1550 number, living in this focking house,' and I storm out, roysh, and no sooner have I left the kitchen than I hear the sound of the stool legs scraping off the floor and the two of them – I can't even focking think about it – but obviously going at each other.

I'm beginning to think that maybe Fehily was right. Maybe Ronan *is* better than I was at his age, though I'd never admit that to him, of course, for fear of giving him a big head. Probably one of the things I love most about myself is that I've always kept my feet on the ground.

He's the smallest player on the field – and there's more meat on a focking pensioner's leg – but when he's got that ball in his Christian Andersens, he's un-focking-stoppable.

He scores what I think I'm right in saying is his fourth try, swatting away the final attempt at a tackle with, like, total contempt, even though the goy tackling him is, like, twice his size, and the referee – realizing that this is *supposed* to be a friendly – blows up ten minutes early, to save Willow Pork any more suffering.

A beating like that could put a kid off the game for life.

'What do you want to see him for?' Tina goes, except it's not 'for', roysh, it's 'foe-ur', the way skobes say it, and I'm looking at her, with her pot roast hanging over the band of her tracksuit bottoms and I'm thinking, how did I ever go there? As in, how did I ever throw that dog a bone?

'It's just a father-son thing,' I go.

I don't tell her the news about me and Sorcha because, well, I'm not being big-headed or anything, but I don't want her to stort getting her hopes up when she finds out I'm single.

Ronan walks over to us.

I'm like, 'Here he comes, the future Leinster number ten . . . Well, definitely at under-twenty-one level anyway . . .'

His old dear hands him a can of Coke and he looks at it and goes, 'Nothing stronger, no?' and she doesn't answer him, which is the only way to react when Ronan's looking for alcohol.

'What the fook do you want?' he goes to me, totally out of the blue.

That takes even Tina by surprise and you can imagine the shit she's heard in her life, living where they do.

I'm like, 'Lovely way to talk to your old man,' trying to pass it off as a joke. He's pissed off with me about something.

I'm like, 'I just wanted to have a little chat with you, Ro,' and I give his old dear a look, as if to say, beat it, which she does.

Ronan storts putting on his tracksuit top.

I'm there, 'This is going to be difficult for you to hear, on account of the fact that you really like her, but . . .'

'I already know,' he goes.

I'm like, 'Know? As in . . .' and he's there, 'You and Sorcha – Roy Orbison . . .'

I'm like, 'Roy Orbison?'

And he's there, 'It's over.'

Of course, I'm in shock. I'm like, 'How do you know?'

'I rang the gaff,' he goes. 'To find out were yous coming today. To ask would yous bring me little sister to see me play . . .'

I'm there, 'Look, adult relationships can be pretty complicated, Ro. See, when a bird . . .'

Without batting an eyelid, he goes, 'You were caught burying the baldy lad, weren't you?'

I can't lie to him. I look away and just nod. Then I'm there, 'Sorcha told you, I take it . . .'

He's like, 'No – you just did. Sorcha never said a word.'

'Too much pride,' I go.

'No,' he goes. 'Too much class,' and he picks up his gearbag, roysh, and storts walking away, back towards Tina.

I'm like, 'Ronan, come back,' but he doesn't, roysh. Instead, he walks a few paces, then turns around and goes, 'You fooked it up, Rosser!' and I notice he's crying . . . and it's all my fault.

'You fooked it up and now I'm not going to see Sorcha or me little sister ever again . . .'

I want to run after him, roysh, to tell him he's wrong, that Sorcha and Honor will always be port of his life, whether me and Sorcha are, like, together or not. But I don't, roysh, because I hear someone call my name and when I turn around it's, like, Hennessy.

'Ross, I need to talk to you,' he goes and straight away, I've got this feeling of, like, total dread.

I'm there, 'What's wrong? Is it the old man?'

He goes, 'Charles is fine, Ross. Well, in the physical sense. Look, let's talk in my car,' and we head for the cor pork and Hennessy's new Lexus LS 460. The two of us sit in the front.

'Ross,' he goes, 'I've got bad news for you. A lot of bad news. I hope you're big enough to take it . . .'

Well, let's see, my wife has focked me out. Definitely one – and possibly both – of my kids hate my actual guts. My old dear is banging some grey-haired, ponytailed fruit called Lance. And Leinster have got Toulouse away in the next round of the Heineken Cup. It's like, how much worse could it get?

'Sorcha's solicitor has been on,' he goes. 'She wants to make the separation formal, pending the initiation of divorce proceedings . . .'

I'm like, '*Divorce!*' and I swear to God, roysh, it's like every bit of energy has suddenly been sucked from my body. 'Divorce? Fock, it's only been a week. I didn't think it was going to get this heavy so soon . . .'

Hennessy reaches inside his jacket and whips out this massive cigor. He runs his nose along the length of it, then storts patting his pockets for his lighter.

'Look,' he goes, 'are you sure this thing is beyond rescuing, because, from what I hear, you're not without your charms? Why not go up there tonight and sweet-talk her a little, get back in the good books?'

I'm like, 'Something tells me this one's going to take a lot more than the usual. I'll give it a couple of days, then pop around there in my cream chinos and my blue-and-white Abercrombie that she likes . . .'

He nods. He's about to light the cigor, but then he stops and goes, 'You've got to understand, Ross, that in any divorce, she's getting custody of your daughter – and she's getting the house . . .'

I'm there, 'It's Honor. My daughter's name.'

He's like, 'Whatever. If you think there's even the slightest chance that you could go up there, charm the pants off her and make her realize what she'll be missing, then do it and do it quickly. This is me talking to you now, been your old man's solicitor for thirty years – you don't do it, Ross, and it'll be the most expensive ride you never had . . .'

I'm there, 'I'll think about the best way to do it.'

He's like, 'Think about this, too. There's a hundred grand missing from your current account and Sorcha's people, they're curious as to its whereabouts.'

I'm like, 'Yeah, I, er . . . well, I bought a couple of aportments. In Bulgaria.'

For a few seconds, he's in, like, total shock.

I go, 'It's in Eastern Europe . . .' and he's there, 'I *know*
where Bulgaria is, Ross. But you're telling me that you
invested your joint life savings in overseas property . . .
without telling your wife?'

I end up just losing it, roysh. I'm like, 'Spare me! I'm not
taking a lecture, from you of all people. How many times
in your life have you, like, changed your name?'

'Hey,' he goes, pointing the cigor at me, 'I'm trying to
extricate you from the mess that is your life – *your* mess – and
I'm doing it as a favour to Charles. I don't want your fucking
gratitude, but at least use the grown-up voice when you talk
to me . . .'

I seem to be apologizing for everything these days.

I'm like, 'Sorry.'

'Sorry?' he goes. 'You don't know sorry yet. How do you
like this? Your old man settled yesterday – with the CAB
and with the Revenue.'

I'm like, 'What?' and he's there, 'Over my head, I hasten
to add. You know what he's giving them?'

Oh, fock.

He leans in close to me, roysh, and he goes, 'Ev-ery-thing!'
and then he just, like, cracks his hole laughing.

I'm there, 'There's no focking way . . .'

'*Everything*,' he goes. 'Your mother will get to keep the
house. Not that she needs it – she's well-off in her own right
now – but everything else . . .'

I'm like, 'What do you mean by *everything*?' and he goes,
'I mean the money, the cars, the boat, the golf-club
membership, the apartments in Villamoura, the box at
Leopardstown . . .'

I'm there, 'What about . . .' and he goes, 'The money from the nightclub – gone. It's already been seized, Ross. You're not going to see a cent of it . . .'

He's like, 'It's sure to knock some time off his sentence, though I'm not convinced that's why he did it. I think he just wanted to make a clean breast of things. Changed man since he went inside . . .'

He holds the cigor out in front of him and goes, 'The only thing he asked for were these babies – twenty pre-embargo Cubans. Worth a grand a pop – can you believe that? He told me I could have one. Said to offer you one, too . . .'

He can shove his focking cigors roysh up his orse.

'You want a lift to your mother's?' he goes.

I'm like, 'A lift? I've got my . . . *Oh no!* you *cannot* be focking serious?'

My body just goes totally numb – and we're talking totally. It's in my old man's name – my BMW Z4, my beautiful, black BMW Z4 . . .

Hennessy nods, like he understands what I'm going through here. Then he goes, 'I have to ask you for the keys. I'm supposed to surrender them today . . .'

As I'm handing them over, all I can think to say is, 'Dude, what the fock am I going to do for, like, money?' and Hennessy's like, 'I'm sorry if this sounds a touch old-fashioned, but have you considered working?'

I sink back into the seat and go, 'Fock, things really are that bad?'

I'm just, like, staring at him, giving him the filthy of all filthies.

'Hey, Kicker,' he goes, playing the innocent. 'Pull up a pew.'

I'm like, 'Don't worry, I'm not staying.'

He's there, 'Look, I heard the news about you and Sorcha, deciding to part and so forth. Terribly upsetting – I understand . . .'

I'm like, 'Forget Sorcha. What about my dosh? What about my focking BMW Z4?'

'Oh, Hennessy told you . . .' he goes.

I'm like, 'You made sure Jackie focking Collins was alright, didn't you? She gets the house. Her and that focking agent of hers,' which I maybe shouldn't have said, roysh, because that's got to hurt, but this is my focking *life* he's ruined here.

'Ross,' he goes, 'I just had to let it go. All of it – the cars, the apartments, the boat . . .'

I'm like, 'The box in Leopardstown – are you off your focking cake?'

He laughs. He actually laughs. Then he's there, 'Your CAB chappies, they weren't expecting half of what they got. But once I started – oh, it was intensely liberating, Ross – I just couldn't stop. I was giving them things that weren't even on their inventory. My golf clubs, my good watch . . . They knew nothing about the place in Puerto Banus.'

I sit down, roysh, not wanting to sound dramatic here, but just, like, overcome with basically sadness. We were going to go there this summer, me and Sorcha, with Honor and Ro.

He just keeps banging on.

'I never would have believed how much tension is centred around our, inverted commas, possessions. There's a chap in here, three cells down from me – he be me and Lex's new ace dude. He doing an alphabet for armed robbery.'

I'm rubbing my head, going, 'Will you quit it with the focking prison talk . . .'

He's there, 'Sorry, Ross. This chap, Ken, he used to be a fireman. Anyway, he told me that people who stand and watch their homes burn to the ground often break into fits of uncontrollable laughter.'

I go, 'That's because they've probably done it themselves, for the focking insurance.'

He's like, 'You're definitely my son, Kicker, because that's what I said. No, no, he said, it's the release of stress. The relief of knowing that all you're left with is the people you love and the clothes you're standing in. I can appreciate that now . . .'

I'm there, 'You can afford to – you couldn't focking spend it in here even if you had it. What about when you get out? Have you thought about that? No more Berkeley Court. No more Shelbourne Bar. No more *L'Ecrivain* . . .'

'You think I couldn't have it all again?' he goes. 'You think I couldn't get it all back and more when I hit the bricks, as we say in here? You underestimate your old dad. I've a good business brain, you know. I could have it all back again if I wanted it. *If* I wanted it.'

I'm there, 'What about me?' which, if I'm being honest, is the only thing I give an actual fock about. 'I've lost focking everything here – we're talking cor, dosh, gaff, wife, daughter . . . possibly even my son. So, like, excuse me for *not* being a happy camper?'

'Well,' he goes, 'I can only take the rap for a couple of those things. But let me tell you, Ross, you'll find wonderful comfort and peace of mind when you learn to let those things go.'

Let them go?

I end up going ballistic. I stand up and I'm like, 'I've actually got to walk out there, take my life in my focking hands on the North Circular Road – the *North* Circular Road

– to try to get a taxi home. I was only coming here because I actually felt sorry for you. But now you can focking rot in here for all I care,' and I storm out of there, roysh, telling myself that I'm never, ever going back.

'What do you *want*, Ross?'

Believe it or not, she's actually considering *not* letting me in, as in, not letting me into my own gaff?

'To talk,' I go, while giving her the eyes, of course. 'My life's falling aport. I can feel it.'

But she doesn't focking blink. She's there, 'There's nothing left to say,' and it has to be said, roysh, I've never seen her hold it together like this before.

'I might be going back coaching rugby,' I go. 'In Mountjoy Prison, of all places, helping my old man.'

It's a lie, of course – that focker's dead to me – but then again, I've told way bigger than that in my time.

She just goes, 'Good for you.'

I'm there, 'I thought that would have actually meant something to you, as in, I'm involved in rugby again *and* I'm helping poor people . . .'

'I said good for you, Ross,' she goes.

So I up the ante. I'm like, 'I don't suppose you've been following the whole Leinster out-half situation. Gerry Thornley mentioned my name as a possible back-up number ten – although it was in Jury's he said it, not in the actual paper . . .'

'Look, there was a time when that would have worked,' she goes, 'but there's no sweet-talking me around this time . . .'

I look into her eyes and she doesn't look away. She does actually mean it this time.

I go, 'Can I just . . .' but she knows where I'm going, roysh, and quick as a flash she's like, 'She's asleep. Look, Hennessy's told you the agreement – you have her on Sundays,' and I'm there, 'It's just, you know, I really miss her. We were just storting to, like, bond and shit . . .' and even though she's entitled to go, you should have thought of that when you threw Eskaterina a bone, she doesn't. Instead, she goes, 'Look, it's already Friday, Ross. It's just two more days.'

I go, 'By the way, I think Ronan hates me,' playing the sympathy cord, but then I hear the kitchen door open behind her and a voice in the hall go, 'Sorcha, who is it?'

It's her old man – that must be *his* 06 BMW 7 Series outside. He gets a new cor every year.

He's not a happy bunny to see me.

'Nice wheels,' I go, 'did you hear about my BMW Z4?' trying to keep it light, make conversation, a mistake of course.

He goes, 'If I catch you around here again, you're going to be mulching my roses, you little shit,' which, I probably don't need to tell you, is aimed at me.

'Dad,' Sorcha goes, cool as anything. 'Go inside. I can handle this.'

He has to think about it for a few seconds. Then he goes, 'Don't listen to his bullshit. I've seen him do it to you before – like a bloody mongoose with a snake,' and he walks back to the kitchen.

When he's gone, roysh, I pull a face, as if to say, *someone's* lost the plot, but Sorcha just goes, 'Is that everything?' and I'm like, 'No, em . . .' and of course I'm just, like, stalling, because I know, roysh, that the second she closes that door, I'm going to be the loneliest man in the world.

'Actually, the real reason I called around,' I go, 'was to get a, er, DVD I forgot.'

She's there, 'Which one?' and I'm like, 'Well, *Jerry Maguire*,' which I only mention, roysh, because it was always *our* movie.

'Do you know where it is?' she goes.

She doesn't give an actual shit that I'm taking it. I can't believe this is the same girl who used to always go, 'You complete me.'

I'm there, 'Er, yeah,' and she's like, 'Go and get it,' and she opens the door wide enough to let me in, roysh, and I head upstairs, into our bedroom – I still consider it *our* bedroom – and I open the cupboard where we keep the DVDs.

It's way in at the back.

I whip it out, roysh, and stick it inside the old tennis racquet and I stop outside Honor's room on the way down the stairs. I decide to look in on her. I just need to, like, see her, even for ten seconds. It'll get me through till Sunday.

So I'm reaching for the handle, roysh, when all of a sudden the door opens from the inside and suddenly I'm standing eyeball to eyeball with a bird whose boat race I could never, ever forget.

It's Anka.

I take a couple of steps backwards, then I go, 'If it's, um, any consolation, I wish we'd hired you in the first place,' but she doesn't answer, roysh, just gives me serious daggers, which I suppose is fair enough.

I just, like, nod my head, then tip back down the stairs.

'Did you find it?' Sorcha goes to me, still standing at the door and making me feel like the most petty focker in the world for taking a DVD that's half mine anyway.

I'm like, 'Yeah,' and she goes, 'See you Sunday.'

The second I step outside, she closes the door behind

me. And there I am on the doorstep thinking, well, there's nothing else for me to do on a night like this except get mullered.

I hit Tonic. A bouncer on the door who I've never seen before stops me, roysh, and tells me he doesn't know my face. I ask him how long he's been working there and he says two weeks, so I'm like, 'That'll focking explain it then, won't it?' and he thinks about this for, like, thirty seconds and just as I'm about to tell him I'm not focking picky tonight, I'll hit the Wolf just as easily, he tells me I can go in and it's like I'm supposed to be grateful or something.

It's wall-to-wall Celia Holman Lee, as usual. When I walk through the door, of course, every female head in the place turns and the word goes round, as in, *he's* here.

I hit the bor and order a pint of the Dutch stuff and I'm looking around, roysh, thinking, if that's the way Sorcha wants to play it, hey, I've no problem being young, free and single, especially in a bor like this.

So after a couple of pints, roysh, I sidle up to these two Barbies – we're talking Nicole Simpson and Evangeline Lilly here – and I stort giving it what can only be described as loads. I'm, like, nodding at the paintings on the wall and I'm going, 'There's some fine works of ort in this place,' and then, just in case they've missed what I'm saying – because in fairness they look as thick as a couple of tuna sandwiches, these two – I go, 'I'm a sucker for beautiful things – and you two fall into that basic category.'

The one who looks like Nicole – a focking exoskeleton with fake tan – actually turns around to me and goes, 'Sorry, we're not *actually* interested?' and quick as a flash, roysh, I'm there, 'Are you speaking just for you or for the good-looking

226

one as well?' and that earns me half a bottle of Smirnoff Ice down the front of my shirt.

I hit the old TK Maxx and as I'm, like, drying myself off under the hand-dryer, I'm thinking, I've broken so many horts in this port of the world, I'm going to have to expect that every so often.

I hit the bor again, roysh, and get chatting to this bird who's been giving me mince pies since I walked in here. She obviously wants me in a major way and I've decided there's no way I'm working hord tonight.

Her name is Nicci with two Cs, we're talking thirty-four, maybe thirty-five – but a good-looking thirty-four, thirty-five – a *little* bit like Jennifer Connelly, but from the side.

'Tell me a bit about yourself?' I go, cracking on to be actually interested in her – let's just say, a trick of the trade.

She's there, 'Well, I work in the bank, in, like, corporate finance. I play tag rugby. I'm single, which I actually love . . .' and suddenly I can see an opening.

I'm like, 'Rugby? You know I play *actual* rugby?' and she goes, 'Oh my God, I *love* rugby. Brian O'Driscoll, Gordon D'Arcy, all those goys are, like, SO amazing . . .' and I'm thinking, Oisinn's right when he says that rugby has become, like, soft porn for women.

I shrug and go, 'They all happen to be mates of mine,' and then I watch her jaw drop in, like, slow motion.

It's not going to take much to unjam her lock.

She's all of a sudden checking out the old bod and she's giving it, 'You're not going to be playing against England in the Triple Crown match, are you?'

I'm just like, 'Injured, unfortunately. I'm hoping to be back for Leinster for the game in Toulouse. I can tell you this – they're going to need me,' and I'm feeling thoroughly ashamed of myself naturally, but I swear to God, roysh, from that moment on it's like she can't focking wait to get me home. We go outside and we hail a Jo and some other bird tries to take it and Nicci nearly tears her orm off at the shoulder.

The bouncer is just, like, staring at me – he can't believe it's only taken me, what, half-an-hour to score – and I'm thinking, yeah, you'll know my Brendan Grace next time, won't you?

I hop in the back of the Jo and Nicci tells the driver that we're going to Dún Laoghaire, as in those new aportments, just behind, like, Meadows & Byrne.

So she all of a sudden storts sucking the focking lips off me in the back of the cor, roysh, and I've got one hand up her skirt, exploring the uplands of her tights, and the other in my Davy Crockett, writing a text message.

I can actually do it blind these days.

At the traffic lights at Temple Hill, I come up for air, roysh, and sneak a sly George at the old Wolfe. It's, like, word perfect – Hey Oisinn just scord a 35 yr old, total stunner, on d way back to hers 2 sort her out in a major way, TOUCHDOWN! – and then I send it, accidentally-on-purpose, to Sorcha, which is pathetic, I know, but that's exactly how I'm feeling at this moment in time.

I turn around to Nicci then and I go, 'I hope you don't mind my asking, but how come a bird as good-looking as you is, like, unattached?'

I can see the driver watching me in the rearview, obviously a man who appreciates a player.

Nicci's there, 'I was actually going out with a guy for, like, ten years. Turned out to be a total wanker. We broke up, like, two years ago? I haven't actually been looking for anyone since then – I love my single life too much,' and I'm thinking, that's good because you're getting it back in about two hours.

I check my phone while Nicci's paying the fare. Nothing from Sorcha. I'd say she's totally bulling, though – and we're talking *totally* bulling.

This bird must be focking coining it in, roysh, because she's got an amazing view of Dún Laoghaire horbour. She's like, 'I bought it about a year ago. I was going to, like, rent out the second bedroom, but I'd actually prefer to live on my own. You know, you can come and go as you please. Probably why I love being single so much . . .'

You wouldn't need to have passed your Leaving to realize that Nicci hates being single more than anything else in the world.

This might have to be one of those get-in, gut-her and get-out jobs, in other words not a focking sign of me when she wakes up in the morning, except the faint scent of Acqua di Gio and a dull ache in her hort.

I decide to, like, dispense with the preliminaries. She offers me a drink, roysh, but I honestly couldn't sit through another tag rugby anecdote with no actual point and anyway it's like, who are we kidding here? The deal is done. Contracts have been exchanged, as they say in the business.

I throw the lips on her in the kitchen and then I slow-walk her backwards, into the bedroom, throw her down on the bed and suddenly I'm like Keith focking Barry, hitting her with the magic – and in a big-time major way.

I go to grab a raincoat for Columbo, but she goes, 'There's no need,' and I'm thinking, she's on the Jack and Jill – happy focking days.

I give it loads, roysh, the full loving spoonful, but she takes a while to hit her stride, it has to be said. All those years with one goy, I suppose she's bound to have gotten

229

lazy, so I give her a few little tasks to do, just to blow away the cobwebs, and suddenly she's working like a Chinaman.

Twenty minutes later, roysh, it's all over and I'm lying there, waiting for the compliments to stort, when all of a sudden, out of the blue, the girl lifts her legs up, sort of, like, gathers her knees in her orms and storts, like, pulling them towards her.

This goes on for, like, three or four minutes before I decide I actually have to know what the fock she's doing here. I'm like, 'Is that, like, yoga or some shit?' and without even blinking, she turns around and goes, 'No, it helps fertilization.'

So you can imagine me, roysh. I'm out of that bed so fast, I'm practically levitating.

I'm like, 'Are you focking Baghdad or some shit?' and she's there, 'Oh, don't be so dramatic. I'm not *trying* to trap you. I don't want a man. I like my single life too much. I'm just looking for a donor,' and I stort lashing the old threads on, roysh, before she gets a chance to ask me my name.

I can only find one Dube. I'm about to walk out of there in one shoe and one sock when I finally find the other one under the bed. I put it on and I go, 'That thing you've just enjoyed there – you can say goodbye to any more of that,' and I storm out of the bedroom.

I don't know why, roysh – I can't explain it, other than to say it was just an urge – but on the way out I pushed open the door of what I supposed was the spare bedroom and I swear to God, I couldn't focking believe what I was seeing.

It was, like, a full-on nursery. There's a cot in there and, like, cuddly toys everywhere and, like, Disney characters painted on the focking walls. And of course, no baby – yet.

I don't want to know anything more about this scene. I head for the rank on Marine Road, thinking, is this what single life is like for goys my age? And it depresses me so much I can hordly focking breathe.

I check my phone. Nothing from Sorcha.

He says he's sorry to hear about, you know . . .

I'm there, 'Word travels fast. Presumably Lauren's old man, yeah?'

He goes, 'I still can't believe it – there's got to be a way back,' and it has to be said, I'm still not used to this new, mature Christian.

I'm there, 'It's probably for the best. I mean, Sorcha could never really cope with being with someone so good-looking. It's, like, jealousy, blah blah blah. Good of you to ring, though – how's things in Californ-IA?'

'Unbelievable,' he goes. 'The work's, like, a dream come true. We've got an amazing gaff in, like, Nicasio – you *have* to come and visit. Especially now that, well, Lauren and I have a bit of news . . .'

It's like, I already know what's coming next.

'Ross, we're going to have a baby.'

Fock – and here's me pissing on the goy's parade.

I'm like, 'That's amazing. Fock, that's given me a major boost, it has to be said . . .'

I mean, Christian – a father? If I was missing that mental focker before, I'm missing him twice as much now.

'She's three months gone,' he goes. 'It's, like, a honeymoon baby . . .'

They went to Tunisia. He's always wanted to see the place where they filmed, like, the Tatooine scenes.

'You make sure and have its midi-chlorian count taken,'

231

I go, 'the second it's born,' and he laughs at that.

Hennessy's obviously told them a few more things. So much for client confidentiality.

'Hey, I heard about your money from the club,' he goes. 'And your car. I'm really sorry. Look, Ross, if you need any . . .'

I'm there going, 'No, no way, Christian . . .' and he's like, 'Honestly, it wouldn't be a problem, not even with Lauren. I mean, she *wanted* me to say it to you . . .'

After everything that's happened. I have to say, she's one in a basic million, that girl, even if she does hate my guts. I wouldn't want my best friend being with anyone else in the world.

I'm there, 'It's, like, really decent of you goys and shit? But it looks like I've no choice but to get a job.'

'A *job*?' he goes. 'Not that, surely . . .'

I'm like, 'I've no choice. I mean, I've got, like, two kids and no income. And believe me, Sorcha's going to be wanting maintenance. God, it's all so focking working class.'

'Well,' he goes, 'it might not be as bad as you think, Ross. You might never have to do any *actual* work. I mean, you played rugby – that's got to mean something?'

I'm there, 'You *would* think, wouldn't you?'

He's like, 'Of course. There's loads of banks who'd love to say they've got Ross O'Carroll-Kelly licking their envelopes for seventy, eighty grand a year.'

'The first stop is going to have to be the school,' I go.

He's like, 'You're going to have to go through McGahy – he hates your guts, Ross.'

I'm there, 'Tell me about it. There was an incident recently with a porking space as well and I just know that that's going to end up being an issue with him.'

Then I'm like, 'Christian, look, it's great news about Lauren.

I'm so happy for you goys – tell her that, will you?' and he goes, 'I will, and you better come and visit us soon.'

I'm in the gaff watching the England game on my Tobler, and it's one of the most amazing matches I've ever seen. When Shaggy scores right at the end, I text Ronan, roysh, and I'm like, 'Dey kno wot d can do wit der chariots!' but he doesn't reply. And then I'm wondering did he even, like, watch the game. Or does he hate me so much it's put him off rugby for life?

Jesus, he loves the sound of his own voice. 'Ross . . . O'Carroll . . . Kelly,' he goes, really dragging out the words, roysh, as if to say, basically, we meet again.

'What's the crack?' I go, trying to keep it light.

He's there, 'I'm very well, thank you. And would you mind taking your feet off my desk?'

He always focking hated that.

He straightens the little plaque he has on the desk in front of him, which says, PRINCIPAL, and it's like, do you *actually* need that to get a focking hord-on?

Everyone said I was Baghdad coming here. Met Fionn outside in the corridor and he was like, 'He hates you, Ross. It's pathological. How many times over the years did you try to get him sacked?' and I just went, 'What was it Fehily used to say? Castlerock looks after its own. Anything we ever need, he said. Well, I need a job. And in case you haven't noticed, I'm not exactly overfurnished in the brains deportment.'

'So,' McGahy goes, after leaving me sitting outside for, like, twenty minutes, 'what can I . . . *do* for you?'

'Well, believe it or not,' I go, 'I'm looking for a job.'

He nods, roysh, with this sort of, like, half-smile on his boat race. He's actually loving this, but I'm not going to let him see how desperate I am.

He goes, 'Yes, I've been following the case of O'Carroll-Kelly Senior in the newspapers. I wondered how long it would be before I saw you again.'

I'm there, 'When I say *a job*, what I'm actually looking for is something brain-dead. And no heavy lifting. I'm expecting a call from Michael Cheika any day and I'm not sure Leinster's insurance would cover me doing basically donkey work.'

He's nodding and smiling, like the smug prick that he is.

'We never really hit it off, you and I, did we?' he goes, as if that's got anything to do with anything.

See, this is it. This is his moment, roysh, and he's determined to enjoy every focking second of it.

I'm there, 'Look, that shit with the porking space – that was, like, a joke . . .'

'And the credit card was the punchline,' he goes. 'Yes, very, very funny . . .'

He smiles, sits back in his chair and sort of, like, puts the tips of his fingers together, a real teacher thing to do. 'Have you any idea what I earn?' he goes.

I just shrug and go, 'Buttons, I'd say.'

'Not quite,' he goes, 'but it's in that ballpark. Certainly not enough to compensate me for what I've had to take from little wretches like you . . .'

Here we go – he *is* going to go raking up the past again.

'Do you know the reason I endured you and your ilk for all those years?' he goes. 'Because I have two boys and I wanted them to have the best education possible . . .'

I'm there, 'And presumably teachers get their kids in here for free?'

He doesn't answer. He just storts giving it, 'I know it's a few years ago now, Ross, but what's your recollection of that time you humiliated me in front of a large portion of the student body of this school?'

I don't want to be the one to point it out, roysh, but there was more than one time.

'I'm talking about the time I was made to apologize to you in front of the class,' he goes.

I'm there, 'Hey, for what it's worth, I still think you were bang out of order the way you spoke to me that day. I was late for class because I had rugby training.'

'And now you come to *me*,' he goes, 'looking for *my* help . . .'

There's no way I'm focking grovelling. I'm like, 'Hey, I brought glory to this school.'

'Of a sort,' he goes. 'Personally, I never saw it like that. For me, the glory was in turning out well-educated, well-rounded, well-adjusted individuals,' and he lets that hang in the air, roysh, and then, using his finger, he sticks an X in all three boxes for me.

'In academic terms,' he goes, 'those years were a disaster for this school. We fell behind Blackrock, Clongowes, Gonzaga, Belvedere, St Mary's and St Michael's in the league tables . . .'

I'm actually sick of his shit already.

I go, 'Hey, I know my rights. Castlerock is supposed to be, like, a brotherhood. There must be, like, a thousand past pupils of this school who'd be happy to pay me a wage.'

'It doesn't really work like that any more,' he goes, with a big shit-eating grin on his face. 'One of the downsides of the new go-ahead business culture, from your point of view, has been the end of the practice of hiring rugby types with nothing between their ears.'

An obvious dig at me.

Just as I'm about to get up, roysh, and storm out of there, he goes, 'But there is *this*,' and he storts examining the sheet of, like, A4 paper, which he's had on his desk all along. I swear to God, roysh, he *knew* I was coming.

'This fellow,' he goes. 'Gus Williams. He was here before your time. Rugby player, if I remember correctly. You two will hit it off, I'm sure.'

He puts the piece of paper down on the desk and pushes it towards me. I pick it up and stort reading.

'Gus has his own business,' he goes. 'And as you can see, he's looking for someone at the moment.'

I'm like, '*Pearse Street Sanitary Services?* What the fock is that?' but he doesn't answer, roysh, just lets me carry on reading the letter.

I do not *focking* believe this. It must be some kind of joke.

I'm like, 'Collecting tampie bins? You're *actually* shitting me now?'

He goes, 'Gus is a touch eccentric, you might say, but it's quite a business he's built up. Collects from hundreds of offices in the city-centre area. And of course, he has the franchise for all the main fast-food outlets – Abrakebabra, McDonald's, KFC . . .'

And he's smiling so hord, roysh, it looks like his face is about to crack.

This has got to be the worst job in the world. I wave the letter at him. 'And this is *it?*' I go. 'This is all you can offer me?'

He goes, 'Like I said, the marketplace has changed. There's a lot of foreign workers who are prepared to do the jobs that you and your crowd once did so expensively,' and he's so focking smug, I swear to God, roysh, at this moment in time I would SO love to deck him.

I get up and go to leave. I open the door and he goes, 'Oh, there is *this* as well,' and I turn around and he's, like, holding another sheet of paper. He's like, 'Terenure College are looking for a new rugby coach . . .'

I just give him a look. I'm like, 'Oh, *now* you tell me. Coaching Terenure or collecting tampie bins from Supermacs? I would say that's no focking contest, wouldn't you?'

'Of course, it would be wrong to say that sanitary-towel disposal is our *only* business. We deal in all aspects of washroom management – air fresheners, soap dispensers, vending machines . . .'

Then he goes, 'Your job, though, *will* be sanitary-towel disposal.'

Gus has got to be the fattest focker I've ever seen in my life, one of those goys who when he steps on the scales it says, to be continued . . .

He's there going, 'We have a large and diverse customer base, which includes everything from hamburger restaurants to kebab restaurants, from pizza restaurants to fried chicken restaurants. We employ precisely one hundred and twelve people and we have eighteen vehicles on the road. And we have a saying here – which I'm considering having put on a plaque for that wall behind me – that tampons are the lifeblood of our profession.'

I'm there, 'I actually think I'm going to vom,' but he just ignores me and goes, 'The bins are collected twice a week. You'll be part of a three-man crew. I wanted you to meet the other two guys, but they're out.

'Friday is O'Connell Street, see – long day. But you'll have heard of them – Terry Graubard, who was the full-back on the team of 1978, and Felim McEvoy . . .'

I'm actually stunned. I'm like, 'Felim McEvoy? As in, probably the best centre ever to play for Castlerock College? As in, won a cap for Ireland on the 1974 development tour to Argentina and Uruguay? You're telling me *this* is what he's doing now?'

'How the mighty have fallen, huh?' he goes and he seems really focking pleased about it.

'Now, it's up to the three of you, of course, but the way it generally works is that the labour is divided between each member of the crew on a tandem basis. One man drives the truck, one man collects the old bins and replaces them with empty ones, and one man tips the entire bloody mess into the furnace, which is located here on the premises. Usually, the boys take it in turns to do each job. Keeps it challenging, you see . . .'

Challenging? This is, like, a nightmare.

'You have a driver's licence, I take it?'

I'm there, 'Er, yeah. Well . . . provisional,' and he pulls a face and goes, 'Yeah, not *really* the same thing, is it? You're going to need a C category licence anyway. I'll write you a letter, say you need it for work. That way, you skip the queue.'

I whip my CV out of my Davy Crockett, roysh, and I go, 'I don't know whether you wanted to see this or not?' and he takes one look at it and he laughs so hord that I can see his big moobs wobbling underneath his shirt.

'This isn't your CV,' he goes, pretty much throwing it back at me. 'You know what *your* CV is? Your perform-ance against Newbridge in the Schools Cup final of 1999. I've never seen anyone play better – before or since. How did Gerry Thornley describe it? Preternatural. Jesus! Have you any idea what it means to me to be able to say to people, Ross O'Carroll-Kelly is collecting my sanitary bins?'

I'm there, 'Actually, I was hoping we might, er, keep it between ourselves?'

He laughs. A seriously evil laugh as well. 'Are you mad?' he goes. 'Look, I'm going to give it to you on the level – and I hope you don't take offence here – but I always *hated* you guys. I'm talking about the backs. You want to know why?'

I'm like, 'Presumably because we always got the birds?'

'It's *precisely* because you got all the birds,' he goes. 'We – and I'm talking about the forwards – we did all the heavy lifting, we took all the hits so you boys could look pretty. So if, at any point, you sense I'm deriving an almost sexual gratification from having you fetch and carry for me, well, it's probably because I am . . .'

He, like, readjusts his breasts.

Then he goes, 'I'll see you Monday morning – nine o'clock.'

I'm about to tell him that I regard myself as more of an afternoon person, but I don't, roysh, because even I'm smort enough to know that he's holding all the aces here.

He follows me outside and he goes, 'Oh, one more thing. I have, let's just say, something of a reputation around here – for being a bit of a character. My *thing* is practical jokes. Now, in the past, this has been regarded as bullying by some people. And a jury.

'But I'll tell you what I told them – I'm not changing. So ultimately the choice is yours. You can bring your court case, take me for ten or twenty grand and, in doing so, walk away from a career with one of Ireland's leading washroom management companies, or you can suck it up and, who knows, in a couple of years, you might even be filling our soap dispensers.'

There is no explaining how completely and utterly depressed I feel at this moment in time.

I turn my back on him and I go, 'I'll see you Monday.'

I'm on the old Wolfe, roysh, trying to get Ronan, and I end up missing a call from Dick Features himself, who leaves this, like, long, rambling message and it's like nothing has actually happened between us.

It's like, 'Hey, Kicker. Looks like I've missed you. Friday night, of course, I expect you're out enjoying yourself . . . with your friends. Wonderful match, wasn't it? Triple Crown and so forth. Young Shane Horgan was magnificent. And O'Gara, back to his best. I know you're a fan. A rival of sorts, but a fan all the same.

'Just wanted to, em, give you the grapes on what's been *going down* in here, quote-unquote. Let's just say that since the events at Twickenham, which the Governor very generously allowed us to watch, Mountjoy Jail has gone rugby mad. This team of mine is flying. The chaps have picked up the basics unbelievably well. The forwards, especially. A few of them went to the metal shop, ten minutes after the final whistle, and they made a wonderful scrummaging machine from an old trailer. Packed it with weights and so forth.

'And let me tell you something, Ross, after just a couple of weeks, these chaps could already give the Munster pack a run for its money. I mean, Lex is a monster. With a capital M, if you've time. First couple of sessions I wasn't sure he was putting his back into it. Then I told him to pretend it was the Guards at the door, come to arrest him. Armed robbery. Fingerprint *and* ID evidence. You're in the middle of counting the – inverted commas – stash, on the kitchen table. Twenty years. Oh, that did the trick. He could have pushed it around the yard on his own.

'But as you know only too well, Ross, a chain is only as strong as its weakest link. Now, *our* weak link was Binky Burton at loosehead. Somebody said he dislocated his shoulder trying to escape from Pat's as a young man – never right again – which made sense to me, because whenever the scrum collapsed, it was always on his side.

'So suddenly I have a problem, although I chose to see it as a challenge. We had a perfectly good replacement in Pat Scraton, but how to break the news to Binky, that was my dilemma. You see, Binky – how do they put it in here? – he be a three-snap case. That means he has a hell of a temper, Ross. In and out all his life. Drugs, mostly. He doing life on the instalment plan.

'I said to Lex, I've always found that honesty is the best policy – except in relation to business obviously. Otherwise, I wouldn't be in here. What I'll do is I'll sit the chap down, look him in the eye and tell him he's dropped. That's how our friend Eddie would do it. I'll make sure I'm standing nearby, Lex said. This sham doesn't take bad news well.

'I planned to tell him this afternoon after visiting. I had young Ronan in to see me. Anyway, there I was, telling him all about my dilemma, when all of a sudden there's a kerfuffle going on at the other side of the visiting room.

'Seems a couple of screws wanted to do a booty check on Binky, obviously hearing that he's back on the gow. Now, the word is, he got a booty full of chow. He packing a *lotta* dog food up there, man. He got enough hop to keep this joint cool for a month – and he ain't giving it to no screw.

So what does he do? He pulls a gat. No one injured, but now they transpacking Binky down to Cork County.

'Problem solved, exclamation mark . . .'

And that's when he's cut off.

8. Can't Even Feel the Pain No More

In fairness to him, roysh, Terry's sound. He knows what I'm going through this morning. He still remembers his first morning, even if it was, like, twenty-five or whatever years ago.

I'm going, 'I can't wear that – I just *can't* . . .'

I'm looking at my uniform, roysh, hanging up beside my locker and it's, like, a dayglo yellow boiler suit with a huge tampon on the back and *Pearse Street Sanitary Services* written underneath in – get this – blood, like on a focking horror poster.

I'm there, 'I just physically could not put that on my back,' and Terry's going, 'Ross, you have to. He phones around, you see – asks were the bins collected and were the crew *properly attired*, as he calls it.'

I shake my head.

I'm like, 'All this because he hates backs? Because we're the glamour boys of rugby?'

'The only advantage of the uniform is this,' Terry goes and he puts this red baseball cap on my head. 'You can pull the peak down over your eyes,' and then he leaves me alone to put the suit on and I swear to God, roysh, I could be focking arrested for the way it clashes with my Dubes.

It's, like, just when I think I've hit rock-bottom, it turns out rock-bottom has a basement.

Felim's driving, roysh, and he's pretty, like, stand-offish with me, it has to be said. At the stort, I think maybe it's jealousy. He's got that thing that Brian O'Driscoll has –

unbelievable player, represented his country, but he'll never have what I've got hanging around my neck here, in other words a Leinster Senior Schools Cup medal.

I decide to slip it *inside* my suit, thinking there's no point rubbing the goy's nose in it.

'What do you want to do,' Terry goes, 'collect the bins or empty them?' which is pretty decent of him, it has to be said.

I really don't think I could face emptying them, especially with *my* stomach, so I end up going, 'I'll collect.'

We pull up on Westmoreland Street.

He goes, 'Are you sure the shades are necessary, Ross? It's raining,' and I'm there, 'No offence, roysh, but I don't want people knowing I'm doing this – at least not until I get my head around the fact that I'm doing it myself,' and out of the corner of my eye, roysh, I notice Felim shake his head and now I'm pretty sure that he hates my *actual* guts?

I pull open the sliding door and climb out, taking two clean bins with me.

I focking hate Westmoreland Street. It's like a little bit of the northside that's leaked onto the southside.

I pull my cap down and go into Abrakebabra. 'I'm, er, here to collect the sanitary bins,' I go and the goy behind the counter just shrugs, as if to say, why are you telling me, but what he's really saying is, I put meat and lettuce into pitta bread all day, which puts me at least five rungs above you on the ladder of life, tampon boy.

I tip down the stairs and stop outside the ladies. I'm wondering should I knock.

I do knock and no one answers, so I push the door and go in. I'm thinking I haven't been inside a ladies' toilets since the night I was borred from Club 92. I go into Trap One and swap the old bin for a new one. Then I do the same in Trap Two.

I can't believe how focking heavy the old ones are and then, of course, I stort thinking about what's in them, roysh, and I end up having to put them down while I hurl my ring up into the sink.

I'm staring into the mirror, roysh, thinking how much I focking hate my old man for making me do this. Then I drink a couple of handfuls of water, splash some on my face and pick the bins up again.

I don't even give the goy the pleasure of acknowledging him on my way out. I lash the two bins in the back and get back into the van.

'Were you sick?' Terry goes and I'm like, 'No,' and he laughs at me, roysh, like he doesn't believe me.

I don't say anything, roysh, but it's like he can read my mind because he goes, 'You'll get used to Gus. He's harm- less enough. They say his wife ran off with the Clontarf number ten. Or maybe it was DLSP. Anyway, like I said, you'll get used to him.'

I'm like, 'Can't see myself being around that long, if I'm being honest. I'm expecting a call from Michael Cheika any day. I know they made shit of Toulouse at the weekend, but there's no denying they need me. Especially with Munster in the semi-final . . .'

'Would you *ever* stop talking out your arse?' Felim suddenly goes.

It's actually the first thing he's said to me.

Terry's like, 'Leave it alone, Felim,' but he doesn't, roysh, instead he goes, 'I'm not spending the next twenty years of my life listening to this shit . . .'

I'm like, 'Whoa, Dude – what *is* your problem?' and I'm thinking, it's probably that *he* was regorded as the best player ever to play for Castlerock until yours truly came along. 'Is it basic jealousy?'

He pulls in, roysh – he actually pulls in at the bottom of O'Connell Street – and he turns around in his seat and he goes, 'It's because you piss me off. You want to know why you piss me off? Because you remind me so much of myself it embarrasses me.'

He's lost it. He's actually lost the actual plot.

He's there, 'You think I ever saw this being *my* life?' and he bangs the steering wheel. 'You think I wasn't *waiting for a call*? I was waiting for a call from Ronnie Dawson. Ten years later I was waiting for a call from Jeremy Davidson. One morning I woke up and realized there wasn't going to *be* any call. Ten years. Ten years of deluding myself . . .'

I don't say anything, roysh, even though he's the one who's bang out of order here. He's too worked up to listen to reason.

Terry just nods over at McDonald's and I don't need to be told. I get out and take two clean bins out of the back. While I'm in there, roysh, Terry must have a word in Felim's ear because the first thing Felim says when I come back with the two full bins is, 'Look, I'm sorry for going off like that.'

'It's cool,' I go, trying not to sound like I'm sulking, even though I am, like, majorly pissed off with him.

'Let me ask you, though,' he goes, 'who are you doing this for?'

I'm there, 'Meaning?'

He's like, 'Well, it's hardly the end of the rainbow, being a *feminine hygiene professional*? So who are you doing it for?'

I go, 'If you must know, my kids,' and he's there, 'Me too. I got a boy and a girl – fourteen and fifteen,' and I'm like, 'Same as me. Except mine are, like, eight and eight months.'

He nods and he goes, 'Well, take it from one who knows – they're what's going to get you through the day. You think of putting food in their bellies. You think of giving them birthdays, holidays, Christmases. That's what makes the job tolerable, day after weary day. You're not going to get through it dreaming of playing for . . . whoever.'

I nod, roysh, even though I don't agree with him. Then he offers me his hand and, of course, what else am I going to do but accept it?

So it's, like, three o'clock in the afternoon, roysh, and we're a couple of hours away from the end of what has to be said is a pretty exhausting day, when all of a sudden my phone rings and when I answer it it's, like, Gus.

'Where are you?' he goes, no hello or anything.

I'm looking around me. It's all, like, boarded-up buildings and pound shops. I turn around to Terry and I go, 'What's this shithole called?' and he's there, 'Rathmines,' and when I pass that on to Gus, he goes, 'Okay, I want you to drop whatever it is you're doing. The guys can finish it up themselves. I have an errand for you. I want you to find a hardware shop and bring me back a tin of stripy paint.'

'Stripy paint?' I go.

I look at Terry and watch him roll his eyes.

'Blue and yellow,' the lunatic goes. 'And bring it in to me as soon as you get it,' and then he hangs up.

Felim pulls in and Terry looks at me and goes, 'Hey, just humour him, yeah?' and I go, 'Kool and the Gang,' and I tell the goys I'll see them tomorrow.

I hail a Jo and tell the driver to drop me at the top of Grafton Street.

I hit Gloria Jeans, order a white chocolate mocha and sit in the window, watching the world go by, just thinking about Sorcha and Honor and Ronan. I get this unbelievable urge to talk to someone. I dial Ro's number, roysh, but it just rings out. He *is* actually ignoring me.

Then I bell Sorcha. She doesn't answer either, roysh, so I just keep ringing it again and again and again until finally, when I'm halfway through my second coffee, she finally rings me back, going, 'Oh my God, are you *out* of your focking mind? Thirteen missed calls? That's like – *stalker?*'

I'm there, 'I'm hordly stalking you, Sorcha. I was just wondering were you in work. I'm in Gloria Jeans,' and she goes, 'I'm not in work, Ross, and even if I was . . . Look, what do you want?' and of course I can't tell her what I want, roysh, because I'm too scared of hearing her say that *she* doesn't want it, not any more.

'A CD,' I go.

She's like, '*What* CD?' sounding majorly Scooby Dubious.

I'm like, 'Er, I suppose, *The best CLASSICAL album of the MILLENNIUM... ever!*' knowing of course that it was what I bought her for her twenty-first.

I'm making a focking nuisance of myself here. I'm actually making the girl hate me.

I'm there, 'I just want to, like, put it on my iPod? If you're in the gaff, I can call out now . . .' and she's like, 'I'll put in the post tomorrow morning. Is that everything?' and I'm there, 'You don't seem to mind porting with it. Does that shit mean nothing to you any more?' and she just goes, 'I have to go,' and she just, like, hangs up.

I order another coffee – I'm storting to see stors in front of my eyes at this stage – and just as I'm finishing it, my phone rings.

I'm hoping it's Sorcha or Ronan.

It's Gus.

'Well?' he goes and I'm there, 'Er, I've tried six shops so far and, well, no luck actually.'

'*Six!*' he goes, basically bursting with excitement. 'And what did they say?' and I'm like, 'Just that they didn't have any stripy paint left. Bit weird in fact – some of them just, like, laughed in my face.'

He cracks his hole laughing. Then he goes, 'You want to know why that is? Because there *is* no stripy paint. Think about it – *stripy* paint?'

I'm like, 'Oh, no! I don't believe it,' picking up an *Irish Times* someone left on the counter beside me.

'You'd better believe it,' he goes. 'Because I've made a right mug of you here today . . .'

I'm there, 'Oh, no!'

'Oh, yes!' he goes. 'I've embarrassed you! I've belittled you! Disgraced you! You're demeaned! Humiliated!' and while he's saying all this, roysh, I don't know why, but I get the impression that he's touching himself.

'See this wee toblet?' he's going.

Why do they *always* have to be in the same room that I'm in?

'This wee baby is the lost word in molti-cleanse formulas.'

The old dear's not even listening to him. She's, like, sitting at the kitchen table, tapping away on her new iBook, like the stupid bitch that she is.

I'm tipping my Frosties into a bowl, trying to shut out the focker's voice as well.

'Red clover for the bloodstream, molk thistle for the liver, hawthorn for the hort . . . Och, thot's only the stort of it. This has changed laves. It promotes peristaltic action, see. Two to three bowel movements a day, goranteed – or your money bock . . .'

I reach across the table for some reason and slam the old

dear's laptop shut, nearly chopping her fingers off in the process.

'Ross!' she goes, actually considering giving out to me, but she thinks better of it and just, like, flips it open again.

I'm there, 'I don't know what the fock *you* see in *him*. And as for *him*, I can only presume he's not only constipated but deaf and blind as well . . .'

She goes, 'I've had just about enough of your vexatious-ness,' which is obviously her word for the day. I lean across and notice that she has, like, the thesaurus open on her desktop and – focking hilarious – she *has* just looked it up.

I laugh at her, then go, 'Suck it up – there's plenty more coming . . .' and I storm out of the kitchen and upstairs to my room.

On the little table at the top of the stairs there's a copy of the *Sunday Indo*, which is, like, folded in half. On the top half of the page there's a photograph of the old dear and that focking tosser leaving Reynord's, of all places – me and Robbie Fox are going to have words – with the headline, 'Book world's most famous bachelor finally meets his match,' and underneath is a story, roysh, which I read while standing there on the landing. It's like,

Has the most famous wandering eye in Irish publishing finally settled? Lance Rogan, the literary agent whose reputation for bedding beautiful young female authors has earned him the nick-name Dick Lit, is reportedly in love. Friends say the forty-eight-year-old from Bangor, Co. Down, is besotted with his new beau – women's fiction sensation Fionnuala O'Carroll-Kelly, who recently announced her split from husband Charles, who is awaiting trial on corruption and tax-evasion charges.

The pair were seen canoodling in the VIP section of popular Dublin nightclub Renard's last weekend. 'They were making no secret of the way they felt about each other,' said one observer.

Rogan, who was recently named Ireland's sixth sexiest man, is in new territory. O'Carroll-Kelly, the face of Crème de la Mer in Ireland, is a grandmother and let's just say 'mature' by Rogan's usual standards. 'Yes, he usually likes them young,' said a friend. 'But he's never fallen this hard, this fast for anybody. Who knows – he could be ready to write the final chapter!'

I'm like, yeah? We'll focking see about that.

I whip out the old Wolfe and I bell Oisinn. I'm like, 'Dude, where are you?'

'Playing golf,' he goes. 'Elm Pork. What's the Jack?'

I'm there, 'What was the name of that bird I was seeing for a while, wanted to be a writer, Charlotte something-or-other?'

'McNeel,' he goes. 'She did some modelling for me, for the *Eau d'Affluence* campaign,' and I'm like, 'I thought that. You wouldn't text me her number, would you?'

He's there, 'Shit the bed, Ross, you're not going back there, are you?' and I'm like, 'No, it's just, well, she showed me this book she'd written. Pile of shite, to be honest, but I think I know someone who can help her get it published . . .'

Sex with Charlotte was like wrestling a gorilla. The day after, you'd be checking your various bruises and sprains and it was like you'd been in a really hord game of rugby. I know a lot of players – good players – whose careers she ended, and I finished it with her myself after aggravating an old rotator cuff injury trying to find her G spot.

I could have told her there was no such thing.

I aggravated her boyfriend as well. He played for Mary's. Threatened to actually kill me when he found out I was rattling her.

I arrange to meet her downstairs in BTs in, like, the coffee shop. She's there when I arrive, roysh, with a big focking pouty face on her. I was trying to remember on the bus on the way in whether it ended badly or not, and I suppose there's my answer.

'I can't believe I *actually* agreed to meet you,' are the first words she says to me.

Charlotte, I should mention, is a stunner, we're talking an absolute ringer for Holly Marie Combs, probably one of the best-looking birds I've ever scored – definitely in the top ten.

I'm like, 'Hey, Charlotte, how are you? You still working in PR?' just to break the ice, roysh, but she goes, 'Just to warn you, Ross, I am *not* in good form. I wore my Uggs and now it's pissing rain . . .' which probably only means something to women.

I'm there, 'Alright then, I'll cut to the chase. Remember that book you wrote a couple of years ago?'

She's like, 'The one that you described as – what was that really clever word you used? – oh yeah, *shit*?'

Uh-oh, this might take a bit of work.

She's like, 'You were the first person I showed it to. It was, like, a huge deal. You read, like, ten pages, then told me to burn it.'

I'm there, 'Did I actually say that? Look, all I meant was that it wasn't *my* kind of book – not that I like books. I'd much rather watch TV. But it's pretty obvious you have talent. What was it about again?'

She sort of, like, rolls her eyes, then goes, 'Neeraja is this, like, nineteen-year-old girl from India, who flees Mumbai for Ireland to escape an arranged marriage to a man she's never met before. She settles in Clonskeagh, where she eventually meets a really, really good-looking goy called Ashok, who's a medical student and who, it turns out, has also fled India to escape an arranged marriage . . .'

Fock, I remember now – it *was* shit.

'Anyway,' she goes, 'they fall hopelessly in love with each other and get married. But the twist is, it turns out that *theirs* was the marriage their parents were trying to arrange all along . . .'

See what I mean?

'Incredible,' I go. 'Now, you didn't *actually* burn it, did you?'

She's like, 'No, but I have thought about it.'

'Well, don't,' I go. 'I'm going to introduce you to this agent. I think you two are going to get on like a house on fire.'

'Am I going to have to fock this goy?' she goes, straight out with it like that.

I'm not going to lie to her. I'm there, 'To tell you the truth, it would probably help,' and she's there, 'Because you know I have no qualms about that kind of thing. If I have to fock him, I will fock him.'

I love birds with no hang-ups, no complications.

'That's cool,' I go and I give her Lance's name and my old dear's address and I tell her to send her manuscript – if that's the word – to there.

'Might help if you, er, include one or two photos of yourself with it,' I go.

She's like, 'What about those ones you took of me with your camera phone?'

I'm there, 'Yeah, they'll, er, certainly catch his eye.'

*

253

Whoa, it's, like, seriously focking hot today.

If this keeps up, I'm going to have to take off my baseball cap. A couple of times I thought I saw Ronan coming. Thought I recognized the Celtic shirt, which he insists on wearing to Lansdowne, but it turned out it was some kid in an Ireland training top, which looks disgracefully like it.

He hasn't returned any of my calls and I'm thinking, yeah, I bet Sorcha's focking poisoned his mind against me, but then I'm thinking, no, that's not her style, so what I end up doing, roysh, is getting Ronan's Wilson, sticking it in an envelope and sending it out to his gaff in a Jo, with a note just saying, basically, I understand why you're not a happy bunny with me, I know I focked everything up, but I'm trying to, like, put things right, make the best of a bad situation, and it's Leinster versus Munster after all, the famous Clash of Civilizations, and I'd, like, love to see you, but if you don't want to see *me*, then I've no problem giving my own Wilson to one of your mates, maybe Nudger, Gull, or even Buckets of Blood.

But there's been, like, no word since, so I ended up just going into the ground.

It's weird, roysh, but it's like, were Leinster issued with *any* tickets for this match? It's nothing but boggers in red shirts and then the odd die-hord fan like yours truly wearing the Leinster colours – pink shirt with the collar up and shades on the head. I send Ronan a text and it's like, 'Get ur orse here quick – we r seriously outnumberd!'

Two minutes gone and Rog kicks Munster into the lead and then Leamy scores a try and we're in serious shit. Paul O'Connell and Anthony Foley are playing out of their skins, as is Rog, while Contepomi's having a total mare and I'd say Michael Cheika's down there focking kicking himself for not bringing me in as cover.

I send Ro another text and it's like, 'He had my numbr – all he had 2do was ask,' but again there's no reply, but I'm thinking, fock it, this is my kid here, I'm going to keep plugging away, just like Rog does when he has a bad day at the office.

See what I mean? He's banging them over from all angles.

I send Ro another. It's like, '16-3, der pissing on us. Wots ryle sayin?'

Second half, more of the same from Contepomi. I'd give him a few tips except I'm at the back of the Lower West Stand and the noise is un-focking-believable.

And it's like Wardy always says, roysh – cometh the hour, cometh the man. Rog just waltzes through our defence like he's ripping the piss and touches down under the posts and suddenly there's actual cabbage-munchers turning around in their seats, roysh, and laughing at me and shouting abuse, none of which I understand, of course, because of the language barrier. I hear BTs mentioned once or twice though.

Rog is the master. It's an honour to have a kid who shares his name. I text him and it's like, 'Rmembr where u wer when u saw d man do dat . . . ur watchin history here.'

I've got to get the fock out of here, because when the final whistle goes, roysh, my life won't be worth living. Only a handful of muck savages actually notice me getting out of my seat. They're too busy watching Trevor Halstead run pretty much the length of the pitch to completely rub our noses in it.

On the way up to Kiely's, I send Ronan another text and it's like, 'Dey cant keep ignorin d case 4 my inclusion after dat!'

Nothing back.

*

The goy's entitled to his opinion, but I actually don't agree with Felim when he says that this Leinster team is past its sell-by date and it's time to, like, break it up. I think it was more like an off-day. And then I suppose the Leinster goys would have a lot more going on in their lives – movie premieres, porties, blah blah blah.

I take out my lunch and it's, like, prosciutto and goat's cheese on tomato and walnut bread.

Terry goes, 'Will you look at Jamie Oliver here?' as I'm unwrapping them and Felim's like, 'Who made them for you – your mommy?' and I'm suddenly on the defensive, going, 'I wouldn't eat anything that's touched her focking hands. I actually made them myself – this is the only shit she actually has in the gaff,' because the goys are eating, like, cheese and tomato on, I don't know, Brennan's bread.

Felim's there, 'You know what would go well with that? A nice little sauvignon blanc,' and the two of them crack their holes laughing, roysh, and then I stort to see the funny side of it. I know my life isn't in a good space right now, but I have to learn to, like, lighten up?

'Gimme one of them,' Felim goes and he reaches over and takes a sambo and then horses into it.

Suddenly I find myself going, 'So when *do* you let it go, goys – as in, the dream? I mean, I watched Ronan O'Gara score that try against us yesterday and, well, I know he's a God and everything, but I couldn't help but think – if it wasn't for injuries, romantic hassles, blah blah blah – that *could* be me down there. Not playing for Munster, obviously, focking turnip junkies . . .'

Felim gives me a kind of half-smile. Then he goes, 'That's how I used to feel watching *you* play,' and of course I'm like, 'What?' thinking, did he *actually* just say that?

He's there, 'There's more besides me, I can tell you. That

year, the year you won the Cup, you had anyone who'd ever picked up a rugby ball dreaming. I used to come away from Donnybrook thinking, I've just been watching the greatest player I've ever seen.'

I'm there, 'Is that why you gave me such a hord time before? Because I focked it all away, being too much of a ladies' man, too fond of the sauce?'

'Look, is a butterfly any less beautiful because it only lives for one day?' he goes. He's actually a bit of a philosopher, even though I haven't a clue what he's on about.

'You were the best schools rugby player some of us have ever seen,' he goes. 'I gave you a hard time because you're not satisfied with that.'

I go, 'Well, I *am* beginning to think Dorce was ripping the piss when he said to expect a call from Michael Cheika. I wonder does he even know who I am?'

I give him the rest of my sambos. I focking hate goat's cheese.

'Nowadays,' he goes, 'when I watch Brian O'Driscoll or Ronan O'Gara or Shane Horgan at work, I don't think, that could have been me – I think, that could be my son one day.'

And it's funny, roysh, because deep down I was thinking the same thing about Ronan yesterday.

'Two o'clock, boys,' Terry goes and I'm straight up off my orse, roysh, because after a week in this job I've already learned that the quicker you get into it, the quicker you're finished.

I put the key in the door, open and close it as quietly as I can, then tiptoe down to the study and open the safe, but there's, like, fock-all in it. So I stort having a mooch around the place, roysh, looking for the old dear's handbag, like a common heroin addict.

I end up totally trashing the gaff, knocking her *Glamour* Woman of the Year award off the desk and breaking it in two, along with all her congratulations cords and a framed photo of her and that focking dickhead – and believe it or not I'm not talking about my old man for once.

Then I just, like, stand on the frame – accidentally-on-purpose – cracking the glass.

I finally find the bag under her desk. Orla Kiely – you wouldn't focking blame her, would you? And here's me practically storving to death.

I unzip it and turn it upside-down, tipping the contents onto the floor. I pick up her purse, which is focking bulging with fifties. I pull out five or six of them, then I change my mind and end up whipping the whole wad. There must be, like, a grand there. Should see me through the next week or so.

I walk out into the hall, roysh, to the bottom of the stairs, where I notice the old dear has left her shoes. The stupid focking cow – I could have snotted myself.

It's then, roysh, that I notice that there's a focking trail of her clothes all the way up the stairs, across the landing and into her bedroom. It looks like a focking dog got loose in Pamela Scott.

But they're not doing anything, roysh, because I can hear the old dear inside the room going, 'Oh, for heaven's sake – what are you reading?' and then I hear her go, '*Indian Summer*? Who's it by?'

He goes, 'Some wee gorl – it's nat bawd,' and she's like, 'Read it tomorrow,' and then she must make another move, roysh, because after about ten seconds he goes, 'Stap! Just stap!' and she's like, 'What is *wrong* with you?'

He's there, 'I'm just nat in the mood,' and she's like, 'When are you ever going to be in the mood?' and of course I'm out on the landing, roysh, cracking my hole laughing.

He goes, 'Och, don't be lake thot, Finny.'

Finny! This just gets better and better!

He goes, 'We did it twace last nate, remomber?'

She's there, 'Twice? Pah! That might be enough for you! Don't touch me! It's those pills – they've taken away your libido.'

'You're being ridoculous.'

She's lost it now. In this, like, high-pitched voice, she storts going, 'You and your focking arse,' which is probably the only funny thing she's ever said in her life. 'You and your *focking* arse . . .'

And the next thing, roysh, before I have a chance to even move, she storms out of the bedroom and I'm suddenly face to face with her on the landing.

Thankfully, she thought to put on some clothes first this time.

I just look her up and down and go, 'Love's young dream, huh? *Finny!*'

'What time are you finished work?'

Fionn seems pretty John B. to talk to me. I just presume it's about JP, as in, should we call out to his gaff, see how he is.

I'm there, 'I'm pretty much finished now,' and he goes, 'Three o'clock?' and I go, 'Yeah, Gus sent me out to get a bubble for the spirit-level. Long story. Do you fancy a coffee?'

So half an hour later, roysh, he walks in through the door of Insomnia, the weight of the world on his shoulders. I'm thinking, maybe it's actually Aoife, roysh, or something to do with school.

He goes, 'Ross, I need to talk to you about something,' and of course I'm there, 'Shoot.'

He's like, 'Look, this is a really difficult situation. Aoife asked me not to say anything, but, well, you're a mate. And I know we haven't always seen eye-to-eye over the years, but, well, you know what I think of you . . .'

I don't actually. Well, I just presumed it wasn't much.

'Sorcha's with someone,' he goes.

I feel like I've been punched in the guts. Hard.

I'm there, '*With* someone?' but it's like someone else has said it, not me. 'I mean, *already?*'

He just nods. He looks really uncomfortable. I'm wondering is it someone we know. I actually don't want to ask, but I end up going, 'Who?'

He just, like, fixes me with a look and goes, 'Cillian.'

I'm there, 'Cillian?' thinking, I've never focking heard of him. Then suddenly I'm like, 'Cillian! *Cillian?*' and he doesn't answer, roysh, just pushes his glasses up on his nose, which I take as a yes.

I'm there, 'Cillian, as in Cillian who she went to Australia with?'

'For what it's worth, I think he's a bit on the dull side,' he goes and he shrugs. 'Aoife's not a fan either . . .'

Dull? And that's coming from Fionn.

I'm there, 'You mean, you've met them, as a couple. As in *actually* socialized with them?' and he goes, 'We met them in Gleason's on Sunday night. Aoife is Sorcha's friend, Ross . . .' and I'm just there shaking my head.

I'm there, '*That* tosser? Pricewaterhouse whatever-they're-called? I mean, when did this happen? As in, when did they meet again?'

He goes, 'Apparently, they've been back in contact for a few months . . . *as friends*.'

I'm like, 'A few months? So this was going on while we were still together?' and Fionn's there, 'Nothing happened. Not then anyway . . .'

Suddenly, roysh, everything storts to make sense. Little things. All those focking sunbeds – I wondered why she wasn't getting any dorker.

In fairness to him, roysh, Fionn didn't have to tell me this shit. I'm like, 'Look, I won't crack on *you* told me . . . if it's going to get you in shit with, like, Aoife,' but Fionn goes, 'No, I'm going to tell her I told you I'm going to go and meet her from work. It's just, when you go out with someone with a history of . . . well, *her* history, it's important that you have no secrets from each other,' and with that he gets up, roysh, and heads for the Powerscourt Townhouse Centre to face the music.

I end up walking down Nassau Street and Westland Row in a total daze. It's like I'm drugged or some shit?

I walk into the Dort station and put my return ticket through the machine. I get on the escalator, thinking about him, about her, about them together. I take an *Evening Herald* from this basically black goy at the top of the escalator and I walk up the four steps and onto the platform and I head for an empty bench at the far end. It's, like, twelve minutes until the next train.

I sit there, roysh, flicking through the paper, my eyes unable to focus on any one headline or picture, even one of Laura Woods. I feel like I'm about to, like, burst into focking tears any second.

'Excuse me,' I hear a voice go. I look up and it's the black goy.

He goes, 'Why did you steal my paper?'

*

Haven't thought through exactly what I'm going to actually do here, but after six or seven straighteners in the Wolf I decide, rightly or wrongly, to confront Sorcha – *and* that loser if he's there.

There's no sign of a Jo, so I walk, believe it or not, sort of, like, reciting what I'm going to say as I turn up Newtownpork Avenue, all the shit I'm going to throw at her, all the names I'm going to call her.

But of course, when the door opens my mind just goes blank.

She looks unbelievably well.

'Nothing happened when you and I were together,' she goes, without me even, like, saying a word. She knows why I'm here – Aoife must have belled her straight away to tell her I knew.

I'm there, 'Oh and I'm supposed to believe that?' but of course it's just something to say. Deep down I know she's telling the truth.

I hear, like, footsteps in the hall behind her, then the door opens wider and it's him, roysh, in his tin of fruit, big focking boring head on him.

'Ross,' he goes, like we've been introduced or something, 'you'd better come in,' and I'm like, 'Oh, that's very kind of you, seeing as it's *my* focking house,' but he doesn't rise to the bait, just shows me into the kitchen, *my* kitchen, the contemporary tobacco one that *I* paid for with *my* money, and I swear to God, roysh, he's got this, like, patronizing look on his boat race.

'Do you want a cup of coffee?' he goes, which is his way of saying, hey, everyone, Ross has been drinking because I've moved in on his wife.

It's like he's actually *looking* to be decked?

Sorcha gives him a look. He takes the hint and goes, 'I'll, er, leave you two to talk,' and he gives me a little nod and this, like, sympathetic smile and I just want to ram his Taylor Keith down his throat.

I'm there, 'Hasn't wasted any time getting his Deep Heat under the table, has he?' and she looks me in the eye and goes, 'I really like him. He's interested in a lot of the things I'm interested in. And he's good with Honor,' which is, like, really twisting the knife.

'Is he still working for whatever-they're-called?' I go. I don't know why the fock that's important to me.

She's there, 'PricewaterhouseCoopers,' nodding her head. She switches on the kettle. 'He's in Auditing and Assurance now.'

I'm there, '*Wow!* Sounds really, really interesting!' which is childish, I know, but she doesn't give me a response anyway. It's like she's letting me say whatever I want, letting me punch myself out. Of course, it's no good saying shit unless you're getting a reaction.

I go, 'I probably should, er, apologize to you – Eskaterina, blah blah blah . . .' and she's there, 'It doesn't matter. That's like, oh my God now. What I really don't want is you carrying that guilt around with you for the rest of your life. I mean, if we're honest, we'd both have to say it was over way before that.'

I'm there, 'Yeah, but if I hadn't let her basically throw herself at me . . .'

The phone in the kitchen rings suddenly and I answer it, roysh, without thinking. It still feels like my home – it's, like, habit.

Some bird from, like, India or somewhere, goes, 'This is Raisha from Perlico. I'm ringing to tell you about FreeCalls and Freetalk Anytime, our two new great value home phone deals. Have you considered the savings you could make by switching from eircom?'

Sorcha's going, 'Who is it?' and I'm like, 'Perlico,' at which point Cillian comes crashing into the kitchen, going, 'What are they offering?'

I'm thinking, typical focking accountant.

'What are you offering?' I go, and the bird is like, 'Well, Freetalk Anytime offers you unlimited local and national calls, while FreeCalls offers you free calls to other Perlico subscribers,' which I pass on to Cillian, feeling like a focking tool.

'Is there a connection fee?' he goes.

I'm like, 'Any connection fee?' and the bird's there, 'No connection charge – and you can keep your existing number.'

I'm there, 'No connection charge. And you can hang on to the old number.'

He's like, 'So what kind of savings are they offering?' and then he obviously cops how ridiculous this whole scene is, roysh, because he turns around to me and goes, 'Would you mind if I . . .' and he takes the Wolfe from me.

I look at Sorcha as if to say, you've traded me for *that*?

Then I realize I have to get out of here because this scene is actually killing me.

I'm there, 'I better hit the road.'

'Can I give you a lift somewhere?' she goes, when we reach the front door. I'm like, 'No, I'll get a Jo Maxi – it's cool.'

It's, like, pissing rain. I zip up the old Henri Lloyd, go out the gate and stort making my way back down Newtownpork Avenue. I stop after only a few yords to look back, but by that stage she's already back inside the gaff.

I think about going back to the Wolf, or maybe the Hot,

but I see a Jo with its light on and I flag it down and tell the driver I want to go to the Ice Bar. I don't know why – it's just, like, where I've got to be.

I ask him to stop off in Blackrock, the grumpy focker, to hit a drinklink and I put my cord in, roysh, and I'm thinking about Cillian, swanning around my gaff, *my* gaff, his *Business & Finance*s on the coffee table where my *Loaded*s used to be, then I key in my pin – it's, like, 1999 – and I ask for a hundred snots, thinking, that girl will die of boredom with a goy like that, just wither up and die like . . . *insufficient funds*.

Insufficient funds?

It's never happened to me before, we're talking not *ever*. Maybe I keyed in the wrong . . .

Okay, fifty . . .

Insufficient funds.

FOCK!

Okay, twenty . . .

She's done this – Sorcha, probably with *him* in her ear – and her old man, of course, focking hot-shot family law solicitor, told Hennessy they were going to basically freeze my funds until they find out what I did with that hundred Ks. I didn't think she'd go through with it.

And there she was five minutes ago, being nice as . . .

I rip my cord out of the machine and just, like, snap it in two and fock it on the ground. I put my hand in my pocket. I've got, like, fifty euros and shrapnel left of what I robbed from the old dear. That's all I have, all I have in the entire world, all I have to show for my twenty-four years on this planet is fifty euros plus shrapnel – and Chuckles there is going to want at least twenty of that. He beeps the horn at me, roysh, because I'm just, like, standing there on the Main Street, having a moment.

When I open the door, he goes, 'Monta fook,' which means hurry up, so I get in again and I check my phone and it's, like, half-five and the traffic coming the other way is, like, bomper to bomper, but this way it's fine and suddenly we're zipping past the Frascati Centre and Blackrock College and Vincent's Hospital and that's when, for no reason at all that I can think of – other than, like, temporary madness – I stort going, 'Monta fook!' basically ripping the piss out of the driver.

It's like, 'Monta fook! Monta fook!'

He swings in outside the Merrion Shopping Centre, roysh, and tells me to getouta fook, but to give him twenty fooken sheets foorst, even though the meter only actually says sixteen, and I tell him to cop the fock on and to drop me to the Four Seasons, which is what he's being paid to do, and when he tells me to get out again, roysh, I tell him I want the Feds and I want them here now, but instead of calling the Feds, roysh, he reaches down by the side of his seat and pulls out what I know from listening to Ronan is called A Persuader, and he gets out of the cor and opens my door and of course I stort screaming like an actual girl, going, 'Not the face! Not the face!' but he doesn't hit me with it, he just points it at me and goes, 'Gimme the twenty,' which I do, and then, 'Outta fook,' which I also do and he drives off, roysh, leaving me on the side of the focking road.

Fock him. It's only, like, a ten-minute walk from here. A nice walk. Ailesbury Road. My kind of people. I'm thinking, how could that girl just, like, stand there, knowing she'd screwed me over, knowing she'd cleaned me out and all of a sudden, roysh, I don't believe that nothing happened before, between her and focking Calculator Boy.

It's weird, roysh, but with this little dosh on me, I actually feel underdressed, like I'm trying to get in here in a focking

Fred Perry and a pair of Levis. And maybe it's my imagination, roysh, but I'm sure the bouncer gives me the big-time once-over and I'm like, 'Hi, how the hell are you?' just to let him know, no need to panic, I'm not working class, and he's like, 'Good evening, Sir, you're very welcome,' and I'm thinking, *that's* why this is the classiest battle-cruiser in town, *that's* why they can chorge whatever the fock they want as far as I'm concerned.

'Good evening, Sir, what can I get you?'

There's something, I don't know, reassuringly familiar about the place – the gold drapes, the floor lighting, the flowers, the grey cocktail menus, the way people have been checking me out with no shame at all ever since I walked through the door.

'Sir?'

I glance at the menu, then go, no, I'll actually have a pint of Ken and the bormaid asks me to repeat it, like it's the first time she's ever heard of it, which, I suppose, working here, might well be the case.

Did you say something, Sir? What? I thought you said something? No – nothing at all. Okay, I'll have your drink sent over to you, Sir.

I sit down at one of the low tables in the corner and do a quick inventory of the place. Left hammer, there's a bird who's a ringer for Hannah Spearritt, but she's with a goy, although I'm pretty sure he's Stoke, from the way he's checking me out. In front of me there's a group of three birds, one of whom, I'm pretty sure, is Claire Byrne off TV3 and the other two aren't exactly bad either. Up at the bor, there's a bird whose name, I'm pretty sure, is Molly and who was in Holy Child Killiney and was supposed to have been in love with me for a couple of years, even though I don't remember exchanging two words with her in my life.

The lounge bird brings my pint and puts it down on the table with a bit of a, I don't know, flourish, if that's the word, like it's a focking bottle of Bolly or some shit. She gives me a little smile – I thought she was a bit smitten by me when I walked in alright – then goes off and comes back a couple of minutes later with three little bowls of, like, rice crackers, nuts and mini poppadoms and of course the Jack and Jill in a little leather folder.

Thank you, she goes and I'm there, thank *you*, giving it loads and not giving a fock who notices.

I throw a couple of mouthfuls back and I sit there thinking about Sorcha and I end up ringing her and when she answers I go that was focking low and she goes what and I go I'm broke as in actually focking broke on top of having no wife no kids no gaff no cor and she tells me I'm drinking, like I need to be focking told, and I tell her I need money to focking live and she goes I'd prefer to let our solicitors handle that side of things because it's important for Honor's sake that we don't fall out and in the background I can hear Cillian tell her to come quickly because she's doing her first bum shuffle, Honor's doing her first bum shuffle, and Sorcha tells me I should go home and I'm like I don't have a home and she goes well whatever you do, I don't think you should drink any more and then she's gone.

The place fills up pretty quickly, all the after-work crowd, solicitors and bank staff. I drink my second pint slowly and end up just, like, people-watching – goys in tins of fruit, talking loudly, surrounded by birds, birds from work, flirting their orses off with the goys because that to them is a career move, see, and the older birds – pint-drinkers, most of them – flirt that bit horder than the younger ones because they know that time is, like, ticking on, and they try to impress the goys by talking about rugby and cors, but they can't see what I can, sitting here, like, detached from the scene, that they've actually *become* goys.

Sir, you're going to have to stop shouting. Shouting? Yes, Sir. Was *I* shouting? Yes, Sir – it's just, well, we have other customers to think of. Was I really shouting? I'm afraid you were, Sir. What was I shouting? You were shouting, she's my daughter. Oh, that's right – *my* daughter, not his. Well, if it's bothering you, it's just as well you mentioned it. It's just the other customers, Sir. We have to think of them. Hey, it's not a thing – you won't hear another word out of me. That'd be nice, Sir. Well, as I always say, it's nice to be nice.

These rice crackers are addictive.

I feel unbelievably lonely. I'm trying to think of someone to ring. Christian's away. Oisinn's away. JP's away with the fairies. Fionn – no, I can't involve him and Aoife. I look through my phone. My address book is a register of birds I can't place and people I've focked over and it depresses me so much that . . .

A loud burst of laughter from the corner. Are they laughing at me? They better focking not be, no, they're not actually. Do you know who it is, it's like Drico and Shaggy and a few others and they're sucking up every bit of attention in the place, surrounded by birds – really, really good-looking birds – and even the people who aren't interested in what's going on around them are only pretending to be not interested out of basic jealousy because there's so much energy coming off that group, we're talking positive energy, good clobber and smiles, big focking healthy smiles, that's what pisses a lot of people off, seeing other people that confident, that happy and fit and healthy and I'm looking at them thinking, yeah, that used to be me.

He's holding my daughter, he's blowing out the candles

on her birthday cake, he's teaching her how to swim, he's telling her not to listen to what some girl in school said, she's beautiful and he's walking her up the aisle . . .

I knock back the last of my pint and I stand up. A lot of female eyes turn in my direction – especially the thirty-somethings – but for once in my life any possible pleasure to be had from a one-night stand is outweighed by the hassle of having to escape from her in the morning without telling her a thing about myself.

I put my hand in my pocket and I whip out the twenty – my last twenty in the world. It's a cocktail here or my taxi fare home – shit or get off the pot time.

I tip up to the bor and ask for a Champagne Mojito.

I watch the borman crush the mint with what I'm pretty sure is called a pestle and mortar, though which is which I can never remember. He puts, like, mint in the bottom of the glass, which he then packs with ice, sugar and lime, then pours in the Havana rum, and the Billecart Salmon and it's, like, watching him do it brings back so many memories.

'Hello? Ross, it's Hennessy.'

'Hennessy, how the fock are you?'

'Ross, I've been trying to get you.'

'Well, looks like you just have.'

'They've frozen your bank account and your credit cards – they know about the apartments and they want the money back.'

'Sorry, Hennessy, you're breaking up.'

'Nineteen euros,' the borman goes and I hand him the twenty and tell him to keep the change, which I don't think exactly pumps his nads.

I take two long sips through the straw. My head feels so focking fuzzy.

Rosser. Hey, Ro. What do you want, Rosser? Er . . . to talk. He goes I've no interest in talking to you and I go Ro, I'm a bit scared here, it's finally hitting me, it's like a delayed reaction and he goes what and I go everything. This time last year I had it all and we're talking *all* and he goes why haven't you been to see your oul' lad and I tell him it's because it's only when I see my old pair that I really miss them and he tells me I shouldn't drink any more tonight and I go Ro, I'd really like to see you and he goes, and this hurts, this actually hurts more than anything anyone has ever said to me in my life, he goes no, everything you touch turns to shit.

A voice behind me.

'Hi, Ross . . .'

I whip around, hoping it's Claire Byrne, but it's not.

I'm there, 'Oh, hey, Molly,' and she goes, 'It's Maisy,' and I'm like, 'Maisy – that was it. How are you?' and she's there, '*Way* over you anyway. I can't believe I was *actually* in love with you? All my friends were like, *aaahhh!*'

She sort of, like, looks me up and down and goes, 'Okay, I don't know if this is true, but are you, like, collecting sanitary-towel bins now, because that's what I heard?'

No point in lying. I'm there, 'Yeah,' and she sort of, like, wipes her brow with the back of her hand and goes, 'Phew!' as in, I am SO glad we never ended up together, not that she was ever in with a shout.

I go, 'I collect the odd bin – just to keep it real – but I actually own the company. See, that's what I put my money into – after I sold Lillie's.'

Without batting an eyelid, she tells me that she's going out with a goy – who she's SO in love with – who owns two houses and five aportments, three of which are still being built at the moment, as in those new ones on the

Stillorgan dualler, the Spirit of focking Gracious Living, and he's, like, renting them all out. He's, like, twenty-five and he'll never have to work again.

Fair focks to him, I hear myself going, maybe out loud, maybe not.

'Oh my God,' she goes, 'property is SO the thing to put your money into, but do it now because the whole thing is about to go, *aaahhh!*'

'So my friend reckons,' I go. 'He's putting his money in tomato ketchup – and he knows a thing or two.'

She's there, 'They're saying it actually *can't* continue like this?' and she flicks her thumb in the direction of no one and everyone. 'It's all based on borrowing and it's, like, German money? I don't really like David McWilliams, but he talks an awful lot of sense.'

I'm so hammered now I can hordly see. It can't last, she says. It can't last. It most certainly can't. Every barrel has a bottom and this is mine, sitting here in this bor, surrounded by beautiful people, sucking the last few drops from the tit of the so-called Tiger.

I hold up my drink and, probably more with the intention of frightening her off than anything else, I go, 'This Champagne Mojito is the last thing I own . . .'

9. A Balkan Disaster

Gus rings me at, like, half-eight in the morning, when I'm on the Dort, hungover to fock, and he tells me they're all out of sparks, the focking lunatic. I'm like, 'All out of what?' and he goes, 'Sparks – for the spark plugs. I need you to go to an electrical shop on your way in and pick up a bucketful.'

I'm there, 'Er, yeah, no problem.'

'And two and a half metres of fallopian tube,' and even though he's got, like, his hand over the mouthpiece, I can hear him laughing so hord that he's, like, snorting like a pig. 'And don't come in without them . . .' and then he just slams the phone down.

Which means I have the morning to kill and it's weird, roysh, I don't know what leads me to do it, but I decide to go and see the old man. It kills me to say this, but I've actually missed him.

'Here he comes, everyone, my main man,' and I'm not exaggerating, roysh, everyone in the visiting room looks up and storts going, 'Howiya, Ross,' and it's like they're all pleased to see me.

'How *are* you, Kicker?' he goes and I'm just like, 'Skint and single,' and he's there, 'Yes, me too. But look around you, look at all the smiling faces,' and he *is* right – it's actually quite a happy place, compared to what it was like when he came in here first. There's, like, a buzz that wasn't there before.

'I've discovered what happiness *is* in here,' he goes, 'and it's not cars and houses and possessions. And that ain't me fronting, man.'

I'm tempted to go, God, I can't believe what a total penis you are, but I'd actually feel bad bursting the goy's bubble.

He goes, 'Rugby – that's what's done it. Mellowed this place right out. And if you've noticed an extra felicitousness in the air, that's not your imagination, Ross, because the big news – fanfare please, trumpets, etcetera – is that we've arranged our first competitive match.'

'Who against?' I go and he's there, 'Shannon! Well, their eleventh team. Would you believe it, though, they're letting us *out* to play the match – under heavy guard, of course. Not sure if that's for the public's protection or ours, mind you . . .'

I go, 'Do you not think you'd be better off concentrating on your case? I mean, your trial storts in, like, two weeks' time?'

He throws his orms up in the air and he goes, 'There isn't going to *be* any trial. I've pleaded guilty. It's an open-and-shut case. *Habeas corpus, caveat emptor*, if you'll pardon the French. All that awaits me is my sentence, which I'll face with a manly stoicism when the time comes, fullstop, new par.'

He's madder than JP.

Then he storts going, 'Pardon me for saying it, Home Boy, but you don't seem to be your usual cheery self this morning,' and I end up kind of losing it, roysh.

I'm like, 'Can you *actually* blame me? Not only have I had to get – and I am not exaggerating here – a job. It turns out to be the worst focking job in the world. I'm collecting used tampons from public toilets.'

He just, like, shakes his head and goes, 'Ross, it's temporary. Like everything else. Which brings me on to other matters.

Something you might be able to help us with,' and suddenly he stands up and calls Lex, who's, like, three tables down.

Lex comes lumbering over to us. He's built like a focking tank. 'What's the story?' he goes, which is how working-class people say, how are you? You're not supposed to answer, though.

The old man's there, 'I wanted you in on this, Lex, as my captain. Ross will have an idea or two. Where others have a brain, he has a rugby manual,' which, it has to be said, is actually a nice thing to say.

'Ross,' he goes, turning to me, 'our backs are good – quick, like you wouldn't believe. They *would* be, most of them have been thieving all their lives. But their handling is shocking. No sensitivity in their hands, it seems to me.'

Lex is nodding.

'I told the chaps at training yesterday not to be dispirited. I'll tell you who'll have the answer to this, I said, and I'm sure he'll be in to see me again when he works through his present difficulties. I'm talking my boy, Ross, hero of the hour, 17 March 1999, quote-unquote, and one of the best lateral thinkers in the business,' and I look around me, roysh, and I suddenly realize that all the other prisoners in the room are listening, with their mouths wide open, roysh, waiting to hear what I say, waiting for me to, like, inspire them?

This is pressure, but of course I thrive in, like, pressure situations.

I think about it for, like, twenty seconds, then I go, 'Pretend the ball is something precious that you've just shoplifted. A piece of Lladro, maybe. From House of Ireland . . .'

'Mother and Baby,' one of the other prisoners goes and they all stort nodding, like that's something they understand.

'There you are!' the old man goes, giving Lex a big wink.

Suddenly, I'm in, like, teacher mode.

I'm there, 'Yeah, you've smashed the window of the display case and you've, like, grabbed this expensive piece of porcelain. The security gord is catching up on you, but your mate to your immediate left is faster than you. So offload it to him, as delicately as you can. Keep telling yourselves – mother and baby, mother and baby . . .'

All of a sudden, roysh, they burst into a round of applause and I swear to God, I've never seen my old man look so proud of me.

'We shall put it to the test,' he goes, 'but I think a certain man who goes by the moniker The Dagger had better watch his back!'

Visiting time's over.

'I'll ring you,' the old man goes and, even though he is a dickhead, I actually mean it when I go, 'Yeah, do.'

I step out onto the North Circular Road and manage to hail a Jo. I get in the back and I bell Gus. He's already laughing.

'How are you getting on?' he goes.

I'm like, 'I'm, er, still having a bit of trouble with the order.'

He's there, 'That's because I've sent you on another fool's errand!' and I go, 'No!' and he's like, 'Yes! Think about it – how you could you even *have* a bucket of sparks?'

I'm going, 'I don't believe it. God, I'm so focking dumb,' and he's there, 'Yes, you are. You're so dumb you should be blond. Do you even know what a fallopian tube is? It's in a woman's—'

I'm there, 'Yeah, I've just remembered.'

'In a woman's gee,' he goes. 'I've made you look a fool again – and the worst thing from your point of view is that

I've already told everybody! I have shamed you. I have humiliated you . . .'

'Valerie's sexual appetite had returned with a vengeance,' she's going. 'It didn't matter how often she had it, how many different ways, how many different rooms, her desire for *it* was insatiable . . .'

He's having none of *it*, though. He's going, 'Nat noy – kinda bozzy.'

'Her breath on his neck brought him suddenly to a proud, twitching stand,' she's going, like the desperate bitch she is. 'As she reached for his belt, she could feel his excitement through the canvas of his jeans . . .'

I'm going to have to get the study fumigated when he finally focks off, which I don't think is far off, judging from the way he goes, 'Finny, I'm sorious – I'm trying to read here.'

She's like, 'What are you reading? Oh, not that *bloody* book again. You've already read it,' and he's there, 'Well, I'm re-reading it. There might be one or two themes I missed the first time around,' and then there's, like, silence for ages and I'm actually about to hit the sack when it suddenly kicks off in there.

The old dear's like, 'You slept with her, didn't you?' and he's there, 'Finny, don't talk shate.'

She's there, 'You did, that's who's taken your appetite,' and he's there, 'Och, will you catch yourself awn. We'd tea at the Morrion Hotel – where were we going to dee it? In the moddle of the drawing rim?'

'But you thought about it,' she goes. 'I know you did. I bet you're thinking about her now?'

'Look, the only thing I'm thanking rate nay,' he goes, 'is that this gorl could be the next . . .'

'The next Fionnuala O'Carroll-Kelly?' the old dear goes. 'That's what you were about to say, isn't it?'

She actually storts crying then, the stupid bitch.

I can hear her.

She's going, 'You've gone off me, haven't you?' and I swear to God, roysh, she sounds so focking needy that I feel like going in there and dragging her off to, I don't know, wherever, to have her name changed by deed poll, because no one that focking pathetic should be allowed to call themselves O'Carroll-Kelly.

The next thing I hear, roysh, is him going, *Ooow!* and then, like, howling in pain.

The old dear's like, 'What's the matter with your shoulder?'

He's there, 'Nathing,' and she's there, 'Lance, I just touched you and . . . you've hurt yourself, haven't you?'

No, but I suspect someone else did.

I go into my room and bell Charlotte. She answers on the second ring.

I just go, 'I take it you did that to him,' and she's there, 'Yeah, but it was just to shut him up. *What* is the story with him – all he talks about is shitting. It's like he's obsessed. But . . .' and then she gets all excited and goes, 'I got a book deal!'

'This isn't even *on* our round. That's all I'm saying.'

'I know,' Terry goes. 'But I told Sheets we'd do one or two of his drops. His wife has the shingles.'

We're porked outside Eddie Rocket's in Donnybrook and of course, it's beginning to sound like I don't actually *want* to do the goy a favour.

I have to tell them.

'It's just, well, I *know* people in here,' I go. 'They come here this time every Friday.'

'Who?' Terry goes. He's driving this week.

I'm like, 'You wouldn't know them,' and Felim all of a sudden goes, 'Are they worse than anything you faced on the rugby field?'

When I don't answer, he turns around – he's in, like, the front passenger seat – and goes, 'I saw you play against Clongowes once, just across the road there. The crowd that day gave you dog's abuse. They were in the ground an hour before the game, calling you unbelievable things . . .'

The memory's actually coming back to me now.

He goes, 'I remember thinking, what's this kid going through in that dressing-room? Because that'd be enough to break anyone. Not you. What did you do? You walked to the end of the ground where they all were, the Clongowes hardcore – and you pulled up your shirt and showed them your stomach muscles . . .'

I actually did that before every match, though I don't tell him that because the goy obviously worships the ground I walk on. So there's nothing else for me to do, roysh, except get out of the van and grab two bins out of the back.

Then I stop, roysh, whip off my shades and my cap and hand them through the window to Felim. I'm there, 'I'm not going to need these.'

As I'm walking towards Ed's, he leans out the window and goes, 'You scored twenty-seven points that day, Ross,' and it's like, yeah, I've nothing to be ashamed of, there's still people in this town who think I'm shit-hot and all of a sudden, roysh, I've straightened my back, pinned back my shoulders and my chin is up when I put my shoulder to the door.

There they are – the third table on the left. Chloe, Amie with an ie and Erika.

Actually, I heard that Erika and Chloe are thick as thieves again, like nothing ever happened between them.

I don't even try to hide my boat race. Quite the opposite. I look each of them pretty much squarely in the eye as I pass their table.

The first *oh my God* is from Chloe. She doesn't have time to, like, process the information and work it into some kind of joke, so she just goes, '*Oh my God!*' three or four times and it's Amie with an ie who goes, '*Oh* my God – he's collecting tampon bins . . . *for a living!*'

I hear Chloe sort of, like, snigger and I just stop, roysh, dead in my tracks and wait for whatever it is that Erika's about to say. I can hear it coming. It's as if I'm tied to a railway track and it's thundering towards me, like the Wexford train.

'Why don't you two just shut up?' I hear her go and I turn around in total surprise.

Amie with an ie is there, 'I'm just saying, no one's going to want to *be* with him ever again when they find out that he's . . .' and Erika's like, 'That he's providing for his children? Makes him a real man in a lot of people's books. If you met one or two more of those, you probably wouldn't be eating chocolate every night and listening to Katie Melua,' to which Amie with an ie has no answer.

I just look at Erika and she looks back at me.

'I hate you for what you did to Sorcha,' she goes, 'but I respect you for what you're doing to try to put it right.'

Then she gives me this look, which I take to mean, you saw me at my lowest ebb and you didn't, like, rub my nose in the dirt, so I'm going to resist the temptation to do it to you. Because whatever's been said and done, we've been friends for a long, long time. I give her, like, a nod of thanks, then I go, 'I, er, better get back to work,' and then I head for the jacks.

The first cubicle is empty, roysh, but there's someone in Trap Two, so after I've changed the first bin, I have to, like, hang around and wait for the other. I'm checking out my boat race in the mirror, roysh, thinking I look actually tired, when all of a sudden I hear this, like, retching sound from Trap Two, like whoever's in there is throwing their guts up?

It's a sound I absolutely hate, roysh, so I turn on the hand-dryer to drown it out and by the time it goes through a second cycle, all I can hear is, like, dry-retching, so I decide, fock the other bin and I head for the door. Just as I pull it, I hear Trap Two open and I have a quick George Hook over my shoulder and out walks this bird. She doesn't look in my direction, roysh, she just walks straight to the mirror and storts checking herself out, wiping her mouth, and my hort pretty much nearly stops.

Because it's Aoife.

She turns on the tap and storts splashing water on her face. I turn my head so all she can see is my back, as I slip out the door.

Ronan's storted smoking cigarillos, I notice. I'm not even going to bother asking who he picked that up from.

He's waiting for me outside work.

I'm like, 'Hey,' and straight away he's there, 'I think I might have been a bit hard on you,' and I'm like, 'Forget it,' because it feels a bit, I don't know, awkward listening to him apologize.

'Erika rang me,' he goes.

I'm there, 'Erika?' and he's like, 'She told me about . . .' and of course he just bursts out laughing in my face. 'Rosser,' he goes, 'could you not have got a better fooken job than that?'

He has a point. Of course, I stort cracking my hole laughing then as well.

'You should have rung me,' he goes. 'I know a few fellas, would have put a bit of work your way,' and I'm there, 'Yeah, and I'd end up sharing a cell with my old man – no, thank you.'

He goes, 'You went to see him. He was made up, Rosser, so he was.'

I'm there, 'Yeah, I know,' and then, I don't know why, roysh, I just turn around to him and go, 'I'm after focking up in a major way,' and I end up telling him about the aportments in Bulgaria.

'Where?' Ronan goes, squinting at me, the cigarillo jammed between his teeth.

I'm there, 'Bulgaria. Hey, Ro, you do geography at school – it's not a shithole, is it?' but he doesn't answer, roysh, he just goes, 'Depends. How much?' and I'm there, 'Fifty Ks a piece. The problem is, Sorcha's looking for the wedge.'

He shrugs his shoulders and goes, 'Sell them.'

I'm like, 'How? I mean, I'm almost scared to ask to see a picture of them. I went and Googled the place the other day and you'd want to see the pictures that came up – it's all stonewashed baggy denims and moustaches. Actually it's not unlike that estate where you live.'

He goes, 'Rosser, no matter how badly you've fooked up here, you're gonna have to assess the damage. Let's go over there, have a look at them.'

He sucks the last bit of life out of the cigarillo, then crushes it under his foot.

I'm there, 'Small problem – I haven't a pot to piss in. The old dear's stopped keeping large amounts of money in the gaff since . . . well, someone broke in and emptied her bag,' and I say this last bit with a big shit-eating grin on my face.

'I'll sub you,' he goes. 'I've a few bob coming to me from one of me creditors. Buckets of Blood's collecting it for me tonight.'

Fionn is surprised to hear from me, though not so much to *hear from me*, more surprised that I want to see him. He can tell something's up, but he probably thinks it's something to do with, like, Sorcha.

'Do you want to come here?' he goes, presumably to his apartment in Dalkey. Focking incredible gaff.

I'm like, 'Is Aoife there?' and he goes, 'No, it's Tuesday – she does that wine-tasting thing with . . .' and he stops suddenly, roysh, as if the mention of her name will cause me to, like, burst into flames.

I'm there, 'I'm on the Dort now – can you, like, pick me up at the station? I've no wheels,' and he says he can.

I don't know why I'm so, like, nervous and shit?

I offer him a handshake instead of the usual high-five and we get into his cor – his new Audi – and head for the horbour. I'd prefer to talk to him there than in the gaff.

I'm going, 'So when are you going on this cruise?' and Fionn's like, 'Three weeks now. We're going right up into the Arctic Circle – we're both pretty excited, especially about the *aurora borealis*, which we might still be able to see,' and I'm like, 'Cool,' not knowing, of course, whether it's a focking painting, a mountain or whatever the fock.

He porks up on the side of the road and we walk down to the little pier, roysh, and we sit on the edge of it, our legs dangling over the water.

All my life I've thought I hated Fionn's guts, but I realize, roysh, that my nervousness has something to do with not wanting to see the goy hurt.

But he still has to know.

So with plenty of, like, pats on the back and I'm-here-for-yous, I tell him what I saw and – more to the point – what I heard in the jacks in Ed's. As I talk, he's sort of, like, staring out to sea, but it's only when he takes off his glasses, roysh, to clean them on his Abercrombie that I realize he's crying. We sit there in, like, total silence, except for the occasional Dude-I'm-sorry from me.

He eventually goes, 'Couple of months back, Aoife had this dental appointment. She had an old filling that broke away. I went with her, just hung around in the waiting room for her. So she comes out and the dentist is behind her. He sees me and he says it's a long time since he's looked in my mouth. He's got fifteen minutes till his next appointment – would I like a check-up? I knew something was wrong because I'd never seen the man before in my life. Our dentist is in Donnybrook . . .'

I'm listening, but at the same time watching a fisherman tie up his boat. That's a job I wouldn't mind actually.

Then I hear the horn of the Stena going out.

Fionn's there, 'I go into the surgery with him and he asks me straight out whether Aoife's having treatment for her eating disorder. It's like, focking hell, what do you say to that? It's, like, what eating disorder? I said, look, she *was* bulimic, but she's fine now. She's not fine, he said. The enamel on her teeth has been worn away – stomach acid, see . . .'

I'm like, 'But could that not be from, like, before? I mean, Aoife was at that shit for years.'

He goes, 'He showed me two x-rays, one taken about six months ago, when she was thinking about having a brace fitted, the other taken, well, a few minutes before. Look, I don't know how to read an x-ray, but he said there had been significant erosion since her last visit.'

I'm like, 'Focking hell, Fionn.'

He takes off his glasses and storts cleaning them again – it's obviously, like, a nervous thing?

He goes, 'I didn't even say it to her. Managed to convince myself that I needed more evidence. It's only the last couple of weeks I've noticed how often she leaves the table halfway through a meal. And I've taken to following her in there afterwards, looking inside the rim of the bowl for tell-tale splashes.'

The poor focking goy.

I put my orm around him. It's awkward and I'm sure people passing by think we're a couple of bennies, but it's the only thing I can think of to do when there's, like, absolutely nothing left to say.

Gus tells me to make it quick because he's about to go into a meeting, so I go, 'That new cursor you wanted for your computer?'

He's like, 'Yeah?'

I'm there, 'Well, I'm going to need a few more days to work on it . . .' and I can hear him whisper to whoever else is in the room, 'He says he needs a few more days – he's been all over town looking for it . . .' and then there's all this, like, muffled laughter and then he comes back on the phone and goes, 'Yes, very good. Keep plugging away.'

I'm like, 'I mean, it might even take me a week,' and he goes, 'Take as long as you like, just don't let me down,' and then I hang up on the stupid tool.

I turn around to Ronan and I'm like, 'Okay, before we check in, we need to find out what kind of yoyos they use in the shithole and if it's not the euro, we need to get ourselves some.'

'It's called the Lev,' he goes and then he taps the breast pocket of his Levis jacket and goes, 'and we're sorted.'

So we head for the check-in desk and I go, 'Where did you change that money?' and he's there, 'Nudger did it for me. Currency dealing's his new line,' and then he hands his passport and the flight details to the bird behind the desk and goes, 'Howiya, love?'

I didn't get a lot of shut-eye last night, portly worrying about Fionn, who I texted this morning, just to let him know, if there's anything I can do, blah blah blah.

So it's understandable if I'm a bit norky.

We're standing in the aisle of the plane, roysh, and I step back to let Ronan get in by the window, but he turns around and goes, 'I'll take the aisle, Rosser, if it's all the same to you. I get a bit claustrophobic being boxed in like that – all those years I spent inside . . .'

Of course I end up totally losing it – and we're talking *totally* here. I go, 'Ronan, you're an eight-year-old kid! Will you quit it with the focking career criminal act?' and he looks at me, roysh, like I've just taken away his, I don't know, hip flask.

In the end, roysh, I end up letting him take the aisle seat, but he spends most of the flight with his nose in the new Paul Williams book, and in a total snot with me. See, he plays that whole hard man act so often that I forget sometimes how easy it is to hurt his feelings.

As we're, like, descending towards Sofia, though, I think, roysh, I've got to be the bigger man here, and I decide to make my peace with him.

'Any good?' I go, nodding at the book and he looks at me over the top of those Ronnie Kray half-glasses we bought him for his birthday.

'Not bad,' he goes.

I'm like, 'Did you get a mention in it?' and I watch his little face light up. 'Eh, not yet,' he goes, 'I've only read a hundred pages, but.'

So I'm there, 'He might have a chapter later on the up-and-coming criminals – as in, like, the stors of the future?' and he looks at me for ages, roysh, like he's trying to decide if this is a good thing or a bad thing, then he smiles and goes, 'Yeah, maybe. In anyhow, it suits me to stay under the radar for the moment, if you catch me drift. I've one or two things in the pot that I don't want Plod sniffing around,' and then he goes back to his book.

I'm thinking, yeah, I might actually nail this whole father-hood thing yet.

We get off the plane, roysh, and go into the passport inspection area and I'm looking around me, roysh, reading all the signs, noticing that they've got focking numbers and shapes and squiggles in their words over here. Which is when Ronan reaches into his Davy Crockett, slaps the wad of whatever the money's called into my hand, then goes, 'Might be best, Rosser, if *you* carry this.'

This is when we're, like, two people from the top of the passport queue.

Suddenly, roysh, my hort's beating like a focking souped-up Ford Fiesta. I look at him and he gives me a big wink, roysh, and I turn around to him and I go, 'Tell me the truth – is this dodgy money?'

'*Ssshhh*,' he goes. 'The phrase, Rosser, is funny money. And I think Nudger would take *that* as a personal insult . . .'

Oh, shit! I cannot believe this.

The next thing I know we're at the top of the queue, roysh, and we're being called up to the little booth, where some goy who looks a right bundle of laughs storts giving my passport the serious once-over. He keeps looking at me, roysh, then back at my picture.

Eventually, he gets on the phone and says something in, I don't know, algebra or whatever focking language these people speak.

I end up nearly kacking myself when the dude hangs up, then goes, 'You will go with my colleague,' and I spin around and there's another goy standing behind me, sort of, like, gesturing me towards this little office.

It's like, FOCK! How do they know?

As I'm being led away, Ronan goes, 'Remember, Rosser – a shut mouth catches no flies,' and then I watch him as he's waved through passport control, roysh, and I'm suddenly in this little interview room.

The goy sits down opposite me and it's like this money is burning a hole in my focking chinos. I am *seriously* kacking it – *and* in a major way. I know I wouldn't last ten focking minutes in prison here, especially with this face and this body.

So what happens? I end up singing like Ronan focking Keating.

I'm like, 'We didn't know the money was hot. I can give you the name of the goy we got it off. Nudger, he calls himself, although that's probably just an alias. Doesn't say a lot. He's usually a wheels man, but this is his new sideline . . .'

I'm storting to have palpitations. The goy's just staring at me, roysh, giving me all the rope I need.

I'm like, 'I'll go to court, testify, the whole shebang. Just don't send me to jail, Dude. I mean, take a look at me. They'll think all their Christmases have come at once . . .'

Then I go, 'Actually, I want to talk to my solicitor. It's Hennessy Coghlan-O'Hara. His number is . . .'

The goy finally speaks.

He goes, 'Meester Ocarull-Kalee,' which means me. 'Your pessport wheel expire next week. I hef to tell you that you must go to the Irish embassy here in Sofia – that is, if you like to go home again.' And then he laughs and tells me that I'm free to go.

Ronan's at the carousel, waiting for our luggage. I'm sweating like a focking mugger. Ronan just looks at me out of the corner of his eye and goes, 'I worry about you, Rosser. You might crack under interrogation.'

The taxi driver turns around to me and – get this – he goes, 'You speak Bulgarian?' and I swear to God, roysh, I end up totally losing the plot with him.

I'm like, '*What* would be the focking point?' and Ronan tells me to stall the ball and also to chill, which is easy for him to say. He hasn't just invested a hundred Ks he doesn't have in what is – as is obvious within five minutes of leaving the airport – a complete focking toilet.

I'm looking out the window, watching the city pass by. Everywhere, there's people who look like the *Big Issue* sellers we have back home. Imagine a whole city made up of them and you've just imagined Sofia. It's like the nineties were only a rumour here, we're talking leather jackets, bad denim and big hair. One F would focking love it.

Ronan's got a map opened out across his lap and he's also leafing through the *Rough Guide* that I picked up at the airport.

'I think I'm after spotting your mistake,' he goes to me, taking off his little glasses. 'You see, most people – *normal* people – who buy investment properties in Bulgaria go for Varna or Burgas, or any of the resorts on the Black Sea. Or even a ski resort, like Bankso, which is mad popular, according to the buke.'

I'm there, 'Okay, so what has Sofia got to offer?'

He gives it to me straight. 'Fook-all,' he goes. 'I hate to say it, Rosser, especially about a blood relative of mine, but you've been conned. This fella has stitched you up big-time.'

I'm like, 'Whoa, whoa, whoa – you're yanking my cord! I mean, how far are we from, what's it called, the Black Sea?' and he goes, 'Eight hours. Ten the way you drive,' and I'm just, like, shaking my head, thinking, how the fock does JP's old man sleep at night?

We stop on Sofia's own version of Seàn McDermott Street. I turn around to the driver and I go, 'Er, why are we no longer driving?' but I've already got a sense of, like, dread in my hort before he even goes, 'Knyaz Alexander Donsoukovs,' which might sound like complete gobbledygook to you, but which I recognize straight away as my new address.

I just put my head in my hands. Ronan pays the driver and goes, 'Sorry about her,' throwing his thumb at me.

I get out and look up at the building. It's big and grey, with the paint peeling off it everywhere and those big, ugly air-conditioning boxes underneath every window and a giant sign on the roof that says Bosch.

'Come on, Rosser,' Ronan goes, getting the bags out of the boot. 'Gimme a hand here . . .'

The stairs and landing smell of fish, though Ronan helpfully informs me that it's actually piss and, given where he lives, I think I can take his word for it. All the way up that ugly, grey stairwell I'm thinking, it's a mistake. There *has* to be another 1040 Knyaz Alexander Donsoukovs.

There's, like, three aportments on my landing. Seven and Eight are mine and Nine belongs to fock-knows-who. I put the key in the door of aportment Seven and find, with a sinking feeling, that it actually works.

I walk in first and it's like, welcome to the Cockroach Hilton. If that pen and ink really is what Ro says it is, then someone's had a hit and miss in here as well. The hum is seriously Pàdraig and the place is filthy.

Fully furnished, the brochure said. It's got, like, two beds, one of which someone has recently tried to set fire to, two hord chairs in the living room, the kind you sit on in focking school, no sofa, a fridge that doesn't work and a portable, black-and-white television that does, but which, for some reason, is attached to a cor battery. And whoever was here last took all the lightbulbs with them. It's, like, six o'clock in the evening and in an hour we won't be able to see each other in here.

'This is where I leave you,' Ronan goes.

I'm there, 'What?'

And he's like, 'I've a room booked in the Sheraton,' and even in the fading light he must see the shock on my face, roysh, because he storts laughing and he goes, 'I'm only fooking with your head. I'd a good day at the track on Sunday – but not *that* good.'

I grab my duty-free bag, roysh, and whip out my bottle of JD, which straight away Ronan takes as a sign that I'm falling to pieces.

He points at me and goes, 'I need you strong, Rosser. We're here to sort this out and it'll be sorted, reet?' and I'm like, 'Roysh.'

He goes, 'Reet, I'm fooken wrecked, so I am, so I'm hitting

the sack now. New day tomorrow – all this'll look different.'

'Yeah,' I go, 'dirtier,' and he laughs and goes, 'Probably.'

I switch on the TV and discover there's not even a remote for it. It's one of those really old sets, where there's a button for every channel, roysh, and when you press one, the one that *was* pressed in pops out.

It's like the eighties never happened here either.

I drink solidly for two, maybe three hours, while pressing the fock out of those buttons, unable to find anything I recognize. Then I do. *'Allo 'Allo!* comes on, except over here it's called *Ano Ano!* So I stort watching it, roysh, and I can't help but crack my hole laughing, because the whole thing is, like, dubbed into Bulgarian or whatever. *Leesten vury carefull-ee, I shell say zis urnly once*, is just a series of, like, clicks and whistles when it's translated into whatever focked-up way they have of talking.

It's possibly, like, the funniest shit I've ever heard? Unless of course I'm having a nervous breakdown too.

Probably the only thing I can actually say I like about Sofia is that it's not a rugby town. I can basically walk around, roysh, without people hassling me with questions about whether I'm ever going to go back playing rugby.

One thing I notice as well is that people keep staring at my Dubes. I suppose they won't reach here for another, like, thirty or forty years.

We decide to spend our first full day in the city walking around and basically getting our bearings.

After a few hours wandering around, Ronan suggests we go somewhere for a nosebag. We find a burger bor called Goody's, which is, like, their version of McDonald's. There's a picture of a cheeseburger in the window that looks about as edible as a focking Brillo pad and I'm like, no way.

So we wander around a bit more, both of us seriously Hank at this stage, and a few doors down from the apartment we find – of all things – a KFC and it's like, happy days.

We order a shitload of stuff and sit down.

'Well?' I go. 'What do you think of it so far?'

He's there, 'It's alreet, like.'

He would say that – it's full of focking Umbro shops.

He goes, 'Only problem is, I can't get me usual baccy over here. I've been in and out of a few shops. Marlboro seem to have the country sewn up.'

I'm there, 'Still, it's nice to experience, like, different cultures and shit.'

I don't know why I said that.

I suddenly crack up laughing, roysh, and I end up nearly spitting chips all over the place. I'm looking at the menu, roysh, and a Zinger Meal here is called a зиНsep Meнo. I can't help but laugh at the stupidity of these people.

Ronan wants to go and check out Alexander Nevski Cathedral. How that's going to get my hundred Ks back I don't know, but I agree to go with him, more to humour him than anything else.

What can I tell you about it? It's a church, the kind of place JP might have gone to get his jollies but it does fock-all for me. Outside, there's a gaggle of old biddies with headscorves and no teeth selling flowers and I'm thinking, it's a bit like Leeson Street on a Friday night – except it's compulsory to smoke.

All I want to do is go back to the gaff and spit a few zeds because I am cream-crackered from all the walking around, roysh, not just today, but ever since I lost my cor.

We cross the cobbled roundabout outside the church and on the side of the road there's, like, a whole line of stalls selling Second World War memorabilia – we're talking shit like medals and old guns with, like, red stors on them.

Ronan buys himself a hand grenade, which isn't real. Well, I presume it isn't real. God focking help the kids in his class if it is.

In a little pork behind where we're standing there's two men – two stall-owners – with Russian hats on, having a fight, not a real fight, but, like, a pretend boxing match. They've both got their fists up and they're, like, dancing around in a circle, throwing digs in each other's direction, but only landing them lightly.

'Keep yisser guards up,' Ronan shouts. 'Keep yisser fooken guards up,' he shouts again and all of a sudden the two of them stop moving and they look over. Ronan takes up a boxer's stance to sort of, like, demonstrate and the two goys look at the position of his hands and his feet and they sort of, like, copy him.

Of course, Ronan strolls over to them then. He grabs the older one's left hand and he goes, 'You've got to hold it higher than that – you're open to the right hook,' and he turns to the other one and goes, 'What kind of a fist is that you're making? Keep yisser thumbs outside – otherwise they'll break on impact. Now yisser feet – one o'clock and three o'clock. That's it . . .'

And I'm watching this, roysh, and I'm thinking, the old man's in the Joy teaching them how to play rugby. I captained and coached teams to the Leinster Schools Senior Cup final. And now look at Ro – it's like us O'Carroll-Kellys were born to teach sport.

I sit down on a bench. Ronan steps out from in between

them, roysh, makes a *ding-ding* sound and the two boys go at it again. They look better this time, more like the real boxers do on TV, and a small crowd storts to gather. They circle each other, throwing little punches while Ronan roars instructions and everyone laughs at the sight of it.

After five or ten minutes the two boys are knackered – or dizzy – and they give it up and get a round of applause from their little audience, roysh, and they both grab Ronan by the wrists and hold his orms up in triumph.

I'm thinking, what a great kid. It's true. He makes friends everywhere he goes. One of the goys gives him a medal in the shape of a stor, which he pins to the front of his Dublin football jacket, and for the rest of the day he refuses to answer me unless I address him as General.

I'm suddenly not tired any more and I'm also suddenly not thinking about the aportments – and the two things might be connected.

It's like, fock it, I'm *actually* storting to, like, enjoy myself?

'Let's check out the old Communist Party Headquarters,' Ronan goes and we wander past what he says is the Bulgarian Parliament and hang a right onto Tsar Osvoboditel Boulevard and past the Russian church we were in this morning. I hand Ronan my camera phone and get him to take a photograph of me in front of it.

We keep walking until we arrive in Nezavisimost Square, which even I have to admit is pretty spectacular, especially the porty headquarters, which is like something out of Gotham City – a tall, narrow building with these, like, giant columns. Ronan says there used to be a big red stor on top of it, but they tore it off during the revolution and I look at him as if to say, how the fock did you know that?

'We learned it off Mr de Barra in History,' he goes and

I'm thinking, if this kid wants to make it as a rugby player, he's going to have to empty all this useless shit out of his head.

'Hey, Rosser,' he goes, 'can you imagine what it was like to stand here, back in the day, when all them fooken tanks and soldiers went past?' and all of a sudden he stands to attention and does a kind of salute, which I manage to get on my phone as well.

I tell him we should, like, grab a coffee, maybe in the Grand Hotel and he's like, 'Game ball.'

First, though, Ronan wants to check another shop for his baccy and while he's in there, roysh, I wander over to a news-stand and see a magazine that I think will make him crack up laughing. I pay the woman, who's wearing a mini-skirt even though she has the old sour-milk legs – white and chunky.

We sit in the hotel coffee shop and order a couple of Americanos and I whip out the magazine and go, 'I bought this. It's like *Hello!* except it's for people from your side of the city,' and the joke is, roysh, that it's called *Story*. I hand it to Ro and he cracks his hole laughing. '*Storee?*' he keeps going. '*Storee?*' and then he keeps, like, giggling to himself and going, 'You're a funny fooker, Rosser.'

I open up the picture of me in front of the Russian church and I text it to JP, along with a couple of lines about it from the guidebook – *built in 1912, its onion domes recently repainted in gold leaf donated by Moscow* – and then a line just saying basically I hope you're keeping well, thinking about you, blah blah blah.

And while I'm doing this, Ronan is explaining *Storee* to an American couple at the next table and he's actually quoting me – 'and this fella here says, it's the northside version of *Hello!*' – and it makes me feel great.

We walk back to the gaff across Sofia Garden, where

there's men playing chess at these, like, grey stone tables. And there's another man playing a sort of, like, bagpipe instrument with his hands.

And then I see two birds walking along holding hands – as in, *actually* holding hands – not a bother in the world on them, and I'm storting to think this might not be a bad holiday spot after all.

That's when Ronan turns around to me – out of the blue – and goes, 'Did you notice that fella following us today?'

Of course I'm like, '*Following* us? What are you crapping on about?'

He goes, 'I spotted him when we were in Kentucky. Other side of the road. Fairly big sham, long black coat, had a Ronnie. Was going to say it to you then, but he was gone when we came out. But then he was down outside the cathedral and I'm after seeing him again. In the lobby of the hotel back there.'

I whip around, but of course there's no one there. He has me totally paranoid now. I'm there, 'Do *not* yank my chain – are you serious about this?'

He's like, 'Rosser, there's a reason I've been able to remain at large despite the best efforts of the *Sunday Wurdled* and our friends in the filth. I *know* when I've got a fooken tail.'

But who the fock would want to put *us* under surveillance? And then I'm suddenly thinking about those iffy notes in my pocket and I'm just about to bin them, roysh, thinking I'll get some dosh from an ATM, when I remember that I don't actually *have* any dosh – other than this.

'Let's go in,' Ronan goes, as I'm putting the key in the door, 'get a bit of shut-eye, then hit a titty bar,' and I'm like, 'Yeah, roysh – you're focking dreaming.'

Somebody's been in. The gaff has been turned over – we're talking totally trashed here. And the funniest thing of all is, it's a good two or three hours before either of us notices.

One of the weird things about Bulgaria is that birds under the age of thirty are all, like, total crackers – we're talking catwalk material here. And all the women over fifty look like focking bag-women. So the question is, what happens to them? Is it something they eat? Or does the government, like, export all the lookers?

I'm actually discussing this with Ro over a late breakfast on Vitosha Boulevard, when he turns around to me, totally unexpectedly, and goes, 'No offence, Rosser, but would you mind giving me a bit of space today?'

I'm like, 'Er, not at all,' even though, from my reaction, it's pretty obvious I do.

He goes, 'Me and the boys are always interested in opening up new markets – I told them I'd have a mooch around,' and I'm there, 'Hey, it's cool by me,' and off he goes, eight years old, going on fifty – oh and stiffing me with the Jack and Jill for brekky.

It's amazing, roysh, but I'm bored off my tits within five minutes of him walking off. There always seems to be some, I don't know, edge, always something happening when he's around.

I stroll up Vitosha Boulevard, looking in windows, but they've no equivalent of, like, BTs, Pull & Bear or Tommy over here, so it's a bit of a waste of time. I pass by this shop called Lucky U, which sells, like, ladies' underwear and I'm pretty sure, roysh, that the bird behind the counter, who is the spit of Aoife Ni Thuairisg, gives me the glad eye as I walk past.

So Slick Mick here does his usual trick, he waits around the corner, thinking up a cracking opening line, while letting her think, oh, I've just seen the man of my dreams and he's just walked out of my life . . .

Then I walk back in.

I give her one of my killer smiles, then I go, 'I was just out and about, looking for something pretty – and hey, I think I've just found it.'

Fock me, she's even nicer than Aoife Ni Thuairisg close up.

It doesn't sound like she has a word of English, roysh, because she tries to talk and what comes out of her mouth is such total nonsense that I can't help cracking up laughing in her face.

Then I'm like, 'Hey, I'm really sorry. I just couldn't help but notice you checking me out when I walked past the window. I hope you're not disappointed with the goods,' and again, roysh, she hasn't a focking bog.

So I give it to her in a language every bird understands. I'm there, 'I like you a lot. And my guess is that you like me . . .'

She nods her head. Finally, I'm getting through to her.

'Well,' I go, 'I think you and me could actually make something together . . .'

I look over my shoulder and go, 'Why don't I grab one or two things here – a couple of, shall we say, naughty bits – and we can head back to mine. Actually, better make that yours . . .'

She nods at me again and of course, I move in to seal the deal. I stroke the back of her hand and the next thing I know, roysh, my two feet are in the air and I'm in a headlock and being dragged towards the door by some focking gorilla.

While this is happening, roysh, the bird behind the

counter's going, '*Todor! Molya! Neh! Neh! Molya! Neeehhh!*' and I don't know what it means, roysh, but whatever it is, it saves me from the hiding of a lifetime out on the street, because it turns out that Todor is a former Olympic wrestler, whose name I'll always think of now whenever I try to turn my head fully to the left.

She says something to him in, like, Bulgarian, then he says something back to her and it's back and forth between them for a minute or so before he eventually cracks his hole laughing, then helps me to my feet, or rather lifts me by the belt of my trousers.

Then he goes, 'In Boolgaria, to say yes, we shake our head, yes? To say no, we nod, like zis,' and he nods his head, like she did – *she* as in Margit – his wife. 'You do it other way, yes?'

I go, 'Oh, fock! Look, I'm really sorry – it was, like, a total misunderstanding?' and he's going, 'Is okay, is okay . . . she is very nice, my wife, yes? Very bootiful?' and I'm like, 'Yeah, she's not the worst,' and I'm pretty philosophical about the whole thing, thinking, wait'll she hits fifty, Dude, come and see me then.

'Come,' he goes, 'you haf dreenk with us. No bad feeling, yes?' and I don't think I have the option of saying no. I couldn't nod my head even if I focking wanted to.

We go back into the shop and he disappears underneath the counter, then produces a bottle of something called *rakia* and three shot glasses. It's made from prunes and it tastes like it's been bled from an engine. He offers us a toast in Bulgarian and we all knock one back and it nearly blows my brains out of my ears.

He looks at me, roysh, with water streaming from my eyes and he slaps me on the back and goes, 'You will acquire this taste, yes?' and he pours everyone another.

So eight or nine later, I'm leaving the shop, roysh, totally trolleyed, having said my goodbyes to Todor and Margit and apologized for the thousandth time. And all I want to do now is slip into a coma. I check my phone. It's, like, half-twelve in the day.

I wander back up Vitosha and somehow find my way back to 1040 Knyaz Alexander Donsoukovs. I stagger up the stairs, roysh, and manage to persuade the key into the lock on the fiftieth attempt. I go in, shut the door behind me and find myself staring down the business end of a pretty serious-looking gun.

At the other end, I'm presuming, is the man Ronan described. He's about 6'4", black coat, Ronnie . . .

I'm suddenly *very* focking sober.

I'm like, 'Whoa! Dude, whoever you are, just chillax . . .' and over his roysh shoulder I suddenly hear this, like, laughter – we're talking evil focking laughter – and this older goy, small and pretty much bald, with a sort of, like, beak for a nose, steps out of the shadows and goes, '*Dobar dan* . . .'

I can feel my legs about to go from under me. I haven't had a gun in my face since the day Sorcha's old man asked me about my intentions regarding his daughter.

I don't know how I get the words out, but I manage to go, 'What do you want?' and the little goy goes, 'That is what I am wanting to ask you?'

I'm about to tell him straight out when all of a sudden I hear this almighty focking crack, roysh, and the goy with the gun lets this unbelievable scream out of him, a noise you wouldn't think a human was capable of making. By the time he hits the deck, Ronan's straight on top of him, his foot on his chest and – get this – a sword, a big focking double-edged sword that looks like something out of *King Arthur* at the goy's throat.

301

I look down and I notice that he's managed to somehow kick the goy's kneecap out, but it's the focking sword I can't stop looking at.

I look at Ro as if to say, where the fock did you get that? He goes, 'Ah, I got it up the town. You'd want to see this shop, Rosser – machine guns and every fooken ting . . .'

The little baldy goy laughs. 'Very goot,' he goes. 'Very goot,' and I'm thinking, he'd actually make a great Bond villain, this goy.

Ronan's still got the sword pressed to the other goy's throat. He goes, 'Alreet, start talking Dmitri, or I'm gonna cut this sham a Columbian necktie . . .'

The little goy – I'm sure his name *isn't* Dmitri – goes, 'This man, he is just hired help. What makes you theenk I won't pull out my gun and shoot you all, including him,' but then – and this is focking unbelievable, roysh – quick as a flash, Ronan reaches into his pocket with his other hand, whips out his grenade and puts the pin between his Taylor Keith.

He goes, 'You shoot me and we're all taking the same trip.'

This sends the goy into absolute focking convulsions of laughter and he even storts clapping, which I'm also tempted to do. Then he just nods as if to say, basically, you've got me.

Ronan goes, 'Now, last Christmas a fella who happens to be a personal hero of mine told me that I should be using this,' and he taps the side of his head, 'instead of this,' and he holds up the sword. 'So what do you say we all sit down like clever boys and talk?'

The goy just can't stop smiling. He keeps looking at Ronan, then at me, then back at Ronan again, like he can't believe his own eyes.

'Very goot,' he goes, eventually. 'Come, I know goot rest-aurant,' and on the way out the door he looks back at the goy on the ground and shouts something at him in Bulgarian, which I wouldn't imagine was a compliment.

'The *foie gras*, it is excellent,' he goes.

Ronan's there, 'I'll take your word for it, Boril.' That's the dude's name, by the way.

I can't concentrate on the menu because I keep thinking about the goy back in the aportment. I go, 'Can I just say, I dislocated my kneecap against Belvedere in the Junior Cup, and it was focking agony. You might want to call an ambulance . . .' and Boril goes, 'I haf already arranged for somebawdy to clean up zis mess. The phone call I make in the car . . .' and I'm like, 'Oh, that's Kool and the Gang then.'

So it's *foie gras* all round.

Boril shakes out his napkin and lays it out on his lap. 'I represent certain . . . *eenterests*,' he goes. 'I em a bizziness men. You understend the kind of bizziness I mean, yes?'

I presume it's, like, drugs.

'Loud and clear, Boril,' Ronan goes. 'Loud *and* clear.'

He's really taken to Ro. Like I said – everywhere he goes . . .

'One of my bizzinesses, I operate from 1040 Knyaz Alexander Donsoukovs – apartamunt Nine. I em your neigh-bour, yes?'

I can't help myself. I'm like, 'Oh my *focking* God! No offence, but that's going to knock a few Gs off the value.'

'Hear the man out,' Ronan goes.

Boril's there, 'When I see someone arrive, first I think – is

police, undercover. Then I see you and I think, no, is opposition. You understend what I say by opposition? You have the look of criminals . . .'

Ronan's delighted with that, of course. He nods at me with this big, like, grin on his face, as if to go, what do you think of that, Rosser?

'You thought we were casing your gaff,' Ronan goes, 'to rob whatever you've got in there?'

Boril's like, 'Somesing like zat. Until I see Ross here wizza gun in his face and he about to tell me everysing – zen I sink, no zey cannot be uzzer criminal geng,' and Ronan looks at me and shakes his head, roysh, like I've let him down or some shit.

Then he turns to Boril and goes, 'It seems to me that you need to establish a strategic foothold on that floor, create a buffer zone around you,' and I watch Boril nod, I suppose you'd have to say thoughtfully. 'Now, it just so happens that the proprietor of numbers Seven and Eight is prepared to sell.'

'How much?' Boril goes, straight out with it.

Ronan's like, 'A hundred and twenty thousand of our euros.'

An extra twenty on top. I like his style.

'This is a deal,' Boril goes, no haggling or anything.

We've got rid of those two focking millstones before Ronan's even found out what *foie gras* is. When it arrives, he looks at it like it's something he's wiped off his K Swisses with a lollipop stick.

I tip it onto my plate and ask the waiter to bring him some chips.

After lunch, Boril takes us to his solicitor's office, where we do the paperwork and sit around for three hours, then to the bank, where he wires a hundred Ks to me and Sorcha's current account and gives us the rest in cash, as requested.

And that's it.

'And you,' he goes to Ronan, when we're back in the gaff, packing our bags. 'If effa you need a vurk, I would like very much for you to vurk for me,' and Ronan goes, 'Very flattered, Boril, but I have me own crew back home. Nothing special at the moment, but it's like they say, from little acorns . . . It was good to meet you, but. Fostering links an' that.'

I hand Boril the keys to the two aportments. He shakes my hand and he's gone.

'C'mon, we'll hit the airport,' Ronan goes. 'See can we change our tickets,' and I'm like, 'You want to leave tonight?' and he's there, 'Ah, it's mission accomplished.'

So we take our bags downstairs and out onto the street and we hail a Jo.

When we're queuing at the ticket desk, I turn around to him and I'm like, 'Listen, I just want to say thanks. You know, without you . . . and that twenty thousand sheets – it's yours.'

'No fooken way,' he goes. 'You need it more than I do. Seriously, Rosser, hang on to it. Give it to me sister if anyone. Can I carry it, but, can I?'

I think he likes the idea that it's in, like, a briefcase?

All of a sudden, roysh, my phone rings. I answer it without thinking and it's, like, Gus. Of course he's heard the foreign dial tone and he can't contain his excitement.

'Where are you?' he goes.

I'm like, 'Er, Bulgaria,' and then he turns to whoever's in the office with him and goes, 'He's after going to Bulgaria!

Bulgaria! This is the best *ever*!' and then he turns around to me and he's like, 'You can't *buy* a cursor for a computer, in Bulgaria or anywhere else, you idiot. You've been taken for a mug again. Made to look like a right arsehole,' and he's laughing so hord, roysh, I think he's going to have an actual hort attack.

Before he hangs up, he goes, 'Now get back to the office – on the next available flight.'

I tell Ronan the story as we're walking to the gate and the two of us just crack up. And while we were laughing, I don't notice that I have a missed call. It's from Oisinn and he's left a message telling me to ring him back immediately. And when I do, I end up nearly dropping the phone, because he tells me that Aoife is dead.

10. You Caught Me Smiling Again

I didn't know she played the aeolian horp. I didn't know she loved The Beatles, or that she was learning Russian from tapes, or that she adopted a mountain gorilla who she called George.

I *did* know she was in Amnesty and that she failed her driving test nine times and that her hero was Alanis Morissette and that the rest of the girls wrote to her once – as in Alanis Morissette – when Aoife was really sick and in, like, hospital, and – fair focks to her – she sent Aoife, like, a cord, with a really nice message in it, as in get yourself well, so much to live for, don't let my whiny voice persuade you otherwise, blah blah blah.

I didn't know . . . well, I'd never heard of a gastric tear.

I'm sitting in the sixth row and I'm, like, willing Sorcha to the end of her speech; in my mind I'm helping her along every time her voice cracks, every time there's a silence. She was the best friend Aoife ever had and I'm sure the girl knew it.

It was actually Sorcha who first persuaded her that she had, like, a problem?

The thing is, roysh, I don't ever remember seeing Aoife eat anything other than popcorn when we were at school and I definitely never saw her without a bottle of water in her hand. She always wore big, baggy hoodies over her school jumper, I presume to hide the fact that she was basically skin and bones.

But one day – I'm sure they were in, like, fifth or sixth

year – Sorcha decided to do what Mounties call an intervention, in other words gather a bunch of her friends around to sit her down and tell her to her face that they're, like, worried about her, but they're here for her, blah blah blah.

Sorcha borrowed one of the teacher's offices and told Aoife to meet her there at, I don't know, say, lunchtime, because there was something she wanted to talk to her about. Apparently, by the time Aoife arrived there were, like, fifty or sixty girls in this tiny little office, most of whom she only knew to, like, say hello to – they were just there for the goss. Aoife disappeared under this, like, ruck of birds, who were all trying to lay a hand on some piece of her clothing, just to be able to say they had shared in the moment.

It was, like, Sorcha and Erika who phoned her old pair afterwards, and that was the first time Aoife ended up in hospital.

The first of many . . .

Sorcha holds it together unbelievably well and then she reads a couple of verses from Aoife's favourite poem – something by Dylan Thomas – and then she goes back to the second row and I see Cillian put his orm around her and he whispers something in her ear and what I'm thinking isn't, get your hands off my focking wife, it's, I'm just glad she's got somebody who knows all the right shit to say, today and every day from now on, because fock knows I don't. And never did.

I look at Oisinn. He flew back from Milan for this, just upped and left some fashion show, not a Charlie Bird to anyone. That focking Versace crowd weren't happy, left messages saying he was this, that and the other, unprofessional, blahdy blah, but it's like he says, that shit he can fix. There's no fixing this. No fixing Aoife.

Oisinn taught her how to play golf. I'd forgotten that,

forgotten that we all had our own individual thing with Aoife. I think she was more in love with the *idea* of playing golf than the game itself – especially the four or five hours of walking involved in a round, which she thought about in terms of calories rather than putts. She loved the clobber as well. Turned up for her first lesson in the plus-fours, the golf shoes, the Pringle jumper and a pink beret – and this is for the focking driving range in Sandyford. Her hand–eye co-ordination was hopeless – she couldn't hit a cow's orse with a banjo. I think it was week four before she actually hit the ball. Oisinn said it was one of the sweetest drives he'd ever seen, a fluke of course, but it was the noise – that *thwack* – that had Aoife addicted. She got obsessed with it. Well, you could say that was her personality.

'I played her in Milltown about a month ago,' Oisinn goes, 'and she birdied five holes.'

I tell him we've been to more funerals than weddings in the last six months and that's not the way it's supposed to be at our age. He nods and says we've said goodbye to too many good people.

Behind me, Chloe is filling in Amie with an ie on what she's heard. 'They're saying her brain was swelled to, like, twice its normal size. It was *actually* trying to force its way out of her skull. It's like, *oh* my God, that is SO disgusting . . .'

This is, like, gold dust to someone like her.

'Her stomach basically exploded – it's like, *hell-o!* Her mum came home from the gym and found her, like, naked on the floor of the bathroom. She had all these, like, bruises – as in, like, down below? At first they thought she'd been, you know . . . someone had got her and . . . But that's not what it was. It was, like, all the blood and the food that had emptied into her body cavity and settled down there so it looked like . . .'

I can't listen to any more of this shit.

I turn around, roysh, and I tell her to shut the fock up and it's only when *I* say it that a few other people go, 'Yeah, Chloe, shut the fock up,' but she gives me the evils and goes, 'Don't take it out on me just because your wife is here with somebody else,' which she's obviously been thinking about, because it's not the kind of shit you say on the spur of the moment.

I turn back and face the front of the church again. The priest is doing the 'go in peace' bit.

Fionn stands up first and then Aoife's old man and two younger brothers follow him over to the coffin and the four of them lift it up onto their shoulders and lead the procession slowly down the aisle, while her cousin, who's in, like, the R&R, sings 'Here Comes The Sun', which was Aoife's favourite song.

I'm standing right next to the aisle and I try to catch Fionn's eye, but he just looks straight ahead. See, they had a row before she died, based on what I'd told him. She went off in a snot, went back to her old pair's, and it was there that they found her four hours later – that bit's true – on the floor of the jacks.

I look at Aoife's old dear, who, for some reason, always liked me. Whenever I was in the gaff, she'd go, 'You get a bad press, Ross, and you don't deserve it,' and it hurts me now to see her like this, a broken woman. Her only daughter . . .

This whole scene – too focked up for words.

Erika gives me a sad smile. Then Sorcha passes and I don't know what way to look at her, roysh, so I sort of, like, set my features in this, like, frozen expression, but as she walks by she grabs my hand and gives it a little squeeze and it's like she's going, hey, we might have no future, but days

312

like this remind us that we *do* have a history and don't forget it, because I won't.

I stand there, listening to the song and I like that line where he goes, 'I think that ice is slowly melting'. Because that's how it feels this morning. Nothing like a funeral to remind you that you're still alive.

Me and Oisinn step out into the aisle and shuffle out into the rain with everyone else. I notice Amie with an ie throwing her orms around Sorcha and telling her that Aoife was lucky to have – *oh my God* – SUCH a good friend and it's one of those compliments, roysh, that you give and expect the other person to say the same shit about you. Of course, Sorcha doesn't oblige her.

I spot Lauren. It was good of her to come home. I tip over to her and she greets me a lot more warmly than I would have expected.

'Congratulations,' I go and she immediately rubs her stomach, even though she's not showing yet, and goes, 'Thanks. Christian sends his love.'

I nod. Then I'm like, 'How is he?'

She goes, 'In shock – first the baby and then . . . *this.*'

'The circle of life,' I go. It's probably the deepest thing I've ever said and I haven't a focking clue where it came from.

Lauren looks at me, warmly, you'd have to say, and goes, 'The circle of life.'

I'm there, 'And work's going well for him, yeah?' and she's like, 'Great. He's been given six months to devise six new characters for a possible new *Star Wars* trilogy,' and she doesn't even need to tell me how in his element he is after that. 'Why don't you come over and visit?' she goes.

I'm there, 'I will. One day. I've got, you know, responsibilities . . .'

I feel a slap on my back. It's Oisinn. 'Wise too late, old too soon,' he goes, which sums it up better than I could.

Behind us I can hear Chloe crying, telling Amie with an ie that she's lost one of her best friends in the world and I don't know whether she's being, like, sincere or not. Sometimes it's difficult to tell with birds.

Me, Oisinn and Lauren wander over to Fionn. Poor focker looks like he hasn't slept in days. His eyes are just, like, dead. It's hord to know the right thing to say. There *is* no right thing to say.

'We were going to get married in this church,' he goes and then the tears just stort spilling out of his eyes. All of our eyes, if I'm being honest. Lauren goes to, like, comfort him but he goes, 'It's okay, it's okay,' and he takes off his glasses, wipes his tears with the palm of his hand, then puts them back on again and goes, 'I promised myself I'd stay strong today. If only for Aoife's mum.'

We all just nod.

'I loved her,' he goes. Then it's his turn to nod. He's there, 'I think she died knowing that at least,' and he turns and looks at me, roysh, pleadingly, if that's the word, like he wants to know if this is really happening, whether I can say something to, like, magic it all away.

'Of course she knew,' Lauren goes. 'You made her very happy, Fionn,' but quick as a flash he's there, 'But not happy enough,' and no one, like, contradicts him, probably because what he said is true.

'We're, er, going back to Aoife's house after the graveyard,' he goes. 'You goys are coming, aren't you?' and again it's the eyes. 'I kind of, er, need good people around me today,' and we all end up going, 'Yeah,' even though it's the last place in the world any of us wants to be.

I don't have the words for this kind of scene. It's

grown-up shit. But being there – just focking *being* there – is the closest any of us is going to get to saying goodbye.

I send Sorcha a text, roysh, not trying to get back in there or anything, but just to say I'm really sorry, I know you've lost a really good friend, you're in my basic thoughts and I thought your speech at the funeral touched pretty much everyone. And straight away I get one back going, 'Thanx ross thats v kind. She was ur friend2. I hope ur ok xxx.'

It's, like, half-five on a Friday afternoon, roysh, I'm finished work and I'm in Eddie Rocket's on South Anne Street, wrapping my face around a Classic with, like, bacon and cheese fries, when I notice this bird – think Delta Goodrem except even nicer – staring at me from the other side of Ed's. She's, like, writing something down, roysh, but she keeps looking up, copping an eyeful of the Rossmeister – obviously thinking, I can't stop looking at that guy, even if he is out of my league – and then looking down again as soon as I catch her eye.

Of course, Slick Mick here can't be content with just being adored from afar. He has to go over, have a sniff.

I'm like, 'Hey,' playing it *über*-cool.

'Oh, hi,' she goes, looking up, suddenly all embarrassed. Could be wrong, but I think she's actually a Septic tank.

I'm there, 'I couldn't help but notice that you were giving me loads there.'

She's like, 'Giving you what?' and I'm there, 'You were staring at me.'

'I'm really, really sorry,' she goes, except the way she says it, it's like, *rully, rully*. She *is* a Septic tank.

She's there, 'I was actually *drawing* you,' and I'm like, 'Drawing me?' and she goes, 'Sure,' and she pushes a piece of paper across the table at me, roysh, and I look down at it and it *is* an actual picture of me.

I'm there, 'That's pretty good. I think I'm probably a bit more, I don't know, muscley on top, though,' and she laughs, roysh, like she thinks I'm joking.

'I'm Shauna,' she goes, offering me her hand, roysh, and I shake it and I'm like, 'I'm Ross. And the pleasure is mine . . . believe me,' laying it on like peanut butter and jelly.

I ask her where in the States she's from and she goes, 'South Carolina,' and I've never heard of it, roysh, so I tell her that I was in Ocean City on a J1er a few years ago and I'd tell her some of the stories, except they're pretty X-rated and she cracks her hole laughing.

Then she goes, 'I hope you didn't mind me drawing you. I thought you had an interesting face,' and I'm like, 'Interesting, as in . . .' and she's there, 'Interesting, as in *intriguing*,' flirting her orse off with me now.

I'm there, 'Do you want to get out of here?' hoping she's on holidays and she's staying in, like, the Westbury or some shit.

She goes, 'Hey, we could go to, like, Stephen's Green. It's such a beautiful evening,' and even though it's not quite what I had in mind, roysh, I'm thinking, if I'm going to get into this bird's Alan Whickers, I'm going to have to play along with the whole romantic scene she's obviously got going on in her head.

Of course at this stage, roysh, I haven't copped that there's something NQR about Shauna. I go, 'Okay, let's hit the Green then.'

I stand up, roysh, and she stands up at the same time and something – I don't know, maybe some little voice in my head – tells me to look down, which I do, and that's when I notice . . .

And everyone in Ed's notices . . .

She's wearing rollerblades.

I don't *actually* believe it. I've pulled a focking bird on wheels.

'Where are you going?' she goes as I put the head down and go off in the direction of Dawson Street.

I'm there, 'Er, Stephen's Green,' and she's like, '*Hello?* The Green is *this* way,' and she flicks her thumb, roysh, in the direction of Grafton Street, but there is no way in this focking world I'm going to risk being seen with her like that.

I've a rep in this town.

I carry on walking, roysh, but of course she's faster on her feet than I am and suddenly she's, like, skating circles around me, going, 'Come on, *this* way,' and she grabs me by the hand and storts pulling me in the direction I *don't* want to go and there's nothing I can do, short of spinning her around a few times and focking her through the window of Pia Bang Home.

So I end up letting myself be dragged onto Grafton Street. It's, like, quarter to six on a Friday evening and all the shops and offices are emptying out. Town is focking rammers. I'm thinking, *someone* is bound to focking see me.

My hort's in my mouth the whole way up the street. Shauna's, like, holding my hand and performing, I don't know, pirouettes and all sorts of focking tricks that are drawing a lot of eyes in our direction. She's also going, at the top of her voice, 'All my friends say, *You're crazy!* But it's like, *hey, but that's Shauna! She's wild!*'

There's something seriously wrong with this bird, as in the wheel's still turning but the hamster's dead.

We're standing at the lights, roysh, opposite the Grafton

Street entrance to the Green, and while I'm waiting for the green man I'm thinking, how am I going to get out of this, and then all of a sudden I spot a couple of Clongowes goys I know on the other side of the road, waiting to cross. I'm thinking, those goys hate my guts – I actually can't give them any more material on me, so I end up nearly tearing Shauna's orm out of her socket, I pull her that hord.

'Where are we going now?' she goes as I'm dragging her in the opposite direction, towards TGI Friday's.

I'm like, 'I just want to check out the, er, menu in here,' and she's there, 'But you've just eaten,' but I don't answer her, roysh, I just haul her sad orse up the road behind me, shielding my boat race with my other hand.

I have a quick George Hook in the window, then I go, 'Fock it, you're bang-on. I *have* already eaten. Let's hit the Green now,' and I stort dragging her across the road, thinking, okay, that's that potentially embarrassing situation sorted, now I'm, like, ten seconds away from losing you.

The road is, like, cobbled, roysh, which means she has to, like, walk rather than skate across. I'm holding her hand, roysh, and I'm walking pretty fast. And that's when, all of a sudden, I hear what would have to be described as a sharp scream out of Shauna and when I whip round, it turns out that she's got one of her skates caught in the focking Luas line.

The whole evening is turning into a focking mare and I swear to God, roysh, it's like it's never going to end.

So she's down on one knee, roysh, and she's trying to free the wheels from the track, but whatever way she stepped on it, they've, like, clicked in there pretty securely. So she can, like, move the skate up and down the rail, but she can't pull it out and she's storting to panic now, roysh, because it's rush hour and those trams are, like, every seven minutes or some shit.

'Just take the skate off,' I go, pretty aware of the fact that she's drawing a lot of heat on us here.

She's like, 'I *can't*. They were a present from my *mom*,' and I'm there, 'Well, she's going to be burying you in them if you stay here.'

People are storting to gather around us, roysh, and I have to tell you, I'm not enjoying the attention. All of a sudden some focking Luas worker comes pegging it down the road towards us and he's going, 'Out of the way, everyone! Let me through, let me through,' except it's like, *let me troo*, because he's obviously WC.

The first thing he does, roysh, is he gets on the radio and tells, I don't know, *whoever*, to stop all northbound trams on the green line until further notice. Then he gets down on his hunkers and storts trying to free the skate and all the time Shauna's telling him, 'Whatever happens, I am *not* taking it off . . .'

I look around, roysh. There must be, like, seventy or eighty people crowded around us, roysh, and of course the more people that gather around, the more people get interested.

I'm trying to look like I'm not actually with her, catching various people's eyes – good-looking birds, in other words – and throwing my eyes up to heaven.

Someone mentions the fire brigade and I'm suddenly thinking, oh my God, if this ends up being the funny little item on the end of the *Six One* news tonight, I'm going to have to focking emigrate.

I'm standing there, thinking, maybe I'll just take a couple of steps backwards here and just, like, disappear into the crowd, when all of a sudden the Luas goy stands up, looks at me and goes, 'You're going to have to push her.'

I'm like, 'Excuse me, say that again,' and he's there, 'Push her. If she won't take the skate off,' and I'm like, 'Where am I pushing her? Do *not* say Dundrum Town Centre.'

'Peter's Place,' he goes. 'It's only about a mile. Left at the top of Harcourt Street, then right. That's where the track goes overground again. She should just . . . slot out there,' and I'm like, 'No way – fock that,' and Shauna's suddenly going, 'Ross, you can't leave me here,' playing to the focking gallery, roysh, and suddenly they're all on her side, telling me in no uncertain terms that there's no way they're going to let me abandon her.

I turn to the crowd and I'm like, 'Can we get one thing straight here – she's not even my bird. I only pulled her, like, twenty minutes ago – and straight away I was having second thoughts,' but it makes no difference.

From the looks I'm getting, there's no doubt this crowd will focking lynch me if I even attempt to walk away from her.

So what else can I do, except put my hands under Shauna's orms and help her to her feet, and then with my two hands on her orse – and her standing on one leg – stort pushing her towards the top of Harcourt Street.

Of course, the crowd decides to follow us, and now that the immediate danger of her getting killed by a focking tram has passed, they're all beginning to see the funny side of it.

They're all cracking their holes laughing as I push Shauna past Shanahan's and as far as the traffic-lights just outside the eircom building, which, as it happens, are red.

'Do you stop at Windy Arbour?' some focking smort-orse shouts from the side of the road and I'm going, 'I can't actually believe I'm doing this. If it wasn't for this crowd, I'd be SO out of here – I don't care what you look like,' and Shauna tells me I'm an asshole, which I can live with.

The lights go green and I stort pushing her again and, as

we're crossing the junction onto Harcourt Street, she storts going, 'Look both ways! Look both ways!' which I do.

I hadn't actually realized that Harcourt Street was so uphill and we're not that far up it when I stort to feel it in my back. So I stop, roysh, and of course not one of the hundred or so people following us offers to take over. All too busy laughing.

A southbound tram passes us on the other track and the driver – who's *real* Dublin – shouts something out of his window, which I don't hear, but it makes everyone laugh, so I end up just giving him the finger and he drives on – slowly, I might add, to make sure everyone on board gets a good focking eyeful.

We pass Copper's and I'm thinking, that's where I'm going to pull in future. At least you know what you're getting there. And I can't say this is better than being with a bogger.

For some reason, roysh, I stort thinking about that scene in, like, the Bible, when that guy helps Jesus carry the cross up that focking hill, with all those other people following them, abusing him and basically ripping the piss.

And then JP pops into my head, roysh, and I'm thinking, I need to ring his gaff, see how he is. What kind of, like, mate am I if I don't?

'What's this?' some focking wisecracker shouts from the side of the road, 'transport cutbacks?' I turn around to Shauna and I just happen to mention that this better be worth all this effort, roysh, and she asks me what I mean by that.

I go, 'As in, the sex,' and I'm thinking, she actually has a cracking little orse, in fairness to her.

She suddenly goes, '*Sex?!*' pretty much spitting the word out and almost losing her focking balance in the process. She looks at me over her shoulder and goes, 'Believe me, I

have *no* intention of having sex with you – I don't know what kind of girl you think I am . . .'

And it's there, roysh, three-quarters of the way up Harcourt Street, just outside Little Caesar's, that it's time for me and Shauna to say goodbye – and fock what anyone thinks.

I turn around to the crowd and I go, 'You all heard that, I presume?' and then – and I'm pretty proud of this, it has to be said – I'm like, 'I'm afraid this is my stop.'

'Ross!' he goes, like he's just seen a focking ghost.

I'm like, 'Hey, Mr Conroy,' and he storts giving it, 'Look, if it's about your overseas property portfolio, let me just say, in five years, Sofia is going to be the Paris of Eastern Europe . . .' but I don't actually give a fock about the aportments any more. I'm actually past it.

I just go, 'How's JP?'

He seems a little, I suppose, taken aback. 'Oh, calmer now,' he goes, then he opens the door fully, roysh, and invites me in. 'He's on valium, or one of those.'

I'm like, 'Can I see him?' and he takes a deep breath. Then he breathes out and at the same time goes, 'You're not bringing him any . . . religious paraphernalia, are you? A Bible, for instance. The doctor said . . .' and I'm like, 'How would *I* get my hands on something like that? Look, I believe in God, but up to a point,' and I hold out my orms, roysh, basically telling him to, like, frisk me if he doesn't believe me.

'Okay,' he goes and he lets me past and I tip up the stairs and find JP in his old bedroom, lying there in, like, total dorkness. I try to get a conversation going, but he doesn't answer me. There's, like, total silence for ten, maybe fifteen minutes.

I get up, walk across to the window and pull the curtain open a couple of inches and the light from outside nearly blinds me. When my eyes adjust, I notice Donna Halley, JP's next-door neighbour, who I've always had a thing for, putting her gearbag into the boot of her old dear's BMW 318 Ci Coupé. I know goys who've joined Crunch just to focking stare at her top tens twice a week. It's time our paths crossed again. I'm sure she's forgotten that shit that happened at the Muckross debs.

'There's a newspaper clipping on that desk over there,' JP goes all of a sudden. 'Would you bring it over?' and I'm like, cool, no probs, and I root around the desk for a few seconds and find it.

He turns on the lamp by his locker and I can see that the headline says, 'Man, 28, dies in N4 crash,' and he hands it to me.

I give it the quick west-to-east and I'm like, 'Yeah? So what?'

He goes, 'Read it,' and I sort of, like, throw my eyes up to heaven, but then I do actually read it, just to focking humour him. It's like, twenty-eight-year-old IT worker . . . lost control of his car . . . hit a tree . . . died instantly . . . same old, same old.

'I went to the inquest,' JP goes. 'You know, very few people just *lose control* of their cars, Ross. The coroner said he probably fell asleep. He was commuting to Dublin from Cloghan every morning, then driving back in the evening. A five-hour round-trip . . .'

I'm like, 'Where the fock is Cloghan anyway?' and he goes, 'Just outside Mullingar. According to the coroner, falling asleep at the wheel is the new drink-driving – people getting up in the middle of the night to drive a couple of hours to their stressful jobs, then driving home in the dark. We've all known the feeling, haven't we – when the eyes close for just a split-second. Terrifying . . .'

I'm there, 'Hang on a sec – why do you give a fock about this dead goy?'

'Because,' he goes, 'I sold him his house.'

I'm just, like, stunned into silence. I wouldn't know what to say even if I could talk.

He's there, 'See, *I* told him, Ross. Commutable distance to Dublin, I said. So you tell me – have I not blood on my hands? Two thousand euros was my commission from that sale. He had a wife and a little girl. Three years old . . .'

I end up totally losing it. I'm like, 'JP, will you focking stop!' knowing in my hort of horts, roysh, that I must have told the same lie a hundred times when I worked for his old man. All those people you hear about on the radio, dying in cor crashes, day in, day out – who knows how many of them I've met, and yet their names mean fock-all to me because, back then, all you ever thought about was, like, making the sale.

'So *this* is what's been eating you?' I go. 'Basically guilt over some goy you probably only met two or three times. Dude, *he* bought the gaff. You didn't force him.'

He's there, 'We've lost our moral compass as a society . . .' and I decide I'm not letting him get into his stride here.

I'm like, 'There doesn't always have to be a moral to every focking story. Everything doesn't come back to the Celtic Tiger. Sometimes the moral of the story is just, basically, shit happens!'

'Thank you, St Thomas Aquinas,' he goes.

I don't even smile. That kind of gag might have made him Chris Rock out in Maynooth, but he's not in focking priest school any more.

I stand up and I'm like, 'Look, I'll call in again tomorrow

– see how you are,' and suddenly, roysh, he's giving me the cow eyes and for the first time I notice that he's sweating like a Munster fan in Copper's.

He goes, 'Would you mind just . . .' and I hold my hands up and I'm like, 'No! Don't even ask it.'

He tries to push fifty bills into my hand and he's going, 'Just two books. You'll get them in Veritas. Please, Ross. *If You Want To Walk On Water You've Got To Get Out Of The Boat* and *Insights Of The Psalms.*'

I'm like, 'Dude, no!' and I stand up and walk out of there as he shouts, 'Even my King James, Ross. *Please!*'

But I don't even look back. There are times when you've got to be tough.

I'm supposed to be out getting Gus a glass hammer and a couple of skirting ladders, but instead I'm in Café-en-Seine with Oisinn, the two of us throwing it down our Gregorys today, pretty much horrendufied at, like, three o'clock in the afternoon.

I'm filling him in on my visit to JP, which probably explains why I'm tanning it like I am.

'When's your old man's case?' he goes, changing the subject.

I'm like, 'The day after tomorrow. They're saying *five* years now, because he pleaded, like, guilty and shit?'

Oisinn's eyes follow some absolute focking boiler to the ladies'. The goy can't help himself.

'How will he feel about that?' he goes and I'm there, 'As in my old man? I don't know. He's just obsessed with this, like, rugby team he's storted in there. I don't know if he's using that as a sort of, like, escape from what's happened to his life . . .'

I get another two pints in and a couple of sambucas as well, because it actually feels like we're celebrating something, although I'm not sure what.

'Do you need any moolah?' he goes. Just like that. Out of the blue. He's a good goy, Oisinn.

I'm like, 'Thanks, Dude. No, I've a few grand left from the sale of those aportments. Plus, I actually got paid yesterday,' but then he goes, 'Ross, do yourself a favour – that job's beneath you. You know, I think you only took it because you thought you needed to be, I don't know, punished. I think you've beaten yourself up enough?'

He leaves me with that thought and focks off to wait outside the ladies' for that mutt to come out.

I sit there for a few moments, then I ring the number, without even knowing what I'm going to say, and I end up getting put straight through to Gus. He can obviously hear Gwen Stefani in the background because he goes, 'Where are you?'

I'm just like, 'I'm in a battle-cruiser, getting pissed on your time.'

He's there, 'What?' obviously thinking he's misheard me.

'There's no such thing as a glass hammer,' I go. 'I know that,' and he's like, 'What about the skirting ladders – would you just pick them up?' and I'm there, 'Gus, all those things you sent me for, I knew they were bullshit all along. The left-handed pliers, the box of grid squares, the metric spanner . . . I knew there was no such thing. I just used it to get out of work.'

He's pretty much speechless. 'I gave you a break,' he goes, 'when you had nothing . . .' and I'm like, 'Well, I *still* have nothing – and I'm telling you to stick your job up your focking orse.'

'It doesn't work like that,' he goes. 'You'll have to work

out your notice——' but I hang up on him, just like that.

I put my phone down on the bar and I spot a bird standing just a couple of feet away, with a big smile on her boat race. She's a ringer for Sarah Chalke.

So I'm just there, 'What are *you* smiling at?' but in a really, like, flirty way.

'Nothing,' she goes, still smiling. 'I just wish *I* had the guts to do that.'

She's trying to get the borman's attention, roysh, sort of, like, tilting her head backwards every time she thinks he's looking in her direction, but he keeps missing her, which suits me down to the ground.

'There's really nothing to it,' I go. 'You just need to get enough beers into you to think that you don't need a job any more.'

She's like, 'You think you'll regret it in the morning?' and I'm there, 'Pretty much, yeah . . .'

She asks me what the job was and of course my first instinct is to, like, make something up – mention, I don't know, Davy Stockbrokers or A&L Goodbody – but for some reason, roysh, maybe it's her honest face, I don't. I tell her I was collecting tampie bins. I actually collected the bins from *here*.

'Oh, you'll regret that alright,' she goes and then she points at my empty pint glass and she goes, 'Can I get you a drink?' just as the borman finally cops her.

'Er, yeah, just a pint,' I go. 'I probably should lay off the sambucas,' and she gives the borman her order.

She turns around and tells me not to worry, that the perfect job is out there just waiting for me and I ask her how she knows, roysh, and she says she works in recruitment. She pays the borman for the round – I count the drinks; it must be her and one, two, three, four friends – and while she's waiting for her change she goes, 'What's your qualification?' and I end up laughing in her face, roysh, and then of course having to apologize.

I'm there, 'Look, I don't even have my Leaving. I was always, like, too into my rugby. Always thought I'd end up playing for Leinster, Ireland, blah blah blah. Of course, now I'm, like, twenty-four – in other words, past it. I've got, like, two kids, a broken marriage . . .' and all of a sudden, roysh, she pulls my pint away from me and goes, 'Whoa! You really don't want any more of this,' and we both laugh.

She tells me she's just going to bring the drinks over to her friends and she'll be back. When she's gone, roysh, Oisinn drops by with the Bride of Frankenstein in tow. I must have sobered up a bit because he suddenly seems way more hammered than me.

'I'm taking face-ache here back to mine,' and the bird hears him, roysh, but gives him a sort of, like, playful slap and goes, 'You're terrible,' and Oisinn tells me he'll text me.

Melanie – it turns out that's her name – comes back about half an hour later, long enough for me to know she's not desperate. She's good, this bird, quite possibly a player.

I spend the time knocking back 7-Up, trying to sober myself up, just in case there's any afters.

'Your mates don't mind,' I go. 'As in me stealing you away?' and she's there, 'Hey, you haven't stolen me anywhere yet.'

She's a focking stunner. And the more 7-Up I drink, the more beautiful she gets, which is, like, a reversal of the way it usually works for me.

We spend the whole night talking. She's from Malahide, but she lives in town. She has four sisters – two are doctors and I forget what the other ones do. Her old dear is brown bread and her old man lives mostly in the States. She's twenty-four. She's had two serious boyfriends, but she's never been hurt. And there's, like, loads of other stuff . . .

At the end of the night I offer to walk her home, being the total gentleman that I am. We cut down South Anne Street, onto Grafton Street and then down Sussex Street on Dame Street. She tells me, roysh, that she lives three doors down from Club Lapello, a lappy where, let's just say, my ugly mug is pretty well known. All the way down Dame Street, I'm just praying the goys on the door don't give me away.

Of course, typical focking bouncers, they cop me from, like, fifty yords away and they're all smiles when they see me with a bird. They know my form. I'm crapping it, but in fairness to them, they pretend not to know me, though they do say hello to Melanie, roysh. I ask her how she knows them and she goes, 'Just from walking by . . .'

So she puts the key in the door and she turns around, holding it open with her back, and goes, 'Well, I really enjoyed tonight,' and it's pretty obvious, roysh, that I'm not getting in here.

You don't need a weathercock to tell you when you're pissing into the wind.

'Maybe we could, er, do it again?' I go, trying not to sound too John B. and failing miserably. She says that'd be nice and we swap numbers.

Then we kiss, roysh, and it's not the *Ibiza Uncovered* number that birds usually pull on me. And after, like, ten seconds of that, she says goodnight and closes the door in my boat race.

And of course, now I've got to face the walk of shame

past the two bouncers. I consider pulling a sly one, crossing the road and pegging it up Dame Street, but if they spot me, it'll only make it worse. I walk past, roysh, looking a bit more sheepish than they're used to seeing me, it has to be said.

'God loves a trier,' one of them goes, just loud enough for me to hear, and I end up just giving him the finger.

'Are you not coming in?' the other one shouts after me and the two of them crack their holes laughing.

But then, just as I'm reaching the rank opposite Trinity, my phone beeps and it's a text from Melanie and it's like, 'They were lovely kisses,' and I feel happy, as in genuinely happy, for the first time in a long, long time.

I was expecting something. Don't know what – but *something*. A speech from the dock. All that shit he said to me, I thought he'd hit them with that. This gleaming New Ireland, he told me yesterday, with infrastructure and investment and full employment, that was his vision of the future and the vision of all of those now being pilloried before the tribunals.

I thought he'd go down fighting, not like a wuss, which is what he is in my book.

It's all over unbelievably quickly. Four days. The State outlines its case against him and his barrister – his *new* barrister, who actually doesn't look that much older than me – basically holds his hands up and goes, okay, my client admits basically everything, but please be gentle with him.

'Listen to that cloying sycophant,' Hennessy goes. He's sitting next to me in the public gallery. 'Oh, yes, he's going all the way to the top, that one – got his careerist tongue up all the right holes in the Law Library. If only your dad had let *me* represent him . . .'

Every morning when he's led into the court, the old man shouts some update to us about his focking team — that chap Bowie handles like a BMW 330i, young Liamo Garton might have strained his levator scapulae, Lex would push Shane Byrne hord for his Ireland place if he wasn't serving the best part of a life sentence . . .

Then he just sits there for the day, roysh, with a little smile on his boat, saying fock-all, which Ronan loves, of course. He's on the other side of me, constantly winking at the old man or giving him the thumbs-up or turning around to total strangers in the public gallery, roysh, and telling them that that's his granddad up there and that if he'd named names, he'd be sleeping in his own bed tonight, but he didn't. 'He kept *that* shut,' he goes, pointing at his mouth. 'First rule of the underwurdled . . .'

Which is pretty funny and helps the day pass because the whole thing is pretty boring, it has to be said, most of it taken up by what they call legal argument, which I have no desire to understand.

Then at the end of four days, the judge tells the old man to stand up, which he does. And even though I'm not exactly his number-one fan, I have to admit that this is the most tense I've been since I led Castlerock onto the field against Newbridge College in the Leinster Schools Senior Cup final in 1999.

'Charles O'Carroll-Kelly,' the judge goes, 'whatever private beliefs you hold, the crimes of which you are guilty were not victimless crimes. As a property developer, you admitted paying bribes in order to subvert the proper planning process and you did it in the name of greed. Most of your developments went ahead against the wishes and better advice of local authority planners with vast experience, whose job it was to ensure a sensible and balanced growth for the city and county of Dublin. In doing so, you helped to create a legacy of social problems in many of the city's poorer areas . . .'

One thing I will say about the old man is that he's not taking this shit like a schoolkid getting a bollocking from a teacher – he's standing there with his head up, looking the judge straight in the eye.

'This court takes an especially dim view of this conduct, given your later election as a councillor for Dún Laoghaire-Rathdown, in which position, by your own admission, you *solicited* bribes from property developers.'

He goes, 'Your systematic evasion of tax was part of a general culture of avoidance, which deprived the Irish economy of billions of euros per annum, starving public services such as schools and hospitals of money. . .'

The old man looks at me – he obviously wants to know what I'm thinking.

'However,' the judge goes, 'in sentencing you, I must give due regard to your co-operation in this matter. Once some measure of corruption was discovered, you came clean, saving the Gardaí thousands of man-hours following the complex paper trail that constituted your personal finances for the best part of your life.

'I must be cognisant, too, of your settlement with the Criminal Assets Bureau and the Revenue Commissioners, which will ensure that, when you finally leave prison, it will be to a considerably reduced lifestyle than that to which you are accustomed . . .'

When you finally leave prison. He's definitely sending him down. You can hear this, like, buzz sweep through the press gallery.

Then it's like, 'I note from the report of your social worker that you have been an exemplary remand prisoner and the

Governor and staff of Mountjoy Jail have been lavish in their praise of the leadership role you have assumed amongst your fellow prisoners. You have started, I understand, a prison rugby team, helping at least four long-term addicts to achieve complete withdrawal from heroin. I hope that, upon your release, you will continue to work with those who have never enjoyed the same privileges as you and that this work will be part of your reparation to the community . . .

'However, given the scale of your dishonesty – and in particular your abuse of public office – I *am* going to impose a custodial sentence. And that sentence is two-and-a-half years' imprisonment, with the time you have already served on remand taken off the end of your sentence. You look like you have something to say, Mr O'Carroll-Kelly?' and you can see everyone, like, sit forward in their chairs.

And all the old man says – the only words he speaks in four focking days sitting there – is, 'With respect, Your Honour, it would be wrong to interpret my, inverted commas, co-operation with the Criminal Assets Bureau and the Revenue Commissioners as an indicator of remorse on my part. I feel none. Thank you.'

Hennessy turns around to me and goes, 'He's already done nine months. With remission, he'll be out by Christmas,' and then he shouts, 'Don't worry, Charles, you'll be out by Christmas!' and the judge, who's already not a happy bunny over what the old man said, goes, 'Anyone engaging in triumphalism in my court will find themselves jailed for contempt,' and then suddenly the old man's being led away.

Out by Christmas.

And it might be my imagination, roysh, but he seems, I don't know, somehow disappointed.

*

335

I walk into the gaff. The old dear's in the study, on the Wolfe Tone by the sounds of it. She's obviously on to her focking publisher, roysh, because she's going, 'You're not *listening* to me – I want to change the entire *plot* . . . Well, *stop* printing it. Yes! I want Lovell written out of it early on, maybe even killed off. Yes, he has his head turned by some young Lolita, yes, a little coquette of a thing. He struggles to bridge the age gap and he has a heart attack and dies. But not before he becomes impotent . . .'

Something about the gaff feels different. I peg it up the stairs, push open the old dear's bedroom door and I just crack my hole laughing. All of *his* shit is gone, the ponytailed prick.

I peg it down the stairs, roysh, we're talking two at a time, burst into the office and go, 'Welcome to Dumpsville.'

'Ross, I'm on the phone,' she goes.

I'm like, 'In case you're interested, your husband was jailed for, like, two and a half years today?' but she just goes, 'Ross, this is important.'

I just look her up and down and I'm there, 'You are going to make one sad, ugly, lonely old bag.'

It was actually Fionn's idea. I wondered whether it was, like, too soon for him to be doing, like, morbid shit like this, but he said that getting out of the country for a couple of days would actually do him good.

'And besides,' he goes, 'I made him a promise.'

Which is basically how the two of us end up in Paris on a Friday in May, walking the streets of the Jewish quarter with what's left of Father Fehily in, like, an urn.

'If the school board got word of this,' he goes, 'I'd probably lose my job.'

He's left me in charge of the directions – er, *not* a good

idea? Especially with the map being in French. Okay, we've just left the Metro station, roysh, so this has to be the Rue de Rivoli. *Rue* must mean street.

I'm like, 'Why would you get the bullet over this?' playing for time more than anything.

Fionn goes, 'One or two of the Brothers – Alfonsus and Ignatius, basically – they didn't want him cremated in the first place. They were overruled by the family. Catholics are cool with cremation. But sprinkling the ashes – that's a complete no-no. They believe that cremated remains should be treated with the same respect as a body.'

I'm like, 'Sounds like a focking crock to me . . . I probably should tell you, by the way, that I think we're lost,' and I hand him the map. He looks at it for, like, five seconds, roysh, then he goes, 'We're not lost – that's the Rue Pavée over there,' and as we cross the road, roysh, I look up at the sign and it *is* the Rue Pavée and I'm thinking, should I crack a gag about the name? But then I think, no, it's probably not that kind of day.

'There's the synagogue,' Fionn goes.

Right enough there's a sort of, like, church on the other side of the road with what I think is called the Star of David on the front of it and then four or five young kids with, like, skullcaps walk out and Fionn can't resist it, roysh, he's straight over to them, blabbing away to them in, like, French – you have to laugh at him – looking for, like, facts and figures, as if his brain isn't full enough.

Eventually, I'm like, 'Fionn – come on!' and he turns around to me, roysh, and in this, like, sing-song voice, he goes, '*Oh, zut alors! Je suis désole!*' and he says *au revoir* or whatever it is to his new mates and we walk on.

We stop at the top of the road and Fionn looks both ways.

'This is the Rue des Rosiers,' he goes, pronouncing it the way the French do, half a pint of phlegm in his throat and half a pint down my shirt. 'The heart of the Jewish quarter. Look around you, Ross,' because he knows my attention span wouldn't be the Rory Best. 'Look at the shops.'

It's all, like, Kosher Pizza, Chir Hadach and the Goldenberg Deli, which has a little blackboard hung on the door with loads of, like, French on it, though I do recognize the word hummus, and of course it makes me think of Sorcha.

We pass a little bookshop, which has, like, a postcard stand outside and Fionn stops and pulls out a couple of cards, sort of, like, studying them. 'Look at that one. *Le quartier juif à l'angle de la rue des Rosiers et la rue des Ecouffes – 1939,*' and he hands it to me and I stare at this really, like, grainy picture, taken from the exact spot where we're standing now and the street is, like, teeming with people, all with hats on, even the kids, and there's carts on the road and things hanging up outside shops and then just a random milk churn and a sign that says Café 10, and I suppose I'm getting some idea of what this place was like when Fehily lived here.

I hand it back to him and he goes into the shop and buys it, along with two more – one of a big line of German soldiers marching up the Champs-Élysées towards the Arc de Triomphe, and another of people celebrating and it's like, *'Paris Libre! Août 1944'.*

We walk around for another half an hour and I suppose, if the truth be told, I'm actually storting to chill out and enjoy myself.

It turns out Fehily and Vianne lived on a road called Rue de Thorigny, a narrow little street, roysh, almost opposite where the Picasso Museum is now. Their gaff is a big white building, five storeys high, with pretty big windows, but it's not, like, aportments any more. It's all been turned into offices.

I turn around to Fionn and I'm like, 'So what do we do? Just tip them here, on the doorstep?'

Fionn goes, 'Seems wrong, doesn't it?' and he storts looking up, presumably for some place higher up, where he could empty the ashes out and they'd, like, catch on the wind.

We walk up the four steps to the front door. According to the plaque outside, it's, like, a solicitor's practice now. Fionn presses the intercom button and we're buzzed straight in. We walk up three flights of stairs, no questions asked, roysh, then we come to a glass door, through which this secretary – a real cracker, not *that* unlike Heike Makatsch – cops us, gets up from her desk and storts, like, walking towards us, squinting at us, obviously wondering who the fock we are.

'What'll we say?' I go and Fionn looks at the urn in my orms and he's like, 'I suppose we should maybe try the truth,' and when she opens the door and goes, '*Bonjour,*' that's when Fionn comes into his own and ends up playing an absolute blinder.

He's like, '*Excusez-moi, madame. Je m'appelle Fionn et son nom est Ross. Je sais que c'est très peu commun, mais, ici j'ai les cendres d'un homme qui a par le passé vécu dans ce bâtiment il y a un long temps – notre ami, un pretre, Denis Fehily . . .*'

He points at the urn and I'm thinking, yeah, it's at times like this that that whole listening in school thing storts paying for itself.

He's going, '*Il est mort il y a quelques mois et son souhait final devait faire disperser ses cendres sur la rue de Thorigny. Pouvons-nous verser ces cendres de votre fenêtre, s'il vous plaît?*'

'*Oh la la!*' she goes, like they do in *Ano Ano!* 'First, I must ask Monsieur Dussourd – *oui*?' and Fionn's like, '*D'accord, merci*,' and she keeps looking back at us, roysh, like she doesn't know whether to, like, trust us and shit?

But Monsieur Dussourd turns out to be basically one of the soundest goys I've ever met in my life. It's like, *pas de problème*, and me and Fionn wander around the office, looking for the window with the best view of the Rue de Thorigny. We choose one that looks directly down on the street. I lift it open and Fionn takes the top off the urn. We say a quick 'Our Father' as he tips it upside-down and we watch as one of our oldest friends is swept away on a soft spring breeze – bent and all as that sounds.

When we turn around, roysh, we notice that everyone working in the office is standing behind us and they all bless themselves, which is nice, and then Monsieur Dussourd invites us into his office for coffee.

'Bernard,' he goes, shaking both our hands and sort of, like, motioning us towards three soft chairs by the window.

This goy is, like, the senior portner in this company, but he's so chilled out it's unbelievable. He seems to have all the time in the world. He has good English, in fairness to him, and we end up sitting there for nearly two hours, roysh, telling him basically Fehily's entire life story and obviously all about beating Newbridge in the Leinster Schools Senior Cup final of 1999.

'Ah, a rugby coach!' he goes. 'Rugby is my passion. I am glad to think he lived here. And you play?'

'We used to,' Fionn goes, 'when we were at school,' which is typical him, roysh, totally underselling me.

I'm like, 'I don't want to come across as, like, big-headed, but I'd probably be playing for Ireland today if it hadn't been for, like, injuries, romantic hassles, the sauce, you know the score. The last few years I've been concentrating mostly on coaching.'

He suddenly sits forward in his chair and goes, 'You are coach, too?' and, I don't know why, roysh – I probably just get carried away more than anything – but I end up going, 'I suppose you *could* say that. I worked with the Ireland team for a couple of years, just giving the likes of Gordon D'Arcy and Geordan Murphy a digout with advice, blah blah blah . . . I'd be a hero to a lot of those goys.'

Fionn lets out an actual groan, roysh, but Bernard doesn't cop it. He seems pretty impressed, obviously not knowing my form.

'Part-time,' he goes, 'I am President for the Federació Andorrana de Rugby – the national team of Andorra, you understand?' and I nod my head, roysh, even though I haven't a bog where he's talking about and Fionn ends up going, 'It's a little principality, Ross, in the southern Pyrenees, between France and Spain.'

Bernard's there, 'Yes – my mother, she comes from there. I grew up there. Lot of snow. Not such good weather for rugby . . .' and I'm like, 'Whoa, hang on – are you talking about the place where people go on, like, skiing holidays? You're telling me they've an actual rugby team?'

'You have never heard of *El Isards*?' he goes, cracking on to be pissed off. Then he laughs. 'We have had a rugby team since 1987. Now, we are ranked fifty-eight in the world, but it's difficult, as you imagine, with a population of just 70,000.'

Then, roysh, out of the blue, he goes, 'Would you be interested in coaching the team, Ross?' and this is having only met me – what? – less than two hours ago?

I'm just hoping Fionn doesn't stick his oar in and tell Bernard I'm full of shit.

I'm there, 'Are you offering me a job?' and he goes, '*Non*, what I mean is we are at this moment without a national coach and we are *interviewing* candidates for the job. But you have much experience, especially for one so young. You would have a . . . *significant* advantage. We are doing some interviews tomorrow and some on Monday.'

'Oh,' Fionn goes, 'because we're heading home tonight . . .'

'No, no,' I go, giving him serious daggers, 'it's actually *tomorrow* night.'

'Well,' Bernard goes, standing up and sort of, like, flattening out his suit with his hands, 'can you get some kind of résumé to me some time today?'

Me and Fionn stand up to leave. I'm like, 'You'll have it in a couple of hours.'

'Come on,' I'm going and Fionn's there, 'No.'

I'm like, 'Fionn, please!' and he's like, 'No, Ross. No *focking* way,' but he's suddenly laughing as he's saying it, roysh, which means he's weakening.

So I just force the pen into his hand and ask the waiter for a couple of sheets of, like, blank paper and a bowl of French onion soup, which I happen to know he loves.

He shakes his head, still smiling, like he thinks I'm off my focking cake.

'Only you,' he goes, 'could turn up in France and talk your way into an interview for the Andorra national rugby coach's job,' and I'm there, 'Fionn, what have I got to lose? What am I going back to? See, I don't think what happened this afternoon was a coincidence at all. I think it's Fehily, looking down on me . . .' and he suddenly gets all serious, roysh, probably thinking about Aoife, and I should try to be a bit more sensitive with shit like that.

'So what do you want me to put down here?' he goes. 'Obviously your contact details – I presume it's the Foxrock address?' and I'm like, 'Yeah – worse focking luck. You know my mobile number and e-mail address as well. Whoa, do you think I should put down my Bebo site?'

He goes, 'Considering that you've got a section on it called, *The Head Says, No, Yet The Nuts Say, Whoa! Fat Birds I Wouldn't Object To Boning*, I probably wouldn't. Okay, education – probably should skip that as well.'

'Leaving Cert.,' I go. 'English, A1. Irish, A1. Maths, A1. History, A1. Geography, A1. . .'

He's like, 'In geography? Ross, an hour ago you didn't know where Andorra was. If you're going to bullshit these people, you've got to make sure your lies are at least half-believable . . .'

He has an actual point.

I'm there, 'Okay, put down a B then – but make it a B1. Okay, further education – a sports management course in UCD. Actually, no, leave that off.'

'Why not just cut to the chase?' he goes. 'All they really want is your rugby experience,' so I'm like, 'Okay, captained Castlerock College to victory in the Leinster Schools Senior Cup 1999. Coached Castlerock to victory in the Leinster Schools Senior Cup 2003,' really warming to it now. 'Assistant backs coach for Ireland rugby team for two years, culminating – if that's a word – in the 2004 Triple Crown win. Actually, put down the 2006 win as well . . .'

'Are you sure about this?' he goes and I'm like, 'Fionn, I've been a nice goy all my life and where the fock has it got me?' which is a good point, actually.

Fionn finishes my CV while eating his soup, then we find

an internet café. While he types it up, I get a sheet of A4 paper and write a reference for myself from Eddie O'Sullivan, which makes me out to be some kind of genius – we wouldn't be half the team we are without him, blah blah blah.

While I'm putting the finishing touches to it, Fionn storts fluting around on the internet and that's when I hear him go, 'Focking hell! Have you seen the salary that goes with this job? It's a hundred and fifty Ks a year!' and I'm like, 'Ah, well. It's a stort, I suppose. Beggars can't be choosers.'

I lash the CV and my letter of, like, recommendation into an envelope, then grab my wallet. I've got this little piece that I cut out of the paper, roysh – it's looking pretty tattered now – but it's this, like, question-and-answer thing with Drico, where he's asked to name his toughest opponent ever and he goes, 'Serge Betson . . . and I would have to say Ross O'Carroll-Kelly.'

I put it into the envelope – it's the only thing in there that isn't total bullshit – and then we catch the Metro back to St Paul, find the Rue de Thorigny again and give the package to Bernard's secretary, who, I notice for the first time, actually has a bit of a thing for me.

I send Melanie a text and it's like, 'Hey i no i said id ring u @ wkend but stayin over in paris extra nite, how u?' and half an hour later, roysh, there's still no reply from her and I'm thinking, I am falling for this bird in a major way.

I'm also falling for this country. It's actually my third time in Paris. The first time was with Sorcha when we were, like, whatever, eighteen, nineteen. I took her up to the very top of the Eiffel Tower, roysh, and it was a really, really clear night and you could see the whole city from up there. I remember catching her eye, giving her one of my big mean-ingfuls, then going, 'Sorcha?'

She was like, 'Oh my God, what?'

I suddenly went down on one knee and I watched her little boat race light up. Then I went, 'My shoelace is undone.'

She slapped me so hord that my ears were still ringing on the flight home.

Fionn can't help but laugh. 'No offence, Ross, but how did that girl stick you for so long?' he goes, shaking his head and I'm there, 'Who knows – who focking knows?'

We're sitting at the bor in the Hôtel Concorde Lafayette, half-ten at night and the two of us already half-cut.

I find myself suddenly going, 'I'm over it now. Well, I'm not over it – as in, *over* it. I'll always love her, but I know there's, like, no going back. It's just the thought of another man playing dad to Honor.'

I suppose, since we're, like, bearing our souls, it's time I mentioned . . .

'Fionn, that day when I told you about Aoife. If I'd known that it was going to cause that major borney you had and that you'd never get a chance to—'

He goes, 'Ross, we were going to have that argument one way or another. Look, I'm as together about this thing as you are about Sorcha. It doesn't really matter what me and Aoife's last conversation was about – it'd be worse if it was about something mundane, like *Big Brother*. Life isn't some simple, clean narrative, Ross, with a tidy little resolution in the final act. Aoife knew I loved her. She died knowing I loved her.'

I stort fiddling with a beer mat, which is something I always do when I don't know what to say next.

'All that stuff's not true,' he goes. 'I'm sure you've heard it – about her stomach and her brain and whatever else exploding. Her stomach ruptured, but it was a heart attack that killed her . . .'

I don't particularly want to hear this, and I especially don't want to hear a friend of mine relive it. But I don't stop him because he needs to get this shit off his chest.

'Every time you binge, your stomach, naturally enough, expands, to the point where the vessels that supply blood to the area burst. So the tissue dies and that weakens the stomach, adding pressure to it every time you . . . *purge*. Her immune system tried to deal with the rupture by dilating her blood vessels. Her heart slowed down. That's when she blacked out in the bathroom. Then her heart just . . . stopped.'

I'm wondering would it be wise to let him have another drink.

I'm there, 'She was great, though, wasn't she? Remember how she looked the night of her debs – you must have felt like Brad Pitt that night, Dude. All your Christmases . . .'

'Do you remember Oisinn trying to teach her golf?' he goes.

I laugh. I'm like, 'We were only talking about that the day of the funeral. We're all going to miss her.'

'I knew what I was taking on,' he goes, suddenly all serious again. 'I knew it was quite likely she'd never be fully well again. I knew I could probably never fully trust her. But I'd have taken her on any terms. You know, it was unlikely she was ever going to be able to bear children, with the damage she did to herself for all of those years. But even that . . . well, it's love, isn't it?'

Then all of a sudden he goes, 'Look, Ross, we haven't always been bosom buddies. But what you saw that day in Eddie Rocket's . . . I'll always be grateful to you for coming to me.'

I tell him he doesn't need to be grateful. And though we might not be bosom buddies, we've been through some amount of shit together, good and bad.

'Life would certainly be a lot duller without you around,' he goes and he holds up what's left of his pint and I don't know, roysh, whether he's saying cheers or letting me know it's my round.

'I've a good feeling about tomorrow,' he goes. 'What you said about Fehily's guiding hand . . .'

'Same again?' I go.

And he's like, 'Yeah, same again.'

My mobile rings at, like, half-ten in the morning and of course suddenly I'm, like, wide awake. I answer it and I go, 'Bernard?' but there's, like, three or four seconds of silence, roysh, and I know it's not Bernard at all.

There's only one man in the world who rings me from a payphone.

Then comes the voice. 'Hey, Kicker.'

I know straight away that something's wrong. He sounds suicidal and I wonder has it finally hit him where he is and what's happened to his life outside.

'You away?' he goes and I'm like, 'Yeah, France. Me and Fionn came over to, like, scatter Fehily's ashes . . . What's the Jack? You sound weird.'

He's like, 'Ross, they've cancelled our match.'

I'm there, 'Cancelled it?' wondering would it be rude to nod off again and let him blab on.

'Cancelled it,' he goes, 'with a big, fat capital C. It seems Bunter, our loosehead, wasn't half as interested in rugby as he led me to believe. Seems he had ulterior motives, quote-unquote. He got himself into a bit of bother yesterday, something silly – deserved nothing more than a pencil-whipping. But while they're putting him on report, they do a cell search – it's routine – and they find a mobile phone. Well, they only had to check his text messages to discover that he was going to take the opportunity of our upcoming match to go over the wall. So they've cancelled the match, orders of our friends in the Department of Justice.'

Weird as it sounds, roysh, I actually feel sorry for him because he sounds so focking depressed.

I'm like, 'Just don't do anything . . . stupid,' and he goes, 'I'm afraid the wheels are already in motion, Kicker. I'm a desperate man . . .' and suddenly the line goes dead, presumably because ringing a mobile in France from a payphone in Dublin costs an orm and a leg.

Literally two minutes later, roysh, the phone rings again, while I'm in the jacks, dropping off the shopping, and I answer by going, 'Not a good time, Dad,' and the voice on the other end goes, '*Non, non.* Ross, this is Bernard Dussourd.'

He's like, 'Ross, will you come to see me now? I can send a car,' and I'm there, 'Yeah, that's Kool and the Gang,' and I throw my clothes on, the same ones as yesterday, which is a bit skanky I know, but we didn't think we'd be, like, staying over, and I knock in next door to Fionn and he wishes me luck, roysh, and I can tell from the way he high-fives me that he genuinely means it.

Bernard's sitting behind his desk with a big smile on his boat race. I'm looking around, roysh, wondering where the other, I suppose, candidates are.

'I read your résumé,' he goes, 'and your reference from Eddie O'Sullivan. Lot of spelling mistakes. English is not his first language, no?'

I'm like, 'Well, he *is* from Cork . . .'

He laughs and then he drops the reference into the bin in front of me. 'You do not need this,' he goes. 'We have some candidates for this job, but they are not so good. When you came to my office yesterday and we talked about rugby, I hear passion from you that I don't hear from anyone else. Straight away I have a good feeling about you. So I ring some friends I have in Ireland . . .'

Oh, fock – there goes that dream!

'. . . and they say very good things about you. My good friend George Hook, he say you are a born leader.'

Hooky? I don't believe it. And to think, my old dear has spent the last two years trying to have the part of Foxrock where he lives renamed Deansgrange West.

'I have no intention to interview you here today,' he goes. 'I want to ask you to become the new coach of Andorra.'

I'm in shock here. I don't know what to say. 'I think Father Fehily led me to you,' I end up going.

He nods his head and goes, 'Yes, perhaps.'

Then he's like, 'We play our matches in Andorra la Vella, the capital, and sometimes in Foix, in France. It will be necessary for you to live here for perhaps five months of the year, but you can return home for every second weekend and our sponsors, Air France, will cover your travel expenses. Now, the salary is one hundred and fifty thousand euros a year . . .'

'Doesn't matter,' I go. 'I'll manage.'

He's like, 'For this, we do not expect miracles. We are prepared to wait a little longer for a place in the Six Nations, yes? The teams we play are Denmark, Switzerland, Norway, Luxembourg. We just want signs of improvement.'

I'm, like, so in shock, I don't actually know what to say, other than yes. It's, like, a whole new stort for me.

Then he shows me out.

I'd actually better get my orse in gear. Me and Fionn will need to be hitting the airport in a few hours.

It's weird, roysh, but I get this, like, tension in my neck whenever I step onto Westmoreland Street. Even though it's not *actually* northside, it's what JP used to call the demilitarized zone. He rang last night to congratulate me, roysh, said he was pleased, blah blah blah. I asked him was he going back to Maynooth and he said he didn't think so. He sounded great, not the old JP, but getting there.

Sorcha rang as well. It's funny, but I think I'll always think of her whenever I pass the Bank of Ireland opposite Trinity, because that's where her and Aoife used to stand collecting signatures against all sorts of shit – bullfighting, fishing, putting lippy on rabbits.

She rang to say she got the hundred grand and even though she said she was going to let her solicitor handle it, she wanted to say thanks anyway. Then she said she'd read the piece in the *Times* and she was really happy for me and, as I'm standing outside Abrakebabra, I keep replaying the conversation in my mind, roysh, trying to work out was there something in her voice when she said it – regret, basically – but if I'm honest, I'd have to say there wasn't.

I do remember going, 'I know it's hord, but maybe one day we can be friends,' and she was like, 'Oh my God, Ross, we'll never *not* be friends?' and, after all the shit that's happened, I suppose that's, like, a result.

The goys are late this morning.

At eleven the little van finally pulls in and in a funny way I'm kacking it, it has to be said, because I'm sure they're not happy bunnies with me for walking out on them like I did.

They don't see me for ages, roysh, too busy blabbing away,

probably about the Munster v Biarritz match this weekend. I tap on the window and their two heads turn in my direction. Terry winds down the passenger window and goes, 'There he is – Clive Woodward!' and for a few seconds I don't know whether he means it, like, sarcastically or what the fock.

Then both their faces light up, roysh, and I know that things are cool.

I go, 'Look, goys, I just wanted to say sorry for, like, leaving you in the lurch . . .' but Felim's there, 'Leaving us in the lurch!' and the two of them crack their holes laughing.

Then Felim's there, 'I thought we'd never see the back of you. Every morning, we'd sit in this van, hoping you wouldn't turn up, praying you'd gotten sense. I'd say to Terry, maybe today will be the day. But then we'd turn the corner onto Westland Row and there you'd be, outside the Dart station. Designer shades on.'

Even I have to laugh at that.

Terry pulls down the sun visor and whips something out of it. It's, like, the piece that was in yesterday's paper. It's like, Andorra Appoint Irishman As Coach.

They actually cut it out.

Terry goes, 'Now, don't forget us when you get to the World Cup and we're looking for tickets,' which is a nice thing to say.

'Why don't you goys come with me?' I go, on the spur of the moment. 'I should be able to, like, get you work over there,' and Felim goes, 'You mean, foreign birds have periods, too?' and we all crack our holes laughing.

Women *are* funny when you think about it.

All of a sudden, roysh, Terry goes, 'Alright, young man, do your stuff,' and the back door of the van slides open and suddenly I'm standing face to face with Shawn Hotten, the famous Hottie, former Belvo legend, who was throwing it into Chloe for a while.

He gives me a little nod of acknowledgement, then he puts on his baseball cap, wraps his Leinster scorf around his face, so only his eyes are actually visible, and grabs two clean bins out of the back.

'Be quick,' Terry goes. 'Gus wants you to get him that sky hook . . .'

I shake their hands and tell them it was a pleasure.

Epilogue

It's, like, four o'clock in the morning when my phone rings and it's some tosser who says he's from the Deportment of Justice. I look at the time and tell him this had better be good.

'It's your father,' he goes. 'I think you'd better come down here . . . immediately.'

When I hear that, I throw myself out of the bed. I lash on my threads without even turning on the light and then peg it down the stairs. The Jo arrives about ten minutes later and I'm porked on the North Circular Road half an hour after that.

One of the screws meets me at the main gate – Hugh, a really sound goy, especially for someone from Cork. I know he was always good to the old man.

'In the end, there was no talking to him,' he goes. 'That team, it was his life in here, boy. He told me an hour before lock-up that he was a desperate man. I know I should have kept a watch on him, but none of us realized until, well, the early hours just how desperate he was . . .'

He leads me out into the exercise yard.

He goes, 'It's a quare old thing is hope. When it's taken away from you, you suddenly realize where you are – and where you're not. I've seen bigger men than your father crack.'

I look up. In this light, I can just about make out the figure of a man on the roof. And stretched out beside him, across the slates, is a banner and I can make out the words,

'Mountjoy – Give Us Our Ball Back,' and then underneath there's something else that's too small to read, though I presume it says quote-unquote or some shit like that.

I'm there, 'I really don't see how this affects me?' and the goy goes, 'He said he'd only speak to you,' which is how I suddenly end up climbing up a focking ladder, onto the roof of the prison.

'Here he comes,' he goes, when he cops me, 'the new national coach of Andorra, no less.'

His teeth are chattering.

'I saw it in the paper,' he goes. 'Lex has started taking the *Times*. He's a huge fan of your friend and mine.'

I'm like, 'Are you off your focking cake? Why are you making a tit of me like this?'

'Careful, Ross,' he goes. 'There's a loose slate, just where your foot is. Almost slipped on it myself. I popped it back in, but I'm not sure how secure it is . . .'

I just shake my head.

I'm like, 'Most rooftop protests, they fock the slates *off* the roof – you're fixing them back on!' and the two of us just crack up, roysh, to the point where we can't even look at each other without laughing.

I remember my hipflask, in my inside pocket. I whip it out and give it to him. I'm like, 'Here, this'll warm you up.'

He's there, 'Kicker, you're a life-saver.'

It's no problem – it's *his* focking brandy anyway.

'How's Hughie doing?' he goes. 'I feel terribly guilty, making all this trouble for him.'

He hands me the flask and I take a long drink out of it. I'm like, 'He says he's going to do his best to – what was it? – limit the fallout. But he reckons this is going to add a couple of years onto your sentence,' and there's, like, no reaction from him.

I'm there, 'And that's when I storted thinking, you know, maybe *that's* the reason you're up here. That day in court, when Hennessy said you'd be out by Christmas, I actually saw your boat race – and don't deny it – you were disappointed.'

'Yes, I know that seems odd,' he goes, nodding his head, 'but I've *found* myself in here. Me is clicked up. Me no ready to hit the bricks.'

That's pretty much what I thought.

I sit down. Fock, it's cold for June. Mind you, it is five o'clock in the focking morning.

'How's it all going with Sorcha?' he goes

I'm like, 'We're going to be friends,' and his face sort of, like, drops and I go, 'No, I'm cool with it. I took Honor out on Sunday. Thank fock she can't talk because Sorcha would flip if she found out I took her to the zoo. You know how she feels about that shit. But Honor was, like, fine with me. Didn't cry once. Thought I even saw her smile at one point.'

'And you're standing on your own two feet now,' he goes, '*vis-à-vis* the job, etcetera. Must feel good.'

I'm there, 'Well, I'd much prefer to be spending someone else's dosh, but you're skint. I suppose this is the next best thing.'

He laughs at that.

'Can I ask you a question?' I go.

He's like, 'Anything you like, Kicker. I've no secrets left.'

'The old dear,' I go, 'do you think she set you up? I mean, do you think she put all that shit in her book, all your secrets, to get you out of the way?'

He goes, 'I'd say it's plausible,' which must be hord for him to admit. 'I guess I'll never know. If she did, though, she did me a favour. The things I've discovered about myself in this place . . .'

357

He just, like, stares off into the distance.

I'm there, 'That stuff you said about money and, like, *having* shit, I thought it was all total bullshit until, well, until loads of stuff. I worked with these two goys collecting the tampies – learned a lot of shit from them. And then the whole Aoife thing. I think the word is, like, perspective.'

He nods. Then he goes, 'I'll be honest with you, Kicker. I was pretty frightened when I came in here first. Tell a lie, I was pure terrified. Thought I was in for a bit of a kicking – my background, the way I talk, etcetera. But it wasn't like that at all. The friendships I've forged . . . Lex and the two Gartons and, well, even Bunter when he gets out of the hole, there'll be no hard feelings. They've made me so welcome. Never judged me. It's like poor old Denis used to say about people . . .'

'. . . they'll confound your worst expectations,' we go, at exactly the same time.

I look across the rooftops. It's definitely storting to get bright. I can hear seagulls.

'So, when are you planning to come down then?' I go.

He's there, 'Thought I'd give it another hour. I *did* have this idea that maybe I'd stay up here for the day – and demand that Brian Dobson do the opening sequence of *Six One* from the yard down there. *Tonight, I'm reporting from Mountjoy Jail, where one man – a rugby coach, no less – has taken a stand against repression . . .*'

I laugh at that. Then I stand up. I need to go home. It's still the middle of the focking night for me.

I'm like, 'So, what, I'll tell them you're coming down?' and he goes, 'Yes, just let me get my thoughts together. Tell them an hour. Thanks, Kicker,' and I tell him I'll see him soon.

I walk over the side of the roof and stort climbing back down the ladder.

I was never a fan of heights, it has to be said.

Down below, I can see the yord filling up with people. There's, like, Feds and — believe it or not — soldiers down there, and maybe twenty or thirty screws, which is a bit OTT. Then a fire truck arrives and three or four firemen get out and stort, like, readying the hose.

Hughie holds the ladder steady as I'm coming down and the second I step off the last rung, he goes, 'Well?' meaning, what's the Jackanory?

I fix him with a look of, like, sadness. 'He says he's not coming down any time soon,' I go.

Then I nod at the fire truck and I'm like, 'I think you're going to have to give him the focking water cannon.'

Acknowledgements

Thanks to my editor Rachel Pierce, my agent Faith O'Grady, as well as Michael McLoughlin, Patricia Deevy, Brian Walker, Cliona Lewis, Patricia McVeigh and everyone at Penguin. Thanks to the old man, who, at sixty years of age, put his footprints down on the top of Kilimanjaro – Everest is shitting itself, Dad. Thanks to my brothers, Mark, Vin and Rich. And to my friends. Thanks to Mary for her love and forbearance – and thank God for her endless store of both.